I0593450

ISABELLA'S
MOON

TONI WASS

MMH PRESS

A catalogue record for this
work is available from the
National Library of Australia

National Library of Australia Catalogue-in-Publication data:
Isabella's Moon/Toni Wass

978-0-6456259-3-6 (Paperback)

My very first act of childish rebellion against my parents was to be born two weeks late, during one of Melbourne's worst heatwaves ever in the summer of 1921.

My first major act of adult rebellion was to fall in love with an American GI and move to the other side of the world to be with him.

Can any rebellion ever be truly intentional when romance is on the agenda?

PART 1

1942

War & Romance

Each shapes the other

1

Isabella

Melbourne, Early 1942
Destiny beckons at Luna Park

Little did I know that by making fun plans for a Saturday night to go to Luna Park with my best friend Coral, I was about to meet my future husband.

Who would have thought true love could happen so easily? Well, it did.

As Coral and I alight from the tram for a carefree, easy night of fun, we make our way to the exit gate on the station platform with excited haste, pushing past some Australian soldiers along the way. Despite their usual cheeky wolf-whistles aimed at any pretty girl passing by, we keep on walking. Smirking the whole time, our Aussie soldiers egg each other on to make the first move, but only two of the gaggle of soldiers finally pluck up the courage to be the first to speak.

'Hullo, darlin', fancy a night on the town? Maybe even a dance or two?'

We walk right on past, not even answering them. Our eyes remain diverted.

One soldier is much more persistent. 'Well, girls, if not a dance, then how about we go for a drink instead? Or we can just talk if you want to … Come on, love!'

We still take no notice of them. With so many handsome American GIs to sweep us off our feet, what chance did our Aussie boys have? Besides, with the GIs enticing us with glamour and excitement, it's enough to woo us Aussie girls with a whole new approach to holding our attention. Long enough for us to turn around and say 'Yes!' to them anyway.

I must say though, some GIs can be downright annoying at times when they refuse to take 'NO!' for an answer.

This was something we were about to find out for ourselves very soon.

Further on down the street, we suddenly become aware of quickening footsteps close behind us, followed by the voice of someone with an American accent calling out to us. We don't even bother to turn around to check them out, but we can tell there are at least two persistent guys seeking our attention.

'Hey, gals! Wait for us!'

As with our Australian soldiers who had already tried this approach before, we were all set to ignore these two as well. Before we know it though, one of them has come right up alongside Coral and the other one on my side. Talk about pushy!

Coral and I had made a pact earlier, that if either of us didn't like the looks of any potential date for the night, we would give the other a quick nudge. So far Coral must like what she sees, because she doesn't try to avoid them outright like I do. For some reason I keep on walking, pretending I don't hear a thing.

By this time, we've made it to Collins Street. When we finally turn around to face them, the GI closest to me says, 'Hi, ladies! Would you happen to know where we can get a drink around this place?'

'Well, you could try the Australia Hotel right here behind us,' I suggest, as I turn to point to the pub we just happen to be standing in front of. 'Try the lounge area. There's usually something going in any city hotel.'

Our ploy to be rid of them doesn't work. Unfortunately, it is already past the hotel's six o'clock curfew time. This, of course, also means closing time for *all* city bars, so if we want to make a quick getaway, it will have to be right now. In hindsight, it was all too obvious; the fickle finger of fate—or whatever you like to call it—had other ideas.

Instead, the one alongside me speaks up. 'Stay with the girls, Brad.' And off he went. I must admit, I did like the look of this one, despite my intention to discourage him.

He is back in no time to inform his buddy that the bar is already closed for the night. For Coral and me, this meant that our avenue of escape was no longer possible. To avoid being outright rude to these two GIs, we now have no choice but to tell them our intended plans for tonight, which is Luna Park, of course.

'So, what is this Luna Park you speak of, ma'am?' this same guy asks. He must be the designated spokesman for the two of them. The one closest to Coral hasn't spoken at all yet.

'It's an amusement park,' Coral explains. 'You know … dodgem cars … Ferris wheels … fairy floss … or cotton candy as you Americans know it. Of course, as with most amusement parks, there is always many other fun things to do too.'

'An amusement park?' The one closest to Coral finally speaks. 'Gee, I haven't been to an amusement park or county fair for years. Would you mind if we tag along with you, gals?'

As best friends, we can often read each other's thoughts, so I can sense without her even having to say so, Coral is beginning to have second thoughts. When I chance a closer look at the GI beside her, I can understand why Coral has been a bit put off by his appearance. His face is all pockmarked and he's so much shorter much than his buddy. Knowing Coral as I do, I know by now she'll end up walking away from him in the end, so she isn't about to encourage him so early in the evening.

I soon realise for myself, though, his boyish excitement is genuine. After all, tonight could be the only opportunity we'll have for some fun together. Life is for the living, and we are still young enough to embrace life as it comes. Besides, who knows what's around the corner of all our tomorrows?

Coral has intuitively sensed my lighter change of mood too. I'm pretty sure she's already aware by now of my growing interest in the other guy on my side.

'Sure, I'm happy for you both to come along with us if you like. It'll be fun! I'm Coral, by the way,' she says and smiles as she extends her hand towards the man beside her in a friendly way to seal the deal. 'Your name is Brad, right?'

'Yes, that's right! But how did you know my name?'

'Oh, that's easy,' Coral grins. 'I heard your friend here call you that.' Coral looks over my way to pose her question to me now, 'So, Bell? What do you think?'

'Bell … is that your name?' The taller of the two men interjects.

'It's Isabella, actually, but my family and friends always call me Bell.'

'Isabella? I love that name! Sounds perfect for you. A beautiful name for a beautiful gal. Isabella is what I will call you, then … If you don't mind, that is?'

I find myself blushing now, which I tend to do with some young men. 'Why should I? I suppose we don't always appreciate our own names until somebody else does. So, I don't mind at all if you do want to call me Isabella. I must admit, my name *does* sound different the way you say it. By the way, what's *your* name?'

'Paul is my name. Paul Meier.' He extends his hand in a friendly greeting. 'I am very pleased to meet you, Isabella.'

Oh my, I can barely breathe! The very fact that he wants to spend time with me too thrills me more than I care to admit. After all, it's Paul I want to spend tonight with, anyway.

'Likewise, Paul.' I accept his hand in the friendly spirit to which it's offered. His hand immediately feels so huge as he covers my own slender hand with his. The rough and calloused texture of his palm strikes me as a man used to hard work. A hands-on kind of man I have a lot of respect for. I like him all the more because of it too. Somehow, his warm touch immediately feels very familiar to me. It's almost like I've known him forever, instead of only a few minutes.

He must feel the same too, since we continue to maintain eye contact much longer than is necessary. For reasons I don't quite understand yet, I am now able to accept that my still-raw memories of my ex-fiancé, Eddie, really do belong in the past. Up until now, I'd refused to let go of him completely. To my surprise, Eddie has suddenly become a distant memory.

I don't want to let Paul see my obvious shyness now, so I look down, breaking my eye contact with him. That's when it suddenly dawns on me; he's still holding onto my hand and he seems more than happy to keep doing so! With the tingly warmth of his hand in mine, I'm not about to discourage him.

Apart from our impulsive plan, for two fun-loving girls wanting to spend Saturday night at Luna Park, this night has turned out to be a total surprise for both Coral and me. If a night such as this can happen out of the blue—with our two GI companions thrown into the mix for good measure—then I can't wait for whatever follows, for all of our future unchartered days ahead of us.

2

Isabella

Early 1942
A Ferris ride meant for two

B eing honest with myself now, I never ever want this night to end. I just know in my heart something magical is happening tonight, and why not? A trillion stars must be in perfect alignment, because at last, my wounded heart is ready to open up again.

But to fully accept and embrace a new kind of love again? Well, we shall see ...

At every sideshow challenge and on every daring ride, it's Coral and me against Brad and Paul. Each team is determined to put each other and every ride or attraction on sideshow alley to the test.

Carol and I excel in the knock-em-down category, as with each of the three weighted balls we triumphantly manage to topple the ten pins. Whereas Brad and Paul thrash us so easily at the shooting-duck gallery. We girls are far from beaten, though. Despite our losses, we are still up for any new challenge that lays ahead and that goes for what we both consider to be the hardest challenge of all. When it's my turn to bring a huge hammer down onto the lever of the high striker at our next challenge, I am forced to accept some masculine strength is definitely called for with this particular challenge. Try as I might, I have no hope of lifting the heavy hammer all by myself, let alone ringing the firemen's bell at the top of the tall wooden pole it's attached to.

That's when Paul gallantly steps in. The gentlemanly side of him is only too happy to assist a lady in distress. For maximum impact, he tells me I must first raise the huge hammer all the way up above my shoulders to start with, but I just cannot do it. With Paul's hands over mine, we manage to heave that hammer up as high as we possibly can.

Heaven help me! I swear, the whole time Paul is helping me to lift the oversized hammer above my shoulders, my heart is beating faster than a hummingbird's wings. With his warm hands covering mine the whole time, along with our combined strengths, we finally manage to bang the hammer down onto the steel base so hard we hit the bell at the top of the pole. With a resounding *dong* still ringing in our ears, we throw up our hands in glee. 'We did it!'

Despite our challenge being over, we continue to hold hands for longer than necessary. I'm not complaining.

Along with our triumphant victory of reaching new heights—so to speak—I am now the proud owner of a huge, bright pink, fluffy teddy bear. The teddy bear isn't the only prize I might come away with tonight. It seems my heart has won its own ultimate prize too.

I can tell by now Coral and Brad are having a good time as well, in spite of Coral's initial reservations about teaming up with him. But just as I originally thought at the beginning of our night together, I don't really see anything romantic happening between them. At least they're happy just to be in each other's company and to enjoy this fun night as a foursome anyway.

The ride I love the most is the Ferris wheel, but when our capsule suddenly stalls at the top, I start to feel *rather* apprehensive. While we're waiting for the other capsules to fill up below us, our own capsule starts to swing irrationally. This is when my girlish fear steps in and I immediately start to imagine the capsule we are occupying suddenly slipping from the steel bars holding it in place, plummeting us to the ground.

Paul picks up on my sudden fear and quickly slides his strong arm around me. I love the way he holds me close to his body in such a protective way. Well, as close as he is socially allowed to, anyway, considering we have only just met. Despite this, I still feel completely safe in his arms and secretly relish the closeness of his body next to mine. Towards the end of the ride—using the capsule's last shaky descent as an excuse—I find myself sneakily edging even closer to him, enjoying his warm embrace so much more.

***

The night seems to fly by too quickly and before long, it's time to say goodbye to our two gentlemen companions. Is this one night supposed to be all there can ever be with Paul? I find myself desperately hoping this won't be my last night with him, but then I have this sudden niggling thought; I swear I can hear Grandma Allen whispering in my ear now, 'Remember, Bell! Young ladies should *always* wait for the man to make the next move.'

I know she's right, but I still find myself wishing for something magical to happen anyway.

As we head towards Luna Park's exit gate, I attempt to make light conversation with my three companions, but my heart suddenly feels heavy with the fickleness of love's lost opportunity. Paul will be leaving Melbourne any day now. Maybe never to be seen again. Does this also mean he's destined to disappear from my life forever? I know I'm being overly melodramatic, but tonight, I've allowed my heart to surge forward with new possibilities, only to be pulled back cruelly into an uncertain limbo again.

As we pass under Luna Park's iconic, smiling clown-face entrance and emerge outside the fun park's secure enclosure, Paul suddenly grabs my hand and pulls me gently to a stop. He puts his finger to his lips, requesting my silence. I soon realise he wants to talk to me alone, so of course, I'm only too happy to go along with his request. We stand quietly off to the side for a moment, as Coral and Brad keep on walking, chatting away to each other like two old friends, thankfully unaware we aren't so close behind them anymore.

Paul leans closer to me and speaks as softly as he can so Coral and Brad can't hear us. 'Isabella, would it be too forward of me to ask you for your telephone number? I know we've only just met, but I would really love to spend some more time with you ... Just the two of us, I mean ... Would you be agreeable to spending some more time with me too, Isabella?'

In response, my heart does some impromptu flip-flops. As I answer him, I beam my happiest smile his way. 'Oh, Paul! I was hoping you would say that. I really had such fun tonight as a foursome, but even more so I especially enjoyed being with you. I was beginning to think for a while there I might not ever see you again and I would really hate for that to happen ... So, that would be a definite YES for me too.'

'I had a feeling you were feeling the same way as me.' Paul takes my hand in his now, to hold it gently against his heart. 'I think something magical has passed between us tonight. You've just confirmed that my gut instinct has been right all along. How about we go and see a movie together, just the two of us? Maybe even tomorrow night ... If that's okay with you?'

'I would like that very much, Paul. I think there's a new movie out in the picture theatre this weekend. A western, I believe ... Do you like westerns?'

'Boy, do I ever!' he answers with boyish enthusiasm. 'So how about you give me your phone number and I'll call you in the morning ... I promise, not too early, though. We can then arrange a time for me to pick you up, right at your front gate.'

'No, Paul, please don't worry about picking me up—especially if you have to use public transport to get around. I live on the outskirts of Melbourne, so if you have to catch a train to pick me up, by the time we return to the city again the movie will probably be over. Why don't I just meet you at the picture theatre instead?'

Paul nods his head in agreement as we talk. In the small notebook I always keep in my purse, I jot down my telephone number and the name and address of the picture theatre, before tearing out the page, handing it to him.

'Sounds good to me. It's a date, then!' He kisses my hand, then leans over to kiss me ever so gently on the lips. Even if this little peck is only meant to be a goodnight kiss, it still packs a powerful punch to my heart. I so want him to keep it going much longer, but I still find myself holding back from giving into Paul's sweet kisses completely. Just as well, too, because Coral and Brad have finally realised we are no longer walking behind them. By pure chance, they turn back towards us at the exact moment Paul kisses me.

Luckily, I quickly figure out for myself, if I *was* to return Paul's kisses with his same longing right now, it's bound to raise far too many questions with Coral on the way home.

Questions I am not prepared to answer just yet. With Coral being my best friend, we usually share our future hopes and dreams with each other, but there is still a side to me that likes to keep certain thoughts private. At least until I am able to process these new changes to my life in my own way first. This is definitely one of those times.

***

'So what did you think of the movie, Isabella? Especially with all of those hot-tempered gunfighters as part of the story?' Paul prompts me as we stroll down Collins Street. Just one night after Luna Park, with our arms already linked closely together, we appear exactly like any couple still close after years of marriage would. Just as I'd hoped, Paul hadn't wasted any time in contacting me.

'It *was* exciting, wasn't it? I loved it!' I answer with equal enthusiasm. 'No-one makes movies like Hollywood does.'

As we stroll along, we discuss the movie with all the excitement of two starstruck kids, trying to fill in those awkward, still-nervous gaps of silences between our words at the same time.

'I was desperately hoping that posse would let those men go at the last minute, but they still hung them anyway,' Paul comments before asking me, 'Do you agree, Isabella?'

'Yes, I know what you mean. I can't believe they went ahead with the hanging too. I honestly thought they would let them go. Especially since those poor men weren't even guilty. I must say, despite the unexpected outcome of the movie, I still enjoyed it. The plot itself certainly kept me on the edge of my seat the whole time. Thank you for taking me tonight. I'm so glad you enjoy western movies as much as I do.'

I share with Paul now, our regular family outings on Saturday afternoons at the movie matinees. 'Because my father was good friends with the owner of the picture theatre, we kids were allowed in for free just one day a week. So Saturday afternoons for the Carlisle clan was always reserved for the picture show. Before the main feature movie there'd be some western serial which played for weeks, and even though each episode was only fifteen minutes long, they were always exciting to my brothers, sister and me. We could barely wait to go the following week to see how the hero or heroine could possibly get out of trouble each time. Did you have those sorts of short serials at the picture shows where you come from, Paul?'

'Sure, we did. Although, I had to earn my own pocket money to be able to go as my family isn't rich or anything. My father refused to waste good money on frivolous things such as movies when I was growing up. He told me once, in no uncertain terms, if I want to go to the picture shows, I must pay my own way. So, I saved some money from any odd jobs I had at the time to pay for my ticket. Sometimes if money was really short, my best buddy, Cody, and me would try to sneak in when the girl in the ticket booth went for her break. The last time we tried to do that, we were unaware the manager had his eye on us. He stopped us just inside the theatre door and unceremoniously kicked us out.' Paul chuckles at the memory now. 'Most of the time, though, I always made sure I had enough pocket money to go. So to answer your question, yes Isabella, I did enjoy those Wild West serials too.'

'We haven't even touched on your life in America yet, Paul. Where exactly do you come from?'

'Chicago, in the Midwest state of Illinois. Despite my parents originally coming from Germany, my two sisters, my brother and I have all been raised as Americans. You know, Isabella, even with Germany playing a major role in World War II, our family haven't been rounded up to be sent back to Germany yet. Even if my family aren't exactly rich, they are still highly respected in America. Being self-employed businesspeople, my parents are generally considered to be fine, upstanding citizens in our neighbourhood.'

'Well, Paul, I for one hope your parents are never sent back to Germany. Prejudice and suspicion seem to go hand in hand with any kind of war, don't they? Australia is no exception. We have our fair share of prejudice and ongoing friction here too.'

'That's pretty much the case in many other countries around the world unfortunately. Anyway, let's talk about something else for now,' Paul suggests. He stops walking as if all of a sudden a thought has just popped into his head. 'Would you like something to eat or drink? I could sure do with some coffee right about now.'

'I'm not really all that hungry, but yes, a cup of tea would be lovely, Paul.'

'A cup of tea it is, then. Is there a cafe around here that's still open at this time of night?' Paul glances around the still unfamiliar surroundings, hoping to spot something nearby that resembles a cafe or diner.

'Well, with the picture theatre nearby, there's bound to be something still open.' I too stop to look around and get my bearings. Being a working girl who has had to watch my pennies carefully, I always take a packed lunch from home so I rarely have to buy lunch from any city cafe or restaurant. However, I do have to walk past them all the time on my way to work.

'I think there's one on the next corner that caters to the movie crowds. Follow me.'

We do indeed find a cafe still open called The Silver Spoon, which thankfully, is still thriving nicely despite the war. That's if the cheerful efficiency of their staff is anything to go by. The sudden influx of customers from the picture shows doesn't faze them one bit. After all, there is always going to be couples like us wanting somewhere to go after a movie, or groups of GIs roaming the streets at night after the city-wide pub closing time. Besides, with most cafes or restaurants suffering financially during this tight-fisted wartime economy, The Silver Spoon is only too happy to stay open to meet the demand. We stop at the counter to order a small pot of tea for me, and some coffee, plus a ham, cheese and tomato toasted sandwich for Paul, before settling ourselves into the first available booth along the back wall of the cafe.

By this time, Paul and I have forgotten about our initial awkwardness with each other.

Our shared interest in movies has certainly helped to break the ice. We've already moved beyond movie plots and are now into other casual chitchat as we wait for our order to arrive. Once served, we don't talk at all for a few minutes as we each savour our deliciously hot drinks. Paul takes a tentative sip of his coffee and sighs contentedly. With each mouthful, he takes a moment to savour the aroma of the strong black brew, while on the other side of the booth I take my time waiting for my aromatic Earl Grey tea leaves, in their own little silver teapot, to brew all hot and strong—just the way I like it—strong with less milk and only one sugar. Once Paul's food order is placed before him, he quickly, but cautiously, takes his first few bites of the thick, piping-hot ham and cheese toasted sandwich.

Thank goodness, the silence between us is no longer awkward. In fact, I feel rather relaxed in Paul's company and very interested in getting to know him so much more. Well, before this whole magical night alone with him has to end, anyway.

As we sit together within the warm cosiness of our booth, we start to explore various subjects we're happy to discuss openly with each other; like the impact of this war on the world in general, the reality of food ration stamps and the different types of food we each grew up with. We even discuss the social cultures between Australia and America. As we talk, we are busy checking each other out in less obvious ways.

When it's Paul's turn to talk, I'm happy to maintain eye contact with him the whole time. This is not hard at all, since he has no trouble holding my attention—in more ways than one. His whole body seems to come alive when he opens up to me. I watch him intently, completely mesmerised by the way his beautiful chunky hands move with such animation as he attempts to describe something technical to me. I can tell by just listening to him, he is highly intelligent, but not arrogantly so. When he smiles, his whole face lights up and I swear his eyes actually seem to twinkle with spontaneous humour each time. Even though he wears a military haircut with short back and sides, his hair on top appears to be an interesting shade of reddish brown. It's even a bit curly too. I have already realised by now he isn't as tall as I first thought him to be. When walking beside him earlier, he is nearly a head taller than my own height of five feet, four inches. To me, his stocky build of broad shoulders and barrel chest more than make up for whatever he might lack in overall height.

To tell you the truth, Paul is like no man I have ever met before, so I am not surprised to admit to myself that I'm completely and utterly smitten with him by now. I find myself sneakily studying his beautiful mouth as he talks. A mouth—by the way—that has already thrilled me with his kisses before this moment, and will again by the end of tonight, I'm sure.

I share some other stories with him too about my own family of course, but most of the time, I prefer to listen to him talk about *anything*. Maybe

14

this is because I just love to hear the sound of his voice. Even if Paul's cultural background may be European in origin, his accent to me sounds predominately American. I also realise that every word he utters is ultimately softened by something else. Like a softly spoken Austrian accent, perhaps, with a fascinating hint of an Irish lilt thrown into the mix as well.

'By the way, where are you stationed, Paul? I don't think you've told me that yet.'

'We're camped out in a remote area called Bacchus Marsh. Do you know of it?'

'Yes I do. It is rather isolated out that way, like you say. I would imagine there wouldn't be much at all in the way of entertainment for you GIs all the way out there.'

'That's for sure! Very little, in fact. Because we're quite a distance away from any worthwhile nightly activities, it isn't easy to obtain a pass to leave the base. We're not even close enough to catch a taxi ride into Melbourne during our free time either. Even so, one evening, some buddies and I decided to head for the town of Bacchus Marsh for a beer and maybe even some dancing. The streets were deserted and blacked out of course. To us guys in search of some fun though, the town looked more than a little forlorn for our tastes. Well, at first glance, anyway. There was no action happening at all from what we could see. Except for a local dance hall, which unbelievably was already overcrowded with GIs. To add to our woes, there was no local gals to dance with either.

'The only music available was provided by a woman of some mature years, sitting down at a piano. She was playing these really old, completely out-of-date songs. Nobody could dance much to it, anyway, and to complete this dismal scene for us, she was accompanied by a young guy on drums, who looked like he was bored out of his brain. As you can imagine, the GIs already present weren't too impressed by this whole backwoods social scene either, but they tried to move to the music anyway. Just for the hell of it, no doubt.

'At intermission when the lady took a break, some of my buddies who knew I could play the piano coaxed me up on the stage to play. They didn't have to try too hard to convince me. I was definitely itching to liven up the old dance hall scene by banging those old piano keys with some good old honky-tonk. Once the young drummer, who was on a break at the time as well, heard the music, he hurried back to his drums to join in with me. I tell you, Isabella, this kid sure did come alive! He had this huge grin on his face for the rest of the night. Before too long, the whole joint was jumping with some serious action.'

As I sit listening intently to Paul regale me with his stories, I already know in my heart I am falling deeply in love with him. I truly believe he feels the same way, because whenever it's my turn to talk he hangs onto my every word—just as I do with him.

Whenever it's Paul's turn to talk, I find myself intensely taking in every little detail about him. From the way he sips his coffee and the way the corners of his eyes crinkle when he smiles. Even the way he devours his simple toasted sandwich, not even dropping one tiny piece of food back onto his plate. When we laugh together, my eyes take in the mischievous hazel flecks in his eyes. I even have to admire how perfect his teeth are. When he holds my hand across the table, my own hand seems to meld with his completely. Suddenly, it's as if we have become just one person.

***

After talking about everything and anything in the cosy little cafe, we're suddenly aware there are no other customers left but us. For the past half hour or so, we had failed to notice the waitress giving us a few subtle hints, wanting us to leave so she could go home. Since we've been so completely enraptured with each other, we had taken no notice. When her subtle hints no longer worked, she'd brought out the mop and bucket and positioned them right next to our table. We finally take the hint and sheepishly get up to leave while apologising for holding her up. By way of a response, our cheery waitress merely waves us off with a beaming smile. Maybe she has a romantic soul that senses a budding romance in the air tonight?

As we stroll along Collins Street, my arm once again links with Paul's. We still find lots to talk about along the way. As I have already suspected by now, Paul really is an extremely intelligent man. Such a good listener too. Even though he grew up within the ever-fascinating, infamous metropolis of Chicago, I'm still a bit surprised he wants to know what it's like to grow up in Australia. I can tell by the questions he asks me, he's not pretending either. He seems to be genuinely interested in everything I tell him about my family and life in Australia. He especially wants to hear about my earlier years growing up in Melbourne, right from my birth all the way up until tonight.

'So, tell me, Isabella, were you born in a city hospital or out in the country?'

'No, not in a hospital, Paul. All four of my siblings and I were delivered at home, in our parents' marital bed, by either a local midwife or doctor.'

'There are five of you? So what are their names, and who is the eldest?'

'My brother Robbie is the eldest, me, then Josie, my only sister, followed by my younger brother Kyle. We're all just a few years apart in age. That is until Marty, the baby of the family, came along … a lot later.'

'Homebirths must have been a normal thing back then,' Paul comments. 'My own mother was birthed by a midwife at home too, as were each of my siblings and myself. So what year were you born, Isabella?'

'I was born in 1921, right at the start of this controversial decade—or as we both know it—the roaring twenties. Not that I really cared much anyway. According to my mother, she literally had to sweat me out, since I was born two weeks late in the middle of one of the worst heatwaves In Melbourne's history. *AND* three days after Christmas!'

'You were obviously determined to come when you were good and ready,' Paul says. Then he adds, 'This makes me admire you more, because you seem to be very much your own person.'

'That's for sure! Do you want to know the name my parents had picked out for me?'

'Yes, I certainly do! Please tell me.'

'Roma, would you believe? Always sounded Italian to me and I'm not even Italian.'

Paul chuckles. 'Well, I for one, am so glad your parents called you Isabella instead. What made them change their minds?'

'My mother once told me she was determined to call me Roma all the way through her pregnancy. That was until I was born and she first laid eyes on me. She immediately decided that I didn't look as a little girl called Roma should. After all, my hair was more of a reddish auburn colour, not Italian-black. My father did offer a few other suggestions at the time, but nothing really sounded right to either of them. That's when the midwife couldn't resist offering them a suggestion of her own: "What about Isabella? It's such a beautiful name, isn't it?" she'd suggested. "You might not like it, but honestly, she looks more like an Isabella than a Roma, for sure." That was it! My parents instantly loved the name Isabella … Thank goodness!'

Just as Paul is genuinely intrigued about my life in Australia, I'm equally captivated about his stories of life in Chicago. Up until now, I have always imagined Chicago to be the way it's always portrayed in movies. With gangsters shooting up the streets and Eliot Ness-type detectives in constant pursuit of them. Paul soon sets me straight on that score. Listening to his own personal experiences of Chicago, I soon begin to understand, Chicago is just like any other major world city. Each with its own history of disreputable behaviour and strange goings-on. Paul tells me he grew up in the outer suburbs, some thirty miles away from the expansive metropolis, so I guess that means he obviously missed the worst of Chicago's infamous underworld element. The Chicago he passionately speaks about now is not all about criminals or cops at all. It's more about a city of extraordinarily smart people, leading the way in groundbreaking medical research, the arts, the environment, the outstanding architecture. 'Chicago,' he says proudly, 'also has its own extraordinary share of big-hearted people too.'

***

Before long, we find ourselves already at the train station. According to the printed bus schedule in Paul's pocket, his last bus to Bacchus Marsh is due to arrive in just under twenty minutes. The last train back home for me is due to arrive in just over ten minutes, so it's a good thing we left The Silver Spoon when we did. The thought of being stranded in the city alone together is definitely not an option for me. Once again, Grandma Allen's words persistently ring in my ear: '*Good* girls don't do that sort of thing, Isabella!' I know too, there is no way my parents would ever agree with such an idea, so it really is time for me to say goodbye.

I dare to believe now that whatever feelings Paul has for me, they're in tune with mine. He needs to make up his own mind, though. Any day now, he'll be leaving Melbourne to go fight a war in the Pacific, so what right do I have to ask him to come back into Melbourne to see me one more time?

Once I've bought my train fare, I spot Paul over by the steel gates that allow regular travellers easier access to all platforms. My train usually leaves from platform one, so I weave my way back towards him from the ticket office with my ticket in hand. I'm elated to note Paul hasn't tried to hightail it out of here once I'd left his side to go purchase my ticket. This surely must be a good sign.

'So, Isabella, now that you have your ticket, I guess you're all set to go home at last.' He stands directly in front of me now and squeezes my hands gently, while his eyes study my face so intently. It's almost like he's trying to memorise my face somehow.

'So, how long is your train trip back home?'

'About an hour, then just a short walk from the station to—'

Before I can finish my words, Paul suddenly blurts out, '—Isabella … Do you think, perhaps, you might want to go out with me once again?' All of his spoken words seem to tumble out of his mouth in one long rush. 'Look, I know I have probably talked way too much tonight and I've probably even scared you off a bit too, but I would really love to see you again. If you want to, that is?' There's a bit of an awkward pause to follow, before he asks, 'What do you think?'

'Oh, Paul, I was so hoping you would ask me such a thing. YES! I would *love* to see you again.' My words are cut off by the thundering rumble of my train as it approaches the station. There's no time for us to talk anymore, as my train will be ready to leave within the next two minutes, or at least until its waiting passengers are safely inside the train, before each one of the carriage doors are sealed tight.

Without hesitation, Paul pulls me towards him, then kisses me—in front of everyone!

'I'll call you tomorrow to decide where we'll go. So, until tomorrow, beautiful lady.'

Without waiting for me to reply, he's already heading to the bus stop right outside the train station. My heart leaps for joy with a jubilant backflip, I finally realise our hearts really have been in tune with each other the whole time.

***

His new orders have come through to his unit that all troops currently held at Bacchus Marsh will be departing from Melbourne to Darwin at 0600 the following Friday. This is it! Less than one week to go before he'll be leaving me behind, perhaps forever. Is our one night at the movies meant to be only a bittersweet tease after all?

What am I supposed to do now? Return to my old life, like Paul never existed? Recent news reports serve to remind me of this fact every day. The reality for both of us is Paul is about to enter hostile territories in the Pacific region within the next few weeks. This is no small challenge for him to deal with; no matter how much I try to remain optimistic, in light of his official orders, a certain heaviness begins to pull my spirits down. I keep my thoughts to myself, though. In the words of my wise and wonderful Grandma Allen: 'When trouble comes, Bell, always keep a happy smile on your face to uplift your soul.'

My parents urge me to just accept this inevitable outcome and to be prepared to let go of this new young man in my life when the time comes. Even though I resent them telling me this, I do know they won't want to see me all broken-hearted again like I was over Eddie.

The thing is, I really do believe Paul *is* the man of my dreams. Sure, I thought I would love Eddie forever when I first met him, but I know deep down in my heart now, my love for Paul is the real thing this time. For this reason alone, I now find myself at a loss of what to do about it. Why does life have to be so bloody complicated at times? One thing I do know for sure, there is no way I am going to let Paul see me upset when we meet again next week. I figure he has enough worries ahead of him without me making him feel worse.

Throughout the week, leading up to our prearranged date on Thursday—our last night alone together—every single day I make sure to give myself a good talking to.

I completely agree with Paul's idea too, after we talk it over during one of our nightly phone calls. 'We should just go out and have a good time together, Isabella, regardless of the frightening uncertainties of this new world war.'

We have also come to the same conclusion; if we're meant to be together, then it will happen of its own accord, without us trying to reset the future for purely selfish reasons.

Of course, saying this to myself and actually believing it, is another thing entirely.

3

Isabella

1942
Magic of a moonlit kiss

For our last night together, Paul had said he'd like for us to spend our time somewhere down by the river. I can't think of a more romantic scene than the picturesque beauty of the mighty Yarra River, unquestionably the flowing life force of Melbourne city.

'Do you ever go out for a seafood meal in America, Paul?' I ask him as we stop and admire various intriguing items in shop windows along our way to the river.

'No, not really. Except maybe for a bowl of clam chowder sometimes. Most of the time though, it's usually a quick Chinese meal, pizza, hot dogs or hamburgers. A plate of fish and chips never really caught on—no pun intended—in the USA. At least, not like the tradition it has in jolly old England or Australia. Some people I used to know in California had this crazy idea to open an English-style fish and chip shop close to the beach. Sad to say, they didn't last very long. I do love fish, but most Americans I know prefer to catch their own, fresh out of the lakes and streams—particularly trout or salmon. The lakes back home are almost as big as the ocean anyway. They even have huge waves, I kid you not. Lake Superior in Michigan is one that comes to mind. From what I understand, Lake Superior apparently has about twelve massive shipwrecks buried deep within its depths.'

'Really? It's hard to believe any lake could have that many ships buried within its depths. Why do you think that is? I mean, why *don't* Americans like fish and chips?'

'To be honest, it's probably the same reason why we Americans prefer coffee instead of English tea. I think somehow it all goes back to the Boston Tea Party. After the revolution, we pretty much kicked the British Army out of America, along with their stuffy Victorian traditions as well. Tea parties were one of the first to go, I believe, followed by anything else that reeked of British traditions—including their rigid manners and fussy habits.'

'Ah, yes, of course! Now that you mention it, I do remember reading about that. Anyway, the reason why I'm asking you if you like fish and chips is because just up ahead is one of Melbourne's most popular fish and chip shops. Would you like to try some?'

'Sure! I do believe I am in the mood for some seafood tonight. Although you realise in America, we call potato chips, fries. Same thing really. They all taste great to me! In fact, my mouth is drooling at the very thought of them. Feel free to introduce me to your famous Aussie tradition, Isabella.'

'Okay! I was going to suggest we enjoy it in the traditional Aussie way, which is the whole lot—fish *and* chips—all wrapped up tightly in newspaper. I think it will be really nice, as you also expressed last night, to sit outside. Somewhere close to the river. After all, it's such a beautiful night, isn't it? Why sit inside when we have this amazing full moon beaming down on us? Right under the Southern Cross too. How Australian is that?'

'Yes indeed! Let's do it!' Paul squeezes my hand in eager response. 'Maybe, in honour of the occasion, we could also find a liquor store somewhere nearby where we can buy something cold and bubbly to drink.'

'You know, Paul, in Australia, we don't call them liquor stores. We call them bottle shops, but most of the time we buy our alcohol, or as we Aussies say, grog, from a pub or hotel. Especially out in country towns.'

'It's handy to know these things, especially from a true-blue Aussie sheila, ma'am.'

'No worries, mate!' I joke back, feeling totally relaxed in Paul's easy-going company.

Inside the seafood shop, Paul watches with fascination as the fishmonger overlaps two sheets of newspaper on his counter, followed by a large sheet of white paper over the top. Next, he empties a whole basket full of steaming-hot chips onto the middle and generously sprinkles salt all over them. He overlaps the steamy bundle of chips with the corner of the paper square, deftly tucking in the outer corners of the paper pieces, before rolling the whole lot into one tightly wrapped package. He does the same thing with the two large pieces of crispy, golden-battered fish, but in a separate package this time, along with few fresh slices of lemon. By the time he has handed over both packages to us, Paul's mouth is positively drooling. He can't wait to get into this whole delicious mess of hot food.

We manage to find a hotel close by, across the road, in fact, where Paul buys us a bottle of chilled champagne to share. The barmaid even offers to lend us two champagne glasses, on the condition we bring them back to her at the end of our meal.

'Why the champagne?' I ask as we seat ourselves at a nearby picnic table, as close to the river as possible. 'Apart from the fact that it's very expensive these days, I somehow imagined you'd be more of a beer drinker. Or even a bourbon or rum man.'

'Sure, I love beer and drink it with my buddies all the time. I even appreciate a good shot of bourbon or rum too, especially when sipped slowly by a roaring fire on a cold winter's night. But when I'm in the company of a beautiful woman on a night such as tonight, why wouldn't I want to celebrate all of this magic with you? Especially with our gourmet meal all wrapped up tight and ready to eat down by the beautiful Yarra River.'

'Gourmet meal?' I laugh. 'Now I know you are teasing me, Paul. This meal would be considered to be more of a poor man's meal in England.'

'Well, that's not how I see it. To me, this is a meal fit for a king, and tonight, under this huge golden orb above us, you are my beautiful Queen Isabella.'

I can't help but blush at his pretty kind of poetic speech. 'Thank you, Paul. That's so lovely of you to say. I certainly do believe we will be dining well tonight too, so yes, champagne is definitely called for. But speaking of dining, we'd best eat these fish and chips while they're still hot and crispy. Trust me, it's the only way to eat store-bought fish and chips.'

Paul starts to unwrap the parcel of chips with undisguised gusto.

'Oh no, Paul!' I laugh as I firmly place my hand over his, to stop him from going any further with his reckless paper-tearing quest. 'You must never *ever* unwrap this paper roll like that! Don't you realise, my good man, it's a sacrilege to do such a thing in Australia?'

'Now I know you're kidding me, right?' He laughs at the horrified look on my face. 'So please tell me then, sweet lady, why *can't* I just rip it open?' Paul questions with a cheeky grin.

'Because you'll let out all the steam if you do that,' I answer with mock primness, as I tear open only one end of the chip packet, but through all the layers of paper, until I reach the steamy centre. My eager fingers are finally able to locate the first few chips and extract them with glee. 'See? In order to keep the chips piping hot, you have to dig them out one by one. Besides, that's half the fun of eating them this way. It's different with the fish, of course. You really do have to open up the whole fish parcel, mainly so you can squeeze some lemon juice on top. I'll have you know, Yankee, this is the unofficial law of Australia, and don't you forget it!'

'I'll make sure I remember these rules in the future, then,' Paul chuckles as he digs his fingers into the paper hole. 'This Aussie ritual is kinda fun. Oh, man! They sure do taste good! I could get used to this.'

Paul squeezes some lemon juice onto the fish, then pulls off a large chunk and puts it in his mouth. 'Wow! This fish melts in your mouth. What sort of fish is this, by the way?'

'It's called flake. Not bad, huh?'

'So where do they catch this flake in Australia? It's really delicious!'

'Oh, you can catch flake anywhere in the world, really. You probably don't realise that flake is actually shark meat.' I smile to myself, waiting for his reaction, and he doesn't disappoint me.

'What the? Did you just say *shark?*'

I have to nod my confirmation as my mouth is full of fish.

'We're actually eating shark? Man! Who would have thought shark could taste so good.' He picks up the champagne bottle and pours some effervescence into each of our glasses. 'Let us make a toast, shall we, Isabella?"

'Why not!' I pick up my glass carefully because of my greasy fingers, ready to clink it with his. 'So, what shall we toast to?'

His answer is a long time coming and he appears serious now, his change of mood having the power to silence my unspoken words as well. Silence prevails again when mere words are no longer necessary. We study each other's faces intently, as if we could somehow freeze this moment forever, both of us clinging to this one second. We know all too well that after tomorrow, we'll be torn apart, by both distance and the unfathomable time frame of war. A test of sorts, I guess, meant to extract absolute faith in each other, while being forced apart for however long. So be it! If fate is determined to separate us, then we aren't about to accept this challenge lightly. This one night has the power to either remain as some treasured memory about someone we met all too briefly but still cared deeply about, *or* it could be the start of a whole lifetime together. Only time can tell.

'Let's just make a toast to each other. You first, Isabella,' Paul prompts me.

'May this night be one of many nights we share together.' We clink our glasses together and drink to my simple words. As an afterthought, I then add, 'Even if it may be far into the future before we meet again, hopefully we will get to do this again one day.' We touch glasses again with a resounding clink and sip, the bubbles tickling my nose this time.

My misty eyes look into Paul's own the whole time, with a heartfelt promise shining only for him.

Paul doesn't look away or try to break the spell, then adds a toast of his own. 'For my toast, I hereby dedicate it to this magical night with you under this huge golden moon, Isabella. I also promise you this; if I am lucky enough to return home in one piece after this war, I will be coming back for you.'

Without warning, I start blubbering. I am also laughing too. All at the same time. I immediately dive into my handbag with desperate fingers for my hanky, as I attempt to hide my silly embarrassment.

Paul leaves his seat to come around beside me. He takes my scrunched-up hanky from my hand to gently wipe my tears away. 'You never have to feel embarrassed with me, Isabella. Even when you cry, you still look wonderful to me. You might not realise this, but you have already captured my heart—and after only three nights too. I'll have you know that your beautiful face is stored away inside my heart forever. You cannot escape!'

It's not only with jest that Paul smiles, for just this moment, his smile is more of a reassuring, everything-is-going-to-be-alright kind of smile. As always, when he does smile, his eyes crinkle with gentleness and humour in that familiar way of his I already love so much.

'How can you see me as being beautiful right now?' I sniffle and blow my nose none too quietly this time. 'Especially with my face all blotchy. Heavens above! My nose is running like a tap as well.'

'Well, you are still beautiful to me—even if you are kind of blotchy right now!'

He jokingly ducks out of my way with lightning speed as I deliver a playful punch to his broad chest.

'Oh really! Is that right?' I laugh in spite of myself, my embarrassment completely forgotten. 'You know, I never realised until now what a terrible tease you can be!'

We turn serious again to gaze into the unfathomable depths of each other's eyes. We've been doing a lot of that lately. This must be what happens when two people fall in love for the first time. They simply can't get enough of each other.

The memory of tonight is already layered with intricately woven memories we have already stored away for all of time. Layer upon layer, over months, followed by years of yearning, such moments can be instantly recalled in the blink of an eye. The dawns of tomorrow may force us apart, but in our hearts, where it matters most of all, this new love we share will hopefully remain steadfast forever.

***

We stay by the river for another hour or so, which seems like only minutes really. Why is it, that when you want time to stand still, it just speeds up instead?

We sit quietly, cuddled up together on the picnic bench as lovers the world over tend to do. We cling desperately to each other and speak softly, with the blossoming petals of love opening up for the very first time. With our heads close together, we turn to gaze up at the full moon. This bold luminous moon, as if from some mystical cosmic force, reflects itself unashamedly onto the surface of the river as a huge golden orb. It is so huge, we can almost reach out and touch it. So it's not hard for us to imagine at all, that for one night only, this glorious glowing moon shines *only* for us.

We finally have to acknowledge it's time to head back to the train station. It's back home for me and back to the army base for Paul. Both of us are only too aware all roads from tomorrow onwards will inevitably lead us far away from each other for too many years.

With heavy hearts and heartfelt declarations of love, mere words can no longer fill the void, nor the sudden loneliness threatening to take over. Except for the champagne glasses, we quickly bundle up all of the freely scattered crumbs tightly within the greasy paper wrappings, along with the empty champagne bottle, and toss the whole lot into the nearest rubbish bin along the riverwalk. After we fulfil our promise to return the champagne glasses to the hotel, we slowly work our way back along the tree-lined river, linking arms once again.

In order for us to leave the river behind, we must first cross one road to take a different short track, before we reach the street that eventually leads us back to the train station.

Just before we cross the road, Paul suddenly pulls me back closer to-wards the steps that lead to the water's edge. The water is much shallower at this particular spot where most people choose to swim in the summer months.

'Paul, what's wrong?' His sudden detour back to the river, instead of away from it, alarms me at first.

'There is absolutely nothing wrong, I assure you.' He pulls me closer into his arms with gentle pressure. 'I just need to do this.' He kisses me then with a passion that takes me completely by surprise. So much so, I literally go weak at the knees. So much for our well-behaved, sedate kisses up until now. Even though I'm a bit shocked at first, I find myself responding to him with the same urgent passion. Our kiss deepens even more, until it is Paul who pulls away first. He takes a few deep breaths to calm himself, while my wayward toes are prompted to flex themselves loose again within my high-heeled shoes.

'Man, oh man! I don't know what came over me just now, Isabella. Judging by your response, though, you aren't too upset with me for kissing you like that … Please tell me you're not?'

'I have a naughty confession to make, Paul. I was sort of hoping you would. My grandmother always tells me that good girls should *never* make the first move. Despite her warning, I *still* wanted you to kiss me.'

'We *could* always blame it on the full moon, you know? It's so massive, and just so amazing, isn't it?'

I can only nod in agreement as I gaze up at the moon with the same kind of awe.

Paul continues on, 'It's almost like we can reach up and touch it. What hope do any lovebirds have of resisting each other when the moon has a mind to cast its spell over them in a romantic setting such as this?'

'I totally agree, but it isn't just the full moon, is it? Something special has happened between us tonight, and I wish this moment could last forever, Paul.'

'Me too! I can well imagine, there must be lots of lovers out there tonight, under the same intoxicating lunar spell as us. Right at this exact moment.'

Paul kisses me once more and I, of course, respond in the same way without hesitation. After some unfathomable length of time, we reluctantly pull back, realising at last that it's hopeless for either of us to continue any further.

As we quietly walk for a while, close together, Paul suddenly stops in his tracks and gently turns me around to face him. 'Do you know what? I've decided to give this moon an extra special name tonight.'

'You have? What sort of name did you have in mind, Paul?'

'I've decided I'm going to name this moon after you, Isabella. From now on, every full moon I see while I am away from you, I will forever think of as Isabella's Moon.'

My heart does a double backflip. 'Oh, Paul! Do you really think so?'

'I sure do! Whenever I get lonely or scared from now on, all I'll have to do is think of this magic night with you in my arms, and I know I'll be okay.'

We walk the rest of the way to the train station clinging to each other, stopping every few feet to embrace again, with each new kiss deeper than the one before. Just as well we reach the station, or we could be in big trouble. It's getting harder and harder to pull away from our desperate embraces each time. So much so, that we could even end up embarrassing ourselves in front of these other commuters already waiting on one of the nearby platforms. Suddenly, we're completely oblivious to public opinions. We're still very aware of people whispering to each other, but when we turn to look back, everyone is beaming at us.

As the train chugs into the station and brakes down to its final stop beside us, reality takes hold. We somehow have to pull back from each other through a sheer force of will. Tears are streaming down my face now as I steadfastly try to hold onto his outstretched fingers. How am I ever going to accept the cruelty of saying goodbye to Paul already, especially when I have only just found him? This very question prompts me to make a new pact with myself, right here and right now. No matter what happens from today onwards, I will do my very best to make sure I do find Paul again. Who knows? Maybe our full moon tonight will continue to weave some magic for us. Beyond its intoxicating hold over us tonight, anyway. Yes, I am realistic enough to know a lot *can* happen in a person's life, even within just a few years. But I truly believe I am up for the challenge of finding my Paul again.

Somewhere, somehow …

4
Paul

1942
Movement in the camp

I lay awake for hours tossing and turning, my mind filled with thoughts of my sweet Isabella. *'Oh God help me,'* I almost blurt out. Confusion fills my gut with fear as I try to settle my restless body down into this unyielding, squeaky bunk bed. I have been one of the hundreds of 'Yanks' on R and R roaming around Australia for close on four weeks. The fun times have ended. Our unit is now on the verge of shipping out to God knows where.

I must have finally drifted off to sleep, because the next thing I hear is the heavy door at the entrance to our sleeping quarters being swung open with force, followed by some mighty heavy footsteps stomping on the floor close by. At precisely 0300 hours, our CO marches into our quarters to bellow at us, 'On your feet, ladies!'

We hit the ground running! Bodies all moving in sync, like a wave of giant ants groggily sidestepping each other on their way to the shower block. Ice-cold showers very early in the morning are guaranteed to stir the sleepiest of us into action. Within twenty minutes we're all uniformed, lined up and standing at attention in front of the transport buses.

A convoy of buses provided by the Australian Government await us outside, just beyond the tented area, but within certain designated areas large enough to allow for ten full-sized buses side by side. This army convoy is to transport us all into Melbourne's Southern Cross railway station. When the military machine pass down any logistic movement through the chain of command, it doesn't matter one iota if those orders include dozens of different units as well. As with anything military, we move as one unit in everything we do.

Despite the hidden fears in some and a naive sense of adventure in others, when it comes down to fighting any war, you just do what you have to do, regardless of any personal demons that follow us around. This morning is no exception. There are no grumbles forthcoming, and none expected. Right from the very first moment when we stumble out of bed and onto these waiting buses, everything moves forward as one well-oiled military unit. A regime geared to unfailing efficiency from the get-go. Including one's thoughts and feelings. It's part of the entire package. 'You're in the army, son!'

Once the bus is underway, I look around me, and apart from a few snippets of conversation in front of and behind my seat, I can't help but feel a sense of uneasiness. When a busload of rowdy men all crammed in tight are neither talking nor laughing together, that's reason enough for me to worry. Apart from the usual shuffling of bodies adjusting them-selves on inflexible straight-back seats and the clearing of phlegm from smoky throats, the overall mood is sombre. Usually, on any previous trips together, once we've settled in for the ride, there's always the usual brief smattering of 'mornin'' or 'that was a great card game last night. Won fifty bucks by the end of the night, too'.

Strangely, this morning, after the first ten miles, there is no talking at all. Only a lot of staring out the window, myself included. Along with my silent buddies, I fail to see anything around to snap me out of this apprehension squeezing my gut inside out. There's only my darkened imaginings to keep me in poor company for however long.

My true fears continue to nip away at my resolve to carry on regardless of what lies ahead. Yes, I know we are in Australia only because of a war. Certainly not for a merry holiday, or to enjoy Australia's white sandy beaches. We're not even here to romance the Australian gals. These distractions turned out to be extra bonuses we never expected. Until now, our introduction to Australia has been an exciting time. Our routines and daily schedules fairly laidback. Until now, at least. We still have our daily marches first up every morning, military talks, instructions, plus the usual roll calls throughout the week. Once our duties are out of the way, though, we're free in the evenings and weekends to take leave off base and enjoy ourselves. But all the fun had to stop sometime, and that sometime is NOW!

We soon learn, right from boot camp, once you join the army, the military has you in their grasp. They expect you to toughen up overnight. This naturally includes any mommy's boys amongst us. No exceptions. There is no sympathy or tolerance to be had from any military quarter. Nor expected either. Never mind if some of us, who signed up for Uncle Sam, have never even fired a gun before.

Even if we are *supposed* to be trained fighting machines by now, inside our troubled minds we really are frightened little boys wanting to be back home with our families. In a little under a month's time, we are about to face an aggressive enemy under fire. In this case, the Japanese Army. This unfamiliar reality is too much for any trained soldier to grasp.

When the sun rises early in the skies each morning, as far back as I can remember, it's supposed to bring new promises of hope and adventure. Just not today, it seems. Today's dawning light brings with it a paralysing fear for whatever future we have left to hold onto.

Up until now, we have taken our easygoing freedom and socialising with the golden skinned ladies of Australia for granted. Whether we are ready for it or not, a whole new chapter of our lives is about to begin.

That's if we should survive this Pacific war at all.

***

Once the convoy of buses reaches Melbourne, we are ticked off on the endless list of service personnel and ordered to board a train. This impending trip from Melbourne to Darwin is to be our first leg of what is to be a three-legged journey altogether. According to our itinerary, the first leg of our journey is to be overland, up through the Northern Territory, over an impressive distance of 1,956 miles in one whole day, plus another eighteen hours the following day. My best buddy, Todd, and I look at each other with amazement. We never expected Australia to be this big since we were offhandedly told back home, 'It's just an island, really.'

After a full day of nonstop rail travel (through a desert landscape similar to the state of Texas, we're told), we are to arrive at an overnight stopover in Darwin. The next morning will see us board another train, on the second leg of our inland journey to Townsville, a city on the east coast of Australia, which mercifully also includes one full day of R and R.

Just in case this schedule doesn't exhaust us enough, the last leg of our train journey to the tropical city of Cairns, at the very top end of Australia, should cure one's lingering urge to explore fresh places forever. Thankfully, our last leg from Townsville to Cairns will be a brief run of around four hours. 'Only four hours?' Todd laughs humourlessly. 'Gee! Ain't nuthin' to it!'

5

Paul

1942
On a steamy train bound for war

At Melbourne's Southern Cross station, I hope to slip away to ring Isabella one more time before boarding the northbound train to Darwin. However, unbeknown to me, my staff sergeant has already thwarted this plan of mine. The top brass have given him strict instructions to keep a sharp eye on *all* of his men—just in case some of us get it into our heads to go AWOL. Especially those of us who have recently 'connected' with new sweethearts in Australia. Even if I have fallen madly in love with Isabella, the thought of going AWOL just isn't an option for any of us right now. In spite of the challenge of being caught going against orders, I still try to call her just the same. Even with scrounging around amongst my buddies for some loose Aussie coins to use in the pay phones, I am still not able to escape the eagle eye of our diligent CO. He isn't dropping his guard for anyone—including me. Not even for one lousy minute. *Dammit!*

In the end, I have no choice but to board the train without calling Isabella. As I stow my knapsack away in the overhead luggage racks, I make a promise to myself to try again at some other designated stop along the way.

Plopping down gratefully into one of the few remaining seats still available, I take to staring moodily out of the wider train windows on the right-hand side of the carriage facing our destination. After a few wasted minutes of watching the same damn scene on the station platform over and over, I start to wonder why our train is still stationary, but then I realise why. Everywhere I look, up and down our outgoing platform, there is much frantic activity going on. From what I can gather so far, just beyond the carriage doors, an orderly group of US guys in GI uniforms are still awaiting around for some official clearance from their COs.

After a while, I'm forced to turn away from this endless scene of chaotic delay to ease my bloodshot eyes for a bit. Without consciously thinking about it, I instantly find myself dreaming again of the classic beauty with the sweet-tasting ruby lips who has captured my heart so easily. I wonder for the hundredth time if I will ever get to see her again. I am only too aware, though, my future is out of my hands for the next few years—at least. My life has merely become a tool to be put to good use by not only the US Army, but the Australian and Philippine governments—oh, and please, let us not forget the Japanese enemy forces too. These major factors are about to play an integral part in my life, whether I return home in one piece, crippled for life, or even—heaven forbid—inside a pine box.

***

In order to reach our destination of Cairns, North Queensland, we must first pass through the monotonous, dead-straight centre of Australia, right up through the unforgiving Simpson Desert. Since the train is moving at such an incredibly slow speed, the CO has permitted us to jump on and off the train, to either walk or run alongside the train to stretch our legs. On one of my random wanderings alongside the train, I come across an Aboriginal hunting boomerang sticking up out of the ground. Since there was no-one around to make a claim to it, I decide to take it back onto the train with me. When I show it to some of my buddies, Carl jokes, 'Maybe this is the only boomerang that will never come back, after all?'

We are all quite intrigued by the kangaroos, but then much to my disgust, some of the guys decide to see how good their aim is by using the animals as target practise. I care very little about going along with this kind of mentality. To me, these kangaroos are so unique—the way they race alongside our train, like real-life bullets in motion. The kangaroos, in some ways, remind me of dolphins. Just as dolphins love to race alongside boats and ships in open seas, these kangaroos also love to race trains over this parched land, all in the same carefree, joyful way.

At night, during the long relentless hours on the train, some guys choose to play cards for hours on end, some like to move to music in their own shuffling, loose-limbed way, in small groups here and there. The ABC radio station had previously set up a music program for some entertainment relief for our troops in the dining car. Some of us choose to stretch out across several seats, trying to catch some shut-eye while the seats are still vacant. Some attempt to read books or magazines in the dull light of the carriage, while others, like myself, position ourselves outside every one of the connecting doors of each carriage. The air inside the carriage during the day is insufferably hot and steamy, as it ruthlessly threatens to choke us close to death. If breathing the air doesn't kill you, the thick red dust seeping into every tiny crack in these timber-walled carriages just might. It has the power to either blind us or merely settle heavily, ultimately making every flat surface as gritty as all hell.

Throughout our first night onboard the train, every single carriage becomes unbearable to sleep in as the train rumbles on so painfully slow towards Cairns. It doesn't seem to matter if your carriage is at the front or the back of the train. There is never any escape from the stifling mugginess. Just like a heavy woollen blanket, this dust insidiously continues to settle in over us.

To make our misery complete, when some card game is in progress, the dining car becomes choked by either cigarette or cigar smoke as well. This results in a man-induced dense cloud, wafting upwards, competing for supremacy with the energy-sucking stillness.

Out in the fresh air, just outside the carriage doorways at each end, is where I choose to be for most of the night. The only trouble is, everyone in my carriage has the same idea. Before long, I'm hard-pressed to find my quiet space to escape the obnoxious combination of smoke haze and sweaty, unwashed bodies stinking out every damn carriage without mercy.

***

After a much-needed reprieve at Townsville overnight and four more hours in our carriage, the train is on its last leg to Cairns. As we head closer to our final destination, the passing landscape suddenly changes from the occasional tree and sparse clumps of grass dotted along the railway tracks, to a lush rainforest landscape of towering palm trees, moss-covered logs laying where they fell and tangled vines creeping up anything growing skyward. As we pull into the station, I can't believe I'm seeing tropical plants growing all along the length of the station platform! Even before the carriage doors open wide, some men are already standing by the doors, wanting to be set free at last. These men jostle aggressively with each other to be the first ones out of the hellbox—as we now jokingly refer to our stinking prison on wheels. After being pent up in a steamy, smoky confined space for days on end, good old-fashioned, gentlemanly manners matter very little anymore.

6

Paul

1942
Out of the firebox and up into the steam

How deluded are we to imagine that once we arrive at Cairns, our troubles will be over for at least a week or two? For those of us, including myself, who aren't used to the tropics, we find it extremely difficult to handle the high humidity of Australia's Far North. Even before we left Melbourne, our superiors tried to warn us about the oppressive heat in the tropics, but nothing could have prepared us for the breath-sucking reality of it.

Son of a bitch! I immediately feel like a wrung-out dishrag within minutes of disembarking the train. The sweat oozes out of every pore of my skin. How am I ever going to handle the possibility of such torture of this extreme heat for months on end? Maybe even for years … No way!

What was I thinking when I volunteered for this hell on Earth, anyway? If I ever seriously doubt my sanity to sign up to fight this war, this would definitely have to be one of those times. But it's too late now. I'll just have to learn to get used to it, but it doesn't mean I have to like it.

Upon our arrival in Cairns, our unit CO informs us we are to be bivouacked at the Cairns military base before the boats come to take us to the Philippine Islands in two weeks. We soon find out the army base is much closer to a tropical rainforest than to the city of Cairns. Great!

So that can only mean that not only do we have to endure this oppressive heat every day, but we'll also have lots of time to squash millions of bugs throughout the night as well. This should be fun!

Man! If I'm already grumbling about the steamy conditions in Cairns, what will I be like when we head further north to the Philippine Islands in a few weeks' time?

As with anything run by the military machine, our tent city soon turns into an efficient operation in no time. Before long, our mess tent is dishing out thousands of extra meals for all incoming units arriving at Cairns. To challenge the mess crew's stamina further, they expect many more troops to arrive within the next two weeks.

Even though this tropical heat has zapped even my reserve store of energy these past few days, I know I'm not alone. My buddies are feeling utterly miserable with this relentless oppressive heat as well. All we want to do is to lie around under some shady palm tree somewhere and sleep forever, but we can't even do that. Since we are still part of a wartime military operation we're still expected to keep our sleeping quarters spotless and answer to roll calls at the crack of dawn—every damn morning and on weekends too.

There is one compensation to living in the tropics, though. Taking into consideration the obvious contrasts from the Northern Hemisphere, the army has mercifully swapped our uniforms from our usual heavier-cloth outfits to lighter khaki cotton-drill shorts, short-sleeved shirts and cotton socks. This is, however, where the sympathy stops; they still demand we wear closed-toe footwear at all times.

Once we attend to our usual daily military routines, we're allowed off the base for some well-earned R and R. There are always a few army trucks available to take us into Cairns city each day. By day's end, some other trucks have been assigned to bring us back to base. Most of us choose to find our own way back, especially if we don't want the MPs breathing down our necks all the time. Of course, there is always the option of a few taxis available at odd times and even city buses running at set times of the day during weekdays, but not on weekends. The downside of the buses is that the last one leaves the city limits no later than 2200 each night. Some of our men, in pursuit of entertainment, or even better still, some female company, usually reject returning to the base this early in the evening.

For myself, I'm always eager to head into Cairns with my buddies, but most of the time, I prefer to explore this beautiful tropical city on my own. Even though I still haven't adjusted to this insufferable heat yet, I can still appreciate the tropical splendour of Cairns city itself. This is like a whole new world to me, so far removed from where I grew up on the outer limits of Chicago. Not just with the difference in climate or size comparison of cities either—the people who live here full-time seem to be in a world of their own too.

The locals all seem to be oblivious and exist in a state of happy madness all the time. I can now understand why too. *Man!* If this insatiable thirst doesn't drag you down into an inebriated stupor every night, then the daily perils of enormous crocodiles, deadly snakes or sea stingers lurking nearby in the sea most definitely will. I soon discover in the tropics that the idea of quenching one's thirst takes on a whole new meaning. Swilling beers or downing entire bottles of whisky seems to be the normal thing to do up this way. It's all too obvious to Cairns' recent influx of military visitors too. Drinking any liquid in the tropics must be either very wet, very icy or even better, loaded with alcohol. Preferably all three.

Not only that, but drinking in the various hotels or pubs of Cairns (aka watering holes) is also the fastest way to meet the locals. Unfortunately, when the inevitable effect of too much alcohol takes over—as it does every night—trouble always follows. Brawls are so easily instigated it seems. When drunken fights start to spill out onto the streets every night, I soon grow weary of this whole noisy scene. That's when it's time for me to head away from the nightly drama to a quiet place for my own peace of mind. I always trust that I'll be able to hitch a ride with some local driver heading in the general direction of our base camp. Not all of Cairns' citizens suffer from this tropical madness, thank goodness, and I learn something new about this place every time.

I usually ask to be dropped off close to the base, then I prefer to walk the rest of the way on my own. Even when the army—and the locals—warn me all the time of poisonous snakes, spiders and those huge, aggressive cassowary birds moving freely around the area. Honestly, I still think I prefer to take my chances with the natural wildlife any day than the human variety lately.

***

Within my first few weeks at Cairns, by chance, I get to meet another beautiful girl to distract me from unchartered desires. I'm certainly not looking for female companionship up this way, but because of some twisted idea of fun from the universe, this new temptation came my way just the same.

Just like Isabella, Nina immediately caught my attention. She is completely different to Isabella, of course, but as my buddies soon find out for themselves—just like all the beautiful girls in Melbourne—the girls of Cairns are going all-out to attract the attention of any handsome, all-American GI staying in their local area for however long.

Some guys in my unit could openly take advantage of this flattering attention, if they had a mind to. Especially with their movie-star good looks and gentlemanly manners. Most of the guys I know, though, are very serious about staying below the female radar. They work hard and never consciously try to draw attention to themselves from any women at all. But when you're young, single and thousands of miles from home and these beautiful women are suddenly throwing themselves at you, it's only natural for any guy to be flattered by all this extra feminine attention. That's what we keep telling ourselves, anyway.

In all fairness, though, none of us are safe from these ever-loving, feminine clutches, and I'm certainly no exception. Just knowing my buddies and I are about to enter a war zone soon, has us all feeling more than a little apprehensive. Although none of us are about to admit this openly to each other just yet. Which makes me wonder now; why did I make such a promise of everlasting love to Isabella in the first place? What was I thinking? I never should've promised such a thing to her at all. Apart from the fact that I'm missing her something awful already, I now have to ask myself is it really fair of me to expect Isabella to wait so many years for me to return? Probably not. If only I could've talked openly to my buddies about these kinds of unfamiliar feelings, I would've known they too are having doubts, just as I am now. Instead of talking it out with each other like women tend to do, the powers that be expect us to 'man up' and just get on with this whole war scenario.

Suddenly, the prospect of going off to fight a war and fulfilling a promise I've already made to Isabella hits me! I find myself so totally alone now and so completely out of my depth. If I had to sum up this feeling in just one word, that word would be: loneliness.

So, I too allow myself to get caught up in this intensive dating game, with me and my buddies as the major prize. When we GIs set off from the USA, we were told we were to be stationed in a country called Australia first up. We had absolutely no idea what it was going to be like at all. All we knew was that there would be lots of kangaroos hopping around everywhere and beautiful beaches. Oh, and that some Indigenous people apparently inhabit the island as well.

We never dreamed, even for one minute, there'd be cities, civilised people, or even a whole bevy of lovely girls, all eager to meet us. From what I've seen so far, war quickly changes one's normal perceptions of acceptable rules regarding promiscuity and 'proper social etiquette'. Suddenly, life appears to take on an all-or-nothing existence. This includes almost everyone, in fact—civilians and military troops alike. Despite one's best intentions, emotions and desires can still run rampant within this hot and steamy prewar zone.

One night, on my lone wanderings around Cairns city, I spot a cafe that serves fish and chips. *Man!* There sure are a lot of fish and chip diners here in Australia. My thoughts immediately drift back to that last amazing meal I shared with Isabella under a starry, moonlit sky back in Melbourne. Without hesitation, I enter the shop, ready to recapture the same experience again—or part thereof. The minute I open the wood-framed screen door, the smell of hot oil and raw fish bombards my senses. The very thought of some steaming hot, crispy fish and thick chunky chips, all wrapped up tight in newspaper, has reawakened a happy memory for me.

That's when I see Nina for the first time. There she is, with her glossy black hair, barely restrained within a thick ponytail, a light sheen of perspiration on her beautiful face and her exposed neck above her short-sleeved blouse giving me the impression her smooth olive skin is naturally glowing. She looks up for a moment to see who is coming through the door, and at that very moment, her expressive smiling eyes, the colour of liquid molasses, catches my attention. Just watching her serving a constant queue of customers in such a cheeky, confident way immediately captures my lonely heart.

When it's my turn to be served, she acknowledges me with her head tilted to the side, with two perfectly shaped eyebrows raised by her unspoken question. This signal is, of course, supposed to prompt me to hurry and place my order. To my embarrassment, no words are forthcoming. I'm suddenly rendered tongue-tied in the face of such natural beauty.

'You want to order, sir? Or do you intend to hold up this queue all night?' When she speaks, an almost smoky tone of slightly accented English infuses her words.

'Sorry, ma'am! … Umm, I'd like to order some fish and chips, please.'

'Ah! So you're American, then!' the girl states, as if this explains my rudeness straight away. 'What sort of fish would you like then, Mr

American? Do you even know what you want or you would like me to explain to you what is available tonight?'

'Er, what about some flake? So far, that's the only fish I know of in Australia.'

'Well, yes. We have flake, but you could also try the barramundi, or maybe even some red emperor? I think maybe you might like them. They're all delicious.'

'I'll tell you what, then. Give me one piece of red emperor and one of the barramundi, please. This way, I can try both and tell you what I think later.'

'Would you like some chips to go with the fish, sir? Or maybe some potato scallops?'

I must have looked really vague by her latest question. 'Potato scallops?'

'Sliced potatoes, which we coat in batter and deep fry in oil. Very popular.'

'Well, you know what … I'm hungry enough to have both the hot chips and the scallops as well. Just so I can say I've tried them all.'

She scribbles my order onto a docket, takes my money, then sticks my order onto a nail directly in front of the cook, just like they do at the fast-food joints back home. At least some things are still familiar. I thank the beautiful girl behind the counter and ask her for her name. She tells me her name is Nina. Judging by her olive complexion, she looks like she could either be Greek or Italian.

Once the rush at the counter is over, she calls out to me at my small chrome table setting nearby. 'Hey, American! What is your name?' she asks me in a cheeky, no-nonsense way.

'My name is Paul, and yes, I am American. From Chicago. What about you?'

'I am one of five daughters of Greek immigrants, but I've lived in Cairns all my life. My family owns a sugar cane farm, about twenty miles from Cairns.'

She then tells me she and her four sisters share a small place in Cairns on weekdays, but her parents still expect their daughters to go back to the farm on weekends. To Nina's parents, family is everything. With so much unrest going on outside their home, they try to keep their family as close together as possible. Nina quickly emphasises to me she and her sisters are happy to grant their simple request.

By the end of my meal, I'd already asked Nina out on a date, and after that, a few more to follow. I really enjoy hearing about her family and life as she knows it in Australia. Even though I'm still determined not to get too serious about her, I soon realise, I just need someone I can talk to, and Nina certainly helps me with this. She hangs onto my every word, especially when I talk about my life in America. I can tell she's wanting to know me more, but just the same, I don't think it's very fair of me to lead her on with any false promises either.

I guess the time has come for me to let her go, so I must tell her our friendship can go no further. 'I'm sorry, Nina. But it's just not going to work and I think you know it too.'

Naturally, I expect some kind of resistance, but what I don't expect is for Nina to immediately start sobbing. 'How can you say such a thing, Paul? You must know by now I am in love with you! Why do you do this to me? How am I supposed to live without you now? You tell me that!'

Just as I'm about to turn and walk away, she really begins to load the guilt trip onto me. 'Please, Paul, I beg of you. *Please* give our love another chance.'

When she suddenly rushes forward to stop me from leaving, I realise I have no choice but to physically grab hold of her hands to release the tight grip she now has on me. Despite me carefully having to prise her fingers one by one off my shirt, she's still determined to try and stop me from leaving. Her sobbing, which had started off at a normal voice level at first, is now starting to become embarrassingly loud—within only a few seconds. So much so, that some people across the road are glaring at me with open hostility written on their faces. I have this bad feeling they're about to start hollering for the cops—or rather, the police—any minute now.

If I run away now, these people are really going to be suspicious of me. What to do?

Right at that moment of me deciding whether or not I should stay to placate Nina further, or take my chances and just run for my life—with the bystanders, the Australian police and even Nina all chasing after me—help arrives. What I wasn't expecting though was to be rescued by the American MPs.

There were two MPs in the Jeep, now pulled up beside Nina and me. The MP closet to me must have intuitively taken in my sticky situation with one glance.

The first thing he did was to climb out of the Jeep and to step forward. He moved forward in an intimidating manner and eyeballed me, up close but not so personal. His aggressive body language was meant to convince me—and thankfully Nina too—he meant business.

With a convincing gruffness, 'Shouldn't you be back at the base by now, Sergeant? What part of sticking to curfew time don't you understand, SERGEANT?'

I realised he was deliberately emphasising my rank, to imply I should know better than to linger in town past curfew time. Even if his accusation of my tardiness wasn't exactly true this time, I wasn't about to argue with my rescuer about any military rules at this point.

Instead, I stood silent in front of him with my head bowed, suitably chastised by his dressing-down of me, since he did this in front of Nina too.

Just so there was no more doubt where Nina was concerned with finally getting the message, MP Harrison (according to his name badge on the front pocket of his military shirt) stepped back to salute me. No doubt because he finally realised by the three stripes on my sleeves, I formally outranked him this time.

'I will have to ask you now, SIR, to please climb up into the back of this vehicle, so we can be on our way ASAP!'

I followed through with his military order posthaste. I didn't dare make eye contact with Nina just yet. Not until I was seated on the back of the Jeep, anyway. Only then did I wave to her as we took off, kicking up a mound of pebbles laying loose in the gutter as it purposefully accelerated out of town. Not one word was uttered between the two MPs in the front of the Jeep and me as we drove out of town. I'm guessing—one or both—of these guys, may have been in the same situation themselves at some point since arriving in Australia, hence my timely rescue just now.

As for my time spent with Nina these past few weeks, I think I already knew for myself that Nina wasn't in love with me. She was more in love with the idea of me, really.

I have finally been able to admit to myself—and without any further doubts—that I'm still very much in love with Isabella, and this time there is no infatuation at all.

It seems my heart has already decided for me what I already knew anyway; my love for Isabella to me is what true love is all about.

7

Paul

1942
Some trouble at the top end

These past few weeks spent in Cairns were meant to be a transition of sorts for the troops, but whenever there are any anxious rumours, or even a hint of live action amongst the troops, suppressed fears or tensions are bound to run rampant.

When recurring nightmarish images of dodging live bullets or facing death head-on start affecting the peace of mind of *all* the new troops, something's gotta give. The reality of this war, happening in real-time on some not-so-blissful tropical island, has finally started to hit home, for Australian and American troops alike. As a result, any underlining tensions among the men in the central city area of Cairns alone have inevitably surfaced.

I've soon discovered for myself over these weeks that there is one common denominator between the citizens of Chicago and Cairns: black skin versus white. The racial tensions, because of the white Australian policy regarding the indigenous Aboriginal people of Australia, appears to run parallel to the racial tensions between a great number of pioneer American settlers, in regard to both the Native Americans and the African Americans. Particularly where our US troops from Chicago, New York and the southern states are concerned. The inevitable mix of too much alcohol and unexpressed fear quickly results in fights breaking out in the pubs and city streets of Cairns. Cairns' police force and our own American MPs have had their work cut out for them.

Brawls are instigated by chatting up the wrong girl, having the wrong skin colour or even just opening your mouth at the wrong time. All factors are enough to arouse anger from drunken tongues all around. Fights usually start inside the pub and hotels, but inevitably end up crashing out onto the streets after one too many drinks. Military visitors and locals alike quickly discard good manners in favour of turning the air blue with drunken profanity instead. Every night, the Cairns police and the American MPs attempt to control any rowdiness or muscle-loaded punches thrown in any direction, but with no success. After a while, it's difficult for any man in the middle of these fights, regardless of race or colour, to know who is hitting who. As if on cue, the Cairns cops with their closed-in paddy wagons and the US MPs with their trucks or Jeeps, usually rock up to gather up their own rowdy lot and move them on out, allowing some order of civilisation to take back the city again.

It isn't just the military personnel either, who are totally fed up with all the tension amongst both the Australian and American troops. It was duly reported, to all concerned in the local Cairns paper, that the Cairns City Council will be calling an emergency meeting in the town hall because the current consensus from the townspeople is that enough is enough! The citizens want their city back! All of this noisy brawling in their streets at night has to stop, regardless of which country is to blame. Besides, it is no longer safe for any citizens of Cairns—adult or child— to be out at night.

Shortly after the Cairns council meeting, an impromptu meeting between the concerned citizens of Cairns and the combined representatives of the US military body and the Australian military body based at Cairns, and a plan of action was finally put into place.

Local volunteers magically arrive in their hundreds to set up makeshift kitchens all over Cairns for an entire weekend. They offered all troops, regardless of race or colour, piping-hot tea or coffee, home-baked scones with jam and cream, SAO biscuits with butter, cheese and tomato, and lamingtons. Man, oh man! They tasted so good too!

Lamingtons, I am told, are really just chunky squares of plain cakes, coated in chocolate icing and finally covered all over with desiccated coconut. The ladies have even offered us slices of chunky fruit cake, which are so delicious, I just want to keep eating them. There are also some SAO biscuits, which would be called crackers in America, and I later found out from one of the serving ladies, these light, crumbly SAO biscuits were so named in honour of all Salvation Army officers. The scones served here in Australia are in fact a sweet version of the savoury ones we eat back home with our main meal. The Australian Country Women's Association, or CWA, served up their Aussie version to us with jelly and freshly whipped cream instead. Most of the married women invite us home for a Sunday lamb roast to meet their family, while the sporty gentlemen of Cairns offer to teach us baseball-mad Americans how to play cricket. In return, our American guys have begun teaching the sporting Aussies how to play baseball as well. By Sunday night, the locals and visiting troops are too tired or too full of food to want to fight each other anymore.

The effects of these thoughtful volunteers have been threefold. We have all stopped fighting amongst ourselves and have definitely developed a taste for some real Australian cooking. We also get to see a glimpse of what the true Australian mateship is all about. Most of all, though, we have all calmed down at last. This is what the wonderful volunteers had already figured out, long before the rest of us. We've finally realised what we homesick boys have craved most of all: to know someone still cares about us! Not just the regimented military side of us, but the hometown man or woman, still hanging on for all of us. To them, we aren't just some nameless soldiers who might never get to see their homeland again.

⋆⋆⋆

It's time to go! Our new orders have only just been handed down from the big brass. Our platoon is due to leave at dawn tomorrow. Who would have thought we Yankees, at the onset of this journey, would end up falling in love with this incredible country? Most of all, its warm-hearted people. This certainly proved to be the case for me. I have fallen in love with this island continent called Australia, and I never ever want to leave these golden shores.

***

Lining up with my buddies to board the platoon boats all along the water's edge and waving back to all of our new-found friends, suddenly this frightening image pops into my mind of the possibility of my own death. I can see myself lying on a crowded beach somewhere in the Pacific Ocean, covered in my own precious blood, which is now draining out of my body and onto the sand beneath me. When I take another detached look over the rest of my body, I notice a seeping hole has instantly popped open where my stomach used to be. When I dare to look around me and beyond my own body, I can see other soldiers lying there too, all shot up and broken like me. Some are lying on the blood-soaked sands, with their eyes wide open, staring back towards their loved ones at home most likely.

Is this sudden image in my head meant to be a prophecy of things to come for me?

Once this image of such realism takes hold of my jittery nerves, my heart starts thumping and my legs start twitching of their own accord. I have no choice now but to find some way to escape this impending hell on Earth! What am I really doing here, anyway? *Son of a bitch!* I must have been crazy to even sign up for this war in the first place!

What are my options of getting away from here? I mean, what is the worst that can happen to me? I'll no doubt be charged with going AWOL, or maybe even demoted.

Either way, the question I have to ask myself now is should I go, or should I stay?

Am I prepared to take the consequences of my actions? Yes, I do believe I am!

***

While I stand in line to board the platoon, my mind is racing ahead of me.

If you're going to do it, Paul, just do it! Once you are all crammed in there with the other guys on the boat, there'll be no more chances of escape. You have to go *now!*

So, while we are still waving goodbye to our new-found Australian friends at the wharf, I seize my moment of escape by climbing down the less visible side of the boat. I dive underwater, knowing I will have to hold my breath for as long as possible. Staying under, I know I can only resurface every few minutes to catch a quick breath of air. Ever so slowly, I make my way towards an old storage shed nearby I spotted earlier back on the boat. I already figured out too—when I hatched my reckless plan to jump ship—the shed would be far enough away from the main wharf for immediate cover.

I was wrong! As soon as poked my head out of the water, I knew I was in *big* trouble.

There, awaiting my arrival at the boatshed, are three burly MPs, with the serious end of their firearms pointing directly at me, effectively cutting me off any further avenues of escape. The MP in the middle —and obviously the main spokesmen for the other guys—steps forward, devilishly projecting a truly scary smile my way.

'Ah! Planning a tropical holiday on your own were you, Staff Sergeant?'

Without waiting for my reply, he directs the other two MPs with a few sharp hand movements to heave me out of the water. 'Please allow us to help you out of the water, shall we, Staff Sergeant.' While the two *assisting* MPs pull my waterlogged, fully clothed body out of the water like I weigh nothing at all, the head guy keeps his firearm pointed my way.

'I am sure you were just wanting to take a quick swim to cool yourself off, Staff Sergeant … But guess what? The only reward you're going to get for all of your foolish efforts will be to cool off your heels in our guarded tent instead. In other words—you are now under arrest, so please oblige us—if you would be so kind—by facing the other way for these nice gentlemen.'

Even though I cooperated without a fight, I do feel rather foolish now, even somewhat humiliated, by the unyielding metal handcuffs holding my wrists tightly together behind my back. Deep down, though, my brief moment of freedom helped to boost my rebellious spirit again. As a result of my reckless bravado of impulsively jumping ship, I knew there was bound to be some severe consequences for my actions. As I await my sentence to be handed down to my unit's CO, I'm forced to acknowledge the trouble my foolish actions have gotten me into.

The trouble is, the more I sweat over the consequences of my actions, the less I am able to come up with answers as to what will happen to me once we reach our destination and my fate is officially decided upon. In the meantime, our platoon boats head out towards Mindanao, which is part of the Philippines. That's where we are to be stationed for the duration of this war against the Japanese under the aggressive fierceness of their air, sea and land forces.

As I take in the tight quarters of other guys squashed in all around me on the platoon boat, the sea spray is trying its best to blind me as I look out towards the horizon. Instead of taking in the beauty of the dawning of a brand-new day and the blue-purple silhouettes of the Papua New Guinea smaller islands in the distance, I can only see a dismal uncertain future in front of me. But after an hour of rehashing this crazy worrying over and over again, I have finally come to the conclusion that I'm not doing myself any favours by dwelling on my fate.

I mean, what's the worse they can do to me, anyway? The way I see it, the highly probable answers to the questions I am seeking inside my head right now are turning out to be far too hazardous to my peace of mind.

I mean, what if I *am* sent to jail? Will I be verbally disgraced in front of the big brass—maybe even in front of my whole unit? Most likely. Maybe my pay will be severely docked too *OR* I could have my sergeant's rank stripped away from me completely. I honestly don't see them sending me back home in disgrace at this stage, though, since the army needs all the trained troops they can get to fight this war. But, well, I'm just one soldier, so it's still possible. Seriously, though, I don't think I need to go there at this stage yet.

You never know with the army machine at times. Especially in the case of a soldier deserting his post. Hopefully, the military powers that be won't resort to a firing squad as punishment for me! Do they even do that sort of thing in the army these days?

To my way of thinking, the worst punishment they can dish out to me is to keep on 'stewing' in silence like this, at least for the next few days, until we're set up on the island.

***

Just as I thought. My rebellious actions have certain drawbacks in the army. Just like when I was in high school, in a way. When I misbehaved in class, I'd be kicked out by the teacher and sent to the principal's office with a note. Maybe the headmaster might have even suspended me from school for a few days too—depending on the 'crime'.

With my punishment dished out by the army, it was ultimately carried out in one of the ways I'd already imagined on my way over to Mindanao. At least my punishment was, in my somewhat relieved mind, thankfully the lesser of all the possible options I came up with. No verdict of desertion or firing squad, at least. *This time, anyway.*

Before I jumped ship, I was a staff sergeant, but as the consequences of my 'foolish and impulsive actions' have been dealt with by military law, and I was immediately demoted back to corporal. I don't really mind too much, though. Sure, the extra bit of money is always a good thing, but any rank status amongst us men is a tenuous thing at the best of times.

Even though I may have lost a few stripes on my shirt, it doesn't mean I'm less of a man without them. Besides, I was told in confidence by one of my current staff, who had also lost his stripes for a few months, that by working hard now, I can easily regain my rank.

'Hard work,' Jackson says to me, 'plus your leadership qualities will soon get you back you back into their good books again. Besides, you've already proven your leadership qualities to those who already have their eye on you anyway.'

I soon discover there is another upside to my impulsive rebellious actions that I hadn't thought of before now. It seems I may have gained a certain level of notoriety amongst my buddies. Some of the guys have even admitted to me on the quiet that the thought of jumping ship had crossed their minds as well, but they didn't have to guts to incur the wrath of the big brass like I had to do in order to win my fleeting moment of freedom.

***

The island of Mindanao is to be our new base for however long, which is both good and bad. Good, because of its tropical setting among coconut palms, wide sandy beaches and our tents, surrounded by the always-smiling native families living close by in their self-constructed, open grass huts. Bad, because the same steamy, insufferable humidity still hangs around us, ready to zap our energy every damn day, just like it did in Cairns. To add to this miserable torture, the constant drone of low-flying mosquitos buzzing around your face at night makes every tiny moment of sleep a blessing indeed. It's enough to drive any uninitiated newcomer to these islands crazy with frustration.

As if all this hasn't been challenging enough, the threat of malaria and dengue fever (breakbone fever) are never far from our thoughts either. For our ongoing protection from malaria, we are all issued with quinine pills, along with a dire warning from our medicos to never *ever* miss not even one of our daily doses whilst in the tropics. Unfortunately, the downside to quinine means our skin turns a ghastly shade of yellow after a while.

We soon settle into a routine of sorts and after a few weeks life is pretty laid back most of the time. Thankfully, we haven't seen a lot of action so far, but we're not fooled even for a minute. Circumstances can change in a heartbeat with a weird kind of uncertain regularity. On our first day here on the island, the CO ordered us to dig a large number of foxholes (aka potholes) all over the island—ASAP! We soon learn for ourselves that the Japanese are known to conduct flyovers day and night. So, whenever any bombs are about to be dropped—for our own safety—we're expected to drop whatever we're doing and head for the nearest foxhole immediately. After a few close calls of ducking for cover, this directive soon becomes second nature.

Along with our ongoing firearm, defence and tactical training every morning, there are also the usual rituals of keeping our bunks, clothes and general quarters in an accepted order, even if it is just a canvas tent. We each have our orders for assigned duties, KP duties and guard duty too, of course, but we're also allocated free time each day. We even have a guard house here. Well, an MP-guarded tent, anyway, for any soldiers who step out of line for whatever reason.

Now that I've become acclimatised, the heat doesn't affect me nearly as much anymore. In fact, I'm even starting to relish it. When off duty, we're allowed to wear singlets instead of our khaki shirts and shorts instead of army pants around the base. Speaking for myself, at least, I sure feel an actual sense of freedom—at last.

***

It is the 49th Interceptor Squadron who is responsible for my own specific kind of training as a radio operator since the beginning of my army service. Being a part of this squadron also classifies me as being an integral part of a skilled team that I am meant to fulfil on Mindanao. During training, it is drummed into me repeatedly that I am essential in this war. I am to send out all essential messages to other units within the south Pacific region. It's primarily my role as a radio operator to track any

Japanese planes as they approach the island. While on my watch, if the enemy happens to be within our island's vicinity, I immediately have to warn *all* troops to take cover in the nearest foxhole.

Our communications tent is a vital part of our military operation here on Mindanao. When on duty, I'm required to keep a vigil eye on all enemy activity, either through tuning into any foreign radio signals, Morse code or by a handheld radio in my comms backpack—an essential communication link on any emergency recon trips.

***

I'm beginning to learn real fast about certain things I always need to remember. Every rostered shift I complete as a radio operator anywhere on the island, I could be under fire at any time of the day or night.

For example, the other night I was sitting at my controls, when out of nowhere, there were three enemy planes flying overhead, ready to release their bombs on us any second. *Son of a bitch!* How do they do that? It never ceases to amaze me how the Japanese pilots always know when to creep up on us like this! It was time to evacuate myself from the radio shack ASAP. However, when I try to make a dash for safety, I am suddenly pulled up short by the headset still attached to my ears. Yes, indeed, an excellent thing to remember for the future.

Even though the Japanese are a constant threat to life and limb, I always manage to find some enjoyable distractions to occupy my time away from rostered duties. On one of my walks around the island, I came across a plane shot down at some point. The sight of the old plane suddenly gave me a brilliant idea. I decided then and there I was going to build myself a boat from parts of the fallen plane! After inspecting what was left of the wreck, I noted with glee; the belly of the fuel drop tank was still intact. After a bit of forceful encouragement of manual tugging here and there, I was finally able pull it away from the main frame. With that done, stepping back for a moment, I had time to figure out what to work on next.

Thankfully, the solution suddenly popped into my head of its own accord; I think I need to offer one of the Filipino women some money to make me a simple sail for my little boat.

Rosalie! That's who I can ask. Rosalie always has a smile on her face every time I see her around the island, who's always helping someone with something they need to get done. Not just her native people either, but our soldiers as well. Because of this war happening right here, right now, hundreds of our military units have pretty much taken over her entire island home in a big way. But still, she smiles.

So I go in search of Rosalie, heading in the direction of where I should find her. I never have to look too far either, since she is usually scrubbing floor mats or cooking on the open fire outside her hut. I always know too, that wherever the island children are playing, Rosalie is not far away, as the island children always seek out Rosalie more than anyone else.

'Hey, Rosalie! I need your help!'

'I help if I can. What you need, Mester Paulie?'

When I explain with what I myself hope are descriptive-enough hand movements of length, width and purpose of what I need from her, she immediately answers with, 'You need a sail for a boat?'

When I nod my head in confirmation, with a promise to pay her for her time, Rosalie's smile widens even more than it usually does. She immediately sets about scrounging around her home, the homes of her immediate family and of her many relatives, looking for a suitable piece of material big enough for a sail. Before I know it, she's finished. With her old Singer treadle sewing machine, Rosalie has somehow turned an old mattress cover into a very efficient sail. All in one day too. I couldn't believe it.

***

Once the sail is complete and hoisted onto my makeshift boat, I spend every spare minute on my off-duty days sailing my little boat around the island. I know what I am doing is dangerous, but I don't really care. For a few hours, at least, I feel like I've died and gone to heaven. The sheer sense of fun completely takes over me. My mind is at peace, and even the risk of death is well worth it. Not for long, though.

For some reason, the wind that is effectively pushing me forward up until now, has suddenly decided to pick this moment to stop completely. *Not a good thing at all, Meier!*

Especially when I'm stuck out away from the beach, on a tiny sailboat, within a war zone. Since I have no oars onboard either, my situation is now dire. I need to immediately reassess. Real fast too!

To my horror, I am now stranded out in the bay, completely vulnerable and open for attack from a Japanese flyover. I desperately pray that they don't pick this exact moment to fly over and spot me out in the middle of nowhere—in full view. My boat might only be small, but any boat will probably be good practise for some Japanese pilot, maybe looking to fill up his regular reconnaissance quota with some target practice. I'm not about to oblige him.

What to do? I keep asking myself this very question over and over with no answers, as I wait helplessly for the wind to pick up again.

Soon afterwards, which can seem like forever when one is locked into any life-or-death situation with no way out, after a few more desperate minutes, the wind thankfully picks up again. It's ever so slowly at first, but then my brave little boat catches the breeze and we move faster towards safety ... *At least I hope so, anyway!*

I waste no time in making my way back to shore. I pivot my hands into paddles along the sides of the boat to somehow try to move it along faster. Once back at the water's edge, I quickly hide away my little boat again under the thick mangrove bushes. With my heart still thumping fast, I head back along the familiar, well-worn track to base, uttering a grateful prayer of thanks to God for keeping me safe once again.

I was able to enjoy my makeshift boat for only a little bit longer. The first sign of its fatefully brief life on the water was when a couple of my buddies and I decided to go sailing one afternoon. Maybe there was one too many on the boat, or we overbalanced it a bit too much on one side, but my boat inevitably tipped over and even though we desperately try to right it again, we were not having any luck at all. We were eventually forced to give up on the idea.

I guess I always knew my mighty little vessel was destined to lie beneath the sea, not above it. It's unfortunate and final demise came about because one of the locals made the mistake of trying to flip it over the wrong way. All we could do was watch with mournful misery as it sank even more into the deep depths of the sea, never to resurface again. Ah well! It really was fun while it lasted.

***

After the disappointment of not having my little boat anymore, I needed some other challenge to engage my inquisitive, practical mind. That's when I came up with my next brainwave. Maybe I could try making some wine? That's when I remembered a recipe some savvy hillbilly shared with me years ago. He was infamous for making the best moonshine ever back in the states, so why not try it myself now?

The most important ingredient is yeast, normally used for breadmaking. It helps to ferment the wine. Since I didn't have any winemaking equipment to speak of, the next best thing, I decided, was to make raisin jack instead. Since there is no written recipe to refer to, I had to think back to what I was told by the moonshiner himself.

'The best way to make raisin jack, sonny,' he said, 'is fer ya' to soak some of dem raisins in some water, then ya'll need to git hold of some yeast from somewheres, 'cause ya carn't make wine without yeast! It jist don't taste da same. The most important thung ya gotta remember too, is that once you got dem raisins and da yeast together into some jug or a bottle, then ya gotta ferment the lot together fer a few months to turn it into wine.'

With a rough idea of his recipe in my head, I scrounge some yeast and raisins from an army cook on the island with a firm promise that he would be the very first taste tester of my end product.

If I had any doubts about my efforts to make my wine, I quickly put them to rest by my ever-willing taste testers. In other words: one or two appreciative but discerning individuals in my unit, who know how to keep a secret from the big brass.

8

Paul

1942
Life can be hell on a tropical island

Our camp cooks make their quota of bread for each day, either late at night or early morning when it's still dark. In order to do this, though, they have to prepare each batch of dough under some kind of artificial light. Unfortunately, this light inevitably attracts a swarm of flying insects which always seems to end up in the bread mixture, giving the finished bread a rather unnatural, crunchy texture that you won't find in any shop-bought bread.

Any new unsuspecting recruits to our unit aren't as yet aware of our bugs-in-the-bread joke—until they bite into it, that is. We all pretend not to notice while the new guy watches us sitting close by with a puzzled frown. We each bite into our black-speckled slice of bread with gusto and you can almost hear him thinking, *These guys eat this bread all the time? So surely that means this food must be okay, then.*

That's when it's our turn to watch them, whilst struggling to keep a straight face. We wait with bated breath for the poor suckers to take their very first bite of army-issue camp bread. We can barely keep from laughing out loud at the horrified look on their faces as their teeth bite down into on an extra crunchy piece of 'roughage'.

'What the hell!' we hear, as the poor saps suddenly eject the offending piece of food out of their mouths with enough force it only just comes to a stop on the far end of the mess hall.

'There's a bug in my bread, and it's a big one too!' is the usual shocked exclamation, as they screw up their faces in obvious disgust. This is our cue for us regular guys to crack up and fall about laughing, as the truth finally dawns on them; the joke is on them. Before long, they too learn to ignore the black 'bits' in the insect-infused bread just like the rest of us. When new troops arrive, it's then up to the 'initiated' to keep the joke going.

One evening, after I've finished my assigned duties for the day, I head for the mess tent where we eat all of our meals. There's a poker game in progress, but I'm not really in the mood. I hang around long enough to watch the game for a short while, but then leave. In hindsight, maybe I should have stayed back there after all.

Once outside the mess tent, I immediately find myself disadvantaged by temporary blindness. Due, no doubt, to coming from a brightly lit mess tent out into a rough, uneven landscape now blacked out completely. Any obstacle under my feet is usually easy to avoid during daylight hours, but impossible to see without a flashlight—which, I realise too late, I don't have. Just when I think I'm heading in the general direction of my tent, I in fact find myself immersed in some gooey muck up to my armpits. To my horror, it doesn't take me long to figure it out; I've fallen into a pit which contains both sewerage and kitchen scraps. After crawling back out of the pit with my dignity seriously challenged, I head straight for the nearby river. After throwing my rifle in first, I have no choice but to retrieve it, staying in just long enough to rid myself of the stench of the muck pile before stumbling back to my tent under the cover of darkness.

Ironically, the total darkness before this messy incident I consider to be my most embarrassing moment of all time, may in fact be my best friend, because the following morning, I am relieved to discover that my stumbling fall from grace into that stinking, slimy piss hole has thankfully escaped the attention of the general masses.

***

After losing my former rank of staff sergeant for a few months due to my impulsive jump to freedom back on the platoon, my CO has been authorised to reinstate my rank. This means that sometimes I'm required to take turns at doing extra duties at night. One of these duties entails checking on the sentries stationed around the loneliest perimeters of our camp at night. When it's my turn to go check on the sentries, it's almost like taking my life into my own hands—it's downright dangerous. A lot of these sentries are, in fact, nervous young men with itchy trigger fingers. The slightest sound in the darkness is enough to make them fire their loaded rifles in any direction. So, I learn quickly to approach them with a great deal of caution each time. Often, I just sit and keep them company for a while. I try to think how I'd feel in the same situation. These homesick guys are basically just scared. Particularly with being so far from home and all that used to be so familiar to them.

***

Every military man on Mindanao island finds that life eventually settles into an everyday existence of regimented routine. The powers that be invariably test us daily. Not by any fierce fighting just yet, but challenges they won't normally come across back at home. Any volatile war zone carries its own set of unspoken rules we all must adhere to. My unit is no exception. Troops caught up in any war zone usually just accept their lot and wouldn't even think to complain of trivial things. Most of all, we learn to expect the unexpected at all times. This applies to seeking any medical attention for oneself too.

We are out on a bivouac (camping trip), just beyond our camp's perimeter, and by lunchtime we're finally ready to call a halt to our morning activities of intense combat procedures, survival training, endurance exercises and acting out potential scenarios of what to do if captured. The consensus now for all participants is that it's time to eat.

Distracted by talking to my buddies, I attempt to open a can of beans with a jackknife. In doing so, the tin can somehow slips in my hand and instead of piercing the lid of the can, the knife pierces my hand instead; I can even feel the blade going in deeply, leaving a large gaping wound between my index finger and thumb.

'*Shit!*' I mutter a bit too loudly, more out of shock than anything. There's blood spurting out of my wound and all over the guys sitting next to me. I quickly grab a hand towel nearby and wrap it around my hand. I hold my wrapped hand up against my chest and go in search of my CO, who is somewhere amongst the troops, sitting around with some guys eating lunch. He takes one look at the blood-soaked towel and orders me back to camp immediately, in search of our medic.

I find him in the medical tent as expected, but unfortunately, he has had one too many swigs of alcohol by now and as a result, he's very inebriated and rather unsteady on his feet. After steadying himself onto the nearest chair, he informs me with a slurred tongue that my hand needs stitches, badly.

Predictably, because of his intoxication, his hands can't stop shaking. I am already well aware his usual diagnosing ability is still spot on. Even if my hand is now throbbing from such unbelievable pain, because of the medic's inebriation, I'm now forced to hold the medic's hands in place while he stitches me up. With no painkillers, either. Not an experience I ever want to repeat.

Whilst on the island, we often come across some unusual, quirky behaviours from the natives. During one particular lunchbreak, as we sit around eating rations and talking amongst ourselves, we are amazed to see a local walking past us with a pet atlas beetle on a dog leash, waddling along beside him. My buddy, Brad, elbowed me in disbelief.

'Man! Can you believe this? I sure wish I had a camera right now. The folks at home will probably never believe me when I tell them about this.'

I soon realise this man is obviously showing off to impress us all, but we're more than a little gobsmacked just the same. I've spotted those

huge beetles in my tent sometimes. They're hard to miss, really. I found
out later from a native I have become friends with, that these beetles can
grow over four inches long. Judging by the distance apart of the native's
hands, anyway, as he tries to explain to me just how long the beetles can
grow. Not only are they huge, but I am also told, they can carry up to
eight hundred and fifty times their own weight. Very impressive, indeed!
I have never in my life seen beetles that big before. Compared to normal
insect sizes, they're huge! At a rough guess, one such beetle I came across
would have to be almost the size of the palm of my hand, which I am
often told is rather chunky anyway.

While these oversized creatures are intriguing, I can't help but chuckle
to myself as I suddenly imagine my mother's reaction if she ever came
across one in her house. In fact, I can guarantee they would totally lose
their uniqueness in an instant, since they'd soon become very dead beetles.
She would not think twice about ruthlessly squashing any beetle—big or
small—with her broom, if they should *dare* to enter her kitchen uninvited.

***

Under the same sort of circumstances as the atlas beetle, one further instance of unusual happenings on this island shocked us to our very cores.
There we were, sitting around talking and eating our lunches together
in small groups of three or four guys. This type of short rest, I might
add, is only allowed after we've already been trudging around the rough
island landscape for several hours in search of some more cleverly hidden
Japanese hidey-holes. The designated rest spots are always under the shade
of the nearest palm tree, and believe me, there are a multitude of them
on the island. Sometimes we even take over some fallen log down by the
river, to literally take a load off our backs once we're able to ditch our
heavy haversacks on the ground for a spell.

Suddenly, all eyes swing around as one native casually passes us by. He's
pushing an old wheelbarrow, with its handles bound tightly with palm
fronds. It isn't so much the noise of the rickety wheel on the wheelbarrow

itself that alerts us to his presence, but it's what's in it that shocks us all into total silence. The man is carrying around his own oversized testicles in the wheelbarrow.

One local fisherman nearby who can speak English, explains to us (once the man with the wheelbarrow is out of earshot, of course) why the man is like this, making some hilarious, suggestive movements of cupping his hands around a basketball to emphasise his meaning. In a nutshell, this poor man has 'too bigga balls'!

Being the inquisitive person I am, I went in search of one of our medics. 'Hey, doc, did you see that native with his balls in a wheelbarrow just now?'

'I certainly did, Staff Sergeant. You're thinking maybe you'd like to have balls like that?' He smirks at the disbelieving look on my face as he continues to roll up a whole pile of clean bandages as he talks.

'No way, doc!' I laugh. 'But I must admit since I am both curious *and* horrified about his condition, I just *have* to ask you now; what's wrong with him?'

'That poor man has a condition called elephantiasis. In simple terms, elephantiasis is a disease caused by a parasitic worm, commonly found in the tropics and easily transmitted from person to person by mosquitoes. Basically, it's a hellish disease which affects the legs, the scrotum area and also the breasts. I've got to tell ya how damn impressed I am by the in-flicted native's ability to go about his daily life despite his embarrassment. I'm not sure I could do the same under those circumstances. In front of the other villagers too!'

'Hell no! Me neither, doc! These natives are such resilient people, aren't they? They just accept each other, and us, so unconditionally.'

Doc nodded in agreement. 'We so-called civilised people of this world could certainly learn a lot from these gentle, loving people.'

'That's for sure, doc! They could be openly resentful towards our military troops who have bombarded their island home, American and

Japanese included, but they still welcome all strangers with wide, friendly smiles, happy to share whatever food they barely have themselves. Such open-hearted people, every single one of them. As you say, doc, civilisation could sure learn a lot from these gentle island people.'

9

Paul

1942
I never signed up for this

Despite the breathtaking beauty of this tropical island, the geographical conditions of Mindanao are challenging enough. When it comes down to military operations, it can be a living nightmare of hellish proportions. Such an existence offers very little incentive for our newer soldiers used to the comforts of home. After the initial thrill of being based on a tropical island has worn off, fighting a major war upon its pure white sands in the steamy, sweaty heat, is just too much reality to get the least bit excited about.

Mindanao boasts a long, irregular coastline and the topography is generally mountainous. Rainforests and many crocodile-infested rivers cover most of the terrain and the rest is lake, swamp or grassland, which hardly describes the lush fields I remember from back home in the United States. These island grasslands bear no such resemblance whatsoever to the corn or wheat fields, or the flat, monotonous landscape of Illinois.

No, the grasslands around here are all insidiously choked by groves of abaca plants (a source of hemp fibre), offering a foot soldier the worse obstacles of all. Towering over us at fifteen to twenty feet high, these thick-stemmed plants severely limit our vision and sap the strength of anyone who dares to hack their way through them. Just like dense fields of sugar cane, abaca plants grow close together in the same way, and there are acres and acres of these damn plants to complicate the hell out of any military unit attempting to get from A to B. Combined with the abaca's stalks, their long, lush green leaves are so dense even a vigorous man must fight his way through somehow. Even with sharpened machetes, we have to use the entire weight of our bodies the whole time, for each foot of progress. And if that's not enough of a challenge within these fields, visibility is rarely over ten feet.

No gentle tropical breeze could ever hope to reach us through this gloomy green, choked-up maze. Even soldiers who I'd considered to be the most physically fit amongst us before this campaign started are suddenly dropping like flies. None of us are immune to the rigours of trekking through such an unforgiving landscape.

As soldiers of war, tactical military superiors require us to carry with us at all times: a haversack which contains the usual army-issue water bottles, mess tin, rations, extra iron tablets, quinine pills and spare socks. Even shoelaces. Apart from our haversack, regular foot soldiers carry with them extra ammunition pouches, an entrancing tool (spade) and a groundsheet.

Apart from my own haversack, as the assigned radio operator on reconnaissance treks, I'm also required to carry around a rather cumbersome dark khaki, military SCR-300 radio on my back. It's a heavy thing too, especially when the reinforced straps that wrap around my body start rubbing against my skin, right through to my cotton shirt under my uniform. By the time we reach camp at the end of each day, a blotchy red heat rash has me itching to scratch it furiously for hours afterwards. After a few hours of thrashing our way away through the thick abaca plants, the weight of this lifesaving radio backpack begins to feel more like I'm carrying around one hundred pounds instead of thirty-five. I shouldn't complain, though, because without this radio it'll be damn near impossible to seek out scattered patches of enemy occupation amongst the thick, impenetrable landscape. Let alone be suddenly fired at by the ever-tenacious and the ever-resourceful Imperial Japanese soldiers. These same soldiers, we've quickly discovered, have a tendency to lurk patiently nearby for hours within the nightmarish vegetation beyond the next clump of abaca plants or thick rainforest foliage, just to be able to knock us off one by one. Thank God a troop of jungle-savvy Filipino scouts from the Philippine Army are with us every time we venture forth into unchartered territory. They take the guesswork out of where to place our feet, way before we do, each and every time.

Sometimes, after many torturous hours of slowly hacking our way through the next abaca clump and the one after that, I find myself having to dodge even my own unit buddies falling prostrate at my feet from extreme exhaustion.

To be honest, some days, I think I'd even welcome a bullet to my brain, putting a blissful end to this infinite hell on Earth.

***

As we continue to advance yard by yard, we are constantly guarded with watchful diligence by the trained hand movements of our recon commander. We instinctively know to inch our way slowly forward until we hear gunfire within only three to five yards each time. If our commander suddenly holds up his flat hand with his fingers close together, we immediately all slink down with the intention of making ourselves look smaller. This is another kind of cruel torture within itself, when you don't dare to scratch an itch or even speak until our commander's index finger points forward a few times. It's the signal we literally sweat for. As before, it's our silent cue to start pushing forward again until our next signal to stop. Slow going, yes, but so vital for our survival.

Since our island treks are mostly meant to be for recon purposes only, our commander warns us at the beginning of each mission not to shoot at the enemy unless we are shot at first. Whenever we come across an open area suitable for me to use the radio, I am to use my own discretion as a trained radio operator, for the safety of our men, to send out short bursts of communication to other military units, warning them of anything suspicious nearby. When we make it to an open clearing, we first pull up fast then immediately lay low, to allow our savvy and highly intuitive native guides to stealthily advance forward in search of any hidden enemy camps nearby. Once they have returned and I'm given the signal that it's safe to go ahead, I open up my radio pack, put my headphones on and slowly tweak the knobs on top of the radio until I can pick up any sort of transmission within our immediate vicinity.

***

Today is meant to be the second-last day, according to our CO, of our current mission of five intensely planned days of recons. As I'm busy tweaking my transmission signals, Master Sergeant Mathers chooses this moment to tap me on my shoulder, breaking into my intense concentration. I have no choice but to remove my headphones and turn my head to the left to face him.

'Yes, Sarge?'

'Anything nearby that we need to worry about, Staff Sergeant?'

I can't help but stare back at his worried frown, but despite my own feelings of apprehension, I'm still careful to keep our commander's worried looks to myself. I know well enough by now, that any new soldier with a loaded gun in his hand and a twitchy finger can quickly spell disaster for his whole unit.

'Well, I have to report, sir, that I'm picking up on some Japanese music nearby. About ten yards away. It could be nothing, but it might be worth checking it out anyway.'

Sarge's commanding presence has returned and he's going about his military business again. 'Good work, Staff Sergeant. Okay, men, listen up! I want two volunteers—as if you have a choice, anyway.' The guys gathered around him chuckle at his obvious attempt at humour. Rather than act all heavy with his troops, Sarge is fully aware he could very well be sending any one of them to their death at his command. Not a directive

75

to give lightly at any time.

Once two *volunteers* have stepped forward, he orders them to cover each other as they advance carefully in the direction I'd heard the radio music just before. After a painful pause in time, our two brave soldiers return, all smiles.

'So, what do you have to report to us then, soldiers?'

'Nothing to worry about this time, Sarge, just a couple of Filipino ladies dancing to some music in some shack nearby—even if it is Japanese music. The ladies have assured us they are not connected to the enemy in any way.'

Japanese music seems to be the only music on the radio they can listen to these days, since it's a well-known fact on the island their radio stations have been taken over by secret Japanese propaganda and are therefore almost impossible to control.

'Fair enough. Okay, then, I do believe we have finished here for the day. Pack up your radio, Staff Sergeant, so we can head back to camp before we really *do* get shot at by not just a few trigger-happy Japanese soldiers, but their entire Japanese Army lying in wait for us.'

Speaking for myself, I am indeed grateful we've managed to survive another day of avoiding the inevitable hidden death traps set for us by an enemy skilled in the art of invisibility. If only tomorrow could promise to be a better day. Tensions are rife on the island. With this tension comes uncertainty and jumpy nerves on both sides of the fence, but our ultimate desire is to survive just one more day. One more week. One more year. I soon learn for myself that anything can happen in a war zone. Even on a picturesque tropical island in the middle of the Pacific Ocean, death can still come either painfully slow or instantly to the unsuspecting, with sometimes disastrous consequences to the overall morale of our troops. At least for now, I'm alive, and I plan to stay that way for a while yet.

***

Back at camp, I stare with wonder over an idyllic scene of waves crashing against the shore. A massive full moon seems to hang loose, with the backdrop of a zillion stars in the sky. This huge golden orb still holds a certain hypnotic magic for me. After all, it's the same moon that captured my imagination—and my heart—back in Melbourne, as I held a certain beautiful gal with the curly auburn hair close to me and fell completely in love with her.

There is a definitely magic in the air tonight. As the glorious full moon luminously lights up the night sky in all directions, it inspires me to declare that it does indeed belong to my Isabella.

The enormous moon lighting up the expansive skies and galaxy of stars all around me indisputably must be held responsible for inspiring my next course of action. If I should ever make it back to Melbourne, I already know what I want my future beyond this war to be like. In fact, if I am even able to make it back to our camp tonight, without being shot at by some lone, ambitious Japanese soldier hiding out there somewhere. I've decided that on this very night, I'm gonna sit down and write to Isabella. Yes!

So without delay, I have declared that this letter will be my most important letter *ever!*

*** *** ***

After I somehow manage to make it back to camp in one piece, I jump into the shower to wash away the less-than-pleasant images of the day under a soothing stream of cool water. After scrounging a few precious scraps of paper from the guys in our unit, I settle down on my bunk to send my Isabella a declaration of my love for her *AND* a proposal of marriage.

10

Isabella

November 1942
A letter from the front

Paul writes to me as often as he can, while still based in the Philippines. When the mail gets through, that is. Sometimes, I receive two letters on the one day, even if they are written just one week apart. At other times, I might not receive his letters until a month later. Because Paul is part of an active military operation, his letters to me, of course, are always heavily censored for security purposes. I do try to understand this, but it's a difficult thing indeed to see most of his words blacked out by thick black pen lines. Yes, it *is* frustrating, to say the least, but in spite of this, I still manage to get the gist of what he is trying to tell me. I'm just happy to receive *any* letters at all from him, really. His letters help to reassure me that he's still alive and well, and most of all, that he still loves me. To any young woman waiting at home for the return of her man, that's all you need to know. Especially when he's away for not just a few weeks, but years. This is when his letters offer the most important reassurance of all.

***

After what seems like years after last hearing from him, I come home from work one afternoon to find one of his letters propped up on the sideboard just inside the front door. Mum usually leaves any mail addressed to me in the same spot every time, and as always, it is left unopened. I know I can count on both of my parents to respect my privacy. I haven't received any mail from Paul for over a month now, so naturally, I was starting to feel more than a little anxious. I decided first thing that morning that this is going to be different. I just knew it. So when I did spot Paul's letter propped up on the sideboard at last, I let out an excited squeal and clutched it close to my heart. My mother, who was in the kitchen when I came home, poked her head around the corner and just smiled. She must have been anticipating my reaction all day, right from when it was delivered by our regular mailman before lunch.

I could tell straight away it was from Paul, by his dramatic cursive handwriting and large bold capitals at the beginning of each line or sentence. If this isn't enough to convince me, the distinctive US Army postmark finally confirms it for me. I can barely wait to open his letter, but before I read it, I need to hug my mum and to attend to an urgent personal need.

'I guess I don't need to ask who it's from, then,' Mum laughs. 'Come into the kitchen when you're ready, darling. I'm just making a pot of tea if you'd like some?'

'Okay, thanks, Mum. I'd really love a cup of tea right about now too. Just give me a few minutes to put my bag away and I really need to go to the toilet. I'm busting!'

'No hurry, darling!' Mum calls out to me from inside the kitchen. 'You still have time to read Paul's letter first if you want to. Besides, I haven't even boiled the water yet.'

Dear Mum! Considerate and loving as always. I rush into the kitchen to give her a quick hug and plant a kiss on her cheek. 'Thanks for understanding, Mum. I'll be back soon!'

As soon as I've hung my bag on the hook behind the door and have been to the bathroom, I rush back to my bedroom. Grabbing Paul's letter, I carefully pull back the flap of the envelope, not wanting to tear it open too much. Whenever I receive one of Paul's letters, I like to store them away, with each one in its own envelope in my shoebox, always privately tucked away at the back of my wardrobe. Away from any possible prying eyes. This new letter is no exception. As is my usual habit, I position myself on my bed, prop my pillow behind my back and lean over towards my window to be as close as I can to capturing any natural afternoon light still left in my bedroom, since outside my window it has already begun to darken to its usual late-afternoon dullness. Back in my early teens I soon learnt that I could still read my beloved books by my open bedroom window in this way, without turning on my bedside lamp. Well, at least until each sunset has run its natural course for the day.

After I carefully open the envelope, making sure not to tear it, I unfold the single piece of paper that is Paul's letter and notice immediately the predictable thick, ugly black lines all down the page. It might be my imagination, but I swear these lines have increased even more since last time. In Paul's very first letters to me, only certain key words or sentences, about locations or enemy attacks, had been blacked out. As this war progresses, though, the mail security has tightened considerably. Any mention at all, in any private letters, of how many of men or women are killed or any military plans in regard to Paul's own army unit, no matter how vague, are grounds for an immediate blackout of any careless or misguided communication passed onto loved ones.

Still, there is no use getting upset about Paul's private letters being tampered with, or even the ever-present black lines on the page. I reassure myself once again that it's nothing personal towards Paul or me. It's just one more inconvenience of wartime you have to put up with. You just have to learn to live with it over time, that's all. So I settle myself down at last to read his letter—or what I can read of it, anyway.

To my darling Isabella,

I don't know if ▮▮▮▮▮▮▮▮▮▮▮▮, or even if you receive this letter and even if you do, if you would even want to answer it. I have been doing a lot of thinking these past few days and I have decided that when I get back down to ▮▮▮▮▮▮ I want to marry you. If you will still have me, that is?

As I sit down by the ▮▮▮▮ I can see Isabella's Moon glowing above me again. Do you remember me telling you on our last date together in ▮▮▮▮▮▮▮ that whenever I see a full moon from that moment on, I would name it after you? Well, there was this enormous full moon last night over ▮▮▮▮▮▮.

▮▮▮▮▮, and my heart aches for you all over again.

It reminds me once again of my undying love for you. But most of all, it has made me realise that I really do want to devote the rest of my life to loving you—and only you. When you receive this letter and if you should want to say yes to my proposal (and, honey, I sure hope you do), when I return to ▮▮▮▮▮▮▮ I plan to officially ask your father for your hand in marriage. I look forward very much to meeting your folks when I return. Most of all, though, I long to kiss your sweet lips and hold you in my arms again. You've become my reason for surviving this war, my beautiful Isabella. What more could I ask for now but to know you are still waiting for me? In the meantime, my darling, I'll await your answer to my burning question.

Yours forever, Paul xxxxxxxxxxxxx (plus a trillion more)

My heart does a complete double flip-flop upon reading his letter. I just kind of knew, months ago, without needing any written confirmation from Paul, that I was about to receive his marriage proposal any day now.

This latest letter still reveals the lonely side of Paul, but it also shows me the warm, loving side of him too. This time, I also detect a renewed sense of purpose in him. This one letter alone means so much more to both of us in an undeniable way. It's like an open confirmation to my most joyful heart. It *is* possible, after all, for two hearts to find each other again, no matter how far apart we are.

We have both endured this complicated long-distance relationship so far, but I take heart in knowing now that we're almost on the other side and a lot wiser for it. We both know deep in our hearts we each want the same thing, which ultimately is to spend the rest of our lives together. This time away from each other has been such a momentous step forward. Right from our very first night spent together at Luna Park until now. The fact that Paul wants to make me his wife, after all he has been through these past few years, tells me that our love is indeed eternal. I don't necessarily need proof of Paul's marriage proposal to know it's true, either.

According to current radio reports from all arenas of this never-ending war, the Japanese Imperial forces seem determined to win no matter what. Regardless, I already know my heart's response to his most important question now. When I have some quiet time later, I plan to write back to tell Paul my answer.

In the meantime, I want Mum to be the first to know of my very important decision.

***

'Josie not home yet?' I ask Mum, not letting onto her about Paul's letter just yet.

'No, she just rang to say she'll be home a bit later today. She said something about meeting up with her new friend Elizabeth after work.'

I sit myself down opposite Mum at our long kitchen table. Even though I'm deeply ecstatic about Paul's proposal, I still want to pick the right moment to tell Mum. To me, it's the right thing to do. I already know I can trust her to keep it to herself until our family dinner tonight.

Mum chatters away as she attends to our pot of tea, while I'm only half-listening to what she's saying. My mind seems to drift off into some dreamy state more and more these days. I have to admit, I'm secretly pleased Josie won't be home until later. Don't get me wrong. I do love my little sister very much, but it's still nice to have Mum all to myself sometimes. Plus, just lately, Josie has been slyly hinting to me, without actually saying it outright, of course, 'Bell, you must be crazy to wait all this time for Paul to come back to you!' Then, of course, she always finishes up with her usual projection of a dim future for me. 'What happens if he doesn't come back, Bell? What then?'

Her persistent, thoughtless comments are really starting to wear very thin with me. With all of these endless newsreels at the picture shows lately and the newspapers saying how the war is escalating even more in the Pacific, I'm *almost* beginning to believe her. Honestly, she can be exasperating at times! I'm worried enough over Paul's safety without Josie sticking her two bob's worth in, implying he might not even return at all.

This is why I reason with myself; I can't help but be grateful that I'm able to share Paul's letter with Mum and *only* Mum for now. I can certainly understand where Josie is coming from, though. I have to remind myself over and over, Josie hasn't even met Paul yet, nor have my parents or any of my three brothers. I have to wonder now, if the shoe was on the other foot and such a thing was to ever happen with a sweetheart of Josie's, how would she feel?

I'm confident in my own heart to know that they're going to love him once they all have a chance to know him. I am also aware my family only have my love-sick impressions of him to go by. Being a private person, I don't usually talk about my deep, deep feelings of Paul to just anybody. Especially not my younger brother Kyle, as he loves to tease his sisters over anything at all. Although not so much Marty, thank goodness! I do talk to Coral about Paul, of course, because after all, she was there with me when I first met Paul, so she probably understands more than even my own family right now. Come to think of it, I have talked to each of my parents at different times about him, but as for my inquisitive sister and one teasing brother in particular, not so much.

To be fair to all of my family, to them he's just some American GI who pretty much became absent from my life right from the start. Even if he has been off fighting the Japanese Army somewhere in the Pacific Ocean all this time—he's still not a real person to them yet. It's not hard for me to imagine how resentful they may be feeling towards this unknown Yankee who is going to take their daughter or sister away to some foreign land. Probably forever too.

'Are you still with me, Bell?' Mum is now staring at me with a concerned frown.

'Sorry, Mum! My mind must have drifted away there for a minute.'

'Yes, I could tell. Goodness me! You were a million miles away just then. Maybe to somewhere over the Pacific Islands to a certain handsome GI, perhaps?'

'Something like that,' I grin sheepishly. 'You know me too well. I do apologise. It seems every day now my thoughts automatically gravitate towards Paul without me even realising it. Sorry, Mum … What were you saying?'

'It doesn't matter, dear girl. It can wait.' Mum reaches over and pats my hand in her usual affectionate way. 'Speaking of Paul, I do hope all is well for him right now? It must be such a horrendous thing, being right in the middle of a war zone day after day.'

'He doesn't ever tell me about what's happening with the war. Anyway, even if he did, his words would inevitably be blacked out once the military censorship get hold of his letters.'

'Yes, I can well imagine!' Mum pauses for a moment to sip her tea, already sensing my need to tell her something important. Her motherly intuition, no doubt. She's very good at that.

'Mum, I have something to tell you, and I want you to be the first to know.'

'Good heavens! What is it, darling?' Mum now studies my face for signs of distress. I give her a smile instead. She smiles back, but with a look of confusion just the same. 'I trust all is well, then … Otherwise you wouldn't be smiling at all … Am I right?'

'Yes, Mum, all is good for me … You already know that the letter I received today was from Paul, right?'

'Yes, I've already guessed that. Besides, I can tell by the envelope. So what is it, darling? … What has happened to make you smile about his letter now?'

'Paul has asked me to marry him and I'm going to write back to tell him YES!' After passing my important decision over the kitchen table to my mother, I offer nothing more except to calmly sip my hot tea as I always do at such times. Inwardly, though, I am sweating over Mum's reaction—one way or the other. She doesn't disappoint me either, by immediately coming around the table to hug me.

'I am so happy for you! This is exciting news indeed … I think!' Suddenly, Mum's eyes start to water, and before I know it, she's reaching into her apron pocket for her hanky. I admit I *am* a bit shocked by her tears. *Are they tears of happiness or dread for me?*

'What's the matter, Mum? Please tell me what's wrong … *Please!*'

'Sorry, I knew this was going to happen sooner or later. Once I realised you were serious about Paul, deep down in my heart, I've even started to dread this moment.'

'But why, Mum? Aren't you happy for me?'

'Yes of course I am, darling girl! That's why I am reacting to your news with tears of happiness for you. *Please* don't think too badly of me, Bell. I just can't help it.' A fresh flow of tears run down her face, her already-soggy hanky trying desperately to sop them all up.

'Oh, Mum! I don't think badly of you at all, I promise! I'll probably be much worse with my own children. I would probably be *more* worried if you *didn't* react at all to me leaving home one day. Believe it or not, Mum, I've been worried about the same thing myself at times. Leaving my family to travel halfway around the world is not something one takes lightly. No doubt, when the time does come, it's going to be very hard for all of our family, indeed. From all different perspectives, from each one of us of course.'

Mum pats my arm in that affectionate, distracted way of hers. 'Yes, I know, lovely, but I'm not making it any easier for you by reacting this way, am I?'

'There's no need to feel bad, Mum. I honestly do understand what you must be feeling. Really, I do. The thing is, we both know full well any major decision in our lives is never going to be easy. There will always be consequences—good or bad … Right?'

'That is so true, Bell. You have always been wise beyond your years, dear girl.'

'I remember a saying I heard a long time ago and I've never forgotten it either, "The heart knows what the heart wants." I know for certain, Mum, that my heart really does want Paul. Pure and simple. So much more than I ever wanted Eddie. Even though Eddie did become my fiancé, he was only my first serious relationship, after all. I've since realised for myself I was more infatuated with the *idea* of Eddie, rather than actually being in love with him at the time … If you can understand what I mean by that?'

'Yes, of course I understand. Your father and I did naturally worry about you marrying Eddie because of the kind of man he was. I think you would have really regretted marrying him, Bell—especially with his kind of loose lifestyle. But having said that, at least with Eddie, we knew we would still get to see you sometimes. With Paul, though, at first we didn't want you to marry him for our own selfish reasons really. As your parents, all we've been able to think of lately is the fact that when he returns from this war, he's going to take you away from us for a very long time.'

'Yes, I can understand why too, Mum … So do you and Dad still feel that way now?'

'No, not any more, Bell. Your father and I have both seen first-hand your love for Paul and the fact that you've always stayed true to him while he's been away from you. In your low moments, we've also noticed you quietly worrying about him. At your high times, we couldn't help but notice your obvious elation upon receiving his letters. In my mind, what you and Paul share together is most definitely true love—just like the love your father and I have always had for each other.'

I am so deeply touched by what Mum has just said to me that I soon find myself blubbering into my own hanky too. 'Do you really think Paul and I will have a marriage as strong as yours one day, Mum?'

'Of course, darling. Any couple can too if they really love each other. It won't be easy, though. You'll have a lot of adjustments to make at the beginning, but if you always remain patient and kind with each other, you'll get there over time. Being good friends to start with and having a good laugh together every day has certainly helped your father and me to face our daily challenges.'

We hug each other again and I even join in, blubbering along with Mum now. When our teapot is finally depleted, I quickly wash up the cups and saucers and lay them upside-down on the drying rack, before emptying the teapot for next time.

***

It's time for me to help Mum with our daily meal preparations. As I peel the vegetables, Mum sets about crumbing the lamb cutlets for our evening meal. All the while, we chatter away together about my day at work, any recent happenings in our neighbourhood and lastly my brothers Kyle and Marty's most recent project: home-brewed beer. Kyle's imagination never ceases to come up with some 'brilliant' idea to make *lots* of money, while our placid, easygoing Marty merely tags along, just so he can spend time with his big brother who he adores. How Marty puts up with Kyle always bossing him around, I'll never know. Time seems to fly by, and before we know it, Josie is back home. In her usual confident, stylish way, Josie breezes into the kitchen and plants a quick kiss on Mum's cheek and mine, before asking the same question we Carlisle children have been asking Mum pretty much all of our lives, 'What's for dinner?'

'Hello, darling! Well, tonight, we have lamb cutlets, mashed potatoes, beans and carrots.' Mum obliges without waiting for Josie's usual follow-up question.

'Yum! And for dessert?'

'Steamed caramel pudding with custard and cream. How does that sound, Josie girl?'

'Sounds wonderful as always, Mum!' Josie declares, while dipping her finger into the whipped cream. Mum laughs as she smacks her hand away. Josie always has the ability to make us laugh with her usual cheekiness. 'How are things with you, Bell?' Josie wanders over my way now, stealing a carrot from the bowl of peeled and sliced vegetables. I playfully slap her hand away as well but laugh along with Mum over my sister's infectious sense of fun.

'Josie! If you keep on stealing the food, we won't have any left to cook with, will we?'

In answer, Josie merely grins and shrugs her shoulders in that familiar way of hers, then quickly changes the subject. 'Any letters from Paul today, Bell?'

'Yes, as a matter of fact, there is, Josie, but I promise to tell you everything after dinner tonight.'

'So he *will be* coming back to Melbourne to see you ... Before returning to the States, I mean?'

Sometimes I could wring her neck! She just can't help herself at times. She loves to rile me by planting these little seeds of doubt in my mind. Although, I much prefer these days not to react to her jibes, because it's so much more satisfying revenge for me *not* to react to her silly taunts just to get a rise out of me.

'Yes, I do believe he'll come back to see me before he returns to

America. Now, if you will both excuse me, I really do need to go to the bathroom.' Without another word, I remove my apron and hang it back up on its hook by the stove. As I pass Josie, I can't resist a passing look her way that says it all.

***

After dinner is over with, it's time for our family ritual of sharing our day with each other. The rule is, if anyone has some personal news to share with other family members, nobody is allowed to interrupt during the telling of each other's news.

There was a time when our family dinners didn't always have the rules and we weren't as well-behaved as we should have been. Sometimes, individual points of view weren't really appreciated at all. Teary outbursts, rife with accusations of unfairness or favouritism by any one of the Carlisle children, invariably turning an otherwise peaceful dinner into a verbal slinging match, every single time. Because of this ongoing discord, my father was forced to make it a rule not to interrupt anyone else at the table, until our own turn. Normally it would have been Robbie's turn to speak first tonight, so we all instinctively glance over towards Robbie's designated seat at the family table, but Robbie's chair is empty, of course, since his army unit is still stationed up at Darwin. Even with knowing this, we still miss him very much at our family dinners every night.

Kyle, who is the first one around our family table tonight to speak up, embroils us with his latest *brilliant* idea, in regard to his and Marty's latest money-making project, while Josie shares her enjoyment of a new book she has just finished, called *The Long Winter*, written by the ever-popular Laura Ingalls Wilder. Marty, being as shy as he is, even with his own family, often declines to speak when it's his turn. However, he is more than happy for Kyle to speak again on his behalf. Whatever Kyle can dream up, Marty is happy to go along with, as a way of soaking up quality time with him. I'm actually relieved to be the last sibling to talk this time around. To be fair to all five of his children, Dad declared a while back that a rotation system was also required. So, in order to be fair to each of his children, talking around the table must alternate as to who starts first. In other words, we go clockwise or anticlockwise around the table. Usually, I'm busting to be the first to share something funny or exciting that has happened during the day, but not tonight.

Prior to my turn, a million butterflies have been having a grand old time perfecting cartwheels in my tummy. As I half-listen to my siblings take turns around the table, my anxious mind rehearses over and over exactly how I want to tell them my news. I am only too aware this latest decision of mine could change my relationship with each of my siblings forever.

'Bell, it's your turn!' Dad prompts me from his position at the head of the table.

'Bell? … Bell! … Are you still with us?' Mum whispers, as she gently nudges me now. 'It's your turn to share … Come, on love, I know you're nervous, but just go ahead and tell them.'

'Sorry everyone. My mind drifted for a moment there.' There are a few snickers coming from both Josie and Kyle now, but one glare from my father is enough to stop them.

'I have just one piece of news that I want to share with you tonight, and it has everything to do with the letter I received from Paul today.' I pause and look around the table to each one of my family. My barely restrained happy tears are threatening to undo my resolve to hold them back until the exact right time. *At least until I've had my chance to tell them my wonderful news first.* 'Paul has asked me to marry him and I'm going to write back tonight and tell him YES!'

Dead silence! In fact, too much for my already jangled nerves. Every pair of eyes around the dinner table seems to bore into me, with blank looks to follow. Kyle takes it upon himself to be the first to break the tension in the room.

'Well, it's about bloody time!'

We all laugh together. My parents and each of my brothers congratulate me. Even Josie, who initially shrugs her shoulders in good-natured defeat, comes around from the other side of the table to hug me. My mother and I share a secret smile with each other. She pats my hand, as a way of thanking me for sharing my secret with her before anyone else.

For now, the very fact that I will be leaving our family home for good, perhaps within the next year or two, hasn't really sunk in yet, but I know it will. At least they're happy for me for tonight, anyway, and that's all that matters. I haven't been able to tell my big brother Robbie yet, of course, but when I do, I hope he will be happy for me too. He never really took to Eddie at all, but I just know in my heart he will approve of Paul. Tomorrow isn't promised to anyone. I know it, and I can accept that. Right at this moment, though, I'm blissfully happy and at peace with my decision.

11

Isabella

1942
The waiting game

As promised, I write back to Paul on the very same night I received his letter, since I planned to post it on my way to work the next morning. There is nothing I can do now but to wait for his reply. Whenever that might be during these fearfully disruptive times, is anybody's guess. In the meantime, I go about my normal routine of work, family time and girly time with Coral on the weekends. It's like my whole body is suddenly operating on a stand-by basis while my romantic soul keeps me constantly under some kind of dreamy spell. Even after posting my letter of acceptance to Paul, there have still been many times over the following weeks when the more logical side of me starts to take back its own power. Despite my 'off with the fairies' moments, my *normal* common sense still persistently niggles at me every day about my decision to leave all I've ever known. Why *am* I marrying a man I barely know? Do I really need to go halfway around the world to prove I love this man? Do I really want to live in some strange land, far beyond Australia's shores forever? *Bell, why on Earth are you even thinking about such a thing in the first place? Have you lost your sanity for real this time?*

Each night in my dreams—once my daytime doubts shut down and allow me to sleep, that is—the magic of romance takes over. In one such dream, Paul has his arm around me as we emerge from the church on our wedding day. He kisses me so tenderly as my family and friends crowd around us. They shower us with confetti and wish us well as we drive off into the sunset, as the tin cans, attached to the back of the car, start rattling on the ground. In another dream, I see Paul and myself happy and carefree, strolling around our future neighbourhood. I'm pushing a pram and Paul is carrying another child on his shoulders. It seems strange to me that I don't recognise the neighbourhood in my dreams, or even what sex or ages the children are, but I strongly believe these dreams of mine will one day become a reality. I do hope so, anyway. While I wait in anticipation for Paul's response to my most important letter to him ever, I imagine over and over in my mind the look that might be on his handsome face when he reads my letter. Will he be happy that I answered yes? Or will he be regretting his decision by now? Perhaps he's thinking he's been much too hasty in asking me to marry him, after all? I desperately long to receive an answering letter from him soon, finally squashing all of my silly fears once and for all. With wartime mail being painfully slow these days, I know I must be patient. Besides, I'll probably have to wait another month yet before I get any reply at all.

***

Several weeks later, those anxious projections of mine didn't exactly happen the way I imagined they would. As soon as I'd spotted his long-awaited letter on the sideboard that afternoon, I immediately ripped it open with shaky hands. There was no way I could have waited to read it in my bedroom. I'd already built up this moment in my mind far too much and for so long, there'd be no logic for me to wait for perfect secret conditions now.

My dearest Isabella,
I could barely believe it after I read your last letter. You

said YES to my marriage proposal! I swear I must be the luckiest man in the world right now. No doubt we'll have a lot of challenges to overcome throughout the coming years, but if we keep on loving each other in exactly the same way, we'll be able to take on anything life might throw at us. Unfortunately, I still can't give you any firm details about our marriage just yet, but I did speak to my CO this morning and he has assured me I am due for a week's leave soon. He has also advised me that approval for my flight down to ▮▮▮▮▮▮ *will be cleared within the next few days. I promise I will let you know somehow when I can, but it's all happening, my darling.*

When I reach ▮▮▮▮▮▮ *I plan to formally ask your father for your hand in marriage. I want to make sure that I do this the right way, Isabella. After all, I will be taking his daughter far, far away. Not just to the next town or city, but far across the sea. I can well imagine this won't be easy for him—for your mother either—especially since they haven't even met me yet.*

But if your parents do give us their blessing—both of them— then hopefully, I'll be standing in front of you, in front of the altar, very soon, my darling Isabella.

Love you! From your devoted husband-to-be,

Paul xxxxxxx (plus ten billion more)

Paul isn't at liberty to tell me in his letter exactly when I can expect him, but he did give me a rough idea of it being within the next few weeks. So you can imagine my surprise after exiting my workday bus back home, I just happen to glance over towards the bus stop and do a double take when I see Marty waiting for me. *Marty never waits for me at the bus stop!* My first thought is that something must have happened at home.

My baby brother looks exactly as he always does—all arms and legs—but with a huge grin on his face! I can't work out for the life of me why Marty is grinning so much. That is until I look to Marty's left and spot an American soldier standing beside him—also wearing a happy grin.

For a moment I am starting to believe my eyes are deceiving me, but no, he really is here! I think too, the reason why I don't recognise Paul at first is because of the yellowish cast to his skin, which I believe is due to the quinine tablets he takes for malaria.

I can hardly believe Paul really is standing before me, larger than life. It doesn't seem to matter how many people are standing at the bus stop staring at us, or even the fact that Marty is watching us too, but without hesitation, Paul walks up to me and kisses me just like he did the very first time. Immediately, he has the power to provoke in me a deep infinite longing with just one kiss. This is the kind of kiss I had almost forgotten existed for such a long while. A dreamy kiss, guaranteed to keep my lonely heart beating erratically well into the night. We have been waiting a long time for this moment, and to our surprise, everybody arounds us start to clap and cheer us on. I overhear an older woman nudge a woman beside her and sigh, 'Now ain't that a sight to behold, Flo?' To which I hear Flo answer back, 'It sure is. Wish my old man would still kiss me like that.'

Good sense prevails in the end. Once we finally realise we're effectively putting on a show right there at the bus top, Paul pulls away and grabs my hand instead. Marty, Paul and I walk together back home. Squeezing in closer together on the paved footpath—well, as much as possible—we talk all the way home, and I can tell straight away Marty and Paul have already become good friends. Marty rarely ever opens up to strangers, but he certainly does with Paul. It warms my heart so much to see Marty chatting away to him like they've been mates for years. I'm not entirely left out of their obvious new friendship, though. As we walk along, Paul and I hold hands all the way and can't stop smiling at each other.

Once we're back home, all three of us rush in through the front gate with so much excitement. Even Fonsie (short for Alfonso), our beautiful white husky, looks happy for us. Mum and Dad have obviously been waiting out on the verandah for a reason. Once we reach the front gate, they immediately get up from their cane chairs, positioned right on the corner of our wrap-around front verandah, to greet us.

'Mum, Dad—I would like you to meet Paul.'

Mum speaks up first, 'Actually, we've already met, darling.'

'I had the taxi drop me off at your place, so I've already got to meet your folks.' Paul explains to me. 'We've even had time to have some tea on the verandah before Marty and I walked to the bus stop. We thought we'd surprise you!'

'Well, you sure did!' I laugh. 'For some reason, I didn't think you'd be here for another few days at least.'

'I was lucky enough to get on a flight that was scheduled to leave our military base just two days ago. There were three other guys due to go on leave at the same time as me, so we were all assigned to fly out together in a smaller plane, usually reserved for bringing essential supplies to our island base.'

'Even better!' I laugh, ecstatic over Paul's surprise arrival. I squeeze his hand to let him know just how happy I am. 'Well, when you *do* return to your island, make sure you thank your CO for me.'

'I'll be sure to do that—I promise!' He squeezes my hand gently in return.

Up until now, my father hasn't spoken much as we all talk together, but I can't help but notice him studying Paul intensely. This is my father's own astute way of sensing for himself what kind of man Paul is. Even though my father is quiet by nature, he doesn't miss much when it comes to summing people up. He certainly isn't frowning, thank goodness, as he usually does when he gets a bad feeling about somebody. Like he did with Eddie, for example. In fact, my father looks totally relaxed in

Paul's company, which certainly is a good sign. I've never really realised until now just how much Dad frowned whenever Eddie was around. Unfortunately, Eddie did always have that boisterous way of expecting *most* of the attention from everyone around him.

Mum suddenly stands up to load up the cups and saucers onto the silver serving tray. 'If you will excuse me now, I need to go and do a few things in the kitchen. Bell, would you mind helping me inside, please. Marty you can come and help too if you don't mind. Besides, we need to let your father and Paul get to know each other a little bit more, don't you think?'

Ah, so this was it! Without the need to say anything more, Mum is acknowledging Dad's need to talk with Paul alone, without any interruption from the rest of the family. Including me, it seems.

'Yes, of course, Mum! Come on, Marty!'

'By the way, Paul,' Mum asked, 'where will you be staying while you're in Melbourne?'

'Well to tell you the truth, Mrs Carlisle, I haven't given it much thought. I am sure a hotel or guesthouse somewhere close by, though.'

'Oh, Paul, please do call me Myra. Mrs Carlisle is much too formal, don't you think? As for you staying in a hotel while you are in Melbourne, I simply won't hear of it. You can stay in Robbie's room since he's still up in Darwin right now. Will that be okay?'

'Thank you, Myra! That will be great!'

'Okay, that's settled. You will, of course, be our special guest for dinner tonight too.'

'Thank you again, Myra. I feel very honoured indeed. I've almost forgotten what a real home-cooked meal tastes like these days.'

'I'll have Marty put your knapsack in Rob's room ... You're happy with this, Paul?'

'Believe me, Myra, it's more than okay with me.'

'You're more than welcome, Paul.' Mum, obviously totally smitten by Paul already, beams back at him, before returning to her task at hand.

'Anyway, that's all I need to say for now. So Marty, Bell … Let's leave these two gentlemen to get to know each other some more, shall we?'

There was no way Mum would have asked Paul to stay unless she really liked him!

***

Once Dad and Paul have wandered out onto the verandah for their *little* talk, Mum heads for the kitchen to finish off making the pan gravy for our evening dinner, while I gather together the cutlery and glasses for our evening meal. As we chat together about the everyday things, I can't help but silently wonder what must be going on between Dad and Paul out the front. I'd love to be the proverbial fly on the wall right now.

When I can stand the suspense no longer, I sidle up to Mum and whisper in her ear, 'Do you think Paul has asked Dad that all-important question yet?'

'I don't think you need to have any worries about Dad accepting Paul into our family. I can already tell Dad likes Paul a lot, without him even having to say it.' Mum stops stirring the gravy for a moment, leaving the wooden spoon in the pot to move over closer to me.

'He's such a lovely man, Bell. So polite and respectful. I can understand now why you fell in love with him. He's *very* handsome too, isn't he?' I don't believe it! Mum actually seems to be swooning over Paul. I don't think I have ever heard my mother talk like this before either. At least Paul has no worries about fitting into our family where my mother is concerned. She even asks me to set the table 'all proper' tonight. This will be no ordinary family dinner, that's for sure. As far as Mum is concerned, Paul deserves the royal treatment, so nothing less will do.

After another thirty minutes or so, we hear the front screen door open and the animated voices of Paul and my father talking a mile a minute as they come in from outside.

'Myra, dear! Isabella! Martin! Can you come in here for a moment! We have some wonderful news to tell you!' My father is the only one in our family who still insists on calling all of his children by their given birth names. There will never be any shortened versions or nicknames from him *ever!* Mum and I quietly hug each other, knowing full well what this news will be. Marty is the first to come wandering into the kitchen from his bedroom.

'What's going on?' he queries with a puzzled look. 'Is dinner cooked already, Mum?'

'No, dinner isn't cooked quite yet, Marty. Almost, though. But never mind about dinner for now, son. I do believe your father has something important he wishes to say to us. Let's go listen to what he has to say, shall we?'

Mum leads the way into the lounge room, just as Dad is filling right five tiny sherry glasses right to the top with golden muscat.

'I have an announcement to make, so let's all gather around, please.'

Paul comes over closer to me, his eyes crinkling with mischief, as he stretches his arm around my shoulders. Heaven help me! Even the lightest touch of Paul's hand on any part of my body has me coming out in goosebumps.

Just as Dad is about to speak, we hear the front gate squeak open. It's Josie, of course, with impeccable timing as always. After she sees us all standing around with sherry glasses in our hands, she appears to be somewhat shocked. It's not until she looks over and spots Paul in his GI uniform and his arm around me that she really does a double take.

'What's with the sherry glasses, Dad?' Josie queries in her usual forthright manner. 'Why does our young Marty have a glass of muscat in his hand too? He *is* underage, after all!'

Surely Josie must be aware by now there's a stranger in the house. For some bizarre reason, though, she chooses to ignore his presence completely.

'Come join us please, Josephine.' Dad requests with a quick wave of his hand. Once Josie is standing beside him, he hands her a sherry glass.

'There is to be a very special occasion for all of us, so your mother and I wanted Martin to join in too.'

'What celebration? Will somebody please tell me what is going on?' Josie questions with exasperation. Her eyes move around to each of us within our little circle. Once Josie finally spots Paul, her eyes stay transfixed on him for a moment or two, before speaking to him with her usual directness, 'At the risk of sounding rude here, I don't believe I know you, do I?'

Paul extends his hand in a friendly way. 'Hi, Josephine! My name is Paul and I'm real pleased to meet you.' Just like Dad, Paul much prefers my sister's full name too.

At last the light switches on! Josie finally makes the connection as to why Paul is even here in the first place. 'Ah, now I get it! So you're *that* Paul!' Josie laughs as she lets go of her breath with obvious relief. 'Whew! That explains it! I thought I must be going crazy there for a minute. You know … Suddenly, you're seeing someone nobody else can see.'

We all stare at Josie, but it's Marty who finally breaks the ice, 'Jeez, sis! I think you must be losing your marbles for real this time!'

'Thanks a lot, Marty! That makes me feel a whole lot better!' Josie laughs along with the rest of us. 'Seriously, Paul,' Josie offers by way of apology. 'Sorry if I seemed a bit rude just now. You just took me by surprise, that's all.'

'That's an understatement!' I cut in. 'But in all fairness to you, Josie, we were all surprised when Paul suddenly turned up here today. Especially me!' I declare as I cuddle up a little closer to Paul, my heart feeling like it's about to burst open any second now.

'No need to apologise, Josephine,' Paul reassures her. 'No offence taken.'

'Before we make this toast,' Mum interjects quickly now 'I do think we should wait for Kyle to get home first, don't you? He *did* promise to be home for dinner tonight, so I think he should be part of our celebrations too.'

'Yes, you're right, Myra. Why don't we do that?' Dad agrees. 'We should postpone our toast until after dinner.' Dad looks over our way. 'Is this acceptable with you two?'

'Yes, of course!' I say. 'I don't know about you, Paul, but I'm happy to wait too.'

'Sure! It's okay with me. Besides, I'm all for eating at any time.' Paul jokingly emphasises his agreement by rubbing his belly with obvious enthusiasm.

'Where *is* Kyle, by the way?' Mum mutters out loud. 'Looks like he's going to be late for dinner *again!*'

'Did somebody just speak my name in vain?' Kyle calls out from inside the back door as he removes his grubby boots. 'Don't fret, Mum. I'm here now, aren't I?'

My younger and very handsome, fair-haired brother fills the kitchen with his own brand of magnetism. This, he always manages to do so effortlessly with any women in his immediate vicinity—whether they be family or not. He grabs Josie first, then me, as we both try to avoid the prickly rub of his rough face against our own. Then he sidles over to Mum and nudges her too. Kyle always has the power to make my mother laugh like no other child of hers can. Even when he was a little boy and Mum was mad at him for whatever reason, he was always able to get around her bad moods with one of his crazy, boisterous cuddles, rendering any current transgressions completely forgiven. Up to a point that is. Of course, our mum draws a tough line when it comes down to being late for dinner.

'Go on, Kyle, get out of here!' Mum pushes him out of her way. 'Bell, why don't you take your pesky brother into the living room and introduce him to Paul.'

'Hang on a minute!' Mum's offhanded words stop Kyle in his tracks. 'Paul is here?' Kyle points his finger towards me. 'You mean *your* Yankee Paul?'

When I nod in response, he sidles over to link my arm in his. 'So your Yankee boy has finally come back for you, has he?' He sidles back over to me and puts a brotherly arm around my shoulder. 'Why didn't you say so before, sis? Well, then, let's go and meet this Yankee doodle dandy then!'

After I've taken a few moments to introduce Kyle to Paul, I excuse myself to go help Mum and Josie in the kitchen again. I must admit, I am *very* concerned about leaving Kyle and Paul in the same room together. For those who don't know Kyle, he can oftentimes offend people with his brash, outspoken manner. Kyle never has any problems winning the ladies over, but he can easily raise the hackles of some men with his more outrageous opinions—just to get a rise out of them. He never makes any apologies for his points of view either. You either like what he has to say, or feel free to leave at any time. It's that simple with Kyle.

I needn't have worried, judging by the laughter I hear coming from the living room. In fact, I'm somewhat relieved to hear them all snickering together over Kyle's more outrageous jokes. Even our painfully shy Marty is obviously enjoying Kyle's raucous company. I smile to myself now, as I hear my youngest brother laughing along with Dad and Paul with gusto over some new joke Kyle has added to his impressive repertoire of jokes or stories used to either shock or thrill his audience.

Even if my fears of my family not accepting Paul have so far proved to be unfounded, my big brother Robbie is bound to be a different story. Especially when he finds out about Paul's German heritage. Knowing Robbie's quick temper as I do, he might even kick him out of the house. Just like Kyle, Robbie too can be rather opinionated at times over certain controversial subjects, so I wouldn't put it past him.

According to Robbie in his last carefully worded letter, it could be a while yet before he is able to make it back home, so I don't see him coming to our wedding at all. Same as with Paul's letters, Robbie's are also heavily censored, of course. It seems our government is in complete agreement with America when our own homeland security is at stake.

***

'I tell you, Myra, you are one fantastic cook! I've never had lamb cutlets before—especially all crumbed and crispy on the outside like that. They're so delicious! And that dessert! Oh boy! This bread-and-butter custard, I believe you call it, along with your own bottled fruit *AND* real whipped cream too. I'm really gonna enjoy making my buddies back in my unit jealous when I tell them about this. Man, oh man! I'm so full now.'

Over dinner and dessert, Paul keeps us regaled with some funny stories of the troop's everyday life on Mindanao. Even with his retelling of the lighter side of life on a tropical island, to his attentive dinner companions, we're still aware just the same, Paul is attempting to spare us the heavier realities of his war experiences for now.

***

While Paul is talking, I happen to glance over to notice Josie watching him. She seems to be hanging onto his every word. I smile to myself, as I remember Josie's insistence that I shouldn't be waiting around like I do for some handsome GI who might never even come back to me. She sure has changed her tune, judging by the starry-eyed look she's directing Paul's way right now. It makes me smile even more to see Josie just as smitten with Paul as my mother. Could it be his American accent? Whatever it is, Mum can't seem to get enough of Paul's company—nor his heartfelt compliments. That's if his overloaded plates for both the main meal *AND* dessert are anything to go by!

Once Paul's stories during dinner have enthralled us enough and all the oohs and aahs have died down, Dad picks this moment to chime a silver fork against his crystal glass. 'Okay, everybody, I believe the time has come. We have a toast to make.'

That does the trick. We quickly regain our composure, ready now to listen intently to whatever Dad has to say.

'Josephine and Kyle, you weren't here earlier when Paul formally asked me if he can have Isabella's hand in marriage. I have, of course, given him my blessing. So without further ado, I would like to make a toast to the official betrothal of Isabella and Paul. May they have a long and happy marriage—just as your mother and I have.'

We all scrape our chairs on the wooden floor now as we stand to clink our glasses together. Even young Marty. All around the table, when I hear the words of 'To Isabella and Paul!' as my family toast to our future happiness, everything suddenly seems so very right at this time of my life.

'Thank you, folks!' Paul adds, before turning his full attention to me by his side. 'Now, Isabella, I do believe I have something in my pocket for you … just a minute I've just got to find it first, what with it being so small and all.' We all laugh as he pretends to search frantically through all of his outside pockets. After an exaggerated light-bulb moment, he dramatically dives into an inside pocket to extract a tiny red velvet box, which up until now, had been sneakily hidden from view.

Paul, with a lovely sense of ceremony, takes hold of my hand and turns it over to place a little red box right in the centre of my palm. The tingly sensation of Paul's hands folding my fingers around it has the power to send delicious shivers of anticipation pulsing through my whole body. Totally mesmerised, I return his look of undisguised love.

Before he prompts me to open it, he stalls for a second before adding, 'Isabella, before you open this little red box, I really do need to ask you something vitally important first.'

I swear I can hear Mum and Josie sighing with anticipation, knowing full well what's coming next. I do believe Paul is drawing this moment out for their benefit too.

Paul crouches down onto one knee in front of me. 'Will you, Isabella Maisie Carlisle, in front of your beautiful family, but with the exception of Rob of course, do me the honour of becoming my wife?'

I need no further encouragement. Sensing full permission from my heart, I'm happy to let go of any unshed tears and allow them to flow freely down my face at last. Not that I would want to hold them back, anyway. Especially when these first tears are responsible for allowing a whole happy waterfall of tears to completely enfold me and my joyful heart in pure happiness.

'Oh, Paul, YES! I would *love* to marry you! More than anything in this world. I love you so much.' I stare at Paul, back to the ring, then back at Paul again.

Upon my acceptance of his marriage proposal, Paul takes me in his arms and kisses me, rather sedately this time in front of my family—which is the right thing to do.

When Paul pulls back a bit, he says, 'Well, I suppose I should let you open the box now!' I'm delighted to see his twinkling eyes are just as misty as mine too.

'Oh, you!' I give a playful thump to his upper arm, as deliriously happy as a giggly teenager. 'Don't mind if I do.' As I open the box, I deliberately take my time, just like Paul did, knowing full well Mum and Josie are waiting close by me already bursting with the same anticipation they had with Paul earlier.

I finally open the little red box. As I feast my eyes on what's inside, I truly believe this must be the most exquisite ring I have ever seen in my life. The ring itself is made from a yellow gold band—but not a garish yellow gold. A single pearly white opal is clasped exquisitely within a tiny heart-sharped setting, with two melee diamonds set either side.

'Oh, Paul! This would have to be one of the most exquisite rings I have ever seen in my life. It's just so beautiful!' He slips it on my hand as my family look on. It fits so perfectly too!

My father and brothers pat Paul's back with their congratulations, even Marty, which is an unusual display of affection for him, whereas my mother and sister dramatically sniffle into their dainty little hankies, barely large enough to cope with their copious tears, as they clutch their bosoms and sigh happily. Heads touch and fingers intertwine with each other as if this one occasion allows their romantic hearts to run free at last.

'I bought it at a jewellery shop in Cairns before going over to the islands.' For some reason, Paul feels the need to apologise to me for having an opal instead of the expected diamond on most engagement rings. 'It's an Australian white opal, and when the jeweller up at Cairns explained to me that because of the war, diamonds are really hard to come by these days, I thought you might like this one instead. I know this ring is not very big either, but I promise to make it up to you by buying you a real diamond ring someday.'

'No, Paul, please don't! This one is just perfect and it fits like it's made especially for me. I promise you, Paul, I really do love it! … Just out of curiosity, how *did* you know what ring size to buy me?'

'That was the easy part. After I noticed the jeweller's daughter's fingers looked pretty close to your size, she tried on all the rings for me, until I found this one. As soon as I saw this little beauty, I somehow knew it was the right one. I'm so happy you love it so much.'

'Love it? It's absolutely gorgeous, Paul! Mum! Josie! Come and take a look.'

Mum and Josie respond with lots more oohs and ahhs, just as I knew they would, which gave me a sudden thought. 'Maybe I should pop over and show Grandma Allen too. What do you think, Mum?'

'No, I don't think that's such a good idea, Bell darling. Your grandmother takes to her bed quite early these days as you know. She's probably already asleep by now. We can all go over tomorrow to see her. She can meet Paul and you can tell her your good news together, *then* you can show her your beautiful ring. I'll bring Grandma some of my fruit cake she loves so dearly for morning tea as well.'

'Yes, you're right, Mum. It's not good to stir her up with too much excitement before bedtime. I tell you, Paul, you're just going to love Grandma Allen and I'm quite sure she's going to love you too. She's such a gentle soul … isn't she, Mum?'

'Yes, she certainly is,' Mum agrees. 'And her mind is as sharp as a tack too. Anyway, Bell, I'm excusing you from kitchen duty tonight. I imagine you and Paul have lots to talk about. Especially about your plans for the future. Besides, even though Paul has only arrived in Melbourne today, you still haven't really had any time alone together. Being summer, it's always pleasant out on the front verandah away from the build-up of heat inside the house. Bell, why don't you make a cup of tea for you and Paul and take it outside?'

'Thanks, Mum, I think I will. Do you like tea, Paul, or would you prefer coffee?'

'No, I think a good hot cup of tea would make a nice change, thank you, Isabella. Besides, I drink far too much coffee these days.'

'You head on out the front, then,' I tell him, before planting a quick peck on his mouth. 'I'll follow you out shortly, I promise.'

'Yes, ma'am! See you soon!' Paul responds by giving me a mock salute before heading for the front door.

As my eyes follow him out, I smile happily to myself. It's now official, we really are going to be married! We do have a lot to talk about.

And a whole lot of kissing to catch up on.

***

We sit on the front steps together with our steaming cups of tea on either side of us so we don't accidentally knock them over.

Once we are alone at last on the verandah, Paul wraps one strong arm around me and kisses me so deeply I can't help but respond with equal feeling. We mustn't allow ourselves to become overly passionate with our kisses, though. We can't help but be aware that both of my parents are inside, trusting us to behave ourselves. Of course, being in full view of our neighbours across the road, we don't need to put in a show for them.

'I've dreamt of kissing you like this for so long now, Isabella, especially when I first saw you again this afternoon,' Paul confesses, as he reluctantly lets me go now to take a sip of his tea. 'We'll just have to remember to behave ourselves for now. I have a sneaky feeling one of your brothers might be watching us from one of those front windows.'

'I don't think so, Paul,' I reassure him. 'They wouldn't dare! You can bet your best boots Mum will be keeping a sharp eye on them, for sure.'

'Your family have all made me feel so welcome, Isabella—even Kyle. I must admit, I wasn't sure how to take him at first, but already, I feel like I'm part of your family.'

'I already knew you would get along with each of them. We Carlisles can be a noisy bunch at times, but we all get along so well together … most of the time, anyway. Like I said before, you'll love my grandmother too, Paul. My father built the house next door for her after Grandfather Allen died. I didn't tell you this before, but Grandfather Allen used to be the warden at Pentridge, Melbourne's major jail, for years. My grandmother is such a treasure really, and she never tried to interfere with my parents' marriage, or with the way they raised us kids either. She's a real lady in every sense of the word. In fact, to know my mother, is to know Grandma Allen too … What about your own family, Paul? Are you a close-knit family too?'

'Not really all that close when I stop to think about it. I am the big brother of our family, with Vanessa coming a few years after me, followed by my other sister Lillian, a few more years after. I also have a younger brother called Benny, who unfortunately, has always been confined to a wheelchair from an early age. Even though Benny is unable to communicate verbally to anybody, he's still an essential part of our family. My father is of a quiet nature—just as your father is. He is a second-generation German as is my mother. Despite them both being of German heritage and their home country is still at war with America, they are still highly respected citizens in our local community just the same. My mother was always the strict parent when we were all growing up under the same roof, but in all fairness, she's had a whole lot of heartache to deal with over the years. Anyway, enough about our families for now. We have something very important to talk about as we don't have a whole lot of time together for this visit of mine. I'm allowed only one week's leave.'

'*ONE WEEK!* You're only allowed *one week* to fly down to Melbourne to be married? That's not long at all!'

'I would have to agree with you on that,' Paul says with a drawn-out sigh. 'But even with knowing this to be true, Isabella, I would still love for us to be married before I go back.'

'You want us to be married during this week? Oh my goodness, Paul! That doesn't give us much time at all to organise *everything* in just one week!'

'Believe me, I know, but the thing is, Isabella; I don't think I will be able to get back to Melbourne again for quite some time. Once this insidious war is finally over, we'll have to pack up everything on the island in readiness for *everything* to shipped back home shortly afterwards. I know how the army works, and believe me, they don't mess around once they set things in motion. As far as you and I are concerned, this one week away is all I have for now. There'll be no second chances. My question to you now, my darling, now that you know of this short time frame, do you *still* think you might want to marry me?

'Oh, Paul, of course I want to marry you! Please believe that. My hesitation is not a sign of me backing out on you. Besides, you already know how much I love you. It doesn't really matter in the end if we only have one week or even six months to organise things, we can still do this!'

Paul pulls me back into his arms and kisses me again. 'I thought you'd say that, but I dared not hope so. This short notice thing is a bit much to expect of you and your family just the same.'

'We'll work it out. My parents are both great organisers, so I'm sure they'll be able to sort out the church and a small reception within this time. I'll ask Coral to help me too. She's usually pretty good with this sort of thing. Besides, she *is* my best friend! But let's not worry about this tonight, please? We can talk to Mum and Dad in the morning. To quote another of Grandma Allen's little gems right now, "Difficult problems are best solved in the light of day. If not tomorrow, then in due time." It goes something like that, anyway.'

'What a wise and wonderful woman your grandmother must be. I love her already! You're right, though, we really should talk it over with your parents first thing tomorrow morning. *And* Coral too, of course.' Paul breathes a visible sigh of relief. 'I must admit, this kind of impossible time factor definitely has me more than a little worried.'

'Since you are sharing some of your worries with me now, Paul, I have also been having a few worries of my own.' I pause for a moment, wondering if maybe I'm making too big a deal about my own worries, when Paul is obviously doing his best to understand his own part in this wedding of ours. In the end, though, I decide to get it over with and I say what I need to say just the same.

'For one thing, what will happen *after* we are married? How or when do you think we're likely to be reunited after this war has ended?'

'Ah! Now it's time for me to reassure you. According to my superiors, it is now up to me to organise the necessary details, not just for myself, but for both of us. Once the US Army know we're married—and we have our marriage certificate to prove it—they will then step in to organise your passage by ship to the United States, through the US Embassy right here in Australia. As you probably already know, there has been a whole lot of Australian women marrying our GIs lately. Any wives of *any* US servicemen, as well as any children from these marriages, will be entitled to a free passage to the States after the war.

'Here in Australia, you will be officially recognised by the US Government as an Australian war bride. It is the US government's role then to move you to your new home in America. Free of charge too! This not only includes your passage to America, but this includes a whole shipload of war brides—from Australia and the world over—sailing to the USA with you as well.'

'So all of us war brides are to be transported over to America together on *one* ship?'

'No, not necessarily one ship. I understand there will be several. All with the same purpose in mind: to reunite all the new wives and children with their long-absent husbands back in the United States—wherever and whenever that may be. It could still be quite a while before you are assigned to a particular ship within these Australian waters. As you can well understand, it's going to be a mammoth undertaking for the military bigwigs to not only move *all* of their armed forces back home, but also thousands of its new citizens over to America too. If all goes well, within a year or so, you and I will be together again. You might even get to experience a white Christmas. How do you feel about that?'

'Really? How wonderful! … But white Christmas or not, Paul, I know for sure that I *do* want to marry you, so it's only a matter of time before we'll be together as husband and wife forever and ever.' I lean over to kiss him, to which he responds by pulling me in even closer—just as I hoped he would. 'I truly love you, Paul, with all of my heart, and I can hardly wait to be your wife. Any day soon, *please!*' I add with a loving hug to follow.

'Your wish is my command. It shall be done, my sweet Aussie beauty. I love you too!'

Paul starts kissing me with feather-light tenderness on my forehead, each of my cheeks, then finally over to my lips, thrilling me beyond my wildest dreams. How I've missed the touch and feel of his arms around me and his desire for me, so obvious in his eyes tonight.

Thank goodness common sense steps in, forcing me to pull away from Paul at last.

'Whew! I think maybe it's time for us to head off to bed—*separately!* The way I'm feeling right now, we could be heading into dangerous territory if we stay here any longer. Besides, darling, you must be so tired. You've come a long way to be with me today.'

'Yeah, I sure am.' Paul immediately lets go of me, realising at last what I'm trying to hint at. 'I never realised just how much either, until I sat out here with you to relax. And yes, you are right, my darling. There will be lots of wonderful moments like this awaiting us. This is neither the time or place to step out of line with your parents, is it?'

'Let's just say goodnight for now, then. Tomorrow can take care of itself … right?'

'Right! Our tomorrows offer many promises, but tonight we need our sleep!

12

Isabella

December 1942
How to plan a wedding in one week

The next few days were all of a bit of a blur for Paul and me. Once we'd told my parents of our urgency to be married within the next week, plans were set in motion with Mum and Dad really fast, with Paul and myself feeling somewhat relieved to know the must-do list of legal details (Dad's department) and catering needs (Mum) were soon to be taken care of.

***

The fact that Christmas 1942 has also been thrown into this whole insanely crazy time factor hasn't entirely escaped our attention either. Because food supplies during wartime have been predictably scarce for most family celebrations for the past few years, Christmas is bound to be the same for the Carlisle family this year too.

Thank heavens my father had planted all of our fruit trees when we first moved out of the city and into the country when I was just a few years old. Because of Dad's foresight and Mum's ability to turn all of our abundant supply of citrus, apricots, peaches, nectarines and apples into pies, preserves, sauces and Christmas puddings over the years, our family has fared very well indeed throughout the lean twenties, the financially disastrous years of the thirties and now here we are again, toughing it out during the war years of the forties.

With Mum being such an excellent cook and a brilliant planner of meals, she has already made the Christmas pudding—loaded with all of her saved pennies inside the pudding, of course—at least six weeks before Christmas Day too. Our Christmases wouldn't be complete, though, without our Christmas cake made from Grandma Allen's secret recipe. Still her proud contribution to every Christmas Day our family has ever celebrated together over the years. One of the very first things I must do this morning, though, is tell Coral I'm getting married. So, after breakfast—before I get caught up with something else first—I phone her immediately. Luckily I'm able to catch her just as she is about to rush out the door with her mother to do their favourite thing: shopping at the markets on a Saturday morning.

'Bell? What's going on and why are you even calling me on a Saturday morning in the first place? Are you sick? Or are you ringing to tell me you can't make it tonight?'

'Hey! What's with all the questions, Coral? Which one do you want me to answer first?'

'The one about why you're calling me on a Saturday morning will do for starters.'

'I promise to tell you in a minute, but first, I have some extra-special news for you.'

'Really? Okay then … Well come on, then, Bell! … Don't make me drag it out of you!'

'Okay, okay! … Guess who was waiting for me at the train station yesterday?'

'Judging by the excitement in your voice, I'd have to say Paul … Am I right?'

'Yes! You are right, my dear friend. Paul *is* back! Even if it is for only one week.'

'One week? Gee! That's not very long, is it? … Hang on a minute … I don't get it … How come he's back so soon? Dad says the war is still

114

raging up in the Pacific area.'

This is exactly why I wait to deliver the punchline, because I am so looking forward to the reaction I know I will hear from Coral. She doesn't disappoint me either. 'Well, my friend. Here is my big news ... Paul has asked me to marry him, and I have said yes!'

There is a silence for all of about ten seconds before my best friend nearly pierces my eardrums over the phone line with one of her most excited screams ever! I mean, to me this scream goes way beyond Coral meeting someone famous in person *or* the ending of some soppy movie where boy meets girl (or vice versa) and they drive off into the sunset together. To say she's happy for me is an absolute understatement.

'Oh, Bell, how lovely! I must say now, I knew from the moment Paul first made googly eyes at you at Luna Park you were a goner! No doubt about it!'

'Yes, well, you're probably right, Coral. I *did* fall head over heels for him. Pretty much from the first moment I laid eyes on him. I'm still just as smitten with him too.'

'I knew it!' Coral piped in, confirming for the umpteenth time her intuitive skills are alive and well.

But then the phone line stays quiet for a moment and I can almost hear her brain ticking over. 'I've just realised, Bell. It seems a bit strange to me that the US Army allow him to come to Melbourne to propose to you, but he's only allowed to stay one week? How bizarre is that?'

It's time to put her out of her misery.

'Paul didn't just come to propose to me, Coral. He has come here to marry me!'

'What? Say that again! ... How can *any* couple get married in one week and still have time for a honeymoon as well? ... Sorry, Bell, but none of this makes any sense to me.'

'That's what I thought too when Paul told me last night, but now that I've had time to think about it; one week or one year for an engagement?

What difference does it make? Especially during wartime. Besides, that's all the time he's got. One week.'

Predictably, Coral starts firing off more questions for me to answer immediately.

'But what about the wedding preparations? What about your parents? How do they feel about you going to live in America for good? Do they even like Paul? Will you even have time for a honeymoon?'

'Please, Coral!' I laugh. 'One question at a time, *if* you don't mind! Okay, Mum and Dad are happy about me marrying Paul and I can tell they love him like a son already. They haven't said anything about me moving to America yet, but they do know how much I love him, and to them, true love is what counts.

'I *think* Dad already has Reverend Parker onboard for our marriage ceremony, but we should know for sure by the end of today. In the meantime, Mum is busy organising a simple reception at home. Grandma Allen, Josie and my aunts are all happy to pitch in and lighten the load too. Dad will also be roping in Kyle and Marty to help get everything done in the shortest possible time.' I pause for a brief moment before continuing, 'There is, however, just one more person I really need to be around to help me on the day, and that is you, Coral.'

'You do? ... You really do? But how can I help? I'll probably just get in the way.'

'Well, I *am* going to need my own personal assistant on hand for my hair, make-up and dressing me on my wedding day, and *that* person is you, Coral ... Please say you will?'

There is silence at the other end of the line, then a sniffly sound before she finally replies, 'I will be honoured to help you in any way I can, Bell ... In fact, try and stop me!

***

My father has somehow arranged for us to be married in the presbytery of our local church on Friday 31st December—New Year's Eve—and just three days after my twenty-second birthday on 28th December. It's just so hard to believe it will soon be 1943 already!

Once my father has explained our urgent circumstances to Reverend Parker, our local minister, thankfully he wholeheartedly agrees with my father's sentiments on this matter.

'After all, during these dark days of wartime in Melbourne, I do believe certain rules and regulations are meant to be set aside for special circumstances,' Reverend Parker declares before adding, 'Harvey, if these two young people want to be married and declare their love to each other in the eyes of God—and indeed to the whole world—then who am I to stand in the way of that?'

Unbelievably, Mum is about to match my father's magic trick of already securing our wedding service at the church, by finding a suitable wedding dress for me as quick as the proverbial wink.

***

Here we are—just Mum and me—sipping yet another cup of piping hot tea from our nearly depleted teapot, munching on small slices of rich fruitcake, as we mull over our dilemma of urgently finding me a wedding dress. I hate to admit it, but the initial excited grins we wore when we first sat down here this morning are fast being replaced by worried frowns.

Knowing by now how difficult it is already to acquire any kind of fabric during these frugal years, Mum is soon beginning to realise the hopelessness of our mission.

'Trying to find any kind of evening wear in the city stores these days, Bell, is almost impossible. Most likely,' she adds, 'whatever they *do* have in stock will have been sold by now on a first-in, first-serve basis to whoever walks through their doors.'

'Oh dear, I see what you mean! Does that go for shoes and accessories as well?'

'I'm afraid so, Bell,' she admits. 'Even bridesmaid dresses and the simplest of accessories such as flowers and shoes are going to be difficult to find in one week.'

But it is while we are glumly staring into our teacups that Mum's eyes suddenly light up. 'I think I might just have a perfect solution for you, Bell!'

'Really, Mum? Let's hear it, then.'

'I think, perhaps, I can do even better than that by showing you what I might have for you … If it's still in my trunk, that is.' Mum suddenly shoots up out of her chair and tugs at my hand with an excited urgency. 'Come with me, please, Bell, so I can show you what I mean.'

I suddenly realise where she's heading. Her box of tricks! I should have known.

***

Once in the side room, she almost pounces over to her own personal wooden trunk (also known by her family as her magic box of tricks). By the time she throws open the lid with energetic fervour, you'd think it was made of paper and not heavy wood. Since she has to bend over to find whatever she's looking for, Mum now has her bum in the air, obviously in search of yet another one of her inspirational ideas buried in there. This huge wooden trunk of Mum's usually resides in the corner of a small room at the end of our side verandah, conveniently close to the kitchen so she can still keep an eye on the progress of the evening meal at the same time. Mum only ever had time to do her dressmaking while we kids were at school or work. Over the years, the only dresses she admits to ever stowing away in *the* trunk, are the ones she's hoping she might be able to fit into again one day.

'Come on, Bell. I have a feeling I might just have something in here you can use. You look about the size I used to be … even if it was a long time ago,' she chuckles to herself. I follow Mum into the sewing room and hold the lid open for her as she rummages amongst the various items inside.

'Yes, I was right! It's still here!' Mum declares, triumphant to have finally found what she's looking for. Mum pulls out a mysterious parcel from the bowels of her treasure chest. Little by little, she carefully peels back the last layer of tissue paper—just as if she's about to wave a magic wand, which literally makes me gasp with wonder. From within the flimsy folds of the soft white tissue paper, she gently lifts out an ivory satin dress and lifts it up towards the outside light seeping into the darkened room in order for me to see it better. At first glance, it looks to be slim fitting and about my size for sure. 'It's hard for me to believe I ever fit into this dress, isn't it? I did, though, and I used to get compliments whenever I wore it.'

I run my hand over the soft silky fabric with awe. 'Oh, Mum, it's so beautiful! Look at the shine in that fabric! It seems to have a life of its own, doesn't it?'

'Yes, it certainly does! Why don't you pop into my bedroom and try it on. If it fits you, it's yours.'

'Really, Mum? Do you mean it?'

Mum's smile widens as she nods in confirmation. I can't resist holding the dress up against me to swivel around like I'm really dancing. 'I simply *have* to try it on now. Be right back!'

In the privacy of Mum's bedroom, I quickly throw off the simple, flowered dress I've been wearing all day and slip the delightful ivory creation over my head and let it slide all the way down my body in one silky movement. The skirt itself swirls around my legs and finally settles at mid-calf with a generous, flouncy fullness.

I study my reflexion in Mum's full-length mirror, turning this way and that, delighted by the way the dress makes me look and feel. Not just by the silky touch of the satin against my skin, but the whole cut of the dress and the way it clings to my body in all the right places. The bodice is buttoned down the front with tiny pearl buttons sewn close together, all the way to the waist. Cleverly placed darts sewn in at the front and back of the dress appear to emphasise the roundness of my breasts. An added bonus is the clever styling in the way that it also pulls in my waistline in such a flattering way. The sleeves puff out beautifully too, only to gather softly together again into a delicate lace band, designed to wrap snugly around my arm, finishing just above my elbow.

I can hardly believe how perfectly the dress fits my own shape. It's almost like it has been made especially for me, instead of nearly a quarter of a century ago. *And to think, my own mother once wore this very same dress in her youth.* 'I knew it!' Mum couldn't resist sneaking into her bedroom to catch a glimpse of me in her own dress. 'I was right! Oh, Bell, the dress looks so perfect on you. You'll probably find it hard to believe I was ever able to wear this gorgeous dress at one time.'

I wrap my arms around Mum's full figure. 'I don't see it that way at all, Mum. Let's not forget, you've also had five children and a whole lifetime of looking after us all.' I'm prompted to hug her again. 'Anyway, Mum, you're still beautiful to me just the way you are.'

'Thank you, darling!' Mum pats my back in her usual affectionate way. 'It really does mean a lot to me to hear you say that. Now, please, Bell, take the dress off for me. I need to air it out in the fresh air for a while. Being in an old metal trunk all of these years, it's bound to smell all musty. I think I might have to give it a bit of a sponge down and carefully iron it too. Anyway, Bell, leave it with me for now.'

'Thank you so much for suggesting this dress, Mum.' My eyes now flash-flooding with tears. 'Oh, Mum!' I hug her one more time. 'Wearing this gorgeous dress on my wedding day will make me feel like I'm the luckiest bride in the world!'

'You're very welcome, darling ... Oh my! Speaking of luck. We must be *very* careful not to let Paul see this dress before your wedding day. There must be absolute secrecy between us now, my girl! This goes for the excitable duo of Coral and Josie too, of course.'

Once the dress is hidden away securely out of sight, we leave Mum's bedroom and head for the sound of laughter in the lounge room.

'What have you two been up to?' Dad queries as we enter.

'Never you mind! Just woman's business, that's all,' I reply.

Judging by Mum's conspiratorial smile, I can tell she's having so much fun with our little secret.

13

Isabella

Late 1942
When a family reunites

On the eve of our wedding, we all happily find ourselves sitting around the kitchen table in the afternoon, drinking tea and all talking a mile a minute. Even Grandma Allen is vying for some vocal attention. Especially from Paul. I can tell my grandmother is just as enthralled with Paul as my mother and sister are. She can't seem to get enough of his soft American accent and keeps asking him endless questions. Just as long as he keeps on talking. A quietly spoken lady normally, I laugh to myself now to hear and see her suddenly acting like a schoolgirl. He seems to be equally taken by my grandmother too. It's clear to me there's a mutual admiration between the pair of them, right from the very first moment they met. This gladdens my heart for sure. My Aunt Violet has even decided to come over with Grandma Allen to meet Paul, but I suspect it's only to check Paul out and to see what the fuss is all about. Aunt Violet has always been one of my least favourite aunties throughout the years. She has this really annoying habit of always talking over Grandma Allen. She even finishes her sentences for her. I must admit, though, that for today at least, even Aunt Violet seems to be enjoying herself. That's if the rare beaming smile I see on her face is anything to go by.

***

Just when I thought nothing else could possibly surprise me on the eve of my wedding day, something else most certainly has.

'What's this I hear about my little sister getting married?' comes a familiar voice that booms forth from just inside the narrow back passageway. 'Did you really think I wouldn't try to be here for your big day, little sister?'

Without turning around, I realise I already know this voice so well. Even if it is just one more added to the mile a minute mix of voices already filling up the kitchen, it's still enough to start me blubbering all over again.

'Robbie! Oh, Robbie! You're really here!' I rush around the table to hug my big brother, crying and laughing at the same time. 'What are you doing here? I thought you were still up in Darwin?'

'As soon as I heard from Dad via my CO that my eldest little sister was getting married, I applied for some special leave, and wouldn't you know it, there just happened to be a transport plane flying back to Melbourne today. So long story short, I was able to catch a ride on it.'

Robbie, standing at just under six feet and of a stocky muscular build, suddenly gathers me up into one of his affectionate bear hugs. 'I've missed so much these past few years. How could I not be here for you, Bell? I wouldn't miss your special day for anything, sis. War or no war!'

I blubber even more soppy tears all over his neatly pressed military shirt. 'Oh, Robbie! Thank you for coming! I've been trying so hard to imagine this day without you, but now that you are here, the happiness of my wedding day will be complete.'

We hug one more time before Robbie starts to look around the room in earnest, searching for something. Or rather some*one*.

'Now where's this handsome Yank I've been hearing so much about?' His eyes finally settle on the kitchen table and he laughs out loud as he spots Paul happily sandwiched in-between Mum and Grandma Allen.

'You had better watch out for these two, mate! Once you get a taste of their cooking, you'll soon be the size of a house.'

'Too late! I'm already hooked. There's no escape now,' Paul jokes back. He politely excuses himself from the ladies to rush over and shake Robbie's hand. 'Paul Meier. It's a pleasure to finally meet you, Rob. I've been hearing a lot of good things about you from your family.'

Before accepting Paul's proffered hand, Robbie is already intent on subjecting Paul to one of his infamous, highly suspicious glares. In effect, Robbie's piercing look can only mean one thing; to effectively pin Paul on the spot, like some disgusting, crawling insect foolish enough to openly submit himself to Rob's potential wrath.

'Did you say your surname was Meier? ... That's German, isn't it?'

I hold my breath, hoping Robbie isn't about to raise any hackles in regard to Paul's German heritage. There is, of course, a sudden deadly silence in the kitchen. If Paul can pass Robbie's intense scrutiny at this point, he'll do okay with the other boys in the family—including Dad, who, privately, may even have some doubts of his own.

In spite of what Robbie must think of Paul wanting to marry his little sister, he'll have to give Paul credit just the same for remaining calm in the face of fierce opposition. I love Paul all the more too, as I wait for some kind of defensive retaliation from him—*like an all-out, hot-headed fistfight for starters*. Particularly since Robbie is openly accusing Paul in front of everyone, of him secretly fighting this war as a German and not as the bloody Yankee he claims to be.

Thankfully Paul is ready with his answer, 'Yes, Rob, I *am* German by birth, so I can definitely appreciate where you're coming from. Particularly with that madman Hitler at the helm of the whole German nation, but I am myself a second-generation American and I haven't even been to Germany. *Ever!* My parents moved to America as newlyweds and only ever think of America as being their true home. Just to reassure you, Rob, they don't like what's happening in Germany either. My parents are both hardworking people who started their own business in Chicago, even before I—their firstborn—came along. They are also well respected and accepted as valued members of the neighbourhood.'

Robbie at least has the grace to look embarrassed now. 'Sorry, mate, if I may have offended you. Put it down to the usual gut reaction we Aussies are often guilty of. We tend to shoot our mouths off first, before putting our brain into gear. All too often, before we even get to know the full facts, we pig-headed Aussies really should take time to get to know other types of people, when we're completely ignorant of their way of life in the first place.'

'No apology necessary. To be honest, Rob, we Americans tend to do the same thing. To me, it's more of a human failing, than a cultural one … Wouldn't you agree?'

Robbie shakes Paul's hand warmly at last. 'Hear! Hear! Couldn't have said it better myself.'

Now this awkward episode is finally out of the way, to break the tension, Robbie starts tearing around the room, happy at last to hug everyone along the way, finishing up as always with an extra-long hug for Mum. She clings to him for the longest time, not wanting to let him go. Anyone can see she's so happy to have her whole family back together again. All of her family in this room know of the deeply religious woman my mother is. This one day alone will be proof enough for Mum to know, without a doubt, that answers to her questions she has been seeking from God in her nightly prayers have hopefully been answered today.

Robbie suddenly raises his voice way above all the excited chatter in the room. 'Hey, everyone! What's the go here? It's as hot as blazes today and for some bloody bizarre reason, here you all are, sipping tea in the kitchen, for God's sake! Hey, Kyle! Marty! I need something cold to drink. I'd really like to try some of my two little brothers' famous home brew that I've been hearing all about lately … Come on, how about it?'

'You only have to ask and you shall receive!' Kyle grins. 'But don't take my word for it, big brother. The proof is in the tasting. Come on out to the shed, then, if you're game!'

Kyle and Marty, the home-brewing duo, don't need any further en-couragement to promote their product. Especially Kyle when it comes down to impressing Paul or Robbie with his plans to make *lots* of money.

14

Paul

Late 1942
With this ring, I thee wed

I never should have gone out into the back shed with the Carlisle boys yesterday! Man, oh man! Whatever Kyle and Marty did to make their beer taste so damn good, they did it well. Too damn good, if you ask me, and now I'm paying for it this morning with the worst hangover ever! It appears I'm still in bed and suffering something awful. Serves me right, I guess, 'cause I think it might be a bit too late to undo last night's activities by now. I really should've quit while I was ahead, but *NO!* I had to go ahead and drink that last beer offered to me by the ever-persistent, and at times, the overenthusiastic, Kyle. So, why then, didn't I listen to that nagging voice inside my head last night? When I dare to lift my throbbing head up to look around me, it looks like I'm lying on a different bed to Robbie's. In a totally different room too! Not the one back at Isabella's place. Nothing is familiar to me this morning ... How in the hell did I get here, anyway? *Oh hell!* A heavy feeling somewhere in the vicinity of my lower body region is urgently warning me I need to pee, real bad. *Where the hell is the bathroom around here? Wherever it is, I need to find it NOW!*

***

After flushing the toilet and washing away the escaped dregs from under my sleepy eyes, I exit the bathroom—which I have finally figured out is attached to a hotel room—only to find another sleeping form sprawled out on the bed next to mine. Thankfully, one look at his morning-stubbled face is enough to remind me that this face actually belongs to Rob, my soon-to-be brother-in-law.

Brother-in-law! … Isabella! … Wedding! … I'm supposed to be getting married today!

In spite of my rude awakening in such unfamiliar surroundings, I'm in full wake-up mode at last. It seems to me my first order of business should be to give Rob a good shaking to rouse him from his equally drunken slumber, *immediately!* I don't care how rough I am with trying to wake him up either, but all he does is roll over and sprawl out on the bed even more. This calls for drastic measures, so I drag him off the end of the bed by his feet. That works! As Rob gets up from the floor, he immediately looks around impulsively for someone to punch or kick, but finds me standing over him instead. He quickly realises that I'm not looking all that thrilled with him either.

'Paul?' Rob mumbles, as he shakes his head in disbelief. 'What's happenin', mate?'

'Sorry about the rude awaking, Rob, but I really do need you to you answer some of my questions right now … Like why are we sharing this cosy hotel room together when I'm supposed to be getting married today?'

'Okay, okay! … Shit, mate! You had me real worried for a minute there.' He chuckles good-naturedly. 'How about you help me up and while I attempt to aim a tinkle into the loo in my present state, you can make us some coffee, then we can then sit down together and talk. *Then*—and only then—can I explain everything to you … Okay?'

'Fair enough … But it better be good!'

While Rob attends to his urgent bladder needs, I go ahead and boil the kettle to make some coffee, all the while, I just want to get out of here and back to Isabella again. All the same, I don't want to upset Rob with my impatience or I could make an enemy of him before we're even officially related.

Speaking of Rob, he finally emerges from the bathroom, rubbing his unshaven chin as he sits down beside me.

'Coffee with milk and two sugars ... right?'

'Bloody perfect, mate! Just the way I like it.' Rob cautiously takes a few sips of his steaming hot brew before continuing, 'I know you must be feeling a *bit* anxious about getting to your wedding on time—so to speak—but it's all in hand, mate. I promise you.'

Rob pauses again to take another quick slurp of his coffee in order to say what he needs to next. 'Don't take this the wrong way, mate, but the reason why you and I stayed in this hotel last night is because ... well, your future in-laws have kicked you out of home.'

'I don't understand, Rob. Why would your folks do such a thing in the first place? Did we disgrace ourselves, with maybe sampling too much of the home brew yesterday?'

'Nope! Nothing like that, I assure you. In case you've forgotten, Paul, the groom isn't supposed to see his bride until they meet up inside the church. Because you're staying in the same house as your wife-to-be, there's not much chance of you avoiding each other, is there?'

Finally, the reasoning of Isabella's parents makes perfect sense to me. 'Ah I get it! *And* with you being home too, no doubt the womenfolk will be wanting to make use of your bedroom before the wedding ... Am I right?'

'Right on the knocker! So we're supposed to make ourselves scarce for the day. Well, until it's time for us to head for the church after lunch, that is.'

A moment of sudden panic hits me, 'But what about our clothes for the wedding? ... My uniform? ... My shoes? My cap? My travel kit ... *The rings?*'

'If you check in the wardrobe over there—or closet, as you Yankees like to call them—you'll find everything waiting for you, along with my army uniform *and* even a pair of clean undies.'

After impulsively rushing over to the closet to check that everything is accounted for, I can finally slow down my erratic heart at last. 'Thanks, Rob! You're a lifesaver!'

'No problem. That's why I'm here … Besides, I'll be in *big* trouble with the women in the family, including your future wife, if I—as your best man—fail to get the groom to the church on time. I tell you, mate, my life won't be worth living if that should ever happen. Anyway, enough of this wedding talk for now, I don't know about you but I'm starving! I reckon I could eat a wild bullock this morning. How about you? You hungry? By the way, we are presently staying at a historical pub in the city called the Mitre Tavern. Believe me when I say their reputation for delicious pub food is next to none.'

'Sounds great, and after a bite to eat, maybe I can work on adding a lining to my overloaded belly again. Perhaps even find me a hangover cure as well … Any ideas?'

'Yep, I sure have … Vegemite! Trust me, works every time.'

'Surely you don't mean that black goo you Australians love to spread on your toast in the morning?'

'The very same! I read once that the combination of malt, B-group vitamins and salt in Vegemite works like a charm against hangovers.'

'Mmm … I think I might prefer to have the hangover, after all, but I'll take your word for it, Rob. Since we're in the city, I want to go buy a special wedding gift for Isabella, in honour of our marriage today, of course. Would that be possible?'

'Yes, for sure! Anyway, let's escape this hotel room before it's too late. You'll be an old married man soon, so this will be your last chance as a single man to soak up some good old-fashioned pub atmosphere. I assure you, mate, you won't be disappointed.'

'You're on!' I agree. 'Maybe even some hair-of-the-dog might just cure this damn hangover.'

15

Isabella

New Year's Eve 1942
Church bells ring out again

There is nothing quite like a country wedding to bring a family or neighbourhood together. Even though this wedding is of such short notice, without the required months of meticulous planning factored into making sure this one single day goes perfectly, it doesn't seem to matter much at all. Our wedding is like a beacon of light and hope within a tight-fisted everyday reality for friends, family and neighbours alike and helps to take away the doldrums for all of us. Of course, when you throw in the fact that our wedding day is also on New Year's Eve—the last day of the year 1942—this calls for a special celebration. For this one day alone we can forget about the doom and gloom of a world war hanging over us.

Besides, there hasn't been a wedding in our local church for quite some time now, so there is so much more excited chatter filling the air than usual.

Even Phonsie, our pure white Siberian husky with his romantic soul—who moves around the house a lot slower these days—is to be part of our church service. As a younger dog, Phonsie was rather famous for inviting himself to any wedding ceremony in the neighbourhood and standing silently (if possible for any dog) almost starry-eyed behind the bride and groom. After the ceremony was over, he'd simply leave the church as quietly as he came. There was not one bridal couple over the years who objected to him being there either. Somehow, Phonsie always seemed to add a certain touch of elegance to any wedding. So how could we not include him as part of our own ceremony?

***

As I emerge from our family's Ford Model T, the first thing I hear is the familiar oohs and aahs of the host usual country wedding onlookers just outside the church gates, hoping to catch a glimpse of the lucky bride. To think that used to be me, eagerly watching all those other brides as I was growing up. Not so long ago, after all, when I think about it now. This time around, though, it really is *me* on my own wedding day.

Is this one day meant to be just a dream? No, Isabella Maisie Carlisle—this day is real. If I have any doubts, I only have to look at all the joyous faces smiling back at me.

After taking a quiet moment inside the church entrance to gather my nerves, with my arm entwined with my father's, I chance some baby steps down the aisle to the time-honoured tune of Wagner's classic bridal march. Outwardly, I try to affect a smile of pure confidence for all to see, but inwardly I desperately pray I don't trip, or even worse, end up flat on my face in front of all present inside this quaint little church. Why, even my bridal bouquet of lilies of the valley shakes just that little bit more at the very thought of it.

As soon as my eyes lock onto Paul's at the front of the church, my nerves calm down instantly. My steps are still slow, but much more confident now. Through the gossamer-thin veil that covers my face, my eyes are locked onto Paul's, and I'm smiling only for him. Paul looks even more handsome in his GI uniform—if that's even possible. He smiles back at me with a look of awe, like he can't believe this is happening to him either. We are about to enter into a whole new chapter of our lives together as husband and wife. Inside this beautiful church, with bunches of delicate flowers tied with satin ribbon down each side of the aisle, they are in effect welcoming me as their new bride into their spiritual bosom. Paul and I are about to declare our love for each other in front of family, neighbours and long-time friends. As I reach the alter, Dad symbolically takes my hand and places it under Paul's. As we face the altar together, Phonsie suddenly makes his grand appearance and sits directly behind us, just as he has done so many times before.

Paul whispers to me, 'Oh, Lordy! You look so beautiful, Isabella! I love you so much!'

I squeeze his hand in response, knowing in my heart I'm *exactly* where I'm meant to be.

Throughout the ceremony, as if in some living dream, we solemnly swear to honour our marriage vows, entwined within our spoken vows to each other, before we each slip our plain gold wedding bands onto each other's fingers. Once Reverend Parker has declared us to be husband and wife, Paul wastes no time in sealing the formal part of our marriage ceremony, by lifting the veil to kiss me—his newly wedded wife.

If this really is all just a dream, then I never want to wake up from it. As a young girl, on the threshold of womanhood, I always tended to lose myself in fancy daydreams of a happy future with my future husband. The reality of my own wedding right at this very moment—and most importantly, the man who is standing beside me as my husband now—is more than I could ever imagine my wedding day would be.

I can hear Mum, Grandma Allen and Aunt Violet all sniffling together along the front pew allocated to the bride's family. I think I might have even heard Josie, Kyle and Marty sniffling amongst themselves too, so much in tune with my own tears of happiness. I notice my tough, but gentle, Robbie at the altar, standing on the other side of Paul, shedding a tear or two as well. Robbie, as my oldest brother, had solemnly accepted Paul's heartfelt request be our best man today. Phonsie merely looks on, in his usual dignified way, of course. Once our marriage ceremony is officially over, it's Phonsie's time-honoured cue to stand up and quietly leave the church ahead of the bride and broom. I couldn't have asked for a better bridal 'attendant' really, since there just wasn't even time to find a bridesmaid dress for Josie or Coral at such short notice.

After our ceremony has finished, it's time to sign our marriage certificate in the little alcove off to the side of the church altar. Once it is signed and documented, Paul and I finally emerge from the church arm in arm, as husband and wife.

After what seems like hours, we are suddenly surrounded and kissed repeatedly by each of our wedding guests and lastly by wellwishers from around the neighbourhood. Once all the smiles, kisses and good wishes are exhausted, we head for our bridal car, for Dad to take us back home again. Laughing happily together as we aim for the open doors of the car, past the last of our guests and onlookers, we somehow try to dodge the inevitable shower of brightly coloured paper confetti from ending up in our mouths.

Mum, Grandma Allen, Josie and Aunt Violet have all put together some light refreshments of sandwiches and sponge cake, since we at least have a good supply of fresh eggs on hand. Naturally, there are the inevitable pots of tea and coffee. There is an unwritten golden rule that most family and neighbourhood celebrations must always stick to, even with our wedding being in the middle of an Australian summer and between Christmas and New Year—huge pots of tea or coffee must always be full and ready to pour the first cup. Keeping in mind the reality of wartime, certain foods such as butter or sugar are an everyday challenge to obtain, so our family catering team must make do with whatever is available. In the absence of champagne, we, as the bridal couple, are toasted with small glasses of golden muscat instead.

All in all, our wedding day has been filled with much love, laughter and so many memorable moments for Paul and myself to never forget. Despite the rush to get a wedding organised so quickly, it was still an amazing feat for my parents and eager helpers to do what they did.

***

The time has finally come. After milling around our family and guests for a few hours, my father quietly hints to us, with a touch of a finger to his watch, that it's time for the bride and groom to leave the happy gathering behind. In other words, to make their romantic escape so everybody else can clean up and get to bed.

As a special wedding present from my parents, my father—God bless him!—has quietly organised for us to spend three full nights in a city hotel. He and Mum wanted us to have at least a real wedding night to remember—even if it is wartime. Since we don't have a car of our own—and with Paul not having an Australian driver's licence—Dad suggested we catch the train into the city and back home again on Sunday. Since Paul is due to fly back up north early Monday morning, this makes our honeymoon a very short one, but with the current circumstances, it can't be helped.

Paul and I manage to sneak away together from my family and invited wedding guests, into what will be forever known now as my *old* bedroom, to grab my pre-packed overnight bag hidden way back under my bed. I am so glad now I had thought to pack my bag earlier with a few items of clothing and enough essentials for three nights. As Paul is required to stay in uniform at all times, he really only needs to take his underwear and his own bathroom essentials in my bag.

I had opted to wear one of my absolute favourite outfits as my going-away ensemble. It really is just a mid-calf-length two-piece outfit, with a soft pleated skirt and tiny pearl buttons down the front of its matching blouse. I decided on this particular outfit because it is so similar in style to my wedding dress, which Paul loves so much. He kept whispering to me all afternoon how beautiful I looked in it. In my mind, no other dress could possibly match up or make me feel as glamorous as my wedding dress, but its equally flattering, waist-clinching style still comes pretty close to making me look and feel that much more desirable for my husband tonight.

***

Once we are alone at last for the first time today, Paul quietly locks the door behind us. As he turns back to face me, I move into his arms with no hesitation whatsoever. I truly believe we have both been waiting for this moment all of our lives, only we never realised it until now.

Since we aren't *officially* on our honeymoon yet, we know we shouldn't even be thinking about stealing a few quick kisses all alone in my *old* bedroom, but we do anyway.

When Paul lures me into the irresistible power of his loving arms, how can I possibly resist him? So I move in willingly, knowing it's where I want to be forevermore.

After a few fleeting, but still barely restrained, kisses, Paul pulls back to completely enrapture me with his beautiful smile, 'Hello, Mrs Meier, it's a pleasure to finally meet you.'

'Likewise, Mr Meier, and I must say, I can't wait to meet *all* of you later tonight too.'

'Cheeky, very cheeky, Mrs Meier! I'll hold you to that thought later, but in the meantime, I am thinking perhaps the bride and groom really should be saying goodbye to their wedding guests first, otherwise they might come looking for us.'

'You could be right, Mr Meier. Let's take a few minutes, then, for each of us to use the bathroom and for me to repair my make-up before we leave this room. After all, we don't want them sniggering behind our backs later, do we?'

The scene when we return to in the living room is a human chain made up of family and friends, that stretches from the front door, all the way back to the kitchen door. We are both amazed and delighted to realise they've all gathered together in this way to say goodbye to *us!* As we each move on down the line, the easiest part for me is smiling and saying quick goodbyes to our wedding guests, as they each wish us a long and happy marriage. I'm surprised there are no tears from me so far, but as I reach my family, I can tell it's going to be a different story.

It all starts off as I suspected it would, with some predictable teasing from each of my brothers. Being my older brother, Rob is first to speak. 'Good luck, sis! Have lots of babies and don't forget to remind them they're half-Australian.'

'I will, Robbie. I promise.' I hug him ever so tightly, trying hard not to cry yet.

'I'm about to miss my big brother all over again soon. Especially since you'll be heading back to Darwin on Monday.' Mere words don't come easy anymore. We hug each other again, even more tightly this time.

Robbie shakes Paul's hand warmly. 'All the best, mate! I hope you realise you've got a special lady in this one.' Robbie points his big thumb my way.

'I surely do know this already, Rob. I promise to take good care of her,' Paul solemnly assures him.

'Good luck, Paul.' Kyle shakes Paul's hand, then adds, 'You're gonna need it. Hey, sis! Have you told your husband you can't cook yet?'

'Thanks, Kyle! Just because I'm married now doesn't mean I can't thump you still.'

'Ha! You and what army? I *am* happy for you though, big sis.' I notice his tears now as we hug, which is starting to make me tear up now too.

It's Marty's turn, 'Hey, Bell, does this mean I can have your tennis racquet now?'

'Not a chance!' I laugh. This is a new Marty teasing me now. 'You've obviously been hanging around Kyle too long. Don't forget, Marty, I'm still going to be around for a while yet, or at least until this war is over. Come on and give me one of your extra special hugs, you cheeky thing!'

Josie can't resist teasing me either. 'So, Bell! I guess I can look forward to taking over your side of our bedroom soon too.' Josie whispers in my ear as she hugs me.

'True, but not quite yet, little sister. You'll still have to put up with me for a while.' I hug her for the longest time. 'I love you, Josie! To me, you are the best sister in the whole world.'

'That's right, and don't you forget it!' It seems that Josie can no longer stop the sniffles neither. *What hope do I have, then, by the time I reach the end of the line? None whatsoever.* One last hug from her is enough to tip both of us over the edge. Josie is fully sobbing now, as she desperately searches the side pockets of her skirt for a dry hanky. Paul offers Josie one of his own hankies, along with an affectionate, brotherly bear hug to go with it. Josie accepts both, no longer caring about embarrassing herself in front of Paul. 'Look at me, I'm a complete mess !' She sniffles louder as she swipes her runny nose with the hanky again. 'My new and *only* brother-in-law. Welcome to the family, Paul! I'm just so happy for both of you!'

'Same here, Josephine! I guess you will be the only sister-in-law I'll ever have.'

Grandma Allen surprises both of us by grabbing Paul to hug him warmly. 'Welcome to our family, Paul!'

To me she says, 'Come here and give me a big hug, Bell, and I will give you some advice in return. I know you and Paul won't get to live together as husband and wife until after the war, but as time goes by, you will see these next difficult months ahead of you as a mere pause in your future life together. Love will win out!'

'Thanks, Grandma Allen, for everything, and most of all, for your wonderful advice. I know Paul and I *will* get through all of this.'

My parents have never been the kind of people who expect any special attention, not even as parents of the bride. Due to current circumstances, my parents are the *only* parents at our wedding, but they still wait at the end of the family line to be the last to farewell their newly married daughter. 'Last but not least' has never be a truer saying than it is today.

'Mum, thank you *so* much for all of your hard work these past few days! This day would never have happened without yours and Dad's help. Thank you too, of course, for my beautiful dress! Knowing this was the dress that you used to wear yourself has made today so much more precious to me.'

'You're very welcome, my darling girl! We'll see you in a few days, then ... Right?'

'Yes, you will! I love you so much, Mum!' We both start bawling together. Without my father having to say a single word, he offers a clean hanky to each of us. The look I catch him giving to Paul says it all: 'Better get used to this!'

My new husband merely smiles back at Dad with an equally knowing look. No words are necessary. Mum hugs Paul now with obvious affection. 'Welcome to our family, Paul! Oh, and by the way, despite what Kyle said before, Bell *can* cook!'

Paul swipes his hand across his brow with mock relief. 'Phew! So happy to hear that, Myra!'

Dad is next in line for me to hug—and hug him, I do. I have always been very close to my father. Even more so now, and I immediately realise why. The church and organising the legal side of our wedding are classic examples of my father's innate ability to make all sorts of good things happen in the shortest possible time. I have always felt safe in my father's arms, even more so now as he holds me close to his heart one more time. All the while, I continue to bawl my eyes out. The emotional floodgates are fully open for today it seems.

'Dad, you are my hero ... Do you know that?' I stop talking for a moment. Well, long enough to take another swipe at my sniffly nose, before waffling on, 'What you and Mum have achieved these past few days has been nothing short of a miracle. Seriously, I don't know what I would do without either of you. Thank you so much!'

'Well, my dear child, that's what parents do for their children.' Dad pats my hand affectionately. No doubt to settle me down. 'I'll be doing exactly the same for each of my other children. You already know by now how very important my family is to me.'

'Yes, I do know this, Dad, and I love you all the more for it.'

'What Isabella says is true,' Paul adds his thanks to his father-in-law, while shaking Dad's hand. 'We really couldn't have done it without you, Harvey.'

'No thanks are necessary, Paul. Anyway, I have one more thing I want to do for you two young people. To save some time at the other end for you, I would like to drive you to the railway station.'

'No, it's okay, Dad,' I protest. 'It's only ten minutes to the station. We'll be fine.'

'No, your father's right, Bell,' Mum interjects. 'Please allow us just one more thing that we'd like to do for you both. After all, darling, it *is* your wedding day.'

'Well since you put it that way, we'll take you up on the offer then … Right, Paul?'

'Yes, thank you! Your kind offer is very much appreciated by both of us.'

After we've said goodbye to my family, there is still just one more person at the end of the line. Coral has been my best friend throughout most of my teenage years and beyond. So, to me, she qualifies as an extra special person in my life, and after all, she *is* family to me and always will be.

'I've attached myself to the end of this line, instead of at the beginning, because I wanted to be the last to say goodbye to you both. Especially you, my dearest friend, Bell.'

My hug with Coral instantly starts off a virtual torrent of fresh tears for me again and the same goes for her.

'I love you, Coral! Just as well this goodbye isn't meant to be a final farewell for either of us. If it was, I'd really be an emotional wreck! I'll be seeing you at work next week as usual.' We hug again before I move on and it's Paul's turn to say goodbye to Coral.

'Bye, Paul!' Coral hugs Paul with an easygoing brother/sister kind of affection that has developed between them. 'Who would have thought our day at Luna Park would spark your romance with Bell the way it did? Pity it wasn't the same for Brad and me. How is Brad, by the way?'

'Not real sure, to tell you the truth, Coral. He was posted to another unit right after our stay in Melbourne. I pray to God he's alive and well, though.'

'That's okay, just wondering, that's all.' She hugs us both one more time. 'I'd better let you two go. I do believe you have a honeymoon to get to. I guess it'll be a waste of time for me tell you both to behave yourselves.'

'You've got that right, Coral!' I give Paul a cheeky smile and receive one in return.

'So I can count on a full report next time I see you then?'

'Not a chance, my dear friend! What happens in the bedroom stays in the bedroom.'

'Spoilsport!'

As is the custom for most weddings that I'm aware of, it's now time for me to throw my bridal bouquet. Apart from my sister Josie, my happily unmarried Aunt Violet and my best friend Coral, there isn't really any other eligible unmarried women in the room, but I throw it anyway.

Aunt Violet doesn't even bother to try and catch the bouquet, but both Josie and Coral do. In the spirit of fun, they both try to push each other out of the way to be the one to catch it first.

I hoist it over my right shoulder and wait for the usual eager responses from the only two qualified bouquet-catchers behind me.

'Sorry, Josie, but the fastest catcher always wins,' Coral gloats with glee.

'Yes, especially when she cheats! I should've tripped you when I had the chance!' Josie answers with a cheeky grin on her face, not looking at all upset about the outcome.

***

As soon as Dad pulls up in front of the railway station, we have no time to waste. With a quick goodbye, we run like crazy to try and catch the city train already at the station. We make it with only seconds to spare. Once onboard, we collapse gratefully into the two nearest seats available.

Thank goodness the carriage isn't as crowded this time, as it usually is during my weekday working hours. Apart from another couple three seats back and three couples further forward on the other side, we're delighted to realise we are almost completely alone at last.

Now that we have these next three nights together, we plan to make the most of every minute of it. Once settled into our seats, we snuggle in close to each other as we hold hands and gaze longingly into each other's eyes, oblivious to the other passengers in our carriage. It's like we are really seeing each other for the first time and we obviously love what we see so far. I am quite sure the other passengers have already suspected we're newlyweds, so they're obviously happy to just leave us be.

'Have I told you already what a very beautiful bride you were today, Mrs Meier?'

'Yes, you might have a few times, Mr Meier, but I don't mind you telling me again.'

'You literally took my breath away when I saw you coming down the aisle towards me. I am one lucky man, that's for sure.'

'That's a coincidence, then, because I thought the same thing about you. As I walked down the aisle, you looked so dashing and handsome in your uniform. There you were, waiting just for *me* too! Well, I know for myself now that I must be the luckiest woman in all of Melbourne tonight … In fact, I'm the luckiest woman in the whole world, really.'

'I can't wait to have you all to myself in our hotel room tonight, Mrs Meier. Just you and me and not one single wedding guest in sight.' We chuckle at the memory now of us each circulating around the room, trying to talk to all of our guests at our reception. Oh, and the smiling! There was so much smiling going on, our faces started to ache after a while. Apart from our quick escape to my bedroom to grab our overnight bags, there hadn't been any time at all really for us be completely alone together as husband and wife.

'Oh yes, indeed, Mr Meier! Not long to go now. Just one more station and we're there.'

'Even better!' Paul kisses the two rings on my left ring finger. My heart-shaped engagement ring and now my yellow-gold wedding band to complete the set.

'I feel so proud to see you wear this wedding band, along with my own wedding band too, of course,' Paul declares. 'They will bind our hearts together forever into just one heart, my darling Isabella.'

'These rings symbolise our love, Paul. Nothing can ever tear us apart for long.'

'I wholeheartedly agree. I truly believe if we can get through this next year of being apart, we can come through anything.'

As I place his hand still clasped within mine, I'm fully aware this is indeed a symbolic journey we are taking together right here, right now. At dawn this morning, we awoke as two separate individuals, but now it's like we are just one person. We both lapse into a quiet companionable silence together. Our golden bands of marriage are touching each other and all the time, our hands remain clasped together, as we each acknowledge that these two golden bands signify an undeniable proof of our unbreakable bond of love for each other.

16

Isabella

New Year's Eve 1942
Honeymooning in wartime Melbourne

Once our train pulls into Southern Cross station, we waste no time in making our way to the Regent Hotel, situated right in the heart of Melbourne. Since it's still only five o'clock on a Friday night, people are still milling around the city streets, long after the shops have closed for this coming long weekend. Even if it is New Year's Eve, when most people the world over may be still wanting to see in the new year with a bang, our nightly blackout curfews have almost become second nature these days. From just after sunset each night until just before dawn the following day, we know well enough by now—for the safety of our city—that we all need to stay indoors. The resilient people of Melbourne, though, still insist upon keeping up appearances. Graciously, Melbourne city dwellers still believe a united happy front is always preferable to sitting out this war indoors, miserably locked away in fear. Despite the gloominess of these ongoing wartime restrictions, most of the people I know living within Melbourne city perimeters still believe that keeping up appearances is just as important for one's soul and overall morale than only thinking of one's own safety or the safety of their city as a whole entity.

After dark, wherever there is music playing, that's where most fun-minded people can be found. The mayor of Melbourne is happy to

144

oblige, of course, but only with the stipulation that all external windows and doors be blacked out at night to the outside world. There are no exceptions. Despite these rigid wartime restrictions, most fun-loving people are still determined to enjoy themselves anyway. Music, indeed, any kind of partying after dark, has to be taken down into the bowels of some deep basement or the darker floors of certain establishments, usually available to 'selected' clientele only. On weekends, especially during the daylight hours, music still plays on somewhere in the city. Whether that be in a pub or under some awning or tree-shaded shelter close to the shimmering life force of the Yarra River, nothing can hold back a true Melbournite for long.

While there may not always be any audible evidence of some underground rousing band music happening between the blackout hours, there is, however, still some secret enjoyment of carefully hidden liquor or maybe even some lucrative poker game being played in secret behind some heavily guarded door, deep down within the bowels of the city.

Having made it this far through these deceptively abandoned city streets of Melbourne's central area, we enter the elegant reception area of the Regent Hotel, hand in hand and obviously eager to reach our room in the shortest time possible. Once we have identified ourselves to the concierge and our reservation is confirmed, we are immediately escorted to our room on the fourth floor by a smartly dressed hotel porter.

Once we reach the door to our room, number 429, we stand aside to allow the hotel porter to unlock our door. Once it is opened wide, Paul surprises me by easily scooping me up in his arms to carry me over the threshold. The porter, all businesslike and with his impeccable manners, merely gives us a knowing smile as he moves around our stylish suite at a brisk pace, checking to make sure all is in order. He takes a moment to explain to us some features about our suite, but most particularly, he reminds us once again about keeping the shades drawn from sunset to sunrise for each of our three nights at the hotel. Once he has completed the formality of welcoming us to our room, he briskly heads for the door, but not before looping the 'do not disturb' sign on the door handle outside. We soon realise this is his way of discreetly leaving us alone for rest of the night.

After he leaves, we're finally free to wander around and check out exactly what this very elegant honeymoon suite has to offer. We gleefully open and shut every cupboard or alcove, fridge or glass cabinet, as we admire every little thing at our disposal for the next three nights. Over on a small table, a bottle of champagne is chilling nicely in an ice bucket with two crystal glasses beside it. Along with the champagne, there is also a complementary bowl of luscious grapes, fresh strawberries, polished apples and plump rosy apricots on offer.

'I can well imagine most hotels here in Melbourne—and indeed around the world, for that matter—must find it very difficult to offer champagne for their guests under these wartime restrictions?' Paul queries as he removes the bottle from its bed of crushed ice to study its label. 'It's not Don Perignon, but it will have to do this time, my dear,' Paul hilariously declares in his best snobbish voice.

Picking up on his silly mood, I take a handful of grapes and gleefully shove a few into his mouth, stopping any further words escaping. 'Quite right, Mr Meier.' After slipping a few luscious strawberries into my own mouth, I snobbishly add, 'One cannot be expected to fritter this night away on mere grapes or strawberries either … Even if they are supposed to be the food of love.'

'They probably have a few cases of champagne from some black-market source, hidden away for their exclusive clientele,' Paul observes. 'I'm quite sure some city hotels must have some sort of reliable source for certain hard-to-get items.'

'Yes, I think you're right, Paul. I've often wondered the same thing myself with hotels and how they always seem to obtain any so-called 'luxuries' for their more discerning guests during wartime. The trick must be to honour these special requests for *certain* items, while still keeping ahead of the competition at the same time … For an extra price, of course.

'I don't mean to sound cynical here, Paul, but I hate to think of what my parents must have paid for this room. Not just one night, mind you, but three nights.'

'I'm sure your parents are more than happy to pay the extra price to give us a honeymoon to remember—particularly since we might only have these few nights together for a long, long time. Besides, I get the feeling your parents are true romantics at heart and they certainly seem to be a lot closer as a couple than most other folk of their generation.'

'They certainly are, always have been. You know, I've never ever known them to be angry with each other. Not only are they as close as a husband and wife can be, but they are the best of friends too.' I wrap my arms around Paul from behind now and snuggle into him. 'We can only hope to be as happy as they are when we've been married for as many years as they have been.'

Paul twists himself around within my grasp and wraps his own arms around me to kiss me. 'So, let's do them the honour of appreciating their romantic hearts by just accepting this amazingly generous wedding gift from them and worry about the cost later. Do we both agree?'

'Yes, of course I agree, Paul. I, for one, intend to fully enjoy their generous gift tonight. I know I can be a bit *too* practical at times. Anyway, I don't know about you, darling, but I would absolutely *adore* some of that sparking champagne right now! If you will do the honours and pop that cork—*Pretty please?*'

'Why, of course! Your wish is my command, me little darlin'. Let us thoroughly enjoy this scrumptious feast, then, shall we? Tonight, let us drink champagne and partake of these tempting love fruits. Let us consider this as a magic time, all alone together, to be a sort of a quest; A quest we must fulfil, to make those nasty war scenes outside this room fade away—well, if only for the next three nights, at least.'

'My! We *are* being poetic tonight, aren't we?' I giggle happily at Paul's lighthearted craziness.

With his champagne glass held high in the air, Paul exaggerates a sauntering walk, as he makes his way over to the radio and turns it on. After tweaking the controls a bit, he finally settles on Artie Shaw's 'Moonglow'. He remembers to turn the volume down, so only us two can hear it, then turns around to face me. On his way back to me, he starts to dance ever so slowly, swaying his hips so easily to the smooth rhythm of the music, looking deep into my eyes the whole time.

'Do you like Artie Shaw?' Paul takes me in his arms as we move in real close together, lost to the music.

'I *adore* Artie Shaw! Glenn Miller too. In fact, I love the sound of all of the big bands.'

'I saw Artie Shaw in Chicago once. Unbelievable! If you ever get a chance to see him playing, don't miss it.'

'I *nearly* did get to see him right here in Melbourne a few years back, but something went terribly wrong on the night, so I didn't get to see him after all. Anyway, remind me to tell you about it some other time. It's hardly important right now.'

'Sounds intriguing. In the meantime …' Paul starts to nibble at my neck with gentle little nips. I think I might as well just lie down, to die blissfully in his arms, especially with the very thrill of him touching my skin in such a pleasurable way. His lips move on up now to my eager mouth. Our kisses start slowly at first, then so much deeper. We are still moving to the music the whole time, but it's like we're in some kind of hypnotic trance now. As the delicious combination of clarinet and saxophone stirs our souls, our bodies respond with a passion to match.

'Oh, Paul, I love you so much!' Each kiss is more arousing than the last, our wandering hands seeking each other out so much more. Paul undoes the back of my dress, while I, in my own haste to reconnect with his lips, fumble with the front buttons of his shirt. Next, off comes my brasserie and down goes the long pants of Paul's uniform. I continue to sway to the music against him but am now only in my panties and Paul only in his jocks. As the song intensifies, so do our kisses. With the rousing, dramatic crescendo of Artie's Big Band reaching its final peak, so too do we yearn for the ultimate crescendo of our love-infused vision and the sublime touch of each other's entwined bodies.

Any previous apprehension either one of us might've been feeling about our first night alone together, this niggling worry is no longer a problem anymore. That was last night. This is tonight and we are truly ready for each other.

'Do you think we should perhaps adjourn to the bedroom, Mrs Meier?' Paul asks me between kisses. By this time the music has stopped and we are down to no clothes at all, but still on our own private dance floor. We stop kissing long enough to look around the room for a moment.

'Good idea! Perhaps we should do that, Mr Meier. Besides, I do believe the other dancers have already gone home.'

'I've never realised just how funny you can be … my beautiful, funny Isabella.'

'You make me laugh too, and if I may say so, you are so very handsome tonight too, my dear!'

'Why, thank you, kind lady! But enough talk for now. It's time for some real lovin'!'

Paul takes my hand and leads me to our private bedroom within the luxurious suite. I most definitely do love this idea—especially from a woman's private point of view.

Paul suddenly stops in his tracks now. 'Are you nervous, Isabella? … I'm sure you must be.'

'I was last night, of course, thinking about our first night together. But not anymore. I *want* you, Paul. *So* much!'

He squeezes my hand in silent agreement. Our true honeymoon hasn't even started yet.

***

I awake the next morning to the sun streaming in through our balcony doors. The glass is stylishly covered by light gauzy curtains in soft biscuit tones to show off the highly polished French doorframes to perfection.

I can see that Paul has already pulled the curtains aside, allowing a gentle breeze to waft in ever so softly from the Yarra River nearby. It deliciously caresses my naked body, reawakening my newly aroused passion once again. Will my desire for Paul's touch ever be sated enough?

In my naivety, I fully expected my wedding night to be as I dreamed, as young girls tend to do, imagining *exactly* what happens when a girl loses her virginity. Privately, my mother sat me down the night before my wedding and explained to me that a little bit of bleeding can be expected the first time, but it doesn't usually last for long. Whether from modesty or the reluctance of her generation to talk about sex at all, Mum never did get into the nitty-gritty of sex itself. I'm sort of glad she didn't. It could have been very embarrassing for both of us. Anyway, some things are better experienced firsthand rather than merely talked about.

Three nights of our honeymoon is all we have together, but we are trying not to think about that. My father once told me that nothing is promised to anyone in this life. Even if that *is* true, fate still seems somewhat cruel to me now. Is any long-term separation really meant to be the true lesson of our own love story? Why does fate *allow* us to awaken our passion for each other, only to snatch it away from us again for who knows how long?

This remains to be seen, I guess.

Speaking of Paul, where is he? 'Paul? … Paul? … Are you there?'

The door to the ensuite quietly opens and Paul pokes his head out. He is wearing nothing but a bath towel around his waist and his face is half covered in shave cream. 'Ah! My gorgeous wife has awakened at last. I didn't have the heart to disturb you, I thought I might as well attend to my morning ablutions first, before waking you for breakfast, which if

I'm not mistaken should be here very soon.' Paul comes over to the bed, gathers me up in arms and kisses me tenderly. He smells deliciously fresh of soap from his shower, but some of the shaving cream that is still on his face rubs off onto me as I kiss him back, and of course, I find myself giggling like a schoolgirl once again. My impulsive giggling only makes Paul eager to make me laugh even more, so he tries to rub even more shaving cream onto me. To avoid it getting all over my face, I respond by ducking under the bedcovers while I move my naked body quickly over to the other side of the bed. Once out of reach, I manage to grab one of the pillows and start thumping him with it, both of us laughing the whole time.

'Good morning!' I squeal, as I thump him one more time with the pillow. 'So, this is how it's going to be, is it? You cover me in shaving cream, while I try to ward you off with a pillow each time.'

'No, only every second time. Come closer, my dear. I'll behave myself.'

'Oh, sure!' But I do anyway. Our lips find each other as we move even closer. 'What time is it, by the way?' I interject quickly as we come up for air.

'Nearly 8:30. Do you remember when we booked in yesterday, we ordered breakfast for around this time?'

'Ah, yes, I do remember now, and just as well too, I might add. I don't know about you, darling, but I think my body needs some nourishing food to replenish me right about now. I'm starving!'

Right at this very moment, there comes a knock at the door and a friendly voice calls out, 'Breakfast!'

'I guess that answers our question, then,' Paul says as he heads for the door. One of the hotel's waiters, dressed in a pristine white jacket and black pants, greets Paul with a welcoming smile. 'Good morning, Mr and Mrs Meier! I believe you ordered breakfast for 8:30 this morning?'

'Yes, we certainly did!' Paul takes one look at the full tray and can hardly believe his eyes. 'Is this all for us?'

'Yes, sir!' the waiter declares with a friendly smile as he wheels in a heavy wooden trolley laden with two medium-sized plates, each with its own silver cover to keep our breakfast hot. There's also two chilled glasses of orange juice, four slices of toast with tiny curls of butter, two pearly white bread-and-butter plates, along with a tiny pair of silver salt and pepper shakers. A floral China teapot and two matching cups and saucers, milk jug and sugar bowl take pride of place on the tray, along with a small silver pot of aromatic coffee. Last, but not least, there are two carefully folded, white linen serviettes bearing the hotel's logo with a fancy gold embroidered letter R on one corner, laid together neatly beside a cute crystal vase containing one exquisite valentine-red rosebud.

The whole fancy presentation creates a delightful picture for us two ravenous honeymooners, indeed. The waiter quietly lays our breakfast out on the small dining table just inside the French doors, and as he leaves, asks us to leave our breakfast trolley just outside our suite door so that when he comes by later he won't need to disturb us again. Without saying a word, his knowing smile tells us he understands the honeymooners' need for privacy.

We can barely wait to tuck into our breakfast and all that's on offer. Lifting off the silver covers, we are delighted to find generous servings of mushrooms on a bed of toast slices cooked in a creamy sauce, grilled tomato and fluffy scrambled egg on the side. When we first checked out our breakfast fare, upon its delivery to our room, we failed to see a small card tucked in under the bread-and-butter plates. The beautifully embossed card reads:

We at the Regent Hotel sincerely hope you enjoy your breakfast, made exclusively for you!

It was beautifully handwritten and signed with a flourish by the manager of the hotel.

'Oh, how lovely! Can you believe all of this is just for us, Paul?'

'I know, honey! It sure is hard to believe, isn't it? Man! I haven't seen

152

a breakfast as fancy as this for a long, long time. How do they do it? Especially with the war? Well, I don't know about you, Isabella, but I don't intend to just stand here and look at all this wonderful breakfast. Let us eat, eat, eat, then sip tea or coffee until we can't take in another thing!'

And that's just what we did. Apart from my mother's home cooking, this would have to be the best breakfast I've ever eaten in my whole life. Especially sharing it with my new husband. How lucky are we?

***

We laze around in bed as much as we want to on our first morning alone together. While Paul drinks his third cup of coffee, I am perfectly content to sip my English breakfast all posh-like from a dainty China cup, as I leisurely gaze out over the picturesque Yarra River. After our coffee and tea supplies are finally depleted, we each sit back to breathe a sigh of contentment. Before too long, though, we can't resist playing footsie under the table, which of course leads to mad frantic sex back in bed. All before lunch too. We can't seem to get enough of each other. Well, after all, that's what honeymoons are all about, aren't they?

***

On our first full day alone together, we stroll lazily around the city streets, arm in arm. Over coffee, we stare dreamily into each other's eyes and kiss at every opportunity. To the other people around us, we probably look like we don't have a care in the world. They aren't to know, though, that come Monday morning, we are to be separated once again for who knows how long? But for now, we dare not think of our imminent separation, but we make a firm promise to enjoy this time together and our moments alone as husband and wife.

At lunchtime, we are content to devour chunky toasted sandwiches and our usual tea or coffee choices at a leisurely pace under a shaded tree at a quaint little cafe in one of the city arcades. In the afternoon, we amble around the Melbourne Botanical Gardens and the delightfully picturesque river walk, always walking close together. When we've had enough of sightseeing, we make our way back to our hotel room to cuddle up together, before drifting off to sleep for the rest of the afternoon. After all that food since our lavish breakfast this morning, walking around the summer-kissed city streets in the afternoon, and let's not forget our lovemaking last night and again this morning, it's time to recharge our inner batteries again. Before drifting off to sleep in the afternoon, we take the precaution of closing our bedroom curtains early. Along with the closeness of our bodies entwined together, by the time the sun sets over a golden horizon, we're already completely oblivious to the outside world.

When we do awake hours later, the room is completely dark. After showering, we put on the one good set of clothes we brought with us and take the lift down past the foyer and into the hotel dining room. It seems strange at first, to have all the windows in the dining room blacked out, but after a while we don't even notice. We are too much in love to even care about what is happening in the world outside this hotel.

Would God really mind if we allow these few moments of precious time for ourselves? Are we selfish to even think this way? I think not.

After a superb meal of beef Wellington and roasted vegetables, a wine trifle for dessert, finishing up with a tall glass of Irish coffee with whipped cream on top, we make our way back to our room. On our last night, we enthusiastically honour the title of the honeymoon suite, by first stripping each other of any distracting clothing before literally falling onto the bed. Making bittersweet love on and off throughout the night finally exhausts us and we drift off to sleep, well into the early hours of the morning. We allow ourselves to slip back to a moment before we even knew what each other's skin felt like to caress so freely, the thrill of each tiny hidden crevice, arousing the senses of each desperate lover. We never want to let the other go. I'm learning firsthand what all of those romantic movies have been hinting to me for years, which is the sublime feeling of looking into your lover's eyes and seeing your own love reflected right back at you. Ultimately, we want the sweet memory of these two nights alone together to keep each other going for as long as it takes to win this war to its final battle.

***

All too soon, our honeymoon is over, but what a wonderful, magical few days it has been. So much more than this girl—with all of her starry dreams still ahead of her—could ever hope for, anyway. We check out of our hotel just before ten on Sunday morning and within twenty minutes of reaching the train station, we manage to catch a train heading back to Coburg. We are both very quiet on the journey, not really talking much, just firmly holding hands, never wanting to let go of this tangible, but at times elusive, lifeline between us. On the other hand, we're just as happy to embrace our silences too. Normally, we never have any trouble talking openly to each other about practically anything—when we're not busy having sex, that is.

We keep to ourselves on the train and just want this time alone—as most newlywed couples tend to do, when they are so totally wrapped up in each other to the exclusion of everyone else around them.

Once we arrive back home, my family will no doubt surround us with hugs, kisses and boundless love. I also suspect Josie will probably be busting to drag me into our previously shared bedroom to ask me lots of burning questions about what my honeymoon was *really* like—and for me to answer her ultimate question of what Paul is like 'in the sack'. Although, I have a feeling our parents will have warned her about respecting my privacy by not asking me any inappropriate questions once I'm back home. I know my little sister too well, though. She may hold off while Paul is still here, but come next week, she's bound to start grilling me for the answers she seeks. I can pretty much guarantee it. She won't let me off the hook either, I'm sure, until I have mostly satisfied her curiosity once and for all.

I stare out the window of the train now, sort of half-observing tumbled cityscapes of houses and shops close to the railway tracks finally giving over to verdant country fields and little creeks flowing under wooden bridges. Even though I already feel settled within my new role as a married woman and am ready to head back home, I still find myself holding onto Paul's hand like my life depends on it. If his silence for the past fifteen minutes is anything to go by, he too must be having a few reflective thoughts of his own.

As for tomorrow? Tomorrow is destined to be a day for teary goodbyes. Today? Today is still ours to hold close to our hearts, to cherish forever and to add a whole lot of newly chartered memories onto the pages of our book of life.

17

Isabella

January 1943
Hidden effects of war

Just as I had anticipated, my family have been expectantly waiting around for us to arrive home. As soon as we swing open the creaky gate, they are magically out the front door and down the steps with lightning speed.

Before my honeymoon, I never gave a thought about me being somehow different with my family afterwards. But I *am* different, and my siblings soon realise this. Particularly Josie. She seems somewhat reserved with me now, which is so unlike her. Normally we can talk for hours about fashion, movies and we even touch on the never-ending mystery of men—even if we have lived with three brothers in the same house our whole life. With me being a married woman now, I guess Josie wonders if I really am still her sister as I was before. Josie being Josie, she no doubt thinks that just because I know what being with a man 'in that way' is all about now, any discussion about sex will probably be out of bounds and even discouraged from now on by our parents and even me. I make a silent promise to Josie—and to myself—to talk to her again after Paul has left and when we are alone as sisters. Happily, I have nothing but good things to tell her now about this oh-so-intriguing taboo subject. I won't be telling her *absolutely everything*, though.

Later, after all the fuss of our homecoming has died down, Mum and Dad try to talk us into sleeping in their room, but we won't hear of it. We also turn down the offer of my old bedroom too, because we'd have to kick Josie out to do that. Thankfully, Robbie volunteers his room in the end. For one thing, his room is towards the back of the house, which makes it more private for us, and with Robbie being over six feet tall, his bed is longer and wider than Kyle or Marty's beds. Robbie insists he is more than happy to stretch out on our comfy couch in the lounge room for the night. 'Besides,' he argues, 'our family couch is so much more comfortable than my army bunk bed up in Darwin. Believe it!'

So that's where we end up for the night. Despite Kyle and Marty sleeping in the room next to us, we still manage to fool around under the sheets, while always being mindful to be as quiet as we can. Luckily, Kyle and Marty have always been sound sleepers. Besides, we don't fancy being the main focus of Kyle's discussion around the family breakfast table when tomorrow morning rolls around.

Little did we know how quickly our best-laid plan could change in an instant.

***

'NO! NO! … I CAN'T LEAVE! … PLEASE DON'T MAKE ME LEAVE, SIR! … I'VE GOT TO GET THIS MESSAGE OUT! I'VE GOT TO WARN THEM! *PLEASE!*' Paul shouts out loud within his fitful sleep, before vigorously thrashing about, forcefully awakening me out of a deep contented sleep. Without warning, he bolts upright.

As I anxiously watch Paul, I'm still struggling to kick-start my befuddled brain into waking up fully. What on Earth could have happened to Paul for him to be shouting out in his sleep like this? I quickly realise he is, in fact, having not just any old nightmare, but a hellish one at that.

'Paul, darling! It's okay, it's okay!' My instincts tell me to wake him as gently as I can. 'You're having a bad dream that's all.' There is no response, though. Paul keeps thrashing about anyway, totally oblivious to me lying next to him.

I turn on the bedside light, completely shocked to realise Paul is sweating profusely, his white singlet soaking wet. My calm, quietly spoken reassurances have no effect on him whatsoever. He doesn't seem to hear me at all and just continues to thrash around from side to side, still pleading to whoever is dominating his hellish nightmare to '*STOP RIGHT NOW!*'

I am at a total loss as to what to do. Up until now, I'd only ever heard my brothers, or even Josie, break the silence of the night when they suddenly call out in their sleep when trapped within some childish nightmare, because some scary monster is chasing them or some huge spider is about to devour them alive. The kind of nightmare Paul is having is entirely different. I sense this one is more like some living nightmare to Paul, that for some reason he is forced to relive again.

Many hours later, I prove to myself that I am spot on with my own kind of reasoning.

Paul's shouts are heard throughout the house and probably all the way over towards the surrounding suburbs as well. That's how loud he sounds to me, as I lie close to him. I need to get some help for him! At least that's what my mind is telling me, but my body suddenly freezes with fear. I must be in shock or something because my body is immediately paralysed. I can't seem to move at all. Even while my still-sleepy brain is trying to make sense of it all, Paul continues to shout and thrash around in bed. *What can I do to help him?*

I don't have to wait long. Before I know it, my entire family are all trying to rush into Robbie's bedroom at the same time, trying to understand what all the ruckus is about, all with shocked expressions on their faces. Thank goodness, though, Robbie is able to immediately recognise Paul's symptoms for what they are.

By way of explanation, Robbie proceeds to gives us the condensed version of what Paul is suffering from.

'I have already seen this kind of thing before, Bell, with some of my mates in Darwin, and Paul is showing these exact same symptoms to-night.' Rob takes a quick look at Paul then shakes his head. 'This, Bell, is the result of some *real* wartime experiences replaying over and over again inside a soldier's mind. These constant nightmares and hellish visions never really leave an affected soldier, even in their waking hours. That is, until they have to admit they have a problem and to seek help. Sadly, they often don't know they need help. One thing is for sure, though, Bell,' Robbie adds, 'Paul *does* need immediate help, before he flies back up to the islands tomorrow … By the way, does Paul have any emergency contact numbers in his knapsack we can call for help?'

I snap out of my shocked state to galvanise my reluctant limbs into action. After rummaging through his knapsack, I'm able to lay my hands at last on a crinkled leather folder, safely tucked away in one of the inner pockets.

'I think this folder might be what you're looking for, Robbie.' I quickly rifle through the various items inside. 'I've got his passport, pay book, social security details and yes, here we are! A list of contact numbers for his family back at home … And yes, his emergency contact numbers: a medic, the MPs and the big brass—as Paul calls them—right here in Australia.'

Robbie takes the list from me and heads straight for our phone on the kitchen wall. 'I'll speak to them if you like, Bell. Maybe with me being in the Australian Army, they might be more willing to talk to me about Paul's condition. You might be his legal wife now, but you're also a woman, so they usually only ever give family members the absolute bare facts.'

While Robbie speaks to someone on the other end of the phone, Dad quietly orders my two younger brothers and Josie back to their rooms before seating himself on one side of the bed to keep Paul from rolling himself onto the floor. Somehow, despite my worry over Paul, I continue to sit beside him on the other side of the bed, speaking quietly to him, hoping the sound of my voice can somehow calm his troubled mind. Even though Paul is still calling out and thrashing around, Mum also sits closer to the head of the bed and gently mops Paul's brow with a soft, moist hand towel, wiping away beads of sweat on his forehead whilst cooling his fever down at the same time.

Robbie must have set something in motion real quick, because the next thing we know, there's a knock at our front door. I am somewhat surprised when I open the door to find two robust female ambulance officers ready to storm into Robbie's room with a metal stretcher, which clatters loudly as they wheel it with haste along the hallway's polished wood floors towards Robbie's bedroom. With so many of our men away at war, I guess there just isn't enough burly men around to load their patients onto stretchers, let alone drive the ambulances. With women in their thousands being left behind by their menfolk, they've been quick to put their hands up to help the war effort. Women from all around Australia, of all shapes and sizes, have all happily stepped into the essential roles of emergency services without complaint. In their usual no-nonsense Aussie way, the newspapers proudly remind us all what a wonderful job they are doing of it. Especially if these two take-charge women are anything to go by.

With a bit of assistance from Dad and Robbie, the ambulance ladies, Gwen and Lola, shift Paul over onto the wheeled trolley, tie him in place with leather straps and are ready to transport him off to hospital in double-quick time. As his only legal next of kin in Australia, I am allowed to travel with Paul in the ambulance. I'm pretty sure I would have kicked up a stink anyway if I wasn't allowed to go with him. I can't bear the thought of leaving him on his own now without me. After all, I am his wife, and he needs me with him.

On the way to the hospital, with me beside Paul in the back of the ambulance, Lola immediately takes on the role of ambulance driver whilst Gwen sits in the back with me, attending to Paul's immediate needs. Gwen speaks quietly to me when she can in-between each observation of

Paul's vitals. 'Mrs. Meier, we're now heading for Parkville Hospital in the city. You might not know this yet, but Parkville Hospital is now under complete control by the US Army and probably will be for the duration of the war.'

She continues to explain that the US Army have set up their own major military tent hospital on the corners of Lonsdale and Swanston streets, for the overspill of patients they expect to take up these beds for the duration of the war. It seems amazing to me how you can live in a city all your life and never really be aware of what's happening beyond your own neighbourhood half the time.

***

Robbie and Mum follow the ambulance to the hospital, mainly for my sake and for Mum's sake too, as she doesn't have a driver's license. Besides, I could tell Mum didn't want me sitting for hours in a waiting room on my own while the hospital staff attended to Paul. Once we're at the hospital, Robbie has volunteered to be a sort of spokesperson between me and the military personnel. Still feeling shaky and numb with shock, I'm more than grateful to hand over any stuffy military protocol to him. Dad, of course, has elected to stay at home with my sister and two brothers, who are no doubt already back to sleep by the time we've reached the hospital.

Once we reach Parkville, our ambulance is met outside their emergency ward by a team of army medics ready to receive Paul into their expert care. Our two women ambulance drivers are instructed to wheel him into the first available partitioned cubicle on the left. After wishing us both well, Lola and Gwen are off again, making way for some other similarly no-nonsense medical person to step in and take over. And he does. With equal efficiency, a stocky US medic in dark blue overalls immediately steps in with expert care and assumes his task of assessing Paul's ongoing medical condition. Before long, he's barking out orders to nearby medics to grab various items *instantly* for him. To my way of thinking, *everything* seems to move up or down the chain of command ASAP when it comes down to any kind of military business. According to Robbie, the same sort of military mindset happens in our Australian army too.

Mum and I have been sitting around on some painfully hard wooden benches for an hour or so before the US medic assigned to Paul's case *finally* makes it out to the waiting room to advise me of my husband's condition. I must admit, I am at this stage beside myself with anxious worry, so I am somewhat relieved to be formally acknowledged by the US medical team in Australia, as Paul's new Australian wife.

'Mrs Meier?' The new medical person is standing directly in front of me now, dressed in a khaki uniform. He taps the front of his army cap for me to acknowledge his presence, just like I've seen troops do in all the Western movies. 'Ma'am! I'm Captain Charlie Waterman. I will be your husband's medic during his stay with us at this hospital. I just want to reassure you that I will do everything in my power to help bring your husband back to his normal good health again.'

'What exactly is wrong with my husband, Captain?' I ask without hesitation, completely ignoring Robbie's not-so-subtle facial signals about the *correct* protocol between military personnel and their servicemen's families.

'In simple terms, Mrs Meier, your husband is suffering from a condition known as combat stress reaction or CSR. It's when a soldier is too stressed to return to his normal duties and is therefore considered to be temporarily unfit for combat duty. Unfortunately, men like your husband tend to keep any kind of traumatic active war experience strictly to themselves, thinking it will just go away in time. Unless they deal with it head on, or talk it out with someone, his hidden phobias will inevitably be pushed down to bump around inside his head, until all that stress has nowhere else to go but out into the open. Usually this happens in the form of stress-related symptoms such as nightmares, body sweats and fever—exactly what your husband had been experiencing tonight. Our treatment for now will be to keep him under sedation. I am also ordering complete bed rest for him for the next forty-eight hours. Only then will we be reassessing him.'

'So, do you think he'll be in hospital for a long time, then?' I ask tentatively.

'It'll all depend on how quickly he responds to his initial treatment, of course, but I will be strongly recommending a few weeks rest in Melbourne. Depending on his recovery levels, we can then let you know what happens after that.'

'But will he still have to return to the war … I mean once you get him all better again?' I ask Captain Waterman.

'Bell!' Robbie cuts in now. 'Paul is only in Australia because of the war. Even if he *is* unwell, he's *still* a soldier. When he's fit enough to return to the front, then that's what he must do! After all, that's what he signed up for. You can't change these facts to suit yourself.'

'I understand what you're saying, Robbie, but it doesn't mean I have to accept it … do I?'

'In answer to your question, Mrs Meier,' Captain Waterman cuts in. 'Yes, your husband will most certainly have to return to his unit again. Rest assured, though, we will be keeping a close eye on his condition from now on.'

I can tell the medic has had enough of giving polite reassurances to his patient's wife for now by the way he shifts his feet impatiently. He's probably itching to get back to the job at hand.

'I'm sorry to hold you up Captain and I'm sorry if my rudeness has offended you in some way. Thank you for taking the time to explain Paul's condition. Just one more thing, Captain, could I see my husband for a moment, please?'

'Yes, of course, Mrs Meier, but please be aware that your husband is under heavy sedation for now, so don't be too upset if he doesn't respond to you right away. But by all means you can go and see him. No longer than five minutes, please. I also recommend that you try and get rest some yourself. You can come back tomorrow and sit with him for one hour to start with. That's if we're all still on the same page in regard to our plan for his immediate recovery.'

'Thank you again, Captain.'

'My pleasure, ma'am.' He touches the corner of his cap again and is on his way.

When I do go in to see Paul, I can tell he is already drifting off into a deeper state of sleep. Just like the medic said, he'll probably be too sleepy to respond to me by now, so I just squeeze his hand to let him know I am here with him, before whispering to him, 'Paul, darling, please know that I'll be heading home with Rob and Mum very soon while you sleep. I promise to return as soon as your medic says I can. Your medic has also suggested to me that since you will be under heavy sedation for the next few days, I should go and get some sleep myself. So that's what I will do.' I squeeze his hand one more time. More for my own peace of mind really and the comforting knowledge that he's being taken care of without me having to be here all night.

I am immediately relieved, of course, when Paul weakly squeezes my hand in response. I have to move my ear much closer to his mouth, though, to try and catch his faint, drug-induced whisper back to me, 'I love you, Isabella.'

With my voice all choked up with emotion to start with, I suddenly find myself unable to speak, so my only response for now is to squeeze his hand gently again. When I do return here in the morning, I fully intend to make it up to him. Even if he won't be awake for a few days, I still want to be here for him, if he should happen to awake earlier than anticipated. Before too long, I can tell the sedative the doctor has given Paul has kicked in. He is most definitely out for the count now, leaving me reassured, at last, that I can't expect any further response from him tonight.

As I leave his room, my tears start to flow, either from exhaustion or sheer relief, I'm not sure which, but I can at last accept that Paul is in good hands tonight. However, once I allow my first tears to escape, the dam walls burst open and I can't stop them. I no longer care what people think of me. I'm officially an emotional wreck! At the first sight of my tear-streaked face, Mum immediately enfolds me in her loving arms and pats my back all the way back to the Model T.

I can't help but wonder, as Robbie remains silent all the way back home, if Paul's condition is perhaps weighing heavily on his mind too. Could he be thinking that Paul's mental illness could happen so easily to him as well? I wish I could talk to him about it, but somehow I don't think he'll be open for discussion any time soon.

***

I slept fitfully last night. This is no doubt due to my already stressed brain suddenly becoming a reservoir overnight, with a whole lot of other anxious imaginings for the taking.

I won't even get a chance to talk to Robbie after all, because while I slept, Dad drove him back to the Williams Air Force Base for his return to Darwin early the following morning.

Seeing the disbelieving look on my face, Mum hugs me gently when I burst into tears yet again. As is Mum's way, she thoughtfully slides a comforting hot cup of tea over towards me and insists that I come and sit down beside her at the kitchen table. This is her way of explaining to me *why* Robbie had to leave without saying goodbye to me this morning.

'Robbie did poke his head into your room as he was leaving, Bell, but because you were finally sleeping more peacefully, he didn't have the heart to wake you.'

I burst into tears again, even after I had already cried myself to sleep last night. I never really imagined waking up this morning without Paul beside me, so I find myself really wallowing in self-pity.

This is all too much to take in. It's like a bad dream taking over my waking hours.

166

'Oh, love, don't go upsetting yourself like this.' Mum continues patting my hand as she attempts to console me. 'Robbie did say he'll try and ring you in the next few days for a progress report on Paul's condition.'

'It's okay, Mum. I'm just crying on behalf of my own miserable self, really.' I'm suddenly finding it so difficult to accept that not only is Paul battling this frightening mental illness right after our honeymoon, but now my big, beautiful, brother is also facing an uncertain future as a fighting soldier. Right here on Australian soil too. I can't help worrying that Robbie might also suffer the same fate as Paul.

I lay my head against Mum's chest to cry even more tears of frustration and misery.

Why does life have to be so complicated?

18

Paul

January 1943
Out of a nightmare, into a hospital bed

Where the hell am I? Just like some cartoon character, I can almost feel my own eyes bulging out of their sockets as I look around me in sheer panic. When I try to sit up, I come up short. It's only when I look down at my body I realise it's a wonder I can even move at all. My awaking mind instantly plunges me into another bizarre moment of disbelief as I see my body is literally wired to some annoyingly persistent beeping machine, positioned just behind and slightly to the left of my now-throbbing head. Come to think of it, this bed is so *very* unfamiliar. *Son of a bitch! What's going on here?* I must admit, I'm at a loss to even understand what is happening to me, and most of all, why. *Am I still asleep?* Maybe this all just one crazy nightmare that I'm still part of?

As far as I can tell, these intrusive little wires are all converging together into the machine at the back of me. Another wave of panic takes over me as a different kind of frightening thought finally invades my strange reality.

Maybe I've been captured by the Japanese and now they are conducting all kinds of bizarre experiments on me?

Don't go thinking like that, man! My inner voice attempts to reassure me.

Back off! This is my nightmare, not yours! … Anyway, what could the enemy hope to get from me … some secret Morse code, perhaps?

Still, *it* persists. *Ease up, man. You're just having a very bad dream that's all!*

It's only a bad dream, you say? More like a living nightmare if you ask me. It's only when I risk a tentative look beyond my immediate vicinity that I really begin to question my sanity … What's left of it, anyway. *Fuck!*

There's one long row of white-painted metal beds to left of me, and damn if there isn't another row of beds to the right of me too! If this isn't bad enough, when I look over towards the opposite side of the room, that's when this whole nightmarish scene really starts to mess with my head. All along the opposite wall of this huge open-ended room, with its high ceiling, there is another row of exactly the same kind of beds. Not only that, but there are some other people in those beds too—along with at least half a dozen people—both men and women, all wearing what appears to be mid-blue overalls, hovering around.

Frankly, Meier, this whole sterile hospital scene doesn't thrill me at all!

Assuming, of course, this is a hospital room and not some experimentation facility for enemy patients …

'Ah! You're back with us at last, Staff Sergeant!'

I immediately stop my erratic visual wanderings of this whole other-worldly kind of movie scene, when I suddenly hear a commanding voice right up close to me demanding my full attention. I turn towards the voice, which is coming from the left side of my body, where I appear to be forcibly wired onto a horizontal prison, for whatever reason.

When I look up to where the authoritative voice is coming from, slowly, my befuddled brain begins to make out a more human shape before my eyes at last.

He is wearing the exact same blue overalls I'd spotted earlier—just like all the other strangers moving around this room.

The welcome-back smile this individual is giving me now, though, is not quite your typical 'gee, we missed you' smile I was looking for, but more of a 'it's about time you woke up' kind of thing.

My still-disbelieving eyes are finally able to focus on the rather stocky guy who is, at a rough guess, in his forties, and wearing a blue cap on his rather large, rounded head. If there is one particular thing that stands out about him, though, it would have to be his impressive pair of bushy eyebrows arching proudly over the most penetrating brown eyes I would ever want to hide from. *Man! I swear this guy can see right into the very core of me. Do I even have a reason to cower before him? … I don't think so, but you never know.*

'Mornin', Staff Sergeant Meier! I am Captain Charlie Waterman, but you can call me Doc if you prefer. I'm the medic who has been assigned to your care.'

Without asking for permission from his temporarily tongue-tied patient, he takes hold of my wrist closest to him with two chunky fingers, checking my pulse against the time shown on his silver wristwatch. He says nothing more for a minute or two as he professionally checks the beat of my pulse then scribbles down his findings onto the clipboard at the foot of my bed. Once this is done, Doc grabs a chair from the other bed beside me while he continues to spear me with those penetrating, know-it-all eyes of his. It seems I have no choice now but to just shut up and to listen *carefully* to 'The Wise One'.

'Do you have any idea, Staff Sergeant, what has happened to you or why you are even here in this Melbourne military hospital?'

Finally, I find my voice. 'I'm in a military hospital … In Melbourne?' My head suddenly feels like it's spinning out of control. *What's with all of these questions trying to knock themselves out inside my befuddled brain?* 'How did I get here and *why* am I here? Sorry, Doc … what I mean is, *when* did I get here—and as you just stated, why am I in this hospital in the first place?'

'I understand you must be feeling somewhat disorientated by now, so I will endeavour to answer each of your questions in due course. I can at least tell you *why* you are here. As a special bonus, I can even give you the correct medical name of your condition, if it helps?'

'Yes, thank you, Doc. That would be most helpful at this stage.'

'Your condition can be best summed up in just three words: combat stress reaction—or more simply CSR. Have you ever heard of it?'

'Yes, I have, Doc, but I must admit, all I really want to know right now is why is this happening to me and how can you fix it, so it doesn't happen again, I mean?'

'Both very good questions, indeed, Staff Sergeant. The easiest way I can explain this condition to you is for me to break down the cause. There are two main factors that sets it off in the first place.

'With any war, there's bound to be some tough conflict going on between you and the enemy. Whenever you step into a war zone against any imposing force, conflict is inevitable. It's a foregone conclusion, really. So when you face the enemy with a gun in your hand, fear steps in too, along with the rock-hard determination of a fighting soldier to defeat the enemy no matter what … You with me so far?'

'Yes, I get what you're saying, Doc. Please carry on.'

'When you add the seemingly endless hours of combat fighting, that's when the fatigue factor comes into play. Hour after hour, day after day, and even if the fighting *is* called to a halt for however long, a soldier's mind and body will still continue to relive the insidious fear in his head of being shot at—or worst-case scenario, seeing your best buddy get shot to pieces beside you. Long after the guns are silenced, your mind will continue to replay the experience over and over again in your head. So even in your case, where you are carrying a radio into battle instead of a gun, you're still determined to keep those lines of communication open no matter what. The worst fear for you, as a radio operator, would most likely be the guilt that comes from failing to complete your mission, therefore letting your team down.

'To sum it all up, Staff Sergeant; if you can no longer let go of the battlefield replaying in your head, your whole body will effectively retaliate by blowing a fuse. In your particular case, order had to be restored ASAP by your assigned medico—as in, myself—by firstly putting you into an induced sleep state, or coma, followed by complete bed rest for at least two weeks to start with.' Doc pauses for a bit, no doubt to give me a moment or two to digest all he has told me so far.

He continues with a sly grin on his face now, 'Besides … I do believe—as of New Year's Eve *last year*—you are now a newlywed. Only two nights before you were admitted here into this hospital, do you remember this at all?'

Isabella, my darling wife! How could I have forgotten about her already? Where is she? I need to talk to her ASAP!

As if reading my mind, Doc sets about reassuring me on this score. 'Don't worry, Staff Sergeant, your pretty wife is still around the hospital here somewhere. I had to send her away for now to get herself something to eat or drink before the poor girl fades away from exhaustion. Besides, I did need to talk to my patient in private too. Don't worry. Normal procedure, I assure you. When you were first admitted two nights ago, though, the staff practically had to prise her fingers away from yours each time they asked her to leave this room. She is one determined woman, that's for sure. A hell of a good woman to have by your side.'

It's uncanny how a mere smile has the power to instantly transform an outwardly serious demeanour, and Doc Waterman has the ability to do this so easily. The wide-open grin he's sharing with me now certainly proves this theory.

'So, Doc, what's the next step for me? … I mean, now that I have come through the first forty-eight hours under sedation? I guess what I am really asking is do I really have to stay in this hospital for the next two weeks?'

'I'm glad you asked me that. The answer is that no, you don't. All I'm saying is that you won't be a going back to the island until I am completely satisfied you are ready to do so. You will most likely be staying here in Melbourne for the next two weeks or so, depending upon your overall recovery, of course.'

I can only stare blankly at Doc now. I'm sure the horror of knowing I'll be confined to this *lonely* hospital bed and this damn machine for the next two weeks must be written all over my face. This is precious time I would much rather be spending with my beautiful wife. This diagnosis doesn't thrill me one little bit.

Not only that, but I am beginning to feel I may have embarrassed myself big time in front of Isabella and her whole family. What must they think of me now? I wouldn't blame Isabella, either, if she wanted to annul our marriage. She certainly didn't sign up for this kind of deal with me. Surely it's worth asking Doc to send me back to the island, instead of staying here to embarrass myself all over again?

'Are you sure it wouldn't it be better to send me back up to the islands and be assigned to light duties for a while?'

'Nope! I'm afraid not, Staff Sergeant. That's not happening! In fact, I am ordering you to stay here in Melbourne for the duration of your recuperation.'

'But if I'm not going to be here at the hospital, where will I be staying?'

'Why with your new family, of course, young man. I am hereby ordering you to be discharged from the formal care of this hospital and into the loving care of your pretty wife and your new Australian family. Besides, your mother-in-law, Mrs Carlisle, has promised me she will be looking after her new son-in-law for as long as is necessary.

'I believe her very own words were—and I quote, "Doctor Waterman, I assure you that while he's in my care, I will be filling him up with some good old-fashioned Aussie cooking and plenty of rest too. I'll have him back to his normal good health in no time"—end quote. So, who am I to argue with that? Until you are fully recovered, Staff Sergeant, I am more than happy to entrust your life into your mother-in-law's diligent care

… Well, at least until you are able to return to your full duties, that is.'

19

Isabella

1943
Back into the war zone

Instead of the two weeks allowed for Paul's recovery time, it takes three weeks for him to be declared fit enough to return to the islands. He slowly but surely resurfaces from the deep, dark hole he has dug for himself. I had been warned by Captain Waterman, at the beginning of Paul's hospital stay, that shock therapy *might* be used as part of his treatment if Paul didn't show any signs of snapping out of his induced coma on his own. Thank goodness, it wasn't required after all.

Whether it was because of Paul's strong will to live, or because of his love for me, day by day he gradually managed to pull himself back from the brink of self-destruction. Once he was weaned from the heavy sedatives in gradual stages, he started to eat again and is now almost back to his old self. He certainly looks a whole lot better.

The deep tropical tan he had acquired on the islands is somewhat faded by now. His skin tone has most certainly lost most of the yellow tinge from the quinine tablets and is finally returning to a more healthy colour. *Thank goodness, I say!* Once his overall outer appearance has improved, his inner workings return to their normal function as well. His handsome face has already lost its gauntness and his ready, cheeky smile is back to its full wattage. *How I have missed his beautiful smile.* Slowly but surely my handsome GI—the Paul I fell madly in love with—is back where he belongs. *With me, for now, at least.* During the last week of his forced bed rest in Melbourne, Captain Waterman gave Paul advance notice of his imminent return to his unit.

The big difference between the first time he entered the war zone in the Philippines and his return there now can be summed up in two words: firsthand experience. What a difference a year or so can make. Going into a war zone as an uninitiated first-time recruit, to now returning to the same war zone as a seasoned soldier. Undoubtably, Paul is not only a little bit older, but a whole lot wiser the second time around.

In the meantime, Captain Waterman has decided to release Paul into the tender loving care of his new Australian family for the final week of his recovery. Naturally, my mother is thrilled to bits to be given free rein to fuss over her new son-in-law again. During this past week, Mum has been more than up to the challenge of 'putting back some meat on Paul's bones'. On a daily basis, she fills him up with a huge cooked breakfast, meat pies or quiches for lunch and his favourite lamb cutlets for dinner during the week. Of course, on his first weekend out of hospital, Mum went all-out, with a scrumptious roast dinner for his first Sunday back home. Just in case this hasn't been enough to fill him up, she also tempts him between meals with homemade sponge cakes, lamingtons and scones, followed by steamy puddings, fruit preserves and fresh cream for dessert. All guaranteed, of course, to reawaken his almost-forgotten appetite. After all, with Paul being so appreciative about *everything* she dishes onto his plate, with him enthusiastically singing her praises, why wouldn't she want to keep the food coming?

'This roast lamb is so amazing, Myra! Oh man, and your peach cobbler is out of this world! Real cream too! I have never tasted real cream this fresh since … well, since the very first time I came to dinner here.'

Mum blushes every time Paul compliments her, which only makes her want to please him even more.

Where Mum leaves off with impressing Paul with her cooking exper-tise, Grandma Allen is only too happy to take over with her knitting skills. Before his three weeks are up in Melbourne, she has knitted him a pair of socks, a beanie and also a vest to complete her trifecta. Even though Paul is heading back to a tropical island, where wool clothing is as foreign as snowshoes, Grandma Allen argues he will still need them anyway, once he returns home to America.

Even Josie is smitten with Paul and hangs onto his every word at the dinner table, whereas my father is just happy to have Paul around to talk to. Now that Paul is officially part of the family, Dad finds it just that little bit easier to accept Robbie still being away up at Darwin this past year or so. Apart from being father and son, Dad and Robbie have always been best mates. Even though Dad isn't one to talk about his private feelings to even Robbie, he still sorely misses his eldest son.

As for Kyle and Marty, Paul has become the official taste tester for their home brew. After he regales them of his own rough 'home brew' experi-ments with some raisin jack on the islands, Paul's status has immediately elevated to lofty heights with my brothers.

According to both Kyle and Marty, Paul has been happily declared to be 'one of the boys'.

Even with all the fussing and loving heaped onto Paul by my family, when it comes to our alone time together, they are nowhere in sight. This includes Josie. Even though Josie loves to ask Paul endless questions about America—particularly Hollywood—she too makes herself scarce when Paul and I want some time alone. After dinner has been cleared away right down to the last teaspoon, the rest of the family are more than happy to talk and play games together without us. Besides, we know we'll be instantly forgotten once there's a pack of cards or game board on the table.

Even though my family are only a few rooms away, this doesn't stop us from fooling around. In fact, we have become very *creative* with our moves—even after only one week.

***

Saying goodbye to my husband at the base is a challenge of epic proportions, but there is no way I'm going to let him go away fretting about leaving me behind. Heaven knows he'll have enough to worry about just surviving this war once he's back there.

So, I put on a brave smile and joke about having to go back to my old single bed. I even joke about having to put up with Josie's loud snoring again. Despite my teasing and joking, though, my heart fails to find the significance of my humour attached to this particular occasion.

Well, how else am I supposed to come to terms of living my life without him in it?

***

The engines of the wide-bellied cargo plane on the tarmac are starting to kick over now, eventually settling into an ear-splitting rhythm of sorts. This deafening pre-flight warm-up is Paul's cue to say his goodbyes and board his flight within the next few minutes. For the purpose of maintaining my hard-won composure for now, I stand aside to give Paul a chance to say his goodbyes to his new Australian family first, plus Coral too, of course. After all, as my best friend, she was there with me when I first fell in love with Paul.

'Bye, Mom!' Paul hugs his new mother-in-law with obvious affection. 'I'll look forward to some more of your home cooking when I return.'

Mum hugs him with equal affection—just as she would with one of her own sons, 'If you promise to return to us all safely, Paul, I'll cook you anything you like.'

'I aim to. I know I've already said my goodbyes to Grandma Allen last night, but please give her another big hug for me when you're back home this morning.'

'I'll be sure to do that, Paul. She's so going to miss her talks with you too. Bye, son!'

178

He hugs Josie next with brotherly affection. 'Bye, sis, I'm sure gonna miss you! Even your highly original questions!' he laughs.

This prompts a cheeky response from Josie. 'Not only do I already have three brothers, but I now have an extra one to thrash in a game of backyard tennis. My victory will be swift, whereas your humiliation is bound to be painful.'

'You're on! Just be warned though, little sister; just because you're a girl, doesn't mean I'm going to lose so easily to you.'

'I'll look forward to the challenge, then,' Josie promises as she hugs him once more.

Coral is next down the line. Paul hugs her with brotherly affection too. 'Bye, Coral!'

'Bye, Paul! It's been lovely getting to know you again. Oh, before you go, if by chance you should ever run into Brad again back in America, please say hello to him for me.'

'I will, I promise. I also wonder where he is these days. Take care, Coral!'

My father steps forward next to shake Paul's hand. 'Don't worry, Paul, we'll take good care of Bell for you. You just worry about getting back home safe and sound.'

'Thanks, Dad … You don't mind if I call you that? Since you're my Aussie Dad now.'

'Not at all, son. We're proud to have you as part of our family. May God always keep you safe in his loving arms!' Upon hearing this, Paul instinctively dispenses with formalities by hugging his new father-in-law. My heart is overjoyed now to see my father—normally of a reserved nature—respond to Paul's spontaneity in the same affectionate way he would with each of his sons.

Paul affectionately shakes hands with his two young brothers-in-law at the end of the farewell line, teasing them about being careful not to let the cops catch them with their 'Aussie moonshine'. Surprisingly, both of my younger brothers, just like my father, dismiss formal handshakes with Paul in favour of some serious backslapping brotherly hugs instead.

It's my turn now. I step forward with a shaky smile. My barely contained tears are threatening to spill forth any minute now. Paul pulls me into his arms without any hesitation and we cling fiercely to each other, then kiss for the longest time, neither of us wanting to let the other go. That is until the groundsman, moving quickly all around us with his two directional paddles, starts yelling out to Paul over the roar of the engines to hurry up and 'Get onboard this goddamn aircraft *NOW*, soldier!'

'I'll write to you as soon as I can, darling … I promise!' Paul declares as he pulls me closer to him yet again, as reluctant to let me out of his sight as I am with him.

'I know you will. I'll write to you too—every night, in fact. That's a promise!'

Paul kisses me one last time before leaning down with one hand to pick up his haversack still on the ground near his feet. He soon realises he can't move though because I am still firmly holding onto his hand, so reluctant am I to let him walk away from me.

'I love you so much, Paul! Make sure you come back to me, okay!'

'Rest assured, our hearts *will* find their own way back to each other. Love you!'

He finally picks up his army haversack and heads for the metal steps leading up into the giant military Hercules aircraft that is about to ruthlessly take him away from me for much too long. He waves to us from the top of the stairs and my family wave madly back to him. Standing off to the side a bit, I touch my fingers to my lips, madly blowing him kisses. I'm beyond caring about appearances right now. Even my blotchy, tear-streaked face has in some way become a declaration of my love for him and I can't hide my tears from him any longer. Nor would I want to. This is not the time for me to act all prim and proper on today of all days.

All too soon, Paul, after ducking his head to clear the aircraft's low doorway, has already disappeared from sight, but we still continue to wave him goodbye. At least until we can see him no more. Once the aircraft door is locked and bolted from the inside and the portable stairs rolled away, the huge wide-bellied aircraft starts to move ever so slowly like some oversized, sluggish caterpillar, towards the runway for take-off as its powerful engines roar with a distinct throb of impatience. Once the old flying machine takes to the skies, just by tucking away its wheels at last, it's able to shed its heaviness to become a young bird in flight again. The big bird soars on towards the once-tranquil Pacific Islands, now heavily cloaked in military armour against wartime bullies wanting to claim them as their own.

20

Isabella

1943
Leaving one's childhood behind

L ife must go on, even while one's heart still continues to be in a state of suspended animation. There is nothing left for me to do now but to try and get back into some semblance of a normal routine. If that's even possible anymore. If I do know one thing for sure, though; I don't think my life as I once knew it—before Paul came into my life, that is—will ever really be the same again. As far as I can tell, I still *look* the same as I always do, but inside I am *definitely* not the same Isabella Carlisle I used to be.

I am now Mrs Isabella Meier, and I must admit, my new name does have a nice ring to it. Maybe, even way back to when I was first born, this is who I was truly destined to become. Who knows? Anyway, there doesn't seem to be much point in me dwelling on the complexities of fate for a year—or possibly even longer—for me to wish I could go back to the way my life used to be.

Not that I would ever really want to, mind you. In the past, I could never have imagined in a million years how the changing of one's name can have such a profound impact on one's whole outlook on life. Now it isn't just me in a singular sense anymore. Oh no! It's always going to be Paul and I, or my husband and I, from now onwards. We are a team—albeit a team on hold for now—but a team just the same. When we *are* finally reunited after this war, with the grace of God, we'll have the rest of our lives to plan everything together. Just as my parents have always done. I mustn't even think about Paul never coming back to me. In order for me to go on living life without him, I'll just have to think of him as merely being away on an extended military leave for now.

***

Now that I am officially a war bride—complete with a new passport and a printed marriage certificate on hand—it's time for me to register with the United States Consulate in Australia. This registration is necessary, I am told, so my name can be added to an already long list of other US servicemen's wives all travelling back to the United States together after this war has officially ended.

In order for me to submit any required documents to the US government, I must fill out all the necessary forms relating to my new status as Paul's wife first. As part of all these drawn-out procedures, I am also required to have my fingerprints taken and a complete medical check-up done (*I do hope my fingerprints don't end up on America's Most Wanted list by mistake*).

In the meantime, I'm still determined to resume my usual lifestyle as much as possible. I even allow myself to go out with Coral to listen to some music sometimes or go to the latest picture show on a Saturday night. I will, naturally, continue to travel into the city each workday and to enjoy my family times at home while I can. Especially when Josie, Kyle and I play tennis together. Watching us play tennis one afternoon, with the winner of each pair playing the person left over, Marty asks if he can play with us as a foursome. With Robbie back at Darwin, we are, of course, one player short of a foursome. Even though Marty is still painfully shy, we all agree. To our surprise, it isn't long before Marty gains a lot more confidence, making us realise far too late that our baby brother is indeed becoming a force to be reckoned with on the tennis court.

***

As the war finally shows signs of winding down, I decide to quit my job in the government office as a typist with shorthand skills. After all, I reason, once a ship becomes available, I will only be given a few days' notice to make my way to the wharf for boarding my designated passage to North America. This short notice of only a few days will mean, of course, that once I give notice to leave my present job, there won't be enough time for my employer to train someone else to take over my qualified position. Since I don't relish the idea of sitting around at home all day, just waiting for the phone to ring, I've decided to take on a temporary job instead, at the Myer Emporium department store in the city.

Thankfully, it's a sales position that doesn't require much training at all. Even before I begin my employment at Myer, I'm dreading the thought of standing on my feet all day in high-heeled shoes. My feet will probably hate me for inflicting such toe-crunching pain upon them by the end of each working day. Even so, I'm starting to look forward to each new day anyway. I particularly love talking to the store's customers face to face, helping them make good choices with each of their purchases.

The department I am currently assigned to sells the necessary school uniforms for most of the private colleges around Melbourne. Each college, I learn quickly, has its own distinctive uniforms along with their own school colours, pocket badges and hat bands, etc. The month of January can be a very stressful time of the year for our Melbourne mothers, since they have to outfit their daughters *before* school resumes at the beginning of February. This means, of course, that any staff working in this department are kept very busy the entire day. Having said that, it's a challenge I enjoy immensely. Even if the pace can be rather hectic at times.

One of the newly hired girls in the same training group as me is a war bride too. She tells me her name is Evie Stilton and she also had to quit her office job like me. We hit it off straightaway and become good friends in no time. After January is over, we are no longer needed in the school uniform department, of course, so we're both moved elsewhere to other departments. Evie is assigned to haberdashery, whereas I'm sent to the woollen department, selling jumpers (sweaters), cardigans, etc., as well as scarves and gloves.

The first day after our transfer, Evie and I meet up in the Myer cafeteria for lunch.

'I can't stand being in haberdashery, Bell!' Evie complains. 'Those tiny buttons are so darn fiddly, especially when you have to count out dozens each time.' While she talks, Evie is stirring the sugar into her tea in a distracted way. 'But, do you know what I'm going to do, Bell?'

'I'm not sure, Evie.' I stop stirring my own tea for a moment to give her a questioning look. 'I'm all ears, though. What *are* you going to do?'

'I'm going to go up to the employment director to ask her if I can transfer over to woollens. *That's* what I'm going to do, right now, Bell, because I honestly don't think I can stand one more day in haberdashery!'

'Gee, I don't know, Evie, I don't like your chances, really. What I mean is, our employment director must have hundreds of staff to shuffle around the various departments each day. Do you really think she is going to listen to any special requests from *any* individual staff member?'

'When you put it like that, Bell, probably not, but I'm going to give it a go anyway.'

Evie suddenly shoots up and grabs her bag from the back of the chair. 'The way I see it, there's no time like right now to try. Wish me luck!'

I watch as Evie heads for the lifts to take her to the top floor where our staff department is situated. I can't help but admire the stylish way Evie always presents herself with her tall, slim figure, her glossy black hair falling in soft waves to just above her collar and her beautiful, beaming smile she shares so readily with everyone. I like Evie a lot, and I must admit, I do like the thought of working with her again. An hour later, I find myself once again standing at the counter of the clothing department trying to look busy. Now that the school rush is over, there doesn't seem to be much of a call for customers to come my way. Who wants to buy woollens during the summer months, anyway? Not even in cold old Melbourne. Which is another reason why I can't ever see Evie being transferred to the woollen department.

You could've knocked me over with a feather, though, when I just happen to look up from straightening a pile of jumpers for the hundredth time to see Evie coming towards me with a triumphant smile on her face. She got her wish to change departments, and from that day onwards, she and I spent a lot of time trying to stay out of sight from the department supervisor, as we hide behind fixtures, whispering or giggling the whole time. I'm often surprised how we ever manage to get away with such outrageous behaviour.

***

I know it's only a matter of time before this war is over, but even so, my carefully reigned-in patience can be a bit fidgety and even downright crotchety at times.

In my present restless mood, I would much rather this next period of my life came around sooner rather than later. Is it just my imagination, or have all the clocks around the world suddenly slowed down lately? Perhaps some invisible hand is 'out there' somewhere, merely waiting for God himself to kickstart all the world clocks again.

When I find myself awake in the middle of the night and back in my childhood single bed, without Paul by my side, it stirs up my most restless moments of all.

I do crave Paul's gentle touches and his ever-loving kisses, of course, but when we both wake at the same time in the middle of the night, when he makes it very clear he wants to make love to me, this is when I crave his persuasive touches most of all.

PART 2
1945 – 1947
And praise be the war is over

21

Paul

1945
Pack up the war

It's official! The war is over! Since being told of this latest news via our CO, my buddies and I have stayed rooted to this same spot for the past hour or so in a state of total disbelief. It kinda baffles me now why we even have to question any good news reports with so much scepticism. Human nature, I guess.

Whatever the reason, we're almost expecting our CO to line us up any minute now to tell us, 'Scrap that last directive, gentlemen! I'm here to inform you, that due to circumstances beyond our control, the war is still on—and yes, we are still part of it!'

Even if we know this new directive to be true, it still doesn't seem real enough yet to be accepted as the absolute truth, much less acted upon with the usual 'yes sir, no sir!'. As trained army soldiers, we are automatically expected to live an erratic existence of survival at all costs—we pray we'll each get to experience even one more hour of living. It's just too damn easy to become even a bit cynical these days, when every one of us starts to question just how 'official' these news reports are supposed to be.

In my prewar years, waking up on a tropical island every morning would be a man's most popular dream. After all, every day on an island is supposed to be all about luscious tropical fruits, ripe for the picking.

189

Not to mention expanses of white sandy beaches to mark your every footstep. *AND please*, let's not forget the best fantasy of all: beautiful girls waiting by your very own grass hut to dance just for *you*. Unfortunately, fantasies fade away instantly once you add the horrific images of guns, aerial bombs, hand-to-hand combat and sweaty jungles to the scenario. Your average island fantasy now has this uncanny knack of turning into a living nightmare.

***

During these past few months, the Japanese Imperial Army have stepped up their attacks on Mindanao and surrounding islands. So much so that now when I watch the waves crash upon this war-ravaged beach, instead of the idyllic, picture-perfect scene I used to dream of, I'm served a reminder of the absolute uncertainties of my tomorrows. Even though the Japanese forces have their backs against the wall, the stigma of failure is a powerful thing for the average Japanese military man, when their ever-resilient, ever-tenacious resolve is ultimately to win this war at all costs. To the enemy, they show no intentions of ever backing down. Japanese foot soldiers still stalk this island with deadly intent. They must know by now, with the intense stepped-up defences of US, Australian, New Zealand and Philippine forces against them, Japan is essentially being nipped at the winning post.

Even if they are our enemy, you can't help but admire the Japanese people for their tenacity, bravery and sheer stubbornness in the face of such fierce opposition. Even with the writing on the wall, this doesn't stop the Japanese military leaders from effecting one last-ditch attempt to come at us with all guns blazing, despite our combined Allied forces pushing them further back into a tight inescapable corner. The powerful message to the Japanese military machine these days is very clear in its simplicity: 'We *will* defeat you. *You cannot win.* It's time for you to back off and go home.'

Same goes for Europe too, I hear. Although, with fighting our own fierce war in the Pacific, Europe seems like a whole different planet, a long way away from us.

So, the rumours *are* true!—A final ceasefire has been declared. The war *is* over and YES! We *are* going home! All that's left to do now is pack up this war like it never even happened and be on our way, back to where we came from.

Well, that's what the military bigwigs are telling us anyway. We're outta here!

***

You'd think the actual packing up of an island battlefield would be a lot easier than initially setting up a well-planned war zone in the first place, but as it turns out, this whole packing-up process can be just as strategically involved—if not more so—than at the beginning.

Son of a bitch! When I think of all of those damn holes we had to dig out when we first arrived on Mindanao. Especially under a merciless tropical sun blazing down on our raw uninitiated skins. This alone nearly sent us stark raving mad from the scorching effects of blistering sunburns for days afterwards.

Those early days soon taught us all a valuable lesson we will never forget; after such an unavoidable initiation upon this island, whenever we had to dig any further holes for the disposal of food and human waste, we soon learnt to dig these endless holes in the early morning or late afternoon light. Unless under threat of an arrest if we didn't, we never dug *any* holes under a midday sun ever again.

***

Once a permanent ceasefire was declared, our daily agenda was suddenly thrown into reverse. Before we leave Mindanao (which over time, has become a home of sorts), we've been ordered to fill in *every* single hole. The main reason we are doing this is out of respect to the Philippine people. In other words, we are to leave this island *exactly* as we found it.

As well as refilling the holes, we also have to dismantle *every* one of the tents—including the massive communication tent our war commanders have used on a twenty-four seven basis to conduct the 'business' end of war. This part of dismantling, however, always includes packing away confidential details about certain top-secret duties and strategic moves against the enemy. Because of the nature of our various secret sources, a strict code of confidentiality is required. This, of course, also includes our unit's radio communications (where I come in), inventory of all weapons and all miscellaneous stores, strict procedures must be adhered to. And when I say strict, I mean strict in every sense of the word. *Every* scrap of paper must be stowed away securely in locked trunks. After all, as any postwar history declares, all war statistics must be itemised thoroughly, before being locked away, analysed and picked apart one page at a time back at Washington. All in a day's work for the army.

As with the communication tent, our sleeping quarters also have to be dismantled, along with every last metal bunk and footlocker. Then, of course, let's not forget the latrine and shower tents as well.

Man! The list goes on. At least we won't suffer the effects of this humidity for much longer.

Last, but not least, our mess tent—damn near the size of a circus tent—which includes all dining settings, food storage and cooking utensils—will have to be dismantled in the shortest possible time. All available army units will have to be on hand for this one.

***

Our army troop carrier is due to arrive tomorrow morning at 0600 hours, so we, as a tight-knit squadron, are spending one final night together to say our goodbyes. Come tomorrow, we'll be sent back to our home states, somewhere in America.

To the outside world, America is often referred to as the 'home of the brave'. Well, the truth is, not all of us are feeling all that brave when it comes down to facing our families, neighbours or even long-time friends again. After all, the friendships we have made here are naturally going to be different. Any friendship forged from pure guts, essentially means there ain't nuthin' we wouldn't do for each other, when our lives depend on it every single day.

After all, there has literally been times when we've had to walk into open fire to save one of our buddies from even just one lethal bullet. I doubt any of us will ever forget that.

We have all changed in so many ways. We are no longer those wide-eyed youngsters we once were. Right from when we first signed up, with our chests full of patriotic fervour, to go fight a long, long way from home. This war has irreversibly shaped us in ways we could have never envisioned during our childhood years. Of course, we know well enough by now not *all* of our troops will be returning home with us. Due to the inevitable realities of war, the injured and the missing *may* eventually return home one day. Whereas the fallen never will. True, some of our fighting men and women are lucky enough to be going back home *almost* the same as when we left America—with all limbs accounted for. As for the insidious hidden experiences of war—deeply embedded forever within our troubled minds—that is another thing entirely. Whether we like it or not, our eyes will forever remain fully open to the true realities of conflict. For our last night on Mindanao, our CO has allowed our unit to relax outside the tents (the ones still standing, that is), to have one last drinking session together. He has even supplied us with some leftover beer from the mess hall as well, as part of his generous deal of letting us say goodbye to each other for perhaps the very last time.

Unbelievably, I even have a few bottles of my raisin jack to finish off too, so we may as well make a night of it. Some of the more easygoing commanding officers are only too happy to share a glass or two of my infamous concoction, but other tight-assed COs definitely will not. I may even be arrested for making moonshine during wartime, but I figure that since I can't take it home, I may as well come clean about my 'wayward sins' and share the last of the brew with my whole unit.

***

Sitting around, drinking beer beneath a leafy canopy of palm trees under a tropical sky filled with a trillion stars, my mind now turns to more serious thoughts. Even with my buddies around me in various states of inebriation—from openly sobbing to spewing long-winded declarations of love for everyone—I have already begun to separate myself from this new rampant crowd.

With this ongoing restless feeling prompting me to be alone with my thoughts, I have no choice but to get up and move around to relieve my stagnant body and to stop my cramped leg muscles from seizing up altogether. I carefully ease myself off an inflexible tree stump that's been propping me up for the past few hours to go for a walk along the beach. The war may be officially over, but I'm still cautious enough to stay close to our camp just the same. Even if I know any lethal bullets won't be whizzing past me anymore, I'm fully aware, just the same, of my sluggish reflexes from all the alcohol I've consumed tonight.

As I walk barefooted along the moonlit sand, my thoughts automatically drift towards returning home. A mixed bag of endless questions that has been chipping away at my peace of mind these past few days is now suddenly vying for my attention.

I knew they would, of course, and even though I've tried desperately to push them to the back of my mind, I have no choice now but to face each problem one by one, before I board the ship taking me back home tomorrow.

My solitary time by the ocean has suddenly come to an end as I hear four of my buddies heading this way. After our intake of alcohol, along with some big band music on the island's nightly radio show, the guys' voices are getting louder by the minute. Any louder and the natives on the next island will be able to hear their off-key singing. As the guys weave their way precariously down the beach towards me, I chuckle to see their arms around each other in a bond of friendship they'll probably remember for the rest of their lives.

As they reach me, Logan, one of the guys on the end of the foursome, rushes up to me with a lopsided grin on his face. Being six feet, four inches tall and as solid as a rock, he quickly grabs me in a spontaneous bear hug, 'Hey, buddy! Whatcha doin' out here all by yerself?'

'Hey there, Logan! Thomas! Chad! Sam! … Oh, just thinking about things … So what are you guys up to, then? … Apart from waking up this whole island with your loud singing, that is—including the island's human *AND* animal occupants.'

Logan is one of those intuitive guys who can usually always pick up on someone's need to go real deep into their thoughts. He obviously plans on taking some time out from the guys with me, because he suddenly turns to his fellow singing buddies and says, 'Keep on walkin', guys. I'll catch up with you soon.'

'Come on, buddy!' Thomas slurs. 'This ain't the night to sit and stare at the waves. It's time to celebrate, man! We're goin' on home, so come on! Let's party some more, man!'

'Yeah, we know this already, guys, and we will. I promise, but Paulo and me just wanna talk for a while.'

'Party poopers!' Chad scoffs as he weaves his way off down the beach with an obvious impatience to keep the party going. Even if it means leaving us behind. 'So which of you shits are still comin' with me?'

'Yeah, yeah, Chad, old son, we're coming!' Thomas slurs. 'Keep your shirt on, will ya?' Thomas yells back at the slow-moving forms of both Chad and Sam attempting to climb up the thick build-up of sand at the top of the beach. We can hear Thomas laughing out loud now at the sight of Chad and Sam slipping, sliding, then climbing over each other in an attempt to be the first to reach the top. Thomas turns back to us, still laughing as he too precariously starts his ascent up the same dune. 'See you guys back at camp, then.'

'Yep! See you soon, buddy!' Logan and I yell, along with, 'Be seeing you guys later, then!' to the darkened form of Thomas as he disappears out of sight altogether.

'Man! I am sure glad you were here to save me from those guys, Paulo. I swear those guys are hell-bent on keeping this party goin' until the sun comes up tomorrow.'

Funny, I could have sworn Logan was more than happy to party on with these good buddies of ours until he saw me sitting here all alone. I get the feeling this is his way of sticking around just in case I have a mind to bare my soul to him one last time.

'So, Paulo, what's happenin' with you and why are you looking so glum? ... You *do* want to go home, don't you? ... Or are you thinkin' you'll be missin' this tropical island a mite too much to ever settle for the madness of Chicago's suburban hell again?'

'You're right on the mark, buddy. Leaving these kind of starry island nights behind for the chill of another frigid Chicago winter is going to be so damn hard to get used to again. I can't believe how much I even hated the thought of coming up to these islands in the first place, Logan.'

'Yeah, I know just what you're saying, man! I had the same reservations as you, Paulo. I tell ya, when we first stepped off that smoky, dusty train at Cairns, I thought I was stepping down into a full-on sauna! Man, oh man! Soggy tea bags had nothing on us back then. How we were all supposed to get used to it in five minutes, I dunno.'

As we both stop talking for a moment, I sense Logan is quietly biding his time, hoping I'll finally open up to him. He'll be waiting for a while, then.

'Look, Logan, I know what you're doin', but it's not going to work. Even though I appreciate you being here for me, man, this is one of those times when I really do need to mull over things in my own way.'

Logan's only answer to me rejecting his help is to place his huge paw of a hand on my shoulder and smile his famous smile. 'I sorta had a feelin' you'd say that, buddy, so I'll leave ya be. I might go and find the guys again for one last drink, before I fall dead drunk into ma bunk for the night. I kinda suspect, good buddy, it's gonna be a full-on madhouse around here the minute the CO rouses us out of our bunks in the mornin', so I best go and git some shut-eye while I can.'

Logan stands up a bit too quickly and sways precariously on the spot until he's able to maintain his balance again, '*Fuck!* Might be best if I skip that last drink and head straight for my bunk instead.' He starts to head off, but then suddenly stops to turn back to me. 'You gonna be okay here on yer own?'

'I'll be along soon … I promise … Besides, it's not like we still have the enemy lurking around here to shoot us down anymore … Do we?'

Logan weaves off along the beach, reassured at last that *I'm* safe … 'Night, buddy!'

'Night, Logan!'

***

Alone, with no distractions at last, I'm finally able to focus on those persistent thoughts constantly disrupting my hard-won peace of mind.

The best advice my father ever gave me during my growing-up years, I've never forgotten, 'Son, to fix any problem you might have—now or in the future—go to some quiet place so you are completely alone, but only after you've gathered together all the facts in your head first. To me, this is the only way you can nut everything out. All in one go.'

Easier said than done, Dad. The way I see it, once I do get back home, I'll need to sit down to inform my folks about a *few* changes that are about to happen to their well-ordered way of life. The first thing I'll need to tell them—since my last letter back home—is that my Australian wife is going to be arriving at their place too. Just a few months after me, most likely towards the end of this year. I don't imagine my mom is going to be happy about this at all. The worst thing for me, though, will be me having to tell them that *both* of us will have to stay with them for maybe a year or so until we find our own place. This news isn't going to thrill them at all!

Since Mom is notoriously averse to accepting strangers—American or foreign—into her home at *any* time, my poor Isabella is bound to feel her wrath *immediately!*

Unfortunately, there is nothing I can do about this, since my family home is first and foremost my folks' home too. Like it or not, we'll have to respect their feelings. All I can do at this stage is be a peacemaker of sorts between Mom and Isabella for a while.

The miracle of me even surviving a world war in the first place could well become like a walk in the park for me, compared to the inevitable verbal explosions I can expect back on the home front. Anyway, once I *am* home, *maybe* I can start to act on my gut feelings rather than over-think what might or might not happen down the track.

When fighting any war in life, it's always good to have a battle plan in place first.

22

Isabella

Early 1946
Leaving one's childhood behind

The war is over! I can hardly believe it myself! At first, the news in all of Melbourne's newspapers of World War II ending sounds more like somebody could be playing a cruel joke on everyone. It isn't even April Fools' Day. Is it even possible for a world war to finish so abruptly? Particularly after so many years of putting our lives on hold. I mean, surely, just about everybody in Melbourne must have had an inkling that such an event *could* happen any day now. But it is *how* it all unfolded that has no doubt shaken each and every world citizen to the core. According to the latest headlines on the European side of the war, Hitler and Eva have supposedly committed suicide. While on our side of the world, under a sinister cloak of darkness, the Japanese armed forces literally have their backs against the wall, trying to fight off the American, Australian, New Zealand *and* Philippine forces.

Despite this strange kind of ending to World War II, the citizens of Melbourne alone can scarcely believe that the almost-forgotten dream of peace is about to become an everyday reality again.

Once the news of ceasefire in both Europe and the Pacific region is officially confirmed, the people of Melbourne immediately burst out onto the streets to celebrate, Evie and me included. There is music on the streets again, spontaneous laughter and the exuberant hugging of strangers simply everywhere within the crowded city streets and all along the grassy banks of the Yarra River.

Suddenly, there appears to be no shortage of precious paper either, with miles and miles of streamers gaily decorating the crowded footpaths within the beating heart of Collins Street. Happy drivers are sounding their horns continuously as they lean out of their car windows to wave to nearby strangers. Even impatient drivers normally stuck in vehicles on congested roads are for once not protesting over someone foolish enough to make a wrong turn into the path of oncoming traffic.

It's impossible not to get caught up in the excitement of this momentous occasion. Especially when I realise for myself this means Paul will be coming back to me too!

I can well imagine people all over Australia, just like me, are silently giving thanks to God right now for their loved ones returning home after fighting this war. Not only those close to Australia's borders, but those fighting overseas too. It's not just Paul who I give thanks to God for, but for Robbie returning home to us as well.

***

At least today I don't have to work my way through tight crowds at the railway station on the way home. This is probably because most of the commuters I travel with to work each day are still celebrating in the city. When I finally do make it back home, I'm not at all surprised to see my mother waiting for me at the front gate with a stream of happy tears running down her lovely face.

'Oh, isn't this wonderful news, Bell?' Mum says as she hugs me inside the front fence. 'Not only is Robbie returning to his family again, but Paul will be coming back to you too! I am mostly happy too, Bell, darling, because I believe that only now can the world begin to heal itself at last.'

As is often the case, when Mum cries, I cry too. As we head inside, we have our arms around each other and a fresh dry hanky each to sop up our joyous tears.

***

Within the next few weeks, I receive a letter from the US government advising me of my ocean passage on the SS *Monterey*. The letter also states they will be corresponding with me again in regard to my required documentation (especially my marriage and birth certificates), plus a whole list of rules, restrictions and procedures, before I even get to board the first available ship within Australian waters.

I guess I'm just going to have to get used to all of this red tape from now on, where 'the all-powerful military machine'—as Paul often refers to the US military—is concerned.

I'll just have to be patient and wait my turn for now. That's what I keep trying to tell myself, anyway. After all, I'm only one of fifteen hundred other war brides who will also be sailing across the vast Pacific Ocean with me. It's hard to wait, though, when I'm so anxious to be with Paul again. Sooner rather than later, I say.

***

After several months of working in the woollen department together, Evie and I are sipping tea in the Myer cafeteria on one of our morning breaks. After a few other discussions have run their course, we are finally starting to get around to discussing our impending passage on the first ship available. Chances are, the US Consulate could even call us this very week to advise each of us separately. We have been warned that our designated ship could be ready to set sail any day now. We will therefore be required to be ready to leave Melbourne at a moment's notice.

'You know, Bell, when our time is up here, I'm going to miss working with you.'

'Oh, me too, Evie!' I agree. 'I just wish there was some way we could end up on the same ship together. Wouldn't that be fun?'

'It sure would!' Evie agrees. That's when we came up with the same idea at exactly the same time. Evie speaks first, her excitement so evident on her lovely face. 'Why don't we make a pact with each other now, Bell, that if we aren't listed on the same ship together, one of us makes an excuse to stay. Well, at least until we can both go together. We could say to them that we can't *possibly* leave at this time. Maybe because of some family emergency or something … What do you think?'

'It could work,' I agree with equal excitement. 'So, let me get this straight, Evie. Whoever gets their notice first makes an excuse to wait for the other to be on the same ship … right?'

'Darn right! That's what we'll do, then.' We loop our pinky fingers together as a way of sealing our secret pact with each other.

But of course, even the best-laid plans don't always work out exactly the way we want. I receive my call from the US Consulate first, but Evie doesn't receive one at all. May God forgive me, but I make up some excuse of my mother being unwell, which of course isn't true. So when my prearranged passage is immediately cancelled, Evie and I feel secretly pleased with ourselves for being able to fool even the US government with our cleverness.

Several weeks later, Evie gets her call, but I don't, so I ring the US Consulate to ask if I can be on Evie's ship too, but I'm immediately turned down, so that Evie is to leave first without me anyway. Our plan to travel together has completely backfired on us. Serves me right for lying about my mother.

When I finally do get my call early February 1946, a letter from the US Consulate advises me I am to travel to Sydney by train on Thursday of next week. My travel costs and overnight accommodation in Sydney will of course be covered by the US government. Upon my arrival in Sydney, I am to board the SS *Monterey* on Friday morning. The ship's final destination is San Francisco, with scheduled stops at Suva, Fiji and Honolulu in Hawaii along the way.

I am also advised, by a more comprehensive brochure, that all war brides are strictly forbidden to leave the ship at any time during our entire sea voyage to San Francisco.

I naturally wonder why, but I'll probably find out when I'm meant to, I guess.

***

My day of departure for the train to Sydney finally arrives. Despite my outward resolve to remain positive and happy, as I stand before my family and my very best friend Coral, my tightly wound emotions still within the perimeters of my self-enforced stand-by mode for now, I know I'm not fooling anyone, least of all myself. To be completely honest, I have been dreading this very moment. Thankfully, this last week flew by so fast I've hardly had time to catch my breath.

So here we all are—my family, Coral and me—all standing awkwardly on the Southern Cross station platform, on an already sweltering February morning. Even at this early hour, the rest of this day promises to be a steamy one, for sure.

I'm wearing a light summer cotton skirt and a short-sleeve blouse, which I decided beforehand would be perfect for travelling. I've also opted to keep a warm cardigan on hand in my carry-on bag for when it cools down this evening on the overnight express to Sydney. Which gives me pause to wonder now, since I won't be arriving in Sydney until tomorrow morning, why it's even called an express train in the first place.

This first leg of my journey to Sydney will undoubtably test my resolve to keep on moving forward to the finish line—my new home in Chicago. After all, this trip is meant to represent a major step in my life, so I do hope I'm up for the challenge of it all. Deep down, I'm feeling more than a little apprehensive in another way too. Up until now, I've only ever travelled to Sydney with members of my family, but every single time I was able to return home again afterwards. This time I am truly on my own for the first time *ever!* The fact that this journey is meant to be a one-way ticket for me weighs heavy on my mind. Ever since I officially received notice of my impending journey, I have taken great care not to let my parents see what is really going on deep down in the pit of my stomach, while at the same time inevitably changing me into who I am meant to become. Despite these unsettling feelings, I'm ready for this next chapter of my life. Come what may.

I can well imagine my parents must have many of their own personal challenges to deal with as well. Robbie still hasn't returned from Darwin yet and now here they are, saying goodbye to their eldest daughter. They must also be fully aware I won't be just moving to the next suburb or around the corner from them, but to the other side of the world.

Yes, I know they still have three other children at home, but it's still going to be hard for them. Still, it warms my heart to know that even when their job of raising all five of their offspring towards adulthood is finally done, their role as our loving parents will never be.

My parents must have always known this day of emotional upheaval could creep up on them all too quickly, but I also know they'd never think for even one second of holding us back from experiencing life in our own way. When I stop to think about the significance of today, we've been preparing for this moment for a while but didn't fully realise it now.

It's never easy for any close-knit family—or close friends—to say good-bye, but our goodbyes on this sweltering summer morning on a crowded railway platform will have to be enough to sustain us for the years ahead. Memories are what they are, and unlike a scene from a movie, we don't always have the luxury of choosing the perfect setting.

The fact that I might never return home again is really starting to hit me hard now. As I struggle to hold back my tears, I have to wonder why I even thought I could, anyway.

Not a chance! As I hug each of my younger brothers, I find myself clinging to my sweet baby brother just that little bit more. I know I'm probably squeezing Marty far too much, but I can't help it. This first goodbye alone is enough to start the flow of unstoppable tears.

Marty is obviously feeling the same, reluctant to let me go as well. Even though he's supposed to be the baby of the family, at fourteen, he's taller than me now. With his head lowered, he starts sniffling into my shoulder as he clings to me even more. I can barely hear his muffled words now, but their meaning is very clear to me just the same, 'I don't want you to go, Bell! Why can't you stay in Australia with us?'

'I'm going to miss you too, Marty … Gee, when I see you next, you'll probably be all grown up. In the meantime, I promise to write to you whenever I can.'

Even Kyle, despite his efforts to remain manly, sheds a tear or two as he quickly hugs me tight in return. For the ever-talkative Kyle I've always known him to be, he has nothing to say this morning, so I give him one of my special sisterly hugs to let him know I understand.

Josie is next. We make the usual jokes about her having our bedroom all to herself, but our tears can no longer be stopped. We cling desperately to each other for the longest time, promising to write to each other every week. I already know this won't be an empty promise for either of us, because I, for one, am going to miss my little sister so much.

Even if she can be really annoying sometimes, I will always miss her anyway.

Coral is next. My, what a friendship we've had! 'Oh, Coral, I am going to miss you so much! You will always remain the best friend I have ever had. You know that, don't you?'

'Yes, of course I know that, Bell.' Coral's voice is muffled too, because as she hugs me, her mouth is almost covered by my hair. 'I have decided this morning, Bell, that I am going to start a travel fund this week, so I can come over to visit you in America. We'll have such fun together, won't we? You and Paul can even introduce me to a few gangsters in Chicago.'

'Yes, well, I'm not sure about meeting any gangsters, Coral.' I laugh and hug her back even more. Coral always cracks these kind of smart quips whenever she senses I'm about to slip into the doldrums. '*Or, we could* go to see a few live jazz or blues shows in Chicago. Will that do instead?'

'You're on! I'll definitely be up for that. We can dance our tootsies off until dawn.'

My parents are the hardest to say goodbye to of all on this highly emotional goodbye line-up. Even though I might be mature enough to leave the nest, right now, I'd give anything just to be their little girl again. I cling to each of my parents separately, then as a threesome for the longest time, within a tight bundle of protective love. That is until the conductor's whistle signals one last time for passengers to board the train or be left behind.

My swollen heart threatens to leap out of my chest now as I wave to Coral and my family one last time from the step leading into my carriage. I quickly plonk my things onto my allocated seat and rush to the nearest window to catch one last glimpse of them, but already they are no longer in view. Since my rational mind doesn't seem to be functioning anymore, my aching heart steps in to allow any lingering unshed tears—and there are still plenty of them—to stream down my face freely.

When I look quickly around me to see who might be watching, I soon realise there are seven other war brides from Melbourne in my carriage, making me feel I am immediately connected to them since each one of us are wearing the same miserable look on our faces. We study each other more fully now, smiling through our tears. After all, we are bound by the same common bond until our journey's end.

It's all too easy to get caught up in all the wonder of falling in love, each with our own American GI with movie star looks, gentlemanly ways and charming accent. Before we knew it, we were standing at the altar, promising to love, honour and obey each other forever. But now the war is over and here we all are, about to sail away on a great big ship across the ocean. To go live with our new husbands on the other side of the world. Away from everything and everyone we've ever known so far.

This is undoubtably reality time for each of us. Pretty much the point of no return. To be perfectly honest, sometimes true reality takes a while to fully grasp. As much as I love Paul and want to spend the rest of my life with him, the realisation of leaving my whole family behind in Australia isn't settling into the rest of my body as easily as it does with my heart. I think, maybe, it's going to take a *lot* longer to move forward from this initial moment of panic and into the next unchartered chapter of my life.

Thank goodness, I soon snap out of my initial panic! After just a few hours, I do believe I *might* be ready at last to embrace my new circumstances. After all, time is something I have plenty of right now. Time to reflect, shed tears, even time to smile to myself over childhood memories or just gaze out the window and watch the ever-changing landscape flash by.

The cityscape of Melbourne eventually gives way to sleepy little country towns, quaint wooden bridges over tree-lined riverbeds here and there. It's hard for me to believe now, that as a teenager seeking endless fun on school holidays, I blithely took these same verdant landscapes for granted.

The only conclusion I can come to at this point in time is to think of this homesickness as merely one more of life's adventures to be woven into the tapestry of the woman I am destined to become.

***

After our initial reserve with each other, I start to join in with chatting to the other women in my carriage. Before too long, we're chatting to each other like old friends. Throughout the day, we eventually merge into smaller groups, but we all agree, it's so much more fun to eat all of our meals in the dining carriage together. There are a few of us, who are no doubt still coming to terms with their new life that prefer to stick to themselves.

I have been allocated a sleeper compartment on the train by myself. Even though I do enjoy the company of the other women most of the time, I'm still grateful not to have to talk all night long.

As the day comes to an end, I drift off to sleep to the rumble of the train as it rattles on down the line. I allow my mind to shut down, but my heart chooses to remain active, spurring me on with dreams of the future. In these dreams, Paul is sweeping me into his arms once again at a train station somewhere deep within the city of Chicago at the end of this long, long journey.

23

Isabella

Early 1946
Sailing away on a great big ship

I take just one look at the massive ship berthed at the dock, and my adventurous soul immediately does a backflip. No words could ever express my excitement of seeing the monstrous, elegant ship towering over me at the Sydney Wharf. As a little girl, I used to imagine myself travelling over the seven seas one day, but the practical side of me never really thought such a thing would ever happen. Who could ever imagine—especially me—that I, Isabella Carlisle, a quiet modest girl from the suburban backwaters of Melbourne, would ever get to do such a thing in real life? Today, my dream is about to happen, and I can barely wait to get onboard. It seems my patience is to be further tested by the rope across the gangway *still* firmly holding me back.

I soon find out in due time, that in order for me to get onboard, I must first stand in this line for *many* hours, behind all of these other war brides already in queue ahead of me.

After the first hour has already passed, though, I am *still* at the back of the queue and now I can understand why. Military officials have decided that women with children should be the ones to board first, which is a smart move, really.

Looking on up the line now, I can see the women at the front of the queue constantly shifting their crying babies from hip to hip or firmly holding onto the hands of their restless toddlers as they chatter away happily to other women in front or behind them. At least these women won't be strangers after the next six weeks or so. To me, personally, I couldn't imagine travelling with young children on a sea voyage for weeks on end. Not to mention the various challenges that await them at their destinations. I don't have to be a mother myself to understand how daunting this trip must be for these brave mothers. Unbelievably, this ship isn't due to set sail for another four hours yet, so now I can finally understand why we had to be here so early. Organising an intake of a multitude of women and children, all travelling on the same ship together, must be like some kind of living nightmare!

Despite my sympathy for the SS *Monterey*'s crew, this whole tedious process of boarding the ship hasn't been a picnic for us lone passengers either. Our early morning rush to catch our shuttle bus from our designated inner-city hotels to the wharf was challenging enough, but to do all this with sleepy, sometimes-grumpy children in tow must have been downright chaotic for mothers of small children. To add to our early morning woes—even for women like myself with no children—dozens of scheduled stops are tightly thrown into the mix to pick up more women and children at other hotels along the way. This in turn means *more* paperwork has to be filled out by our bus driver at each stop. No wonder these poor mothers already looked exhausted long before joining this tiresome boarding queue.

Despite having a really comfy bed to sleep in at the hotel, even I found it almost impossible to sleep last night. This is no doubt due to one part sadness about leaving Australia and three parts excitement of this ocean voyage itself, stressing my already overloaded mind even more.

While I wait in my bubble of thoughts, I continue to stare at the SS *Monterey* in awe. On the train to Sydney, when sleep eluded me, I had decided to catch up on a bit of reading about the ship itself from the printed information I was issued with weeks beforehand. Thankfully, along with all the printed information I would need to hang onto, there was also a very helpful diagram of the ship showing me where each deck was, along with some basic nautical terms to learn before sailing. Being the inquisitive person I am, I was even more interested to learn about the history of this majestic ship.

According to some of detailed facts and figures I'd been given by the US Consulate, the SS *Monterey* is 632 feet long from stern to bow (length) and 79 feet across the berth (width) of the ship. I was also fascinated to learn that it was even commissioned by the US government during World War II to transport troops to and from various key military ports around the world. As a footnote added to this information, it also stated that the SS *Monterey* had once been a luxury cruise ship and has already sailed the seven seas many times over.

I am equally in awe of all the time and money and planning the US government must have undertaken to turn this elegant iron lady of the sea back into good use again to transport us war brides and offspring from all around the world over to the United States. Love them or hate them, when the highly motivated Americans do anything at all, they don't do it in half-measures. In other words, when they plan something, they go *all* the way. It's perfectly obvious to me too that the men and women who are part of this so-called unemotional US military machine are really romantic softies at heart. Especially when it comes to pulling out all the stops to reunite wives and children with their husbands and fathers at long last. Whether planned or not, the US military have somehow managed to increase their already impressive population statistics by the thousands. Nothing to scoff at.

As with any queue, most people start dropping their reserves to talk and open up more to those around them. This certainly helps to pass the time, what with us all being thrown together as total strangers to start with. But with people being people—wherever we admit it or not—we still crave company. As is often the case, we're more inclined to open up to a total stranger, without inhibitions or past history to hold us back. Perhaps even more so than we do with our own family or close friends. By way of proving this to myself, I soon learn that the person in front of me in the queue is Ruby.

After talking to her for only a few minutes, I warm to her immediately. Being a rather tall, busty girl, Ruby has the type of fuller hips that somehow matches perfectly to her impressive upper proportions. She looks so statuesque to me—but in a more understated, elegant way. With her tightly curled red hair and her friendly smile, she has already won me over so easily. Ruby somehow radiates confidence without even opening her mouth. I just know we could become really good friends by the end of our journey. I'm hoping she feels the same way too, especially if we're berthed close enough to each other on the same deck.

If I thought my trip seemed so long from Melbourne to Sydney, after hearing of Ruby's own travel experience, I have no reason to grumble about anything at all. Ruby tells me she has had to travel pretty much most of this past week to even make it here this morning. Firstly by bus, then by train, all the way from North Queensland to Sydney. She looks to me to be in her mid-thirties but has never had any children. I can't help wondering what her husband is like and what sort of life she has led up until now. As curious as I am about her, she doesn't strike me as the sort of person to talk about her personal life to just anyone, so I steer away from any probing questions. At least for the time being, anyway, and certainly not where we are standing right now, literally surrounded by thousands of women all jammed together in this increasingly noisy queue. There's bound to be time enough later for some deep and meaningful talks. Oodles of time for me to make friends with many more people over the next six weeks too, I would imagine.

***

Once onboard, we are informed by the captain of the ship himself that the first order of business for all of us will be to find our cabins and off-load our carry-on luggage as quickly as possible, before coming back on deck to say our goodbyes to any loved ones still prolonging their farewells on the crowded wharf below. We are also 'requested' to pose for photographers and reporters from several Sydney newspapers who have already lined up along the wharf, ready to record such a momentous, newsworthy event. After all, who wouldn't want to hear about a shipload of fifteen hundred Australian war brides—some with children already—all sailing on the same ship together, to America, to be reunited with their American husbands? If I lived in Sydney, I probably would have come along with the crowd to take a look as well.

After searching up and down the narrow corridors that connect all the numbered cabins on each deck, I finally manage to locate my cabin and am absolutely delighted to discover that it is one of the most desirable cabins onboard. Located on the top deck, it even has its own bathroom. During wartime manoeuvres—I found out later from one of the crew— that this cabin had been specially selected for the officer's quarters during the war. How lucky am I? I find myself thinking of Evie at this moment, wondering if she has been given the same sort of service on the SS *Lurline* as well. I certainly hope so. Anyway, I will no doubt look forward to comparing notes with her by phone, or by post, after a few weeks or months of living in America.

But, for this sea journey, as the old saying goes, 'I'm happy as a pig in mud,' and since I'm one of the first to make it to the cabin, I get to choose my bunk.

There are two bunk beds, side by side, with ample walking space between them. I notice the two top bunks are next to a decent-sized porthole. Just like I've seen in the movies! I've always dreamed of waking up in the mornings on a ship and being able to look out to the ocean from my very own porthole. From where I'm standing at the entrance to my cabin, I choose the top bunk on the left and quickly throw my carry-on onto my chosen bunk. I have absolutely no hesitation in laying first claim to it.

Once my corner of the cabin is all sorted and the contents of my suitcase are all packed away into my allocated locker space, I don't waste any more time heading back onto the main deck for all the fanfare of the SS *Monterey* setting sail.

Up on the main deck, the air of excitement is infectious. I happily allow myself to be carried along by all of its craziness. I don't mind too much at all, really. Besides, who wouldn't want to be part of such a momentous occasion?

All I can see below and to either side of me is a mass of thousands of faces as they try to look upwards, squinting against a glaring midday sun. In the spirit of fun, everyone on the wharf is having a wonderful time throwing a whole heap of colourful paper streamers up high towards us, making sure to aim high enough to reach the main deck. Most of the streamers fall short, ending up in the water instead. Some of the war brides with small children I already recognise from the embarkment queue this morning are still down on the wharf, saying their last-minute goodbyes to family and friends. Most of the passengers' families have probably travelled from far-flung towns and cities around Australia, just to be here for their departing daughters, sisters, nieces, grandchildren, friends or neighbours.

So absorbed am I in what is going on around me, I fail to realise I've suddenly become crowded in by the other excited women either side of me, all jostling for the best position along the main deck's railing. I join in with their infectious waving to everyone. Just to anyone at all, really, even if I don't know a single soul on the wharf. It doesn't matter at all. In my mind, I'm not really saying goodbye to total strangers today, but to fellow Australians, all bound by a common bond of belonging to one country and one collective history.

After all of the streamers have finally ended up in a crumpled heap on the deck floors, all the excited fanfare has at last died down to a mere animated chatter. After all of the curiously endless questions aimed at the Aussie war brides have been totally exhausted, the captain puts in a well-timed appearance. He politely, but very firmly, kicks all the journalists off the ship, particularly the most persistent ones. The elegant SS *Monterey* is finally able to throw off her ropey restraints and point her bow dead centre between the majestic sandstone heads of Sydney Harbour. After all, the SS *Monterey* is on a special mission to deliver her precious cargo of women and children into the loving, waiting arms of husbands and fathers.

If ships could talk, I'd imagine her blowing her horn and saying out loud to all, 'I MUST LEAVE NOW! I MUST NEVER FAIL!'

***

I stay up on the main deck with some of the other women long after the last massively thick ropes securing the ship to the pylons have been thrown off. I am still rooted to the same spot along the main deck railing. I am simply content for now to watch any activity that is going on in front of me. I am especially fascinated to spot two mighty little tugboats in front and to either side of the SS *Monterey*, proudly towing her out beyond Australia's world-famous Sydney Harbour.

This moment will stay etched in my mind forever as one of those undefinable—but above all—most unforgettable events in one's life. Even if the seas should be choppy, or if I have to spend this whole journey miserable with sea sickness, I'm convinced for now at least that my internal navigation is firmly set on its own course for the future. Over towards the wharf, I watch with amusement as a persistent haggle of journalists and cameramen still intend on capturing that one last photo, that could very well be THE photo to make it to the front page of newspapers and into the history books for all time. As we inch further away from their lenses, I can easily imagine the newsreel footage that will be shown in picture theatres around Australia next week and all the weeks to follow:

'Yes, Australia, these brave women are crossing the Pacific Ocean together, all to be reunited again at last with their long-absent husbands. It will be a reunion for the littlies on board too, since most of them haven't even met their daddies yet. Yes, folks, it's going to be a grand reunion, indeed!'

I really don't know what will happen in Australia next week or even what will happen once I reach America at the end of this sea voyage, but I am content for now to just trust in my own intuition and in the love that Paul and I share with each other.

In the meantime, I fully intend to think of this sea voyage as a once-in-a-lifetime experience, to tell my future children about one day.

What I do know, though, is that I am totally famished! It has been a long time since breakfast, which basically consisted of only a few snatched pieces of fruit to nibble on, provided free of charge from my hotel room this morning. I'll probably regret eating anything at all if any dreaded sea sickness should happen to kick in later, but for now, I need immediate sustenance, otherwise once the ship's galley closes tonight, it could well be a long wait until breakfast tomorrow morning.

Yes! Some food, please! My neglected, rumbling tummy pleads its case.

'Then food you shall have!' I declare as I head for the galley. That's if I can remember exactly where the galley is. *Just follow the crowd!* My tummy urges me on.

24

Isabella

1946
Everyday shipboard life

Pretty soon after, with food in our tummies, followed by some soothing beverages to wash it all down, the deafening crescendo of a whole lot of excited voices together soon fills the dining room (which I quickly learn takes up almost an entire deck of this ship). I do honestly believe this ear-blasting racket might even be enough to challenge the highest sound barrier. The effect of too many people demanding to be heard at the one time suddenly seems to bounce off the walls. With cutlery being carelessly dropped on the floor and ceramic plates being noisily stacked together onto trolleys, it's enough to make you want to run for cover. If you didn't have a headache before entering the dining room, you certainly will afterwards.

Mothers, who have been struggling all day with buses and long queues at the wharf, diligently holding on tight to lively toddlers struggling to run free everywhere, are finally able to sit and relax for a while. I could see for myself from across the dining room the stress leave their faces and be replaced with relaxed smiles as they start to forge some brand-new friendships with other mothers nearby. Pretty soon, a whole chorus of screaming babies and overtired toddlers are joining in too, drowning out any chance of normal conversation as they demand their mother's full attention once again. Total bedlam! It is definitely time to bed down the babies and toddlers for their first night at sea. I can almost guarantee most of these women will probably fall asleep alongside their little ones as well.

***

With my tummy full at last, I'm still not sleepy just yet, so I'm happy to just wander around the unrestricted areas of the ship for an hour or so, before heading back to my bunk for my first night at sea. So far—touch wood—no sign of sea sickness yet. I still feel pretty good considering I've never spent time on any ocean liner before, but I noticed a few of the women in the dining room earlier are already expressing feelings of nausea and disorientation.

Unfortunately, one of those ailing women also happens to be sharing my cabin. Mavis is from Tasmania, which I soon find out after introducing ourselves to each other upon returning to our cabin at the same time. No sooner have we left Australian shores, when Mavis starts to complain of feeling nauseous. 'I never should have eaten that last bowl of ice cream,' she groans. 'I don't feel so good, Bell.'

Mavis has taken to her bunk for an indefinite period of time and steadfastly refuses to leave this safe refuge she has created for herself. Apart from vomiting in the toilet bowl, at least she *does* vacate her bunk to use the bathroom for showers and to clean her teeth—especially after vomiting. She certainly doesn't desire to venture beyond the four walls of our cabin for any meals either. Right now, food is the last thing on her mind.

I am secretly convinced her nausea is all in her mind, but I would never tell her that, of course. I strongly suspect Mavis doesn't really want to go to America at all. After what Mavis related to me about her background earlier, my trusty intuition proves me correct yet again.

'During the war and because my two brothers were both away fighting the Japanese, I was the only sibling left at home. I was expected to stay around the house to help our father keep the family farm going and help Mum in the kitchen.'

218

'That must have been so hard for your parents too, Mavis. Especially with not just one son away from home, but both. Have either of them come home from overseas yet?'

'No, and they never will,' Mavis declares with an expression of the total unfairness of life clearly written on her face. 'My parents were informed—by an official letter from the military—that both of my brothers were accidentally killed when an American destroyer mistook the HMAS *Sydney* for a Japanese warship. As a consequence of this American destroyer's fatal error, HMAS *Sydney* and all of its crew were sent it the bottom of the ocean. Including my two brothers.'

It's clear to me—but obviously not to Mavis yet—that she definitely has a deep-seated dislike for Americans in general. Even if she is married to one now.

Every time I've return to our cabin this past week, Mavis is there already on her bunk directly under mine. Her only companion is a metal mop bucket on the floor beside her, which to me, only serves to remind her of her never-ending misery over and over again. She obviously has it in her mind to stay put for the whole duration of this soul-sickening period if necessary.

After a few days of seeing Mavis looking so miserable all the time, I start to feel really bad for my previous lack of sympathy towards her. During the past few days, whenever I'm heading off to the dining room, Mavis has taken to asking me if I would mind grabbing a small amount of dry food for her eat. So, after each meal, I make a point of grabbing a handful of dry soda crackers, which are always available on every table, to take back to her. This is what Mavis lives on for days. Just dry biscuits and water. She is a heavy-set girl, so going without food for a bit probably won't matter much in the long run. I have tried to talk her into coming with me outside into the fresh air, but I have to accept that no amount of coaxing from me is going to entice her to leave her bunk under any circumstances. It isn't until we are about to reach Hawaii that I finally manage to talk her into leaving her safe haven. I'm beginning to see some positive signs of her good spirits coming back at last.

I think if I hadn't insisted she leave the cabin behind and come with me at last, she would have regretted it later for sure. For her to have missed seeing the lush splendour of the beautiful, tropical Hawaiian Islands up on the main deck would have been a travesty indeed.

***

I have made friends with one of the sailors onboard, and after he finishes his chores, he's allowed to come up on deck. This is when we enjoy sitting and talking to each other in the evenings. There is never anything romantic between us and there never will be either. To me, he is more like one of my own brothers, who I already miss so much. I just like to talk to him about lots of different things, that's all.

His name is Peter—or Pete, as he prefers to be called—and he tells me that when we reach Hawaii, the first thing he plans to do is to go buy himself a case of beer.

'Of course, Mrs Meier, you would be more than welcome to come and join me in a beer or two when I get back onboard … If you want to, that is?'

'You know, Pete, you can call me Bell if you like. All of my friends do. I would hope that we're friends enough by now to let go of formalities … For the duration of this ocean voyage, at least.'

I can see by his hesitation he's still reluctant to let go of his strict military rules.

Noting his discomfort, I quickly add, 'Only if you're comfortable with doing so, that is. In answer to your question about the beer, if it tastes anywhere near as good as my younger brother's home-brew, then yes, Pete, I'd love to have a beer with you. Count me in.'

'I'm sure you already know by now, Bell, that I consider you to be my friend too, so yes, I will be more than happy to call you by your first name. Probably not in front of my immediate superiors though, you understand?'

'Of course, Pete, and yes, I do understand this rule by now. Especially after reading our passenger rule book, which states: *Any fraternising between passengers or crew onboard is to be strongly discouraged.* Your own naval rule book probably says the same thing too.'

'You got that right, Bell,' Pete chuckles in agreement. 'Anyway, how are we going to do this, then?' Pete goes quiet for a moment, before his eyes light up. 'I know! How about, when you see me coming back up the gangplank with my case of beer, that's your cue to meet me near the gear locker. It's where we usually store our mops, brooms and other cleaning products for easy access for the crew. Do you know where that is?'

'I'm pretty sure I do, Pete. I've seen you go inside that metal door near the staircase on the main deck a few times already, until I see you come back out of there soon after with a mop and bucket or a broom. Is that the gear locker you are referring to?'

'Yes, that's the one. So, after dinner and once this ship is underway again, meet me outside the gear locker. But only when you can slip away unseen, okay?'

'You're on!' And why not? Apart from enjoying a few quiet beers together, we certainly aren't planning to meet up for any sinful reasons, that's for sure. As an added insurance against tongues wagging, I ask Pete if I can bring Mavis along, to which he agrees, but then he quickly adds, 'No-one else, though, Bell. It *is* only a small locker ,after all.'

***

I soon find out, on the night before we dock at Hawaii, why certain shipboard rules must never be broken.

'The real reason, Bell, why women passengers onboard this ship aren't allowed to leave the ship once it is docked at Hawaii, is because on previous trips some war brides chose not to return to the ship at all.'

'Really, Pete? So, the women actually walked off the ship and never came back?'

'Yep! To my way of thinking, by the time a ship sets sail at Sydney, Melbourne or wherever, these newly married women are obviously having second thoughts about leaving the only home they've ever known to be with a man they hardly even know. Then there are the women who fall instantly in love with this whole tropical island scene before deciding to stay on indefinitely. Either way, a new rule was enforced, so not even one woman of the fifteen-hundred-plus aboard the SS *Monterey* is permitted to leave the ship. *Period!*'

When the ship does dock at Hawaii, Mavis and I have to be content to view as much as we can of the glorious tropical island from the ship's railing. We're both mesmerised by the sheer majestic beauty in every direction. Up until now, I'd only ever imagined in my dreams that such a scene existed. If it did, I only ever saw evidence of it in Hollywood movies or in some glossy travel book or magazine.

If I *still* had any doubts that I'm really here, the visual proof is right before my very eyes. The myriad of palm trees everywhere and the island people all decked out in their tropical attire has Mavis and me wishing we *could* go ashore. Just watching all these friendly islanders waving back to us makes us long to be active participants of the whole gorgeous scene. Not as onlookers from afar. But we'll just have to accept it's *not* going to happen this time around.

Right on sunset, as we lean out over by the railing, we're completely captivated by it all. Along the horizon, dramatic slashes of purple infuse with the ruby tints of a huge golden orb on the horizon, as it finally releases its hold on the day to slip dramatically below the foaming waves. Mavis and I, along with dozens of other women either side of us at the railing, remain transfixed with wonder. We listen blissfully to the lovely timeless beat of Hawaiian ukuleles and drums from a group of musicians entertaining us from their island port. We can hardly believe it either, when dozens of native women dressed in exotic grass skirts suddenly appear along the waterfront to perform their timeless, sensuous hula dances for us.

To add even more effervescence to this magical moment, the island's palm-fronted pier is magically lit up for us by a string of bamboo torches wedged in the sand all around the pier and along the beach front. The Hawaiian people have come out in large numbers to welcome us tonight with such spectacular magic that I will never ever forget.

When the show is over after sunset and the performers have left us still wanting more, the SS *Monterey* prepares to pull up anchor again. This is about the same time Mavis and I spot Pete struggling up the gangplank with a case of beer slung over his shoulder. After dinner we head down to the locker as prearranged with Pete. I soon realise this co-called locker room has no lockers at all. It is only meant to be a storage room, after all. The interior, instead, is all filled up with a whole lot of large bottles of cleaning fluids on the shelves. Where there is no shelving, there is a wide variety of mops, buckets and brooms, all neatly arranged along one side of an already cramped—but still orderly—room. Pete is already in there waiting for us, sitting in the middle of the room on an upturned mop bucket. In front of him is another bucket, filled with his beer bottles chilling nicely on a bed of chunky ice.

It's very warm and stuffy in the locker, but Mavis and I find ourselves a couple of metal buckets to sit opposite Pete. We waste no time in positioning our 'seats' around him in order to help him drink his beer and get inevitably very tipsy in the process. I can't help but notice how happy Mavis is tonight. Her face is alive with mischief and fun, but it's most likely due to the copious amount of beer we're happily consuming in the gear locker together.

After we have been here for some time, there's a knock at the door. We freeze and try to stay silent until whoever it is gives up and goes away. Much to our disgust, this annoying person just keeps right on knocking. Pete quietly motions with a wobbly finger to his lips for Mavis and me to hide behind the door, before he cautiously opens it. With Mavis being of a larger frame than Pete or me, he can only open the door a crack. This locker is supposed to be off limits to *all* personnel after hours, so Pete, frowning with obvious worry now, soon realises he might be in big trouble for this idea of his.

Sure enough, it's one of the officers who is in charge of overseeing both the sailors and any restless war brides onboard. Apart from women not being allowed to leave the ship at all, navy personnel are strictly forbidden to fraternise with women passengers *at any time!* This officer can obviously see us through the crack anyway, so he somehow manages to squeeze his way into the locker, demanding to know what we are doing. As if he doesn't know, especially with the bucket of chilled beer bottles now in full view. Just when we think we're going to be in big trouble for sure, the officer closes the door, and to our relief, up-ends a spare bucket to sit down and join us.

Erik, who happens to be a very tall, handsome Norwegian, enthrals us for hours with endless stories of his world travels. We could happily listen to him talk all night. Unbelievably, here we are, with the four of us sweltering in the heat of this tiny room, guzzling beer and having a merry old time.

A few times after this night, I run into Erik up on the main deck and he tells me again about all the other countries he's seen on his travels. Of all these countries, though, Erik declares New Zealand to be the most beautiful one he has ever seen by far.

'New Zealand? Really? I would have thought Norway, with all of your spectacular fjords and beautiful scenery, your home country would have to be your first choice.'

'Ah, Isabella!' Erik says, preferring my full name over calling me Bell as Pete and Mavis do. 'One day you must see New Zealand for yourself and you will understand what I mean. To me, it is even more beautiful than Norway. Maybe even more beautiful than Hawaii too.'

***

We never really do get to see much of the other two women in our cabin during the entire journey. Annie, one of our roommates, and her fellow onboard friend Pat spend most of their time together. Every single day, in fact. Each morning, Mavis and I can see them from the dining room or from the deck railings walking around and around the upper deck, taking their 'constitutional', as Annie calls it. I must admit, this isn't an expression I am all that familiar with.

Every evening after dinner, I notice Annie and her friend Pat head straight for the stern of the ship, and I can't help but wonder what they are up to. One night, I decide to follow them. With a little hesitation, I amble on over towards them casually, like I am merely taking a stroll around the deck on my own.

They're surprised to see me, and Annie is the first to acknowledge me as she looks over my way. 'Bell! What are you doing up here?'

'Oh, just wandering around the deck. I don't know about you two, but I find the cabin a bit too stifling on these hot tropical nights. I might ask the same thing of you two as well?'

Pat speaks first, with a melancholy tone to her voice. 'Oh, we just come up here each night to look at the Southern Cross for as long as we can. As we travel more into the Northern Hemisphere, we won't be able to see it so much.'

'In just a few short weeks, we'll be in San Francisco,' Annie adds. 'We still feel very homesick at times, but just seeing the Southern Cross each night somehow makes us feel closer to home. Somehow, the thought of being home comforts us so much more.'

'I can certainly understand what you're both saying,' I agree. 'Like you just said, Annie, pretty soon we'll be in San Francisco and we'll be seeing a totally different sky every night. That's going to take some getting used to—for all three of us.'

I'm so glad I took the time to understand them better. They aren't nearly as aloof as Mavis and I wrongly judged them to be. They're just homesick, that's all, but lucky enough to have each other's friendship, even before this journey had begun. After an hour or so of chatting to them about our home country and sharing stories of growing up in Australia, I start yawning, ready for sleep at last. I finally wish them both a goodnight, before heading for my bunk.

As it turns out, I'm very relieved I had the sense to pick one of the top bunks before we sailed. Once we entered the humid tropical waters, any tiny sea breeze drifting in through the open porthole near my bunk at night has been a huge blessing indeed. I often see women from nearby cabins lying out in the wide passageways on their mattresses and well away from their stiflingly hot cabins as they try to catch some relief from the occasional sea breeze.

***

After a few more weeks onboard, everyday life soon settles into an easy rhythm. The morning sun beams in through my porthole at a ridiculously early hour each day, so I have no choice but to wake up much earlier than I would back home. I soon realise the early hours in the laundry are the least-congested time for washing out my underwear and other delicates before a good number of the other women are out of bed. Understandably, with fifteen hundred women onboard, it's a challenge to be able to find a spare washing machine or dryer at the best of times. Especially with all the young mums with kiddies onboard.

To be honest, I don't mind too much being up and about early. It's such a pleasurable thing lately—after attending to my own laundry, of course—to greet other early risers in the dining room each morning. Invariably, these early risers are mothers talking with other mothers, whilst still keeping an eagle eye on their toddlers who are happy to chase each other around the chairs within our unrestricted outdoor areas.

I can always count on the usual regulars near the coffee machine. I can't believe I have actually taken to drinking coffee. Something I never thought I would do. My favourite steaming hot cup of tea throughout the day is no longer available, it seems. The pots of tea made by the cooks or waitstaff here are really terrible! I doesn't take me long to learn that Americans don't have any clue at all about how to make a decent cup of strong, full-bodied tea. Their idea of making tea is to plop a couple of tea bags into a huge teapot, add lots of hot water then serve it immediately—as it is. The time-honoured English tradition of steeping the brew is sadly lacking here, with absolutely no chance for the brew to develop any aromatic flavour at all. The end result is that each new pot of tea tastes exactly like barely tinted, insipid hot water to me. So, to keep my tastebuds still intact by the end of this sea voyage, I have decided to stick to some of the strong-brewed coffee on offer instead. When in Rome, do as the Romans do, I suppose. At least this shipboard coffee has a bit more taste to it. Once you take away the bitter, stewed taste that is. I'm not trying to be a snob or anything, but it's obvious to me that English traditions die hard and fast in this part of the world.

Speaking of tea again, it suddenly dawns on me: the Aussie thing about tea is more of a symbolic reminder of home to me. It isn't so much the tea itself, but a treasured ritual I've always taken for granted in my daily life thus far. After all, it's something I shared with my family each and every day. Particularly in the afternoons with Mum and Josie after my working day. Sipping our way through a whole pot of tea after dinner is something my family always love to do together, while we share news of current world events or our own daily happenings. Crowding around the wood stove at the kitchen table or by a cosy winter fire is most certainly the place to be during the chilly winter months in Melbourne. Sipping steamy cups with friends during our morning work break is something else I love to do. This is when office gossip or some love life dilemma is always the talk of the day. I don't think I'll ever underestimate the social power of a simple cup of tea ever again.

It's a lonely feeling, indeed, to suddenly realise once again my family and friends are thousands of miles away from me by now. My sudden pang of loneliness in turn gives way to tons of self-pity. For the second time since leaving home, I cry myself to sleep, my sobs muffled under my pillow, to hide my all-consuming misery.

I do run into Ruby from time to time onboard. Lately, I've taken to thinking of Ruby as my-lady-in-the-queue friend.

Goodness me! Boarding the SS *Monterey* for the first time already feels like a million years ago now!

Honestly, all the days onboard this ship seem to meld into each other after a while. I have no clue whatsoever what day of the week it even is anymore. Not that I mind, really. I'm over the doldrums now and back into enjoying some happier days ahead.

Anyway, as I was saying, I've run into Ruby a few times. We chat for a while, but I can instinctively tell she prefers to keep mostly to herself. She is her usual flamboyant self, though, as she strolls slowly around our social deck. Her hair is always well-coiffed, her make-up flawless, her clothes all so beautifully tailored and her accessories all expensive looking. The combination of her outfits and her accessories appear to perfectly match Ruby's secretive persona. So far, I still haven't been able to find out about Ruby's story either, not even who her husband is. Pity! My usual runaway imagination attempts to fill in the blanks, of course, but whatever conclusions I come up with, I decide to keep to myself. Other people onboard are probably curious about Ruby too. Despite my obvious intrigue about her mysterious aloofness, I silently send her my good wishes for her new life in America just the same.

25

Paul

1946
Back to where I belong

Despite what the various news sources try to tell us, welcoming armed forces home again after fighting any world war isn't all about happy smiles or hosting a ticker tape parade in our honour.

Yes, our families, neighbours and friends came out in their thousands all around Chicago to welcome us back home, but our 'victories' soon faded away once the brass bands stopped playing.

It isn't so easy for the fragile minds of young boys to pick up where they left off and start life all over again. The boys who enlisted straight out of high school to go fight a war in a foreign land not only left home in a boy's body, but much later, after returning home as a fully grown man, they were expected to act like one too. To my way of thinking, a huge slice from their innocent boyhood has been ripped away from them to never be given back again.

For me personally, I had at least already left school well before World War II started, so I was able to find work around my neighbourhood for quite a few years before enlisting in the army. Coming back home to the USA for me means that even if I did leave for the war as a single man, now that I'm a married man, I have all the adult responsibilities that go with it. *Man! Am I crazy or what? Well, crazy in love, anyway!*

In love or not, the truth is that I will have my Australian wife following me back home. This means a whole lot of new problems for me that I hadn't thought of before, but then again, I've never been one to walk away from a challenge.

Finding a decent job—with enough money coming in to financially support Isabella and myself comfortably—must be first on my agenda. We will also need to find somewhere to live independently of my parents. I can't see my mother being too happy having a 'foreigner' living in her house for very long. That's a certainty!

Speaking of Mom, I'm going to have to sit down with the folks tonight and ask them if Isabella can stay here with them for now. At least until we're able to find us a place of our own.

Somehow, I don't think this particular request of mine will be very well received by either of my parents—*In fact, I could even be kicked out of home myself!*

***

Well, there's no time like the present to talk to Mom and Dad about Isabella turning up here next week at the latest. I've decided this is going to be the night. There is to be no more procrastinating about it on my part anymore. It *has* to be tonight.

After supper is finished with, the dining table is cleared, the washing up is done and every last dish or piece of cutlery is stored away, I grab a bottle of beer from the refrigerator as well as three tumblers, and as per our usual evening ritual, head for the front porch to where my folks are already waiting for me to join them.

I do believe the right moment for my big talk with them has arrived. I sure do hope so!

'Mom, Dad. There is something urgent I need to talk to you about. Please just hear me out first, then I'll be happy to hear any of your objections or answer your questions … That okay?'

Dad remains silent as he stares down at some spot on the floor, but Mom immediately grunts in that dismissive way of hers, warning me that she already knows what's on my mind and she's not very happy about it at all.

'If it's about this new foreign wife of yours, son, then the jury is still out on that one.'

It doesn't take a genius to see my mother's brick wall is already firmly in place. This is what I've been dreading all along. As for my father, he still seems to be deeply engrossed with that hidden spot on the floor. I guess I'm not at all surprised by either of their reactions so far, but I'm still determined to try and change their minds for the better.

'The thing is Isabella will be arriving in Chicago by the end of next week, so we can no longer avoid her arrival, which is bound to affect each of us in different ways. Isabella especially is totally unaware there is a problem with her staying here. As you both know by now, I haven't been able to find any available apartment for us as yet, due to this current postwar shortage of accommodation, of course.' I take a deep breath before continuing, 'All I'm asking of you both now is to let us stay here for a little while until I can find somewhere else to live. According to you, Mom—as you have already stated numerous times by now—*maybe* I *might* have been better off with an American wife, but I love Isabella very much, so I won't *ever* regret marrying her.

'We can't always choose who we fall in love with, Mom, and even if you don't want her here, she is still my wife. If you kick her out then you will have to kick me out too. I go where she goes.'

Dad surprises me by being the first to speak. Usually it's always Mom who is the first to voice her objections. 'We're not saying Isabella *can't* stay here at all, son, but you have to understand, it's not so easy for your mother to have a stranger staying here. A week or two would probably be okay, but not for months on end.'

Mom speaks up finally, and I honestly wish she hadn't because she reminds me about the complexities involved with my younger brother.

'You know well enough by now, son, since I've been forced to put Benny into that special care institution I'll probably never be able to spend any time with him ever again once *she's* here to stay!'

Hearing my mother speaking about Isabella like this, you'd think my wife could very well be the scum of the Earth, instead of her new daughter-in-law. Just the same, I *can* understand where my mother is coming from. Because of Benny's mental and physical disabilities, Mom has had to be there for most of his ongoing care from birth to his impending manhood and beyond. Ever since her friend Marion had talked Mom into putting him into a special care home for Benny's severe disabilities, she has started to blame Isabella for her decision.

'I know you're still upset about Benny going into that place, Mom, but it's hardly Isabella's fault, is it? It's not her fault, either, that finding an apartment is so darn difficult these days.'

Dad follows Mum's lead now, by also objecting to Isabella living here with them. 'You know, son, I don't think I can handle the strain of having your new wife living under the same roof with us either. For any amount of time, really.'

'Well, how about this idea, then. I've started to check out some trailers on sale recently. The one I like the most, I think I can get the owner to knock down the price for me to a hundred dollars second-hand. I'll park it in the backyard, so this way we won't all be living under the same roof all the time. As soon as I find an apartment, I can sell the trailer and put it towards the rent. So what do you say, Dad? … Do you think you might at least be agreeable to *this* idea?' I hold my breath, hoping Dad will see the sense in my idea and talk Mom into it too. I know it's no good asking Mom at this point, because I know she will say no straight out.

'Yes, this sounds like a good solution to me too, son. What do you think, Erika?'

'I guess it could work, but mark my words, son, she'll not be cooking in *my* kitchen!'

26

Isabella

1946 America
New country for new brides

We finally reach San Francisco Bay after almost a month at sea and we have travelled close to seven thousand nautical miles to get here.

Just like Australia's own beautiful Sydney Harbour, which can literally take the breath away from any wide-eyed visitor, San Francisco Bay does the same for me. Talk about a spectacular first impression of my new country! San Francisco Bay area on the west coast would undoubtably have to be the second most famous city in the United States—with their east coast city of New York with its Statue of Liberty being number one, of course. After all, many unforgettable songs have been written about both of these world-famous, welcoming seaside cities, I doubt if I will never forget the memory of looking up at the sheer, towering splendour of the Golden Gate Bridge as the SS *Monterey* sailed under it. We reach San Francisco in the late afternoon, just as the sun is setting over the bay, casting a breathtaking glow over the magnificent welcoming structure. I can't help but think what a perfect name for this bridge. Golden Gate! Not just a bridge really, but a real gate in every sense of the word, as it spreads out especially for me to welcome me to my new home!

234

Any thoughts of immediately setting foot on American soil after berthing is quickly quashed by the ever-present government authorities once again. We are all destined to become America's future citizens, but not quite yet. For some unknown reason, we are to remain offshore overnight, and I, for the life of me, cannot understand why. Yes, we are finally here in America, but not *really* here in a sense. For some reason, my intuitive gut senses an anxious kind of feeling. It's like being in some kind of limbo, so I am at a complete loss regarding how to express the disjointed feeling in a more flowery poetic way. Even to myself.

Where the SS *Monterey* docks offshore for the night, I am shocked to realise it is right beside the foreboding, gloomy walls of the infamous Alcatraz prison.

It seems ironic to me, that apart from the Golden Gate Bridge, my first impressions of my new country should happen to be of a prison for hardened criminals. It immediately takes me back to my childhood when I used to visit my grandfather who was a warden for many years at the Pentridge Gaol in Melbourne. As is the way, with children being doted on by their grandparents with sweet treats and baby kangaroos to play with, the looming dark prison walls just beyond our grandparents' residence somehow managed to fade away into the distance as we played in their own patch of garden attended by the *good* prisoners.

Alcatraz doesn't demand all of my attention, though. As Mavis and I gaze out together over San Francisco's skyline, we do so in awe and wonder. Even as we watch, clumps of low scattered clouds quickly drift towards each other, completely cloaking the towering bridge in an almost-mystical shroud. We glance over towards the city itself and watch with fascination, the twinkling of a million lights in every direction. Like any modern motorised city, there is a constant stream of traffic over the bridge, with a glowing chain of white headlights on one side and red tail-lights on the other. The glowing line of traffic never seems to pause either. Not even for one single minute.

After watching this spectacular vista of new sights for a few hours, Mavis starts to yawn. She admits she is sleepy enough now, despite the constant chattering excitement still brewing from the other women all around us. Without further ado, she heads off to her bunk bed for the last time. I have noticed, in the past few days, Mavis is talking a bit too much about nothing really at all. After a while, her words tend to run into one long monologue. She doesn't seem to want to talk about what is really on her mind. I suspect she might even be frozen with fear, in a way, about meeting up with her long-absent husband again.

I promise her I'll be along later. But to be honest with myself, I'm not quite ready just yet. I'm simply too excited to go to bed, so I stay by the ship's rails alone with my thoughts for another hour or so. There are simply too many thoughts jostling around in my head for me to give into sleep now anyway.

Well, here I am, I say to myself, tomorrow morning I'll finally be stepping foot for the first time on American soil, not knowing a soul and barely even knowing my husband. For this one moment of sheer panic, I feel so completely alone. Despite my regular pep talks to myself over the past month, I'm not feeling so sure about my future anymore. Suddenly, I feel way out of my depth again.

I know I really do love Paul very much. These past few years of separation from him, while he plays his own important part in this war, really have tested our commitment to each other. Our letters certainly do help a lot, but they can never truly replace the touch and feel of each other. Deep down in my heart, I know for sure, my love for him still runs ever so deep. After all, how else could we have survived this war, separated like we have been? All throughout our time apart I was fully aware that each new sunset meant another day dawning with the blessed wonder of Paul still being alive.

From Paul's last letter from the Pacific Islands, I know that he would be back in America by now and has probably already been back for the past six months or more. Apart from the military servicemen and women who are still recovering from the horrors of war in various hospitals around the world, most of the GIs from all over the USA should be back home long before this very moment. A lot of GIs, like my Paul, will be also waiting anxiously for their sweethearts, wives and children to be reunited with them again.

The new calm state of mind I've worked so hard to maintain is calm no more, and I know only too well this new reality depends on how much my new home country is prepared to open up for me. As a foreigner, I wait here with bated breath at their border for the final approval.

***

The next morning, all passengers onboard the war bride express passage across the sea are all packed up and assembled together in the main dining room, ready to leave the SS *Monterey* for good. After an early breakfast, we are effectively organised into more manageable groups. One by one, each group is expected to disembark in some kind of orderly fashion. Nervous mothers with crying babies and excited toddlers continually running around their mothers' legs are once again squashed together into inevitable, slow-moving queues towards freedom.

Before we all split off into our individual groups, I manage to grab hold of Mavis to say goodbye to her one last time. Despite our shaky friendship at the start, what with her constant seasickness and me listening to her vomiting into a bucket all night, we have still formed a companionable, easygoing friendship regardless.

'Goodbye, Mavis! I'm really going to miss getting around this great big ship with you, walking the decks with you, and best of all, guzzling beer with you, Pete and Erik in the locker room.' We both have a good laugh at the last one as we hug each other affectionately.

'Me too, Bell! Please write when you can, as will I too … If I stay with my husband, that is.' Tears are spilling down her cheeks with such misery now as she acknowledges her true hidden feelings to me at last. 'I am so very nervous about facing him, Bell. I have to wonder too if my love for him is strong enough to keep me here in this strange new country.'

I hug her fiercely, before pulling away to look her straight in the eye.

'Mavis, as your new friend, the only advice I can give you at this time is not to hang onto any unrealistic expectations. Allow yourself at least six months to settle in. If you still feel the same after that time as you do now, then you must be true to yourself and head back home … At least after six months, you would've given it a fair go. Does that make sense? I hope so!'

'Yes! It makes perfect sense, Bell. Thank you for being so understanding from the start too! I promise you that whatever happens in six months, I will let you know either way.'

We hug each other one last time before being literally pulled apart by Pete taking his last opportunity to say goodbye to us too.

'Well, ladies, here you both are, ruthlessly leaving me to get drunk all by myself in the locker room! *And* what am I going to do without you to talk to, Bell? My life is over, ladies!'

'Oh, Pete! Don't be so melodramatic. You know we love you … Don't we, Mavis?'

'Bloody oath we do, Pete. We are really going to miss you!' Mavis is the first to hug him, swiping away her free-flowing tears with an even-soggier hanky.

I'm next. 'Come here, Pete,' I affectionately order him. 'Give your unofficial big sister a great big hug.'

He obliges me with a huge bear-like hug that reminds me once again of leaving my three brothers behind in Australia. It's time to pull out another hanky from my handbag too.

Just before Pete takes off, I remember something important I need to tell him before he leaves us for good, so I grab his sleeve to hold him back. 'Hey, Pete, before you go, would you do a favour for me?'

'Sure, Bell! What favour would that be?'

'Would you please tell Erik, our Norwegian drinking friend, goodbye for me?'

'I surely will, Bell. I must admit I haven't seen much of him since our night of boozing in the locker, but I think I know how to track him down. Bye, Bell!'

'Bye, Pete. The best of luck to you for the future too. I'll never forget you!'

The last image I have of Pete is of him with his wide toothy smile turning back one last time to wave to us before disappearing deep into the crowd.

***

As a member of a group of war brides (six groups altogether), the one common denominator we have is that we all shared the same deck throughout our sea voyage to America. We are about to go our separate ways now, but once again, like last night, we are still not allowed to leave this ship just yet. This whole frustrating scenario is beginning to feel like some kind of torturous anticlimax. Not just to me, but to the other women in my group as well. Essentially, we are all anxiously waiting for this last obstacle to be over with so we can get with our new lives real soon. The latest news we get from our liaison officer is not what we want to hear at all. It appears we are *still* expected to endure another lengthy period of waiting around for several hours before we can even think of disembarking.

***

Finally, we are given the go-ahead to walk down the exit ramp of the SS *Monterey* at last. We manage to break free of the huge 'official' disembarking building, only to come up short against *another* obstacle on our path to freedom. I can't believe we are back in a queue again! Only this time, we are being directed to board the nearest bus, already outside waiting for us with its motor running for its next load of passengers. This bus, we are told, will take us to the San Francisco train station, for our three-day homeward journey to Chicago.

I do believe this whole massive transfer of women from ship to bus is starting to get to the organisers by now. There have been too many delays already, so they are obviously intent on getting this show on the road once and for all. Something must have clicked into place in this whole tiresome passenger-moving exercise, because no sooner do we have our bums on the bus seats, does the bus move into gear and is off down the road to the train station at long last.

After a few twists and turns on roadways we are unfamiliar with— plus the scary sensation of crashing into other vehicles, because of travelling on the 'wrong' side of the road—before we know it, we're almost onto the seven-mile-long San Francisco-Oakland Bay Bridge. Once on the bridge, I'm compelled to take one last look at the grand old lady of the sea from my bus window. This massive ship, the SS *Monterey*, that has safely brought us this far from home, will forever remain our last link to Australia and our loved ones for quite a while.

Right now, I can't help but feel another sense of sadness washing over me. Yes, I'm bound to have bouts of homesickness from time to time. *It's perfectly understandable*, I keep telling myself. But these sneaky thoughts just keep on interrupting my sense of excitement about actually being here, in the famous city of San Francisco.

Here's the thing, Isabella, there's no going back, so you had better get used to it!

Regardless of any spasmodic reservations on my part, *For better or worse, I am here to stay!*

Besides, I never want to forget the one reason why I'm here in the first place and that is my undying love for Paul. He alone is what drives me forward. He *is* my future, and he alone is the *one* reason I need to stay here. To accept this new chapter of my life.

***

The first designated train stop for the War Bride Express (as we have jokingly started to call it) en-route to Chicago is a little town on the border of California and Nevada. As our train pulls into the station, our female liaison officer, Celeste, tells us we can get off the train to walk around if we want to. Once I've stepped down from the train, I look around me with amazement. The town looks, for all the world, like it's caught up in some kind of time warp. It looks exactly as I picture a desolate one-horse scene to be, complete with a rough dirt road running all the way through the middle of the town. In fact, it looks *exactly* like one of those old cowboy movies I've watched as a child. In place of horse troughs and hitching posts, though, there is only a few old pick-up trucks and one very dusty, dirty, great big Cadillac parked in the main street.

One of the stores along the strip, I discover with delight, just happens to be a drug store. I've learnt enough about America to know they don't have chemist shops like we do in Australia. The big difference between such stores, is that the American drug stores all have soda fountains with their movie-famous, padded vinyl seats running the length of the long chrome counter. Of course, we eager Australian women just *have* to go inside to check it out. We aren't disappointed either. We don't get to taste any sodas or ice cream sundaes this time around, but we do enjoy soaking up the fun, nostalgic atmosphere anyway. It's our first introduction to Americanisation and we love it.

Back on the train, we're well taken care of when it comes to meals. We soon discover our meals are the same as on the ship. The US government has pulled out all stops to make sure we're well-fed and happy for every single day of travel. All the way to our new homes.

For our first night on our Chicago-bound train, there is a soup of the day, which is tomato soup followed by steamed vegetables and a choice of either fried chicken or fresh broiled (grilled) trout. If we prefer, instead of the steamed vegetables, we can have mashed potato or fries on the side. The long thin potato strips they call French fries are such a fun new thing for us Aussie girls, who are more familiar with the thick, chunky chips always served with fish as a takeaway treat back home.

After dinner, the rail stewards get busy making up our drop-down beds with four bunks per compartment. Just like on our Aussie trains, each compartment has a curtain to pull across the aisle windows for privacy. I don't know about the other girls, but I feel very much like a queen, all tucked up inside crisp cotton sheets. On my first night, after a hot satisfying meal right before bed, followed by a steaming hot shower, I am instantly lulled to sleep with the rhythmic motion of the train.

I wake up several times from my cosy slumber to the sleep-muffled sound of clanging bells as we pass through little towns throughout the night. When I open my eyes the next morning, I know without being told we are now in the state of Colorado. As far as the eye can see, there are endless corn fields along with some real tumbling tumbleweeds blowing across the flat, open prairies, being pushed along the rough weedy ground by deceptively lazy winds. It all looks so desperately lonely to me out in what is considered to be the old Wild West of America. For a moment, I can almost picture some lonely cowboy or even some famous Wild West outlaw travelling from town to town on horseback across this same, rather uninteresting landscape. Despite knowing the true reality of these desolate scenes in all the Western movies I've ever seen, it's still hard to believe I am seeing this all for real. As far as my eyes can see, though, there is not one cowboy in sight.

For the first few days, the other war brides and I congregate together in one of the compartments to talk about each of our lives and our families back home. We also take the time to admire all of this intriguing, constantly changing scenery along the way. One of us mentions the flashing lights and clanging bells heard every time we pass through towns and all agree, every one of us heard them too. Now, in the light of day, we are still hearing the clanging bells. It soon dawns on us that the bell and lights are a signal, so that each time we come to a crossing, a long wooden arm, parallel to the tracks with a flashing light and siren attached to it, descends automatically preventing any traffic from crossing the tracks. In

Australia, we have gates that open and close, which I learnt long ago are manually operated with levers by the local station masters from inside the station house. I can even remember a time when the gates were handled by a man on foot.

When our conductor, Sam, comes into our cabin on his morning rounds, we pounce on him. He just starts laughing, whilst moving backwards in protest, which is no doubt because of all these women, with a strange way of speaking, are asking him too many persistent questions at once. I get the feeling he doesn't mind too much, though. In fact, I think he may even be a bit flattered about being asked to inform a carriage full of Aussie women of his beloved railway system.

There is definitely a hint of national pride in his voice when Sam explains to us that there is an electrical current that runs along the tracks, called the third rail. When any train passes over this third rail, it automatically sets the stop signals in motion to prevent all traffic from passing over the railway tracks.

Another Americanisation for us to either embrace or discard, depending on where we end up with our new life choices, I suppose. For me personally, I choose to embrace these new changes, and like I said before, treat it all as one big adventure.

***

During our daylight hours, and apart from the usual routine of turning up to the dining car for each meal, we are free to amuse ourselves in whatever way we chose. To stretch our legs and to pass the time of day, most of us like to walk from one end of the train to the other. We have also taken to stopping off at the dining carriage for a cup of coffee and a chat too.

The only other significant break on our train journey across the various states is when our train comes to a station stop on our second day of travel. Some of the girls race to the window of the carriage. The girls on the station-side of our train love to observe each train as they come to a stop at the other platforms closest to us. At one station, the girls continue to watch the other trains load and unload their passengers, but are suddenly very excited when the next train that pulls in is filled with US sailors, all resplendent in their dazzling white uniforms. Some of our Aussie girls begin waving madly to them. They keep doing this from afar, until one of the girls spontaneously yells to the others, 'Let's go!'

Without any further prompting, off they run. One of the girls, Barbara, stops in the aisle by my seat to ask me if I would mind watching her three-year-old boy, Danny, for a little while. He is such a cute little boy, so I am more than happy to play with him while his mother is gone. However, our liaison officer wastes no time in ordering the excited women back onboard, warning them one more time, there is to be no fraternising with these sailors either. It's not like we didn't already know this, since we had been warned about this rule often enough right from the beginning of our ocean voyage.

This rule is reinforced for good reason too, I believe. We had several male liaison officers onboard the ship to provide meals for us, clean our cabins, and of course, keep the ship spotless, but they must be lonely enough to want to seek out female company sometimes. It's not hard for me to imagine their libidos becoming quickly aroused by these equally lonely women, sorely missing the amorous attentions of their absent husbands. All too soon, these new war brides are about to become full-time wives and mothers again. I guess they figure a little harmless flirting isn't going to hurt anyone.

I don't tend to go along with this kind of thinking at all, but I don't think it's my business to voice my thoughts on this matter to the other women. Each to her own, I guess.

To my reasoning, such actions aren't really a harmless thing at all. Any kind of so-called innocuous flirting has a hidden, dangerous element to it, by enticing an already restless soul into doing something impulsive or downright foolish in the end. No thanks!

***

Judging by the constantly changing landscape outside my train window, we've now reached the sprawling metropolis of Chicago. That's if the increase of congested traffic choking the inroads, as well as hundreds of people crowded in and around the tall skyscrapers impressively towering over the beating heart of the city, is any indication.

These obvious signs of our final approach to Chicago Union Station is warning enough for me to check my suitcase and carry-on bag one last time, to make absolutely sure I have gathered everything together that belongs only to me. I don't fancy having to return to the city later because I've left something behind, or worse, have taken somebody's bag by mistake.

As the train enters Union Station, my inner voice attempts to undermine my confidence. *So, this is it, Bell!* There is no turning back now. Once I step off this train, regardless of whether or not Paul is waiting, my life is about to change forever. That's a whole new world out there, after all.

I ask myself, am I really ready to embrace it, or would I rather take a flight away from here and head back home to Australia? What will it be?

Well, I'm here now, and for better or worse, I really need to be with my husband again.

27

Isabella

Mid 1946
Chicago is my new kind of town

Our train comes to a complete stop late in the afternoon of our third day of travel by rail.

The last time I saw my husband was just before he was sent back to the Pacific Islands three weeks after his unplanned hospital stay in Melbourne. This unavoidable fact is starting to hit home to me once again; Paul is still practically a stranger to me!

After all—when I stop to think about it—we really had only spent one week together when we first met, then there was the one week we spent together before our wedding, an impossibly short three days of our honeymoon, then another few weeks when he ended up in hospital right after our honeymoon. While the war raged on in the Pacific, we still kept in touch with our handwritten letters, of course, which was the only way we were able to communicate during this time away from each other. Our loving letters inevitably became our most important links for each of us to cling to.

During my last day of train journey across the United States—from San Francisco to Chicago—I desperately yearn for some solitary space on the train for an hour or two. Even though I have become quite close to a particular group of women onboard, a part of me still craves some *me* time alone. I have to acknowledge that I desperately need to work through my own private, niggling thoughts. In my own way and in my own time. This is the way my mind works. One issue I definitely need to come to terms with is my inner apprehension over my imminent reunion with my husband.

As I stare out over this new foreign landscape, so deep are my troubled thoughts throughout this final leg of my rail journey, that I could just as well be looking out at the most majestic mountain ranges, the most spectacular painted desert sunsets or the wide, fast-flowing rivers of inland USA, and not even see them at all. Regardless, deep down, I know, whatever roads I take in the future, hopefully they will all lead back into the loving arms of my darling husband at last. My biggest question to myself now is how will we react to each other when I do finally step down from this train? I have travelled ten thousand miles to be with my man, but at the end of my journey, what will be the sum of our *real* feelings for each other? Is Paul experiencing the same doubts and fears as I am right now? I'd give anything to know what he's thinking at this very moment. Up until our rushed marriage in Melbourne at least, Paul had been a carefree bachelor of sorts. Will he resent his loss of freedom with a new wife to support and care for? I'm only too aware of the obvious adjustments ahead of us on a daily basis and eventually on a long-term basis. How will we even survive this first week together as a married couple, let alone many years from now?

Our wartime romance never allowed for much discussion about his American family either. It suddenly dawns on me; I know very little about his own family. Apart from the fact that both of his parents are still living, he has two sisters and a younger brother, we never really got around to discussing them at all. How could we have allowed this to happen in the first place? Will they immediately accept me into the family, or will it take them years to even get used to having me around? Could our marriage be based more on infatuation than true love after all? I must admit, what initially attracted me to Paul in the first place was the way he looked so handsome in his military uniform. Not only that, but he's so very clever too. He can fly an aeroplane and has been a radio operator in the army. Why, he even knows how to send messages by Morse code! I don't personally know of anyone else who can do that. Oh my, he can even play the piano beautifully too! I have never met a man like him before. These past few years without him, I have clung so steadfast to these special memories of Paul, which I faithfully keep close to my heart at all times.

I know I am essentially only an office girl, but I feel confident enough to know I am still proud of what I *am* able to do at whatever job I take on. I'm also good at other things too such as sport, especially tennis. *AND* I've always had an unquenchable thirst for learning most new things quickly as well. I just hope our combined talents and interests will be enough to keep our marriage alive and a continual interest in each other for years to come.

Paul swept me off my feet so easily right at the very beginning of our love story, but then again, I wasn't alone there. After all, being caught up in this particular period of history, everything seemed so surreal at times. Especially for the men and women who have had to go off to fight a major war in some unfamiliar foreign land. Most people that I know, have had to learn very quickly to live life day by day and any happiness found, is indeed something to hold onto, no matter how fleeting the promises of love may be. Listening to other war brides, like myself, on the train, I realise by now I am most definitely not the only one to be experiencing these profound moments of sheer panic.

Another interesting thought just popped into my head. It will be Paul the civilian I'll be meeting at the station this time. *Oh dear! Will I even recognise him out of uniform?*

***

As the train runs through the tunnel leading into the station, my heart continues its loud thumping in my ears, but under the overhead cover of the station platform, its beats have increased tenfold once the train comes to a complete stop. As I step down onto the platform with my suitcase in hand, my eyes anxiously search the crowds for Paul, not realising he is already right there in front of me, smiling that same handsome smile I remember from the very first day I ever saw him.

Well, he appears to be happy to see me at least, and his first words to me are like a soothing balm applied directly to my troubled soul, 'Hey, beautiful! Remember me?' before opening his arms wide to welcome me into them.

I leap into his open arms with happy tears in my eyes. 'Oh, Paul! I've made it. I'm really here!'

We kiss with happy abandonment, not really caring about who is watching us. It's like our two separate hearts are one complete unit again. I truly am back where I belong, with all of my niggling doubts about our reunion instantly dispersing into a puff of nothingness. Paul is my *future*, and the future is ours to do whatever we want to dream up together.

'Shall we go? Let us leave these crushing crowds behind, my darling Isabella. We have a *lot* of catching up to do ... In more ways than one, wouldn't you agree, Mrs Meier?'

'You have me completely in the palms of your hands, Mr Meier! Where you go, I go. It's even more wonderful to know we have the rest of our whole lives to do just that.'

***

For our first night together, we head into downtown Chicago where Paul has reserved a room for us at a lovely hotel on Michigan Avenue. After checking in, we drop off my luggage to be in time for an early dinner at a very popular restaurant called the Hoffbrau. As soon as we enter the Austrian restaurant, I embrace the first whiff of delightful smells all around me and suddenly realise just how famished I am. Since early this morning, I have been so churned up inside I couldn't even look at food on the train, let alone digest it.

The atmosphere of the Hoffbrau is so very charming and the Austrian waitstaff never stop smiling. They can't seem to do enough for their new customers either. When the waiter comes over to our table, we order breaded veal cutlets and two glasses of beer. I find it hard to believe I used to hate beer, but after guzzling down that delicious ice-cold drink in that tiny gear locker onboard the SS *Monterey*, I happily accept as I have now acquired a whole new appreciation for a timeless, frothy beverage.

Paul and I talk pretty much nonstop throughout our meal, in-between mouthfuls of beer, veal cutlets with creamy mashed potato, steamed greens and honeyed carrots. At the time of deciding what to order for dinner, Paul thought I might enjoy the veal cutlets. I didn't really understand exactly what they were, but I trusted Paul's choice and he doesn't let me down. Delightfully, I soon realise breaded cutlets in America are almost exactly the same as our crumbed cutlets in Australia. It's the first time I've ever tried veal, though, and now I love it almost as much as my mum's lamb version.

During our meal, a roving photographer comes over to our table and asks us if we would like to have our photograph taken. Of course, we say yes. One day, I can well imagine this photo in a pretty frame, taking pride of place on top of a piano in our new home, capturing our reunion, marking the start of the rest of our lives together.

Upon leaving the restaurant, with our bellies full and completely satisfied, we stroll along Michigan Avenue for a while to walk off all the food and beer we stuffed into our tummies. I immediately fall in love with Chicago. I especially love the beautifully sculptured historical buildings which tower over us. But not in an intimidating way. Openly gaping and oohing and ahhing at all of the magnificent architectural city buildings towering over us, I am suddenly very much aware of all of the infamous history attached to Chicago, right from its unique conception. Despite Hollywood's portrayal of gangsters in drive-by shootings in the streets of Chicago, it all looks so perfectly normal and inspiring to me. The people

I'm meeting in Chicago so far are all so friendly and openly warm to us, as we casually stroll along their city streets.

I can't help but notice that every one of the people who pass by us are so stylishly dressed without even trying to stand out. High-top fashion never looks as good or so naturally put together as it does in Chicago. This not only goes for the women in their exquisitely styled outfits, but also the tall, dapper men in their stylish suits.

After an hour or so of wandering around the brightly illuminated city streets, we don't waste any more time in heading back to our hotel room. After all, we do have a *lot* of loving to catch up on. Of course, there will be a lot more talk of our future, our families or even our own untold personal experiences from the past few years or so. But not until tomorrow's dawn light comes around.

Tomorrow will take care of itself. We're young and in love, after all, with so many possibilities for us to grab and hold onto, as our new tomorrows stretch out in front of us. With passionate and heartfelt fervour, we openly declare to each other we will always be an unbreakable team together and ready to face whatever the future holds for us, come what may. But for now, there is another kind of love we wish to pursue passionately throughout this coming night and most definitely into the wee hours of the morning.

Just like our very first night together, Paul still looks at me in that same desirable way. He still undresses me with that same cheeky eyebrow-raising glint in his eye. He even kisses me and touches my body in the same pleasurable way as before, but somehow our loving is distinctly *different* now. There is a deeper love much more evident this time, binding us together within an intangible bond. Unbreakable against all odds—we sure hope so, anyway. We both know only too well by now, any promises of tomorrow can never be guaranteed. We're not only joined by the bonds of marriage and our willing bodies, but I'm also convinced it's the deep, infinite facets of our love that binds us, where we cease to be separate people.

28

Isabella

Mid 1946
New home, new in-laws

W e check out of our hotel just before midday the following day, all blissfully happy and totally relaxed. Most of all, both our bodies and our souls are completely revived by now after our night of loving. Our spirits armed too with a new resolve to take in our stride whatever comes our way.

Little did we know how much we would need it. Sooner than anticipated, I might add.

Our route out of Chicago is via North Avenue, which Paul informs me is really the only way west. This is as far as we need to go today, anyway.

Before we exit North Avenue, Paul points out the small airport where he used to take flying lessons before the war and where he gained his pilot's licence. I can tell straight away, he is very proud of this particular skill by the tone of his voice.

'When I was growing up in Chicago,' he starts to tell me. 'I had this passion for aeroplanes. Still do. Every spare cent I made from the odd jobs I had back then, I'd spend on model plane kits. My most favourite thing to do as a young boy was to take my completed model planes out onto an empty playing field somewhere to watch most of them crash and burn because of my lack of experience to start with. Later, after a lot more experimenting with structures and glues, I eventually had more successes than failures. I just loved to watch them soar way up high into the clear blue sky for hours on end.'

***

We have finally reached our destination of Villa Park. Travelling along Washington Boulevard, the main avenue leading us directly to Paul's family home, I am completely captivated by the look of this whole area. The huge elm trees on either side of the street have grown so high over the years that the branches seem to fully embrace each other overhead, creating an enchanting cathedral effect.

At last, we are at home! Well, Paul's parents' home, anyway.

'So, we're going to be living with your parents, then, Paul?' I ask him, somehow dreading the answer since I'm not entirely sure about such an idea in the first place. *What if they don't like me?*

'Yes, we *will* be living at this address for a while, but I can promise you, honey, we won't *actually* be living *inside* the same house as my parents. Unfortunately, Isabella, most apartments have become impossible to find after the war. Something I hadn't counted on when first making plans as to where we can live. I hope you don't mind, darling, but I ended up purchasing us a large trailer a few weeks ago for us to live in. I assure you, though, this trailer is only meant to be temporary fix for about a year at this stage. Well, until we find our own apartment, anyway.'

I'm looking at the front of the house now and to each side of it, but I'm somewhat confused. 'So where is the trailer, Paul? I can't see it anywhere.'

'It's parked out back. Behind the house for more privacy.'

'Are you happy with your decision to buy the trailer?' I ask tentatively. 'Do you think maybe your parents won't want me living in the house with them for too long?'

'It's not that, honey. I just honestly don't think it's such a good idea for me to live in the same house as my parents anymore—especially now that I am a grown man *and* married. No, that's not going to happen! Not

254

even for one night.'

I am immediately so touched by Paul's thoughtfulness and for him to consider my feelings in this way. Besides, I don't wish to disrupt his parents' daily routine if I can help it.

***

I soon find out for myself just how considerate Paul really is in regard to his mother. He knows all too well she isn't the easiest person to get along with *at all!* (In fact, that's the understatement of the year!) *Plus*, his father had suffered a nervous breakdown years before, so in a nutshell—even before I arrived here—my new father-in-law had made it very clear to his son that he didn't want me around too much either. *Little did I know—before even stepping inside his parents' place—I was off to a shaky start already!*

***

By the time we've pulled into the front driveway, I must admit I am feeling more than a little nervous. It doesn't reassure me one bit to realise his parents are already sitting out on the front porch watching us approach. They don't even get up to greet us, but just continue to sit there and study me with deep frowns on their faces, making me feel like some tiny insect under a microscope. Their unwillingness to come forward to greet me certainly doesn't make me feel even the slightest bit welcome.

My intuition tells me that by making me come to them instead, this is merely their own sneaky, intimidating way of keeping me at a distance.

Until they get to know me a little better, perhaps? At least I hope this is the real reason, instead of them not wanting me to be here at all.

As soon as Paul removes my luggage from the back seat of the car, he grabs my hand and squeezes it gently. I realise this is his own quiet way of letting me know he understands how intimidated I must be feeling right now. Especially with such a cold reception from his folks. I squeeze his hand back and give him a brave smile. If only to reassure him I'm okay, before we head up the front porch steps together. We're still a united front at least.

255

Still holding my hand, Paul steps forward with a calm look of confidence that I mentally applaud him for.

'Mom, Dad, I'd like you to meet my wife, Isabella.'

Both his parents remain seated and it's perfectly obvious to me no welcome kiss or hug will be forthcoming any time soon.

'Mornin' … So, did you have a good trip, then?' Paul's father is the first to speak, but his mother remains tight-lipped and just keeps right on trying to stare me down. His father at least stands up to greet me. 'You've certainly come a long way, haven't you? It's Hans, by the way. Welcome to the family!'

'Thank you! I'm so happy to finally meet you, Hans.' I move cautiously forward now and give him what I hope will be considered the friendly hug it's meant to be. 'Yes, I did have a marvellous trip, thank you. The US government have looked after me very well, all the way from my home city of Melbourne, Australia, to your beautiful city of Chicago.'

It seems his father is only able to offer me a gruff acknowledgement for now, but I do manage to win a smile from him at least. I can see for myself now who Paul has inherited his stocky build from, along with his lighter skin and his same reddish brown hair. Hans is undoubtably a more mature version of Paul. Same hazel eyes too, I notice.

Paul's mother still hasn't offered any greetings yet, so to break the ice, I speak to her first. 'Hello! I'm Isabella and it's just so lovely to meet you at last, Mrs Meier.'

By way of response, his mother grudgingly offers me a few reluctant spoken words, ever so gruffly, I might add. 'Mornin! … So, you're *finally* here. You sure took long enough.'

She's not even going to tell me her name or even invite me to call her anything but Mrs Meier I suppose! Heaven forbid! Why does she even bother to acknowledge me at all?

Even with her sitting down, I can tell his mother appears to be much shorter in height than her husband or her son. I can also tell she has a fuller, mature woman's figure, very much like my own mother. Especially after many years of birthing four or more children each. Her face is very weathered, and I can already tell this frown she chooses to perfect for my arrival portrays a rather dour disposition that would scare most people away. When I hear of her life's story much later, though, I can certainly understand why. I already know from Paul she's has had more than her fair share of tough challenges that most people wouldn't be able to cope with. But for now, my first impression of my new mother-in-law isn't a favourable one. *It's is only my first day here too!*

I am soon to learn she wears *all* of her misery on her face, *most* of the time. To say she is intimidating is an understatement. I quickly realise, with much dismay, it's probably going to take a *lot* longer than I initially thought it would to win my mother-in-law over, into accepting me into *her* family, that's for sure!

'Did you say your name was Isabella? … That's more of an Italian name, isn't it? But you're Australian! Why then, would your parents give you an Italian name when you come from Australia?'

'My mother told me a few times, Mrs Meier, that she and my father really loved the name Isabella after her midwife suggested it at my birth. As for Australia, even though it's called an island continent, it really is quite a big country, populated by people from all over the world. Just like in the United States, we have *lots* of Italians living in Australia too.' I try to enlighten her about my home country in a friendly way, but the gruff 'hmmph!' is not reassuring me one little bit!

She does however finish up with, 'By the way, you can call me Erika if you like.' But there will obviously be no welcoming hug included. She just stays seated the whole time and continues to throw me these suspicious furtive looks, which are no doubt meant to keep me in my place. At least until she's ready to drop her guard with me I suppose—*if* she ever does.

Paul and I chat away lightly with his parents for a little while—touching on only *safe* subjects, such as the summer weather due any day now.

But when the talk suddenly turns to the elections running towards the end of the year, Paul decides it's time to make a quick exit.

'Mom, Dad, if you will excuse us for a little while, I want to settle Isabella into our new home and give her a chance to make a start on unpacking her suitcase before supper.'

'Fine, son, go ahead, then,' Erika agrees, as she heaves herself up from her porch chair with a grunt. 'While you're doing that, I'll see about putting a meal together for us. I suppose we'll need to buy more food, since we have an extra mouth to feed now.' As she says this, she makes a point of directing a sly look my way. It's only too obvious she really does resent me being here, but I've already decided I'm not going to let her get to me.

'Thank you, Erika. Thank you, Hans. I just want you both to know that I'm very happy to be here and I'm sure we'll all get along just fine, once we get to know each other better.'

As we walk away, I can't help but hear Erika mumble to Hans, 'Well, I'm not so sure about that. But we shall see, Hans … we shall see.'

He replies, 'Come on, Erika. Don't be like that. Give the girl a break *please.*'

By the time Paul and I reach the trailer parked just beyond the rough wooden clothesline, I am trying very hard to hold back my tears. I expected his parents to be a little hesitant about Paul marrying a foreigner, but even at this early stage of being here, Paul's mother's comments have the vindictive power—as she intends, no doubt—to completely throw me off guard. *So much for trying to maintain a positive outlook in the face of fierce opposition.*

***

Once we're inside the trailer and have closed the door, Paul pulls me gently into his arms. 'Don't take any notice of my mother, Isabella,' Paul offers me by way of apology for his mother's gruff behaviour. 'I know she can be so damn intimidating at times.'

'She really hates me, Paul!' I sniffle into my hanky.

Paul takes the hanky out of my hand now and gently wipes away the tears I can no longer hold back. Soon I'm sobbing into his shoulder, still very much in shock.

'I promise you she doesn't hate you, Isabella. Believe it or not, she isn't always *this* bad. When it comes to sharing her home with *any* stranger, she is usually guarded anyway. You have to remember, honey, that's exactly what you are to her at this stage—a stranger. Please just know that it's not about you at all, really. Like I said, Mom can be like this with anyone, at any time. Even with people she has known for years.' Paul pulls me in even closer to him and gently rubs my back. 'I just know that in time, she'll come to know the sweet, caring, funny woman I already know you to be, which of course, is the reason why I fell in love with you in the first place.'

'Thank you, darling!' I sniff a few more times into my hanky. 'It does help to hear you say this, and I'm sure in time, we might at least be friends. But I fear your mother accepting me as her daughter-in-law may take a little longer!'

We look into each other's eyes now and burst out laughing.

'When all else fails, we still have our sense of humour to fall back on,' Paul adds, before turning me around to take a look at our new home for the next year or so.

'What do you think? Will you mind living out in this trailer with me for a short while? I promise you, honey, that by this time next year, I will have found us a place we can call our own. I know Mother can be really difficult to live with, but if we keep in mind it's only going to be for a little while, we can manage. I feel sure that over the next few weeks we can all learn to get along with each other *somehow* ... right?'

'As long as I have you here beside me, I know I can get through anything.'

I kiss him again to seal the deal, before turning to take a closer look around the trailer's compact interior. There is a double bed at one end, and from where we are standing, I can see some generous storage space along both sides of our bed. On the left, there is a small built-in alcove, complete with a radio, portable record player and a stack of LP records. At the other end of the trailer is a well laid out, compact kitchen area, with a gas hotplate and compact oven below it, along with an equally compact refrigerator conveniently positioned alongside the stove, as well as a small benchtop area to prepare our meals. I'm happy to hear from Paul that the fold-out table and L-shaped seating area right beside me quickly converts into an extra bed if needed as well. There is even some cheery, yellow chequered cafe-style curtains at the kitchen end of the trailer, and some plain, but thicker, white curtains covering the window above our bed.

The only thing the trailer doesn't have is a toilet, but Paul quickly reassures me there is a toilet in the basement of the house for our use. Same goes for the laundry. *This should be interesting,* I think to myself, *fitting in with Erika's regular laundry routine could become just one more treacherous challenge for me to deal with on a daily basis.*

'The inside of our trailer looks so cosy, Paul. So romantic too; we can certainly make good use of the bed every night!' I arch my eyebrow a few times to back up my cheeky innuendo.

'Uh-oh! What have I got myself into with you? What a saucy wench you've turned out to be! I love you for being this way though … So, tell me honestly, darling. Do you really do like our new home?'

'Oh, Paul! Honestly, with all jokes aside, I just love it! I really do!'

'Great! Because if you're happy, I'm happy. You ready for some supper now? I don't know about you, but I'm starving! Let's go!' Paul declares as he opens our only trailer door.

As I follow him out of the trailer, I know in my heart I'll always be willing to follow him anywhere he plans to go in the future. *Even to his mother's house for lunch!*

My resolve to fit in with my new family is back in its rightful place.

Regardless of the less-than-welcoming reception from his parents earlier, I know that come what may, I'm still here to stay.

***

I'm too nervous to take note of *exactly* what is served for my first meal with my in-laws, I do recall Erika asking me if I like cottage cheese and I *think* I answered yes. Even if I've never tried it before, there is no way I'm going to say otherwise. After all, I've always loved all kinds of cheeses, so I'm sure I'll probably love cottage cheese too. There may have been some cold cuts served, but with me being so nervous the whole time, I just can't seem to remember.

After tasting the cottage cheese, I decide I'm not so impressed after all. It must be the blandest cheese I have ever tasted in my life, but I decide not to let onto anyone about it. Not even Paul. So I try to eat it anyway, but when I try to force it down, it sticks to the roof of my mouth as I try hard not to gag. When Paul asks me if I'm enjoying my meal, I somehow manage to gulp down my last mouthful without choking on my answer. 'Mmm! It's all so delicious!' I shamelessly lie with a smile on my face.

After supper, which Paul and his parents call their evening meal, I help Erika clear the table and stack the dishes beside the sink. The layout of Erika's kitchen is obviously all about practical workspace. Practical, yes, and totally devoid of any colour as a result. The one and only colour I can see, as I glance discreetly around the room, is the depressing shade of brown on every surface and every wall there is to be seen. To me, brown is not a colour at all really, but I suppose to Erika's way of thinking, her kitchen *does* have a no-nonsense look about it. She keeps it spotless too. There is not a thing out of place either. Nor could I imagine there would be—*ever!*

I start to fill the sink with hot water, then ask Erika for some dish-washing soap.

'Don't worry about it, girlie. Since this is your first night here, I have a mind to let you off any kitchen duty for tonight at least.' Erika tries to sound gruff, but I can tell it's her own way of showing some kindness to me after all. I can't help but feel both grateful and relieved, since I've been secretly dreading helping her in the kitchen. I fear my nervousness might result in me breaking one of her best plates or something. I can breathe a little easier knowing I'm off the hook with trying too hard to please my in-laws. For tonight anyway.

Being a warm spring evening, Hans, Erika, Paul and I move out onto the front porch, which to me, isn't much of a porch at all. I never took much notice of the entrance to the house when I first arrived, but I take it all in now. There is a small closed-in room just beyond the entrance and the steps leading up to the front porch. This is obviously where Hans and Erika like to sit on their comfy chairs after supper. The fact that I didn't even notice this room when we arrived earlier today reminds me of just how nervous I must have been at the time. I finally feel relaxed enough now to take in my new surroundings at a much more leisurely pace. This little room has windows along two sides, with each window fully open now to catch the night breeze. Paul prompts me to take a seat beside him in one of the comfy-looking overstuffed armchairs, just waiting for someone to sink into them. To complete this room as being a favourite family space for summer evenings, a chunky, timeworn, scratched wood coffee table for drinks and treats is positioned perfectly in front of us. Every chair in this room, including mine, is facing out towards the street, obviously to watch life and neighbours pass them by, from their own little domain of domestic bliss.

It's such a pleasant thing to be out here in the gathering twilight. So much so, I'm content enough to want to stay out here for however long this evening ritual is meant to last.

As soon as I sit down, I start to feel this strong need to plant my feet firmly on solid ground, however foreign this soil might be. In response to my new optimism, I take in one deep contented breath to fully relax my whole body. Instead of the sweet smell of fresh cut grass, or maybe even some pleasant whiff of nearby blossoms in the garden, my inner peace is shattered by the pungent whiff of cigarette smoke working its way over toward me.

I've been so completely caught up in my own thoughts for a few precious moments, I failed to notice Erika light up a cigarette right beside me. She doesn't even seem to notice the smoke from her cigarette is blowing directly into my face. On second thought, maybe she *does* realise, but deliberately chooses to ignore it. Maybe it's her own sneaky way of putting me in my place yet again. I'm not quite sure.

Slowly, bit by bit, I manage to reposition my chair—without being too obvious about it—so I can effectively face away from the full force of her cigarette smoke. I'll just have to make a mental note to move further along the row of chairs next time. Maybe once Erika realises I'm not going to react to her intimidation tactics, she might give up. I don't like my chances, though.

Hans has brought a bottle of beer and four tumblers out onto the porch with him. He starts to pour the beer, but stops before pouring the fourth one.

'Sorry, Isabella, I forgot to ask. Do you like beer? We have lemonade if you prefer it?'

'No, I wouldn't mind a glass of beer, thanks, Hans.'

'Here you go, then!' he says as I reach over to take the glass from him. Judging by the look on his face, he's probably a bit surprised I even drink alcohol at all. It obviously pleases him to know I'm not one of those posh ladies who only sips wine to be sociable.

As I sink deeper into the back of my chair, I allow myself to slowly savour the chilled amber liquid with a deep satisfying sigh.

'So you really do like American beer, then, Isabella?' Paul asks with his fingers subtly running these little tingly circles on my shoulder.

'American beer is the *only* beer I have ever tasted so far. I did try some Hawaiian beer onboard the ship, but really, it is still considered to be American beer, isn't it? ... Oh, and the beer we had last night in Chicago, of course. To tell you the truth, apart from my brothers home brew, I haven't tried any commercial Australian beer yet. What I do know about Australian commercial beer, though, is that's well-known for it's strong flavour … Is that right?'

'Yes, it sure is!' Paul agrees with me. 'I did try some English beer at a pub in Melbourne, and to me, it was even stronger than the most popular beers on tap here in the USA. What I didn't appreciate about the English beer, though—especially their Guinness—was that it's always served at room temperature. This kind of beer might suit their quaint little pubs in jolly old chilly England, but not here in the US and definitely not in Australia.'

While Hans, Paul and I continue to explore the subject of different beers around the world, I just happen to glance over at Erika. I don't even know what made me suddenly look her way, but I couldn't help noticing she has suddenly turned quiet. She certainly doesn't seem to be interested in the merits of any beer at all. (Not that I blame her, really). She just sits there, smoking her cigarette, staring out with watchful eyes beyond her front porch into her neighbourhood.

When Paul asks her what she thinks about drinking any brand of beer, Erika merely shrugs her shoulders and replies, 'To tell you the truth, son, I don't care what brand of beer I drink, as long as it's cold and wet. End of story.'

'I'm with Erika on that one,' Hans chuckles as he gulps down a few more mouthfuls.

Erika lights up another cigarette, then deftly changes the subject to politics. She certainly has a *lot* to say on this subject. Before long, she, Hans and Paul are in a heated conversation about the terrible state of the country and the economy. Erika seems to take great delight in berating the present government, the irresponsible people running it and how corrupt these very same politician are. To Erika, they wantonly hand out money to various foreign countries, all at a cost to the American taxpayer. She is probably right too, but I am still surprised just the same. As I listen to

Erika rant on and on, I can't help but compare her to my own mother. My father enjoys an occasional glass of beer, but not my mother. I could never imagine my mother ever smoking a cigarette either. As for talking politics, not a chance! She is always such a lady and I love her and appreciate her or the more for it, even more now.

All I can wonder at this point is what have I got myself into here and how will I ever learn to get along with my new mother-in-law? It's all a complete mystery to me right now.

From where I am sitting, my focus is suddenly diverted to a large open area across the street. There's a parallel row of grape vines growing along the wire netting fences. Once the sky has turned really dark, a myriad of tiny twinkling lights seem to peek out shyly through the vines.

What on Earth? Am I seeing things? I quickly grab Paul's arm to get his attention. 'Paul! What are those lights over there? There are hundreds of them!'

'They're fireflies,' Paul explains. 'Also known as lightning bugs. I gather you don't have them in Australia?'

'Well, if we do, I've never seen them for myself. How absolutely fascinating!' They are just so magical and I can't take my eyes off them. If this kind of natural wonder is supposed to be a regular occurrence throughout the summers here, then I will look forward to lots of future evenings, when these tiny creatures make their timely delightful appearance again.

A yawn escapes me, which Paul immediately notices and stands up. 'Mom, Dad, I think I should take this poor tired girl of mine off to bed.'

He holds his hand out to me, to pull me away from my much-too-comfortable chair, but to my dismay, my body refuses to budge.

'What's happening, Paul?' I laugh. 'I swear this chair is conspiring against me. It's almost like it just wants to keep me rooted to this very spot for the rest of the night. I'm so relaxed, I can hardly move.'

'Understandable, honey. It's been a big day for you and I'm more than ready for bed as well … Let's go, shall we?'

When I finally do get up to leave, I make sure I turn to my in-laws to bid them goodnight. 'Erika, Hans, thank you so much for such an enjoyable time tonight, but I think I am completely done in. I shall talk to you both in the morning. Goodnight!' I lean down to peck Erika on the cheek, but she predictably pulls away at the last minute. All I get is a gruff 'Night!' instead.

I soon realise, that to even expect a goodnight hug from Erika so soon, is really pushing my luck. Hans surprises me, though, with a quick hug which I am more than happy to settle for. One out of two is a still positive sign, and for now, I can live with that.

Paul leads me gently along the driveway running alongside the house towards our trailer. He takes the precaution of guiding us with a flashlight (or torch, as I know it), to make sure we don't trip on any unseen obstacles along the way. When I'm sure we're out of earshot, I whisper to Paul, 'In the morning and before we have breakfast with your parents, I want you to do me a favour, please, darling.'

'Sure! What kind of favour would that be, sweetheart?'

'I want you to tell me what has happened to your mother in her life, that can help me understand why she acts so miserable all the time. Something really bad must have happened to make her act this way. Especially the way she was with me today ... I mean, I'm right, aren't I? I can sense it so strongly.'

'Yes you're right, Isabella. Life certainly has dealt her a hard blow. She's had to deal with more than her fair share of heartache. More than most people could ever possibly comprehend. But I promise to tell you as much as I can tomorrow. Fair enough? In the meantime, our bed is beckoning.'

'Thank you! In order for me to get along with your mother in the future, Paul, I need to understand her better *now*.'

Once I've taken my first step up into our trailer, I spot the bed and immediately throw myself onto it with sleepy abandonment, still in the clothes I changed into before dinner. 'Mmmm! This bed feels so good and I feel so tired! I'll just lie here for a few minutes if that's alright,' I mumble into the pillow.

'That's probably not a good idea, darling. You really should get under the covers and settle in for the night. When I come back from watering a tree outside, I'll help you to settle in ... Okay?'

'Sure thing. You'd better hurry back, though!' When Paul does return, he has no choice but to slide me over to my side of the bed, to try and find some space for himself.

It probably won't be the first time he will have to move over for me, when I stretch out over onto his side of the bed. After all, up until now I've been used to a single bed.

29

Isabella

Mid 1946
Beyond outward appearances

'I tell you, sweetheart, you were out like a light last night. By the time I'd come back from watering the bushes outside our trailer, you were out for the count.' Paul laughs as he nuzzles in closer to my neck. 'I had to try and steal back some of the bedcovers you insisted on hogging.'

'I can't believe I fell asleep so fast. It must have been the beer that did me in.'

'Would you like some coffee? I have some already brewing for us.'

'That would be wonderful, darling! I must admit, it's most unusual for me to drink coffee first thing in the morning. I've always been a tea drinker, but I'm sure I'll eventually come to enjoy your American coffee just as much.'

'How about we steal some of Mother's tea bags? We'll smuggle them out of her kitchen, then bring them back here to the trailer later? Then you'll have a choice of both.'

'Sounds good! Speaking of your mother, you promised to tell me more about her this morning and I'm holding you to that promise, Paul.'

'Only if you can offer me another kind of promise of your own later … If you get my drift?'

'I definitely do get your drift. As if you even need to ask. I'm thinking we might have to take a rain check on that side of things right now, though. We don't want your parents catching us unawares, do we? Heaven forbid! Then we'll have to explain to them, like two naughty children, why we're late for breakfast.'

'Smart thinking! I'll pour the coffee. Then we'll talk.'

***

'My mother was seven years old when she and my uncle, her younger brother who was four at the time, were left at an orphanage by my German grandmother. She herself had been abandoned by her own mother at birth, and then later by her husband—my maternal grandfather. With my German grandmother struggling on her own, she soon had to accept there was no way she could financially support her two young children anymore. Mom's little brother unfortunately died soon after being placed in the orphanage. Most likely due to loneliness and abandonment. For seven years, Mom endured a loveless life, of a strict daily regimen with no affection whatsoever. Often so inwardly lonely, she desperately hoped every day her mother would return to take her back home. Her wish did come true eventually, but not in a good way. As soon as Mom reached fourteen—the age when orphan children are often sent out to work—my grandmother *did* return to the orphanage one morning to reclaim her daughter. If Mom was expecting life with her mother to suddenly improve, she was sadly mistaken. Grandmother Shaufe wasted no time in telling her she was now expected to earn her keep and help pay the bills. There would be no free ride for her daughter and definitely no chance of any innocent childhood.

'When my mother was just twenty-four years old, she met my father. Even though he was thirty-one at the time, my father was still living with his mother, a very dour German woman by nature. After Grandfather Meier passed away years before, my grandmother—as a matter of necessity—soon learnt to rely on her son entirely for financial support. My father's well-paid position as an insurance adjustor kept the two of them quite comfortable for many years. Until he met my mother, that is.

'My father was raised as a strict Catholic, but as far as I know, Mom had never received any religious instruction throughout her childhood at the orphanage. Nor with her own mother. They must have seemed like an odd couple when my parents first met, but they fell in love anyway. After just one year of meeting each other, they were married—much to the chagrin of my grandmother. Now that her son had a new wife to support, she knew her financial security was in jeopardy. From that point onwards and for the rest of her miserable life, Grandmother Meier had very little time for her only daughter-in-law.'

'Oh my! That must have been so devastating for your mother at the time. Your poor mother! How is anyone ever supposed to get over something like that, Paul?'

Paul continued on, 'When Mom and Dad started their family, I was their firstborn, and as I told you back in Melbourne, my two sisters followed, then last but not least, my little brother Benny.

'Sadly—as if my mother hadn't had enough challenges in her life—Benny was born with severe brain damage, and even after endless medical tests were carried out, the doctor informed my parents that Benny had contracted an infection while still in the womb. So, for the whole of his life, my little brother has been totally dependent on our family for *everything*. The day-to-day physical care for Benny was mostly Mom's responsibility, of course. Benny has no control of his bodily functions at all, he has to wear diapers all the time. If this wasn't enough of a daily challenge for my mother, he also had to be fed, bathed, clothed, propped up and be amused by all his family at any time of the day. Since he is also unable to walk, it was always left up to Mom to lug him around from room to room by herself, while us kids were away at school during the day or Dad was at work.'

'So where is Benny now?' I ask Paul, totally puzzled by his absence.

'In a government-run institution, set up not far from here for others just like Benny, who also have special needs. The idea for this place was originally suggested to Mom by a neighbour and close friend, after she learned you were already onboard the ship and on your way here. This friend, Marion Stephens, convinced Mom in the end, it really would be for the best. After all, she suggested, her new daughter-in-law might not be able to accept Benny the way that he is.'

'Oh dear! So that means your mother must be blaming me entirely for having to put Benny into that place away from his family then. No wonder she isn't so friendly towards me. Oh, Paul, I feel really bad now.'

'Please don't blame yourself, honey. It's not your fault. Mother blames herself more than you ever could. She somehow feels she has failed him. You'll probably meet Marion sometime within the next few days no doubt. She's always over here and she'll be wanting to check you out for sure. Never tell her anything private, though. I'll bet my bottom dollar she played on Mother's heartbreaking indecision to let Benny go into this facility against her wishes.'

'Well that may be so, but I still think I will need to tread carefully with your mother for a while at least. Thank you, Paul, for telling me. I understand her so much more now.'

Paul takes hold of my hand across the table and looks me in the eye. 'I'm confident enough to believe that Mom will come to appreciate having you around, once she gets to know you better. Like you said, we'll just have to be mindful of her dark moods for now.'

'Don't worry. I'll be keeping to myself mostly while you're away at work each day.'

'Enough dramas now, Isabella. It's time for breakfast. You ready to face the music?'

'Face the music? Yes well, feels more like a tremulous drum roll if you ask me. Anyway, darling, you go on ahead. I'll be along shortly ...

I promise!'

'Okay I get it. You need some thinking time for now. See you soon then.'

***

Thank goodness Paul understands my need to have some me time. Alone in our trailer at last, I stare out the window, not really seeing anything at all as I try to slot my troubled thoughts into some sort of order in my head. While I'm mulling over all this new information, I start to sip my coffee, but soon spit out the overwhelmingly bitter taste from my mouth.

Aggghhh! Having to give up my precious cups of tea first thing in the morning is another thing that's going to take some getting used to I'm afraid. After a few more sips, I stop caring about the ghastly bitter taste of the brew and drink it anyway, while I allow all of the jumbled thoughts to bump around freely inside my head.

To my way of thinking, Erika's childhood years, compared to my own idyllic childhood, must have been filled with so much loneliness and sheer hard work. After enduring those loveless years at the orphanage, she then had to encounter more loveless years with not only her own mother, but her mother-in-law's coldness as well. Over time, Erika has been forced to push the memory of those sad years from her mind, any way she could. It's either forget the past, or let it destroy her completely. For the sake of self-preservation, she has obviously chosen the former. The consequences of her choice, though, mean she's forced to try and push down all of her hurt and pain into some dark forgotten hidden corner of her soul. 'What goes down, must come up' when it comes to pushing any hard-to-deal-with emotions down. But as I have already learnt for myself in life, none of our futures are certain, at any time. Or for anyone. Unfortunately for Erika, all of her hurt and anger have inevitably been resurfacing as an insidious form of deep resentment and bitterness, which she's now obviously chosen to direct towards me.

Despite me being on the receiving end of Erika's wrath, after hearing of my mother-in-law's sad story, how can I not feel compassion and empathy

272

for the poor woman? I just wish she would try to remember how lost she herself felt when her own mother-in-law rejected her all those years ago, just as she is doing to me now.

***

Breakfast with Paul's parents isn't as uncomfortable as I imagine it to be.

Maybe our relaxed time together out on the front porch last night has gone a long way towards Erika and Hans accepting me. Perhaps Erika might even begin to realise her daughter-in-law really is making a genuine effort to meet her halfway.

A breakfast of ham and eggs over easy, a popular expression in America. Paul tells me it simply means eggs cooked on both sides, but less so on the second side. There is also a small glass of orange juice in front of me and the inevitable cup of strong coffee to the right of my plate of eggs. Even after my first sip of coffee in a real American home, which is basically brewed the same way every time, somehow *still* tastes stewed to me. Perhaps this is because once the coffee pot is completely refilled in the morning, it's brought quickly to the boil on the stove, kept hot and ready to go at all times. It's never wasted though. Every last drop of coffee—Paul tells me—is drained from the pot throughout the day. Once drained, there's no more until the next morning. Not that I will ever worry about that happening. After watching me trying to drink the bitter coffee without pulling faces, Paul squeezes my hand under the table.

However, I don't think this would be the right time to tell him that tea bags can never really be the same as using loose tea leaves—which, according to both my mother and grandmother, should always be steeped for just the right amount of time in a *real* teapot.

***

Paul and I spend the first day of our domestic life doing some grocery shopping at the local store, which turns out to be a real eye-opener for me. I have never seen so many different kinds of food in a supermarket before. Most of the brand names are totally unfamiliar to me, and everything I see or touch is new and fascinating. Since Paul is already familiar with this store, we both agree he should be the one in charge of the shopping trolley and our pre-written shopping list. He already knows where each item is located, and as he finds them, he crosses each item off our list.

As for me, I'm more than happy to let Paul continue shopping without me, while I take my sweet time studying all of the products available on the shelves. I make it my mission to study as many new labels as I possibly can. All in one day too.

I keep asking a nice man named Bob, who is diligently stacking shelves, to explain to me how certain unfamiliar products are used (pestering the poor man is probably more like it). Bob takes it upon himself to patiently explain to me each product in question. I'm sure he must be thinking to himself what a strange person I am.

I must sound a bit funny to him with my Australian accent too, because after a few times of me asking him something, his bushy eyebrows always seem to come together into a worried frown. It's perfectly obvious to me Bob is gallantly trying to process what in Heaven's name I am talking about in the first place! Whenever I open my mouth to speak, my words seem to get lost in translation between us. One such item in question that perplexes both him and me the most is sultanas. Since I had already decided this morning to make Paul a fruitcake, I ask my ever-willing helper, 'Bob, would you happen to have any sultanas?'

'Sultanas?' The poor man does his Bob-thing again with his bushy eyebrows as he tries to figure out exactly what I'm asking him this time. 'Sorry, Mrs Meier, but I've never heard of such a thing. What would you normally use it for in Australia?'

'We bake sultanas into fruitcakes. You probably know it more as a dried fruit really.'

A light-bulb moment brightens up his eyes. 'Ah, got it! Come with me!'

I follow him as any housewife worth her salt would do to the cooking aisle where he hands me a box of dried fruit. It's only after I check the packaging by turning it over to read the back, that it states quite clearly these are definitely raisins, *not* sultanas!

'I think this is what you might be looking for. You might call them sultanas in Australia, but in the USA, we call most dried fruit raisins.'

'Thank you so much for your help, Bob, but I think I need to go find my husband now, so I will leave you to get on with your work.' *(And leave you in peace, you dear man!)*

I'm sure, as I walk away, he's probably dreading any return visits by me to his store.

Ah well! I have to start somewhere, don't I? Early days yet … I have come to the conclusion at the end of my first full day as a new housewife that, like coffee, supermarkets are one more thing that's going to take a *lot* longer for me to get used to.

More than anything else so far, though, I love my time spent alone with Paul. Especially in our new home—even if it is just a simple trailer for now. After packing away all of our groceries together, we decide to have some fun by playing LPs on the record player.

Apart from discussing what kind of music we each enjoy, we talk about everything else under the sun. I feel so grateful that I'm able to be close to Paul in this way. From what I understand—apart from girl talk and reading books—some housewives aren't so 'lucky' in the communication—or sex—department with their husbands.

For our first supper on our own, we heat up a pizza, and I must admit, for a store-bought pizza, it tastes amazing! Everything we do together today is so beautiful to me. Particularly, making love for the first time in our new home blissfully seals the deal. It doesn't matter how small our first home might be, it's far grander than any palace to me.

For now, this time alone is all the more precious to us because we know that come tomorrow morning, Paul will be off to attend to his new business idea. For me, it means a day of learning how to become an American housewife.

There's no escaping this transition into the American way of life, I'm afraid.

30

Paul

1946
A long, long history of family troubles

When Isabella was only a few weeks away from arriving here, it was Mom's closet friend, Marion Stephens, who dared to broach the subject of Benny's future care to my mother. During their regular coffee and cake ritual once a week, Mrs Stephens had apparently suggested putting my little brother Benny into the newly opened, government-run special care facility right here in this area. She must have somehow convinced my mother of the benefits of such a place for Benny, because before I knew it, my parents had formally submitted Benny's name and medical details for consideration for their highly specialised, in-house care at the institution to start with, followed by a full-time residency at the facility—should he qualify as being eligible following all their assessments.

From what I've read about such places myself, though, 'patients' who are considered to be eligible for these government facilities rarely ever return home. I think, deep down, both of my parents were perhaps hoping Benny would be rejected by them after all. Due to the severity of Benny's medical condition, though, he was accepted immediately.

Despite my inner suspicions that Mrs Stephens had been planning this all along, I'm not really angry with her, because I know her well enough by now to know she would have only done it out of love for Mom. I honestly don't believe she tried to manipulate Mom out of any malice either. I think it was more of a case that she was only too aware, that in order for Isabella to live here—for however long—to deal with Benny as he is just might be to much of a shock. After all, Mrs Stephens knows firsthand just how hard it is to watch Benny being spoon-fed or looked after by Mom on a daily basis.

Even as Benny's big brother, as someone I love very much, it isn't very pleasant for *any* of us to watch Benny eat or drink at the best of times. Particularly when he constantly drools into his food. With Isabella being a country girl from a family of five kids, living with someone like Benny might prove to be too much over time, despite her best efforts to please my parents.

I don't mean to doubt Isabella's ability to deal with Benny's condition, but if it's hard even for our own family to deal with it at times, how is Isabella—coming from a family of five healthy kids with no family challenges such as this—supposed to react to our Benny?

Unfortunately, my mom is not the only one carrying around this guilt about Benny. I don't think my father will ever get used to Benny's inevitable fate either. Dad has willingly squandered thousands of dollars over the years trying to find a cure for Benny, but his desperate efforts have proved to be futile every time. The numerous specialists Dad paid to find a cure have all tried to make Dad understand that there is no hope for Benny, but my poor father could never be convinced of such a discouraging prognosis.

With Dad being such a deeply religious man, he always steadfastly believed that God would someday guide him to a miraculous cure, but even God let him down in the end.

Then, of course, there's also the effect that Benny's condition has had on Vanessa, Lillian and me. I remember Lillian telling me once how deeply embarrassed she felt about going to school in hand-me-downs too many times. And even though Vanessa has never openly spoken to me about how she felt growing up with Benny the way he is, I can tell she felt just as embarrassed as Lillian, judging by the eyes-down look I used to see on her face every time we took Benny out of the house on a family outing.

Yes, of course, I did feel embarrassed about Benny at times too, but in a totally different way to the girls. It was never about his physical appearance, it was more about how I felt whenever my friends came over to our house after school or on weekends. Dad would immediately carry Benny into the room and plop him down in the middle of whatever we were playing and expect us to amuse him. I would have loved it if my little brother could have joined in with us, but I just knew that was never going to happen, so I eventually gave up inviting my friends home at all.

Whenever our family ventured out for the day with Benny, people would rudely stare and whisper loud enough for us to hear. The truth is that I really admire my parents—especially my mother—for keeping Benny at home with us for as long as they did. As far as they were concerned, Benny was part of our family and that was that. They always expected their able-bodied kids to feel the same way as they did, but it was tough for us as teenagers to feel repeatedly pushed aside when Benny needed their complete attention, when we really wanted to share something special with them.

I saw another side of Benny on one particular day when I was looking after him for Mom. For the first time ever, I finally understood why Mom had been so protective of him all these years.

I was playing the piano and Mom had positioned his wheelchair beside me. All of a sudden, Benny started doing something I have never seen him do before! He actually started to sway his upper body from side to side. In perfect time to the music! When I looked over his way, he had this great big grin on his face. I couldn't believe it! I have never ever seen him do this before and it was as if he was trying to tell me, 'See, Paulie, I'm not such a dummy after all, am I?'

From that day onwards, Mom and I turned the piano sessions into a regular thing. I played the piano even more for him after that. Somehow, I had managed to bridge a previously unfathomable gap. A true sharing of brotherly souls.

31

Isabella

Summer 1946
Making peace with the in-laws

It isn't always so easy to stick to my resolve to make peace with Erika. Months on from when I first arrived here, before I head over to the house for one reason or another, I have to remind myself of my self-imposed pact concerning my mother-in-law. Deep down inside my gut I can't ever imagine us being all that close. I still don't think she cares for me much either.

In the meantime, a mutual stand-off between us still exists. I can sense in my bones her stand-offish behaviour and frigid, unfriendly mental 'barbs' boring into my unprotected back every time I turn away from her.

Perhaps my normally shy, reserved demeanour intimidates her in some way as well. She's certainly very forthright when it comes to expressing her political opinions, that's for sure, whereas I tend to keep my thoughts to myself. Perhaps for this reason alone, she finds it equally as hard to talk to me. Here I am, a stranger from a country she knows absolutely nothing about invading her safe home sanctuary. Not for a few days either, but the forseeable future.

I've discovered that Americans don't really have any interest in Australia at all. They know so little about such a remote island of sorts, a long, long way away. Oh sure, they know about our kangaroos and koalas. They also know we have lots of nasty 'bitey' things running all over the place, but that's really the extent of their knowledge about my home country.

Paul recalled to me back in Melbourne—it's hard to believe it's years ago now—that when he first stepped foot on Australian soil at the beginning of the war, he was surprised to find real cities existed and to meet a whole lot of people who actually spoke English. After hearing this from Paul, I am even more reluctant to talk about my home, not wanting to bore people to death. If they ask me, though, I'm all too happy to tell them plenty about my wonderful childhood growing up out in the country, with my close-knit family in Melbourne.

Getting back to Hans again; despite the little time I have spent with him so far, I've discovered I really do like the man. He is quite smart in so many ways. Most days, though, I can hear him pacing around upstairs and mumbling to himself. Although, he does like to talk to me about his youth and has even told me I'm a good listener. Thankfully, he seems to enjoy my company as much as I do his. Just as well, because I've noticed for myself that no-one, including his wife, seems to have time for him at all. It's almost like he's invisible to them.

***

Growing up the way my mother-in-law did, she missed out on normal parental love and personal attention. As for myself, I'm ashamed to say, with my own parents, I so often took the unconditional love they heaped on me for granted. Growing up in an orphanage, Erika must have felt unloved and unappreciated every day of her life. If I had to walk in her shoes, I certainly would have felt this way too. I can almost guarantee that when Erika met Hans, she probably believed she'd finally found someone who really cared for her beyond whatever life had thrown at her so far.

Unfortunately, this side of her married life didn't go exactly the way she hoped it would. This is no doubt due to the fact that Hans just isn't a passionate man at all. Erika, on the other hand, is a very passionate woman when it comes to fulfilling her hidden desires.

With Hans being as religious as he is, he thinks sex is purely for the procreation of mankind and not for the wanton 'pleasures of the flesh'. Even though Erika had adopted Catholicism when she married Hans, that didn't mean she was prepared to go along with Han's strict celibacy rules at all. She needed so much more from her husband. More than Hans was willing to give her.

After I'd been at Paul's parents place for several months, I'd often see Ted Velardi's car parked in the street. Ted is the family's insurance agent who comes around each month to collect the homeowner's monthly instalments. It's obvious to me that each time Mr Velardi calls on Erika, he ends up staying much longer than necessary to write out a receipt. I doubt he is trying to sell her extra insurance policies each time. I can't help but wonder to myself what the neighbours must be thinking.

At the same time, I am happy for her. The flirting from this handsome Italian man—and I am certain that's all it is—must give her a certain feeling of femininity, because after each time Mr Velardi leaves, Erika seems much happier, behaving like a blushing schoolgirl. I suspect Erika already knows what I know, but just the same, there is no way I could ever bring myself to talk openly about Mr Velardi with her. Nor would I ever want to give her away to Paul or Hans. Over time, it soon becomes a secret thing between us. Each time, after Mr Velardi leaves, she looks me in the eye and smiles that sly smile of hers. In response, I simply smile back at her and pretend I haven't seen anything at all.

32

Isabella

1946
Everyday life in the 'burbs

For the first few months of married life, I conscientiously begin to acquaint myself with the various tasks necessary for me to become an everyday, happy American housewife.

According to a book I bought at the grocery store, in order for me to become a good wife for my husband, I need to know the most efficient way possible to plan meals and shop for groceries. At the same time, I must also learn the full value of the American dollar. Most importantly, though, before Paul is due home after his hard day at work, I must always remember to make myself look beautiful and greet him at the door.

As well as learning to master the budget, I'm also learning to cook all sorts of delicious meals for Paul, which I've never attempted on my own before. Well, I never really had to before now, since back at home, Mum was always around to cover up my mistakes.

When I think about it now, I realise I must have led a very sheltered life in Melbourne, far removed from the grown-up realities of everyday married life. My lack of experience with preparing meals on a daily basis has turned out to be a real wake-up call for me. But as a new housewife with my very own kitchen to cook in—as tiny as it is—I'm up for the challenge! I want to get it right. First time, every time. Most of all, I want

284

Paul to be proud of me. This daily cooking thing can't be all that hard to tackle, surely?

I must admit, it *did* take me a while to learn to cook even basic meals. From sloppy eggs and burnt bacon in the mornings to boiled-dry vegetables in the bottom of the pan in the evenings. There is no limit to my culinary failures. Tough, over-stewed meat or chicken are definitely my new specialities. For a few weeks now, *anything* I've cooked has soon become yet another victim of my experimental culinary blunders.

After months of determination, my tears of frustration and embarrassment have become a thing of the past, when my first successfully cooked supper is *finally* rewarded by Paul wiping his plate completely clean.

Of course, there is always my *other* reward at the end of the day too. Thank goodness I don't need any book to help with that aspect of my married life. At least in *that* department, everything works beautifully.

***

Not only do I manage to master many necessary housewife skills in the kitchen and keep track of the household budget, I also manage to find my way around town. Gradually, I'm getting used to my new surroundings a little more every day.

I have finally come to my own conclusion—after too many early disasters—that this new learning curve of mine is best approached as a gradual uphill climb, rather than trying to take one giant erratic leap of faith then beating myself up afterwards for any failures.

One day at a time! This is to be my new motto from now on.

Most of all, I tell myself sternly every day that I mustn't get too upset over silly mistakes, every time such things happen. When Paul returns home I don't want him to be greeted by a teary-eyed, dishevelled wife. He deserves to be welcomed home each day by a happy, smiling wife, who no longer secretly dreads him walking through the trailer door to find yet another domestic disaster waiting for him. Instead, I long to be one of those calm, efficient, beautiful American women I have always admired in movies.

Before I came to America, I was under the misapprehension that Americans are so much further ahead than I could ever be. Most especially when it comes to their modern conveniences. It doesn't take me long to realise for myself that I am just as smart and knowledgeable as most of the people around me. Sometimes, even more so, but I'm careful not to let on I know just as much as everyone else. I still ask for advice and even be modest about it, but at home, I just *know* I have the essential housewife rules done and dusted.

While I'm busy learning to be a good housewife, Paul is doing his part by trying to be a good husband too. According to one of the books I've been reading about marriage, *A husband's role is to support his new wife in a way that most well-brought-up young women have become accustomed to before marriage.* In other words, he is meant to bring in the money.

Just before I arrived in America, Paul had already kick-started his new business idea by purchasing a reliable service van. His next step was to contact all the managers of our local supermarkets and various other stores with the idea of home delivering their customers' purchases on certain days with each store within our local area.

At each supermarket, he has asked the store manager to make some space available for him at the front of the store, where customers can leave their groceries to be picked up and delivered by him to their home later that day. I've already noticed that most women in my neighbourhood don't drive, and I soon figure out why. Since there is usually only one car per family and with the man of the house being the sole breadwinner, he basically has to have full use of it throughout his working week to drive back and forth to his job, or to the train station and back.

Paul has cleverly figured out the older women of our neighbourhood are housebound *all* the time. With no family living at home anymore, they're now totally dependent on others to help deliver their groceries to them. He ultimately hopes over time that his idea might turn into a profitable business.

Unfortunately, after only a few months of putting his plans into action, we're barely scraping through. Even with our tight household budget in place, it doesn't take us long to realise his business idea barely brings in enough for us to live on. The dream of saving for our own home from any spare change left over each week is so far slipping away from us.

Despite Paul being a smart, talented man, there is no regular money to be made from his other skills either. Not even being a licensed pilot is going to help him. Even though he used to play piano in a dance band before the war, with the popularity of the jukebox, he and a whole lot of other musicians have quickly found themselves out of work.

When military servicemen first returned from the war, Paul—as well as a significant number of other returned serviceman—found out very quickly there weren't a whole lot of employment opportunities for them to pick up where they'd left off. I personally think it's cruel and demoralising for all of these brave men like Paul, still able-bodied and ready to get back into living again, to be confronted with such an uncertain future.

They are all too often bluntly told, 'Sorry, but you have to understand, gentlemen, your kind of military skills are no longer required these days.'

Even if Paul was a radio operator during the war with Japan—and might I add, under direct fire many times too—what use are those skills to him now in peacetime?

For the first time in his life, Paul feels totally useless. Most of his war-time skills are no longer relevant in this new postwar scenario it seems, so he takes on several jobs here and there. Whatever he can find, really, just to keep the money coming in. The idea of Paul asking his parents for money is certainly not an option for us at this time. Or any other time, for that matter. This desperate option alone would surely destroy Paul's self-esteem, forever I fear.

After being given a tip from a recently employed friend, he also applies at the same local post office for a job as a mail carrier and is at last successful. We are, of course, well aware it doesn't take a whole lot of intelligence to be a mail carrier, but we're still very relieved and grateful all the same to have a steady income at last.

Paul's mail route often takes him through our part of town, so when he does get the chance, he calls in at home to have lunch with me. After all, it's me alone in the trailer most days, with only music on the radio to keep me company. So I love it whenever he's able to stop by for lunch and for whatever else newlyweds can make time for. Even in the middle of the day.

***

Before we know it, summer has turned to autumn and so, of course, winter inevitably follows. I can't help but be concerned whenever Paul goes out in the van now and he comes home at lunchtime with his face constantly red raw from being exposed to the elements. There is a heater in his delivery van, but of course, each time he has to deliver a bundle of mail or bulky parcels, he has to leave the warmth of the van heater. When returning he then has to try to regain some degree of body warmth until the next house comes up. Christmas time is the worst. Even though all the houses in every street look so amazing with their twinkling festive lights, as well as snowmen and Santa sculptures on the front lawns, Paul starts to envy his customers all tucked away, toasty and warm inside, as he delivers to every house on his run. By the time he gets to the last house on his morning schedule, he is often feeling lonely and miserable. But in a determined effort to keep this job, he continues to steadfastly sprint from door to door under such freezing conditions.

'Oh, Paul, darling! Look at your poor face! I just hate to see you go back out into this rotten weather again. I do wish you could stay home with me for the rest of your shift. What is this post office management thinking of, anyway, sending their staff out in weather like this? There should be a law against it!'

'It's okay, sweetheart, as the saying goes, the mail must get through. Besides, I'm used to these kind of driving conditions. I grew up with it, remember?'

'Yes, I know, but it's still not right!' I declare with much indignation. I just feel so sorry for him when he has to go back out into the cold. Each time he has to return to work after his lunchbreak with me, I can't help but imagine him having to trudge through the deep snow with bitter cold winds blowing in his face to simply deliver mail.

Just before I'm about to complain again, it suddenly dawns on me I'm not making Paul feel any better by complaining all the time. 'Sorry! I'll get off my soapbox now.'

Despite being used to bone-cold days in Melbourne, until you've experienced even one of these frigid, icy days in Chicago, you can never ever imagine how cold 'cold' really can be. Once it seeps into your body, you just can't seem to get warm, no matter how many clothes or blankets you pile on yourself. I've learnt very quickly, though, to rug myself up each time I leave the trailer. Even if I am only heading over to Paul's parents' house to use their toilet, I go to the extent of completely covering my face—to avoid frostbite. In hindsight, Melbourne's chilly winds are more like a brisk, ocean breeze compared to Chicago's frigid winds that blow directly in from the arctic chill of Alaska, chilling both body, mind and soul.

On the other hand, winter in the USA can be so very beautiful. I just love to sit by my window, where I'm mostly all cosy and warm, and look outside at the spectacular view before me. The world outside my trailer door has been transformed into a fairyland right before my very eyes. During moments such as these, I am totally enthralled to watch the snow fall as soft flakes until it finally settles like a soft cashmere blanket over the landscape outside.

Just like in the movies, icicles hang from the eaves of the roofs, until Jack Frost takes over with his magic wand. This whole frosty scene never ceases to inspire my soul, as it transforms everything from a miserable frigid scene one minute, to a poetic vista of indescribable beauty the next.

***

After Mother Nature has finally brushed away every last trace of winter's icy fingers upon the land, she allows the welcoming and uplifting warmth of spring to burst open. Exorbitant displays of massive flower blooms alongside the tiniest of perfect little buds, are poking their glorious heads out, happily competing with each other for attention. Every soft summer breeze is an excuse for blooms to flutter their petals, catching the best light for their vibrant colours. The rustling sounds of tiny critters darting in and out of bushes delight me with endless distractions. Of course, when spring finally has its fill of impressing us mere mortals, summer soon follows with a warmth and lightness to inspire one's soul. Well, I for one am completely enthralled by everything new around me. It's hard for me to believe after arriving in America just before summer last year, that a whole year of seasonal changes has rolled around again.

I don't mind Paul going on his mail rounds so much these days, as I know he is much safer once the snow melts away into nearby rivers and creeks. Paul assures me the roads aren't so slippery anymore either. Black ice, I quickly learnt, has the lethal potential to turn his normal daily mail routes into a hazardous death ride every time he ventures away from home.

To me, the warmth of summer goes hand in hand with lots of fun things to do. Particularly on Saturday mornings. This is when I love most of all to head away from the claustrophobic entrapment I often felt in the trailer during winter. It makes me so happy now—even a little light-headed—to be out and about with Paul in the van, even if we do have to use his work van and the gas to fill it for our own personal use for the time being.

It's always so such fun for me to venture forth beyond the tree-lined streets of our neighbourhood and out into the big wide world again. As we drive, Paul points out various places to me, so familiar to him from his childhood, and now this very same neighbourhood is where he lives as a married man.

***

One Saturday morning, Paul has a surprise in store for me. After our grocery list has been ticked off at the supermarket and we are heading back to the van, Paul suddenly gets behind me and places his hands on my shoulders to steer me in the opposite direction.

For the first time, I find myself questioning his normal sharp sense of direction. 'Paul, where are we going? The van is this way.'

'Ah, but we aren't going back to the van just yet, my love. There's someone special I'd like you to meet. She's been dying to meet you for quite a while now.'

'She?' I grab his elbow to slow him down, before raising my eyebrows in question.

'Yes, she. But don't worry your pretty little head about any competition. I just have this feeling that you two are going to hit it off really well.'

Paul takes hold of my hand now and leads me into our local drugstore. Without being disloyal to my own country, I have come to the conclusion that our chemist shops in Australia could never compare to the drugstores here.

Of course, my first introduction to soda fountains was in the small town on my train trip to Chicago. How could I forget? Especially the fact that this drugstore was *exactly* as I had pictured it would be from Hollywood movies. So, I am ecstatic to see that this one, right here in our neighbourhood, is no different. To complete this real-life image for me, *lots* of shiny chrome is featured on the legs and around the padded seats of each swivel stool lined up along the front counter. The shiny chrome effect is also featured along the front edge of the highly polished laminated countertop.

I follow Paul's lead now, to stand with him in front of the soda fountain counter, where a dark-haired, rather tall young woman is busy serving customers. I guess straight away, this is the 'she' he wants me to meet. We sit ourselves down on two of the nearest stools to wait for her to come over to us when she's free. After the sudden rush is over, she starts walking towards us, down the working side of the counter and extends her hand to greet me in her strong Texan drawl. 'Howdy! You must be Isabella. I'm Toby-Lee and I'm just so thrilled to make your acquaintance.' She shakes my hand with so much enthusiasm that I can't help but feel welcome. I have to wonder why she has such a masculine kind of name for such a young woman?

The three of us manage somehow to have a conversation in-between Toby-Lee taking care of her customers. She obviously wants us to hang around a bit longer, so while we talk, she keeps herself busy by making us both a malted milk. All the while, she continues to talk a mile a minute. I honestly think Toby-Lee could talk underwater.

All the time she is talking, she's busy adding chilled milk, scoops of ice cream and powdered malt into two tall glasses. I'm still listening to what she is saying, but I'm also totally fascinated as I watch her do her thing, frothing the concoction up under the milkshake machine before topping it with a thick dab of whipped cream and finally some sprinkles of dry chocolate bits. Toby-Lee plops the two tall glasses of the creamy concoction in front of us before heading back along the counter to serve more of her customers.

Paul informs me, after she leaves us for a while, that our drinks are in fact malted milks and very popular these days. I have never tried one before, not even back in Melbourne, and I must admit, it does look awfully good. After taking a few sips from a red-striped straw, I admit only to myself that I don't really care for it much at all. It's all so sickeningly sweet, but I try to drink as much of it as I can, which isn't much. I leave the remainder in the glass, only to find out later Toby-Lee was very hurt over my rejection of the malted milk. Especially since she took so much trouble to make it extra rich for me, only for me to leave it mostly untouched.

When Toby-Lee is once again free of her other customers, she comes back to talk to us. She tells me she is also a stranger to this area like me, having moved out Chicago way, from a town in Texas, just north of the Mexican border, known simply as Big Spring. Like me, she has a strong accent, although hers is a real Texan drawl compared to my Australian, more nasally twang.

While she works, Toby-Lee continues to fill us in on her background. During the war, she had initially moved to California to begin working at an aircraft factory as a riveter on a large bomber aircraft. At the time, her husband-to-be, Jimmy Brusch, was first stationed at California before being shipped overseas to fight the war in Europe.

Paul interjects here to tell me that Jimmy's parents live on our street, across from Paul's parents' house. It's a sad irony of World War II indeed, for Jimmy to find himself fighting his own people, in the same town in Germany where his parents had originally grown up before migrating to America. His grandmother still lives over there. How conflicting that must have been.

In-between serving her customers, Toby-Lee regales us with a much more personal story about the night she and her Jimmy met. She was on her way home from working the night shift at the aircraft factory and as she stepped off the bus, she noticed a US soldier sitting in the bus shelter all alone. He was quite inebriated and told her he'd accidentally got separated from his buddies and was now lost. He needed to get back to his base ASAP but wasn't sure when the next bus was due, or even if there was a bus going past the base at this time of the night. She took pity on him and made sure he got back to the base before curfew, but not before they arranged their first date for the following evening. The very fact that Jimmy actually remembered her enough to turn up had Toby-Lee convinced they were meant for each other. It wasn't long after their first date that Jimmy was shipped off to war. By that time, Toby-Lee was already madly in love with him.

Even before the end of the war, Jimmy became a wounded casualty and was flown back to England, where he spent many months recuperating in a British hospital.

'When ma Jimmy was finally realised from hospital and due to be sent back home, I was fixin' to get on out to his folks' place to surprise him for when he gits back home, so withou' thinkin' twice 'bout it, I headed for Chicago on the very next bus.'

When Toby-Lee and Jimmy did get to marry, it was due to another impulsive decision. After disappearing for a whole weekend to Las Vegas, Toby-Lee and Jimmy returned home, announcing excitedly to Jimmy's folks, and to the whole damn neighbourhood they were now legally 'hitched'!

***

As time goes by, Toby-Lee and I have become close friends. We duck over to each other's place all the time, as Toby-Lee only lives just a short walk over from where our trailer is. Homeowners around our neighbourhood, and in most parts of the United States, appear to have this unspoken rule about not erecting any fences to divide their properties from each other. They even consider it an insult to put up a fence to keep their next-door neighbour at bay. I must admit, I am inclined to agree with this sentiment. To my way of thinking, it is a much friendlier way of acknowledging one's neighbours every day.

33

Isabella

1947
Where did my real mother-in-law go?

An introduction to my new neighbours initially came about through Erika, of all people, who I must admit, really surprises me sometimes.

For obvious reasons, I was of the opinion that Erika would have preferred to dismiss me as being her daughter-in-law to her friends and neighbours altogether. I was even beginning to believe she might try to keep me hidden away out of embarrassment. Especially in regard to my strange accent or even my most embarrassing ignorances about the American way of life.

Unbeknownst to me—not long after I arrived here—Erika had sneakily invited all the ladies in our street over for lunch. I guess she must have thought with me being a new, young housewife in her neighbourhood, now was as good a time as any for me to meet the other ladies I was bound to come in contact with on any given day.

On the morning of the planned luncheon, Erika came knocking on my trailer door after Paul had already left for work.

'Mornin'!' Erika greeted me in her usual gruff way. 'Do you think you might want to come to lunch at my place today?' There was to be no talk of today's weather or any other frivolous chitchat, Erika came to say what she needed to say and that was that!

This invitation was so out of the blue I wasn't sure how to answer her at first, but in spite of my nervousness, I still responded quickly enough to satisfy her. 'I'd love to, Erika. What time?'

'Please come at eleven thirty, sharp … Oh and don't worry about bringing anything.'

'Yes, of course, Erika. I'll be there.' I didn't think it would be a very good idea to refuse. I had a feeling if I *didn't* accept her invitation, I may never receive another one. I must admit, the very thought of spending *any* length of time alone with Erika still scares me half to death.

'Got a few people I want you to meet!' she adds abruptly, then without another word, turns on her heel and heads off. Before she's gone too far, she suddenly turns around and adds, almost as an afterthought, 'Oh, and wear a nice dress too.'

What's that supposed to mean? Wear a nice dress? This is lunch with Erika, after all. I'm totally puzzled of course, but too intrigued by now not to comply with her request.

***

Once I enter Erika's kitchen, I can hear a lot of unfamiliar voices filling up her house. Much more than the 'few people' Erika had first hinted to me—along with her rather obscure invitation to lunch. In fact, there must be around ten women in Erika's living room and when they realise I have arrived, they all stop talking. I had somehow hoped to enter Erika's living room unnoticed, but there's no chance of that, I'm afraid.

Erika suddenly stops talking to a group of women and without apology, weaves her way through her guests towards me, where I remain frozen with indecision. I know what fear a kangaroo must feel now, when it's trapped in the headlights of an oncoming car at night. By way of defence, I find myself backing up against the doorjamb.

'Ladies! I would all like you to meet Isabella, Paul's wife and my new daughter-in-law. She's from Australia, so she doesn't know much about our American way of life yet. I'm hoping this luncheon today will give us all a chance to welcome Isabella and for her to get to know each one of you as well.'

There is a sudden rush of 'welcome, Isabella!' or 'so lovely to meet you at last' or 'I have been simply *dying* to meet you, Isabella!'

Their friendly greetings put me at ease immediately and once a glass of non-alcoholic fruit punch is quickly pushed into my hand, I'm suddenly bombarded with so many enthusiastic questions.

To start with, the first round of questions for me to answer are all about my trip to America on the SS *Monterey*. Was I seasick? Was I treated well by the US government onboard? What was it like being on a ship for such a long time? Etc. etc. They are all very keen to know how I'm settling into my new life here too. The question that seems to intrigue them the most, though, is about my former life in Australia; how do I feel about leaving my parents and siblings behind to come and live over here permanently?

Without warning, I have become the centre of attention, but I'm more than happy to answer all of their eager questions. When the questions start coming thick and fast, I feel suddenly out of my depth, especially with all of these beautifully dressed, inquisitive ladies crowding around me. That's when Erika kindly steps in to rescue me. I am so very grateful for her well-timed intervention.

'Ladies, ladies! *Please!* That's enough questions for now! I do believe we may be overwhelming Isabella. There will be plenty of time for all of your questions later. After all, she will be with us for a *long* time … right, Isabella? Come on now! Lunch is ready.'

For lunch, there is a variety of dishes, all provided by each of the ladies present, but the dish I love the most is a salad made from canned tuna and macaroni. It's the first time I have ever tried tuna and I quite like its chunky texture. Back in Melbourne, we only ever ate canned salmon, which I remember having a much stronger flavour than the tuna in this salad. It seems a bit bizarre to me that the salmon in Australia is usually imported from the Northern Hemisphere, whereas in return, the tuna from Australian waters is imported up to America. Anyway, I figure it's wise for me to keep my cultural observations to myself for now.

Most of the women I meet from the neighbourhood are so much older than me. There is Mrs Bisby, a lovely, sweet lady who lives at the back of us. I also enjoyed meeting Mrs Helen Bittner too. Mary Lesticow is one of Erika's neighbours that I already knew before today. When Mrs Lesticow first learnt I was about to leave Australia, Mrs Bittner asked Erika for my address to welcome me to the neighbourhood. So I had already been corresponding with her well before I even left home. Evelyn Lantz is another friendly neighbour who has even given me a wonderful American cookbook. Some of the other ladies (I still yet have to remember all of their names), each gave me a small welcoming gift as well.

***

I thought to myself later what a thoughtful thing it was for Erika to organise this wonderful luncheon for me, particularly when I stop to remember her less-than-friendly welcome home greeting on my first day here in this neighbourhood.

But this isn't all she does for me.

Shortly after my welcome-to-America luncheon, Erika takes me to meet her very close friend Marion Stephens, who lives with her husband and their two children in a beautiful Spanish-style home, closer to the 'town centre' (the city of Chicago, that is).

After warm greetings at the front door, we're taken by Marion outside to a lovely grassy area within her rather expansive backyard. It's while we're chatting together that Marion just happens to look down and spot a four-leaf clover near her feet. In the spirit of a welcoming friendship, Marion immediately plucks it gently from its earthy roots, to gift it to me for good luck.

I like Marion right away and her husband too, who owns a flourishing commercial business in downtown Chicago. I can't help but notice as we talk together how friendly Marion seems to be with everyone she comes in contact with. Just like a 'proper' lady, really. Until she opens her mouth to speak, that is. Her speech is generously interspersed with profanity. I have to admit I'm more than a little shocked at first, but funnily enough, I don't find it offensive at all coming from Marion and soon realise it's her natural way of describing things to us.

On the way home from Marion's, Erika and I are chuckling about some of the things Marion said throughout our afternoon with her and the 'unique' way she expresses herself. Erika then told me about a certain evening when Marion's husband had invited one of his business associates home for dinner. He warned Marion beforehand to *please* watch her language as the man was an important customer. So, not wanting to embarrass her husband, she was too afraid to open her mouth at all throughout the entire evening. After the man left, Bob said to Marion, 'For Heaven's sake, Marion, why didn't you join in the conversation?'

'Well, Bob, to tell you the truth, I was too fucking afraid of saying the wrong fucking thing!' After that, he never once asked her to watch her language again.

34

Isabella

1947
Beyond the neighbourhood

Getting to know our neighbours and Paul's friends is always enjoyable for me, plus without me even realising it at the time, I've been slowly initiated into the American way of life. One of Paul's friends we've met from before the war, Wiley James, also played in the same dance band as Paul.

Wiley and his wife Gertie often invite us over for dinner, and Gertie really loves to cook, her speciality being delicious cakes and pies. Wiley and Gertie both taught us how to play pinochle too, which is a card game that is very popular these days. Now I've caught the bug for the game, the four of us love to play it for hours on end, always having so much fun together.

Of course we love to do other fun things as a foursome too. One Sunday afternoon, the four of us arranged to drive up to a town in Wisconsin, where there was a skiing competition being held. Paul decided to invite them over to our trailer for dinner afterwards, and made up a big batch of 'sloppy joes' which we always enjoy. It's basically a whole lot of minced meat between two pieces of bun, but can be very messy to eat, hence the title of sloppy. Paul quickly put the minced beef filling together before we left for Wisconsin, so we'd only have to reheat it when we came back later.

Paul asked me if I would mind baking his favourite dessert of lemon meringue pie. I must admit, I was a bit concerned about Paul's request, as I don't really trust my little oven in our trailer to do its job when the time comes to heat it up later. The oven temperature never seems to stay hot enough for making anything that requires a consistent heat source. Especially with special desserts such as this. But I go ahead and make it anyway, even whipping up the meringue for the topping, so I have just enough time to take it out of the oven before we leave the trailer.

Much to my horror, when the four of us return to the trailer later, specifically, into the kitchen area, there is my pie on the table with its flattened meringue on top. Unfortunately, during the cooling off process, the once-fluffy top has totally collapsed down onto the filling. Naturally, I'm mortified to see it this way, especially since I'd gone to so much trouble making the pie crust and the filling. The crumpled meringue is such an embarrassment to me, I can't help but wonder what Gertie must think of my cooking disaster. Mercifully, she doesn't think it's a disaster at all. She even made me feel better by telling us about some of her own disasters when she first learnt to cook too. Thank goodness, we were able to laugh about my pie later. Besides, once we scraped off the flattened meringue, the rest was delicious.

***

Other friends we visit regularly are Nick and Doris Roccatis, who live on the south side of Chicago. Even if it does mean quite a long drive for us to visit them from where we live in the outer suburb of Villa Park, we still enjoy spending time with them. Nick is another childhood friend of Paul's who also grew up in Villa Park, but Doris is a born-and-bred city girl. Deep down, I'm not all that fond of Nick really. He can be a real loud-mouthed Italian at times, whereas Doris is a sweet demure girl I like very much. So much so that I can't understand for the life of me how Nick and Doris could've even ended up together. They just seem so mismatched to me. But who am I to judge?

Because it's such a long drive into the main city area of Chicago, with the roads being so dangerously icy in the winter, we often choose to stay overnight at their place and head back home the following morning. They own a large house on the south side of Chicago, but to save money they decided to rent out the main part of the house upstairs to a young family. So Nick and Doris live downstairs in the basement where they have set up a compact living area, consisting of a kitchenette, a cosy living room, bathroom and one large bedroom. In the bedroom there are two double beds, so Paul and I usually sleep in one of them each time.

So, here we are again, downstairs at the Roccatis'. After our usual late night of playing cards, drinking beer or wine and talking for quite a while, we're finally ready to head off to bed to sleep for what's left of the night.

However, Nick is in the mood for sex and proceeds to fulfil his need with Doris—disregarding the fact that Paul and I are in the same room as them. Our bed is right next to theirs, in fact. This doesn't seem to register with Nick at all. For some bizarre reason, he just doesn't seem to care, so Paul and I have no choice but to listen to him grunting above Doris for what seems like hours. We both breathe a sigh of relief when Nick *finally* rolls over and snores heavily for the rest of the night.

I can tell by the thunderous look on Paul's face the next morning he is totally disgusted with Nick. I feel so sorry for Doris too. She must be feeling humiliated by Nick's amorous but inappropriate actions during the night. With Doris being so timid, she doesn't dare say no to him, I guess. After that night, we made a silent pact between us to never sleep at their house ever again.

Another late night with them after that, we both insist on heading back home. We stick to our decision too, despite their protests for us to stay with them. Unfortunately, we don't get very far on our journey home before we run out of gas. It's so bitterly cold outside too. Even before we'd left the Roccatis'.

Just in case running out of gas isn't enough to worry us, the heater in the van also refuses to cooperate. To make our situation even more dire, the unforgiving cold temperatures are now plummeting even further into an instant freeze zone. We suddenly find ourselves stranded out in the middle of nowhere, with no other cars on the road to stop for us. We desperately huddle close together in the car, but with no interior heat, we know we simply cannot stay here much longer. We have no choice now but to try and find some kind of help very soon or literally freeze to death overnight.

We make the decision together to leave our car and trudge through the thick snow towards one smallish solitary house we just passed nearby. By this time, it's already around one o'clock in the morning. Luckily for us, we are very relieved to see there is still a light glowing softly in one of the windows at the front of the house. As we knock on the door, we silently pray someone will let us come inside. Eventually, a woman opens the door, and after we briefly explain our desperate situation, we ask if we can use her phone. Paul rings Nick to ask him to bring us some gasoline in a can. Thankfully, the lady of the house has invited us into her home while we wait for Nick to turn up.

Once we enter her living room, we are rather shocked to see the floor covered with children in sleeping bags or just tucked in tightly together under a pile of blankets. I count six children in all. Nope, seven—there's a baby huddled in amongst the whole jumbled mixture of sleeping bodies.

Glancing around, I happen to notice a heater in the room off to the side a bit, but it's obvious to me they have no central heating throughout the house. Or maybe they can't afford to use it if they do.

Looking around the living room, and at the sight of all these children squashed up together on the floor, I feel deeply humbled by what some families have to endure in order to survive life.

***

There is one thing in particular I find very hard to get used to with the

American way of life, and that is their funerals and the common practice of open caskets.

Lillian, Paul's sister, is married to Will Monaghan (Bill, as I have come to know him), who comes from a large family. There are nine children in the family and Will is the only son. I always feel so privileged to be invited to one of their family gatherings as Will's family are such nice people, every one of them.

One of his sisters, Mira, has two sons, one being twelve years old, and the other thirteen. Will's father, a retired gentleman, enjoyed spending time with each of his grandchildren, taking them to all kinds of interesting places.

On one fateful day, Will's father decided to take all five of his grandchildren to an amusement park nearby. There were three children in the car from one family and Mira's two boys as well. As his car approached a stoplight, he got the green light to go ahead, when suddenly from out of nowhere, another car ran a red light from the side, and smashed into the grandfather's car, killing Mira's two boys instantly.

On the afternoon of the boys' wake, as Paul and I entered the funeral home, my first sight is of Mira sitting between the caskets of her only two children. The boys were both dressed in shirts, ties and lovely blue woollen sweaters and each boy was laid out in an open coffin for all to see.

It's not long before I start sobbing. Without a doubt, it's probably the saddest thing I have ever experienced in my life so far. The sight of the two beautiful boys lying there, as if they were sleeping with their mother sitting between them, breaks my heart completely. I feel extremely embarrassed, of course, but there is nothing I can do to stop my uncontrollable tears and spasms of noisy hiccups. Paul is at a loss for what to say or do to help me through. Lillian, my sister-in-law, quickly and discreetly comes to the rescue and takes me into another room, but I just can't be consoled.

In the end, some of the other relatives politely suggest to Paul that perhaps we should leave. Without another word and with an understanding nod, Paul quietly bundles me into our van while I continue to sob all the way home.

Part 3
1947 – 1949
Brand-new family

35

Isabella

1947
A family in the making

Several months after we've settled into the trailer, without letting onto Paul just yet, I have this strong feeling I might be pregnant. Even if deep down I'm feeling really excited about the idea of me carrying a baby inside my own body, I'm still very worried about what Paul's reaction to our unplanned pregnancy will be, plus what it'll do to our plans to find our own place, as right now he's hoping it'll be by the end of this year, or so he says.

I don't really have any idea what symptoms I'm supposed to be having, if I *am* pregnant, that is. My breasts, particularly my nipples, have become very tender these past few weeks. Not only that, but I can no longer stand the smell of cooked food, so it's becoming increasingly difficult to hide my sudden nausea from Erika, let alone Paul.

I'm pretty sure I *am* pregnant, especially since I've missed one monthly period already. Up until now, I've always been able to rely on my 'monthlies' to be as regular as clockwork.

I have no idea of how on Earth I'm going to tell Paul my news, especially when I stop to consider we are trying to save every spare dollar we can. Come to think of it, the thought of raising a child in a trailer certainly doesn't seem like such a good idea either. Regardless of my own secret worries, I will still have to tell him soon. Besides, I've already noticed Paul watching me out of the corner of his eye. He can no longer hide his deep concern for me any longer, especially with my normal healthy appetite on a downward spiral lately.

I have decided to tell him by lunchtime tomorrow no matter what. Being Monday, the first day of Paul's working week, I know he'll be home for lunch, so I figure it will be the perfect time to break the news to him. Besides, absolute privacy is so important for such important news. I really don't fancy breaking the news to Erika or Hans just yet.

Oh dear God, please dont let him be mad with me!

By the time I hear Paul pull up in his van close to our trailer, I've already worked myself up into such a nervous state, I hardly know what to do with my hands anymore. To make me feel better, I've dressed myself up in my best dress for him; the soft apricot one with a row of tiny pearl buttons all down the front. Paul always loves it when I wear this particular dress, so I'm hoping it *might* soften his response to my news somehow. I've even curled my hair in a flattering new way too. As I sweat and wait for him, I wind my frilly hanky around and around my fingers so many times they are now beyond feeling any tactile sensation.

I've rehearsed a thousand times in my mind exactly what I'm going to say to him when he walks through that trailer door, but all of my best intentions fade away the second he steps inside. I just blurt it out, 'Paul, I think I might be pregnant!'

He just stares at me, not uttering a single word for the longest time.

Much too long for my fragile state of mind, anyway.

'Paul …?' I reach over for his hand, grasping it firmly in my own (which of its own accord is starting to shake with pure fear by now). 'Did you hear what I just said? I think I'm pregnant … In fact, I'm positive I am.'

He's still not saying anything yet, but by way of answering me, he

310

simply slides across to my side of the padded seating of our trailer's dining area with a beaming smile on his face to hug and kiss me. *What better answer could I ask for than this? All is well.*

'Yes of course I hear you, silly!' he laughs and hugs me again.

The most beautiful sound in the world to me is Paul's spontaneous, happy laugh, and that's what I'm hearing right now. 'So you're not mad with me?'

'No way! You just caught me unawares, that's all! Especially when you just blurt it out like that!' he chuckles. 'Well, this certainly explains you going off your food, then. I should have realised, honey. I honestly didn't think it would happen so soon, that's all.'

'I thought you might be angry with me. I honestly didn't think we'd already have a baby on the way so soon after us starting our new life as husband and wife *AND* especially with us madly trying to save for our own home.' I just keep babbling on, making excuses for myself as to why I have even allowed myself to fall pregnant so soon.

'No, honey! I promise I'm not mad with you.' Paul kisses me again. 'Knowing that you're pregnant, or might be, just makes me more determined than ever to find us a place of our own for when the baby comes. When do you think you might know for sure?'

'I was thinking of making an appointment with some local doctor within the next week or so. Do you know of any around here?'

'I'm not exactly sure to tell you the truth. I haven't had to go to a doctor since returning home. All of my medical needs have been taken care of by the military for years. Touch wood, I haven't needed a doctor up until now. Maybe Mom will know of one.'

'No! Please, Paul, I'd rather we keep it to ourselves for now, if you don't mind? At least until we know for sure.'

'Good idea! I'm with you on that. Maybe Toby-Lee knows of a local doctor we can go to. I'm sure she'll be able to keep our secret to herself for a few more weeks, don't you think?'

'Yes, you're right! I'll ask Toby-Lee. She's bound to know of one in our area. When you go back to work after lunch, I'll invite her over here for a quick chat. In the meantime, like I said, we really need to keep this quiet for a little while longer with your parents. Although, I have a feeling your mother might already suspect I'm in the family way. Besides, having had four children of her own, I'd be surprised if your mother didn't suspect by now.'

Lucky for us, we've been cooking most of our meals in the trailer lately, except for lunch with Erika and Hans on Saturdays, and of course, every Sunday after church. I know darn well if we were still eating in their house all the time, Erika wouldn't be able to resist commenting about such a thing. As it is, I can already sense her watching me more closely. At such times, I deliberately try to avoid any direct eye contact with her. Although, I don't think I am fooling her for even one minute.

On Toby-Lee's recommendation, I make an appointment with a young doctor by the name of Dr Dan O'Connor. He's tall and lanky, and despite his boyish face, his impressive head of thick, dark hair is already streaked with grey. Most of all, Dr O'Connor has this cheeky grin that immediately puts me at ease. In fact, I think he's the perfect choice for my first-ever American doctor. He just has this easygoing way about him that suggests to me as his patient I'm in excellent hands.

Paul comes with me on my first visit to Dr O'Connor and I can tell he feels at ease with him as well, so we decide to stick with him. Thanks to Toby-Lee, she is prepared to keep our secret safe for however long we need her to. Besides, she can see for herself how gruff Erika is with me most of the time. As it turns out, it wasn't necessary for Toby-Lee to keep quiet about our secret at all, as Paul and I decide to tell Erika and Hans that very same afternoon. Once my pregnancy is confirmed by Dr O'Connor, and with us being so excited about having our first baby, it doesn't really matter who knows now, anyway.

Hans congratulates us and actually seems really excited about becoming a grandfather again as Vivienne and Lillian have given him grandchildren already. Erika, on the other hand, gives me her usual critical response. 'Well, looks like you two will have to save a lot harder for your own place now.'

Inwardly I seethe. *Why can't Erika be happy for us for a change?* I can feel Paul flinch beside me too. This is just one more way for Erika to put Paul back in his place again. She always does this to him. As far as Erika is concerned, Paul is still just a little kid to be bossed around. She obviously isn't prepared to treat him as the man he has become. Not even now, when he is about to become a father for the first time.

Unfortunately, my morning sickness is already having an impact on my appetite, not just in the mornings either. I can no longer keep *any* food down. Whatever I eat lately, I never fail to bring it all back up again.

I eventually overcome this, though, by sneaking off to the bathroom to put my fingers down my throat *before* I sit down to eat. After the initial convulsive gagging, I can finally manage to keep most of the food in my stomach.

***

After going to bed, I'm instantly awake with severe pains in my abdomen. *What's happening to me?*

I'm only three months along with my pregnancy by now. The pains are becoming stronger and stronger, and before I know it, the intense, gut-wrenching pains ruthlessly cramping my stomach have suddenly turned into labour pains. I bury my head into the nearest pillow, my grief all-consuming and too overwhelming to deal with at this point in time. Thankfully, my stressed body finally forces me into an exhausted sleep.

Once the initial shock of my miscarriage has sunk in, a fresh flood of tears leave a lingering message in its wake; *I am a complete failure as a woman.* All too easily I find myself sinking into this unfathomable hole of self-pity, where not even my normal rational thoughts can pull me out of it.

Who am I to even think I could carry a baby past three months, anyway? God has obviously decided I'm not suitable to become a mother after all. Does this mean now I'll be doomed to lose *all* my of babies before I can carry them full-term?

Paul tries to console me, but by wallowing in my own self-perpetuated, miserable state of grieving for our lost child, I can no longer hear his gentle, soothing words anymore. I'm obviously determined to block him out completely and just refuse to listen to reason. When Paul tries to reach me through my fog of despair, I turn my head away every time.

Indeed, I'm determined to block *everything* out beyond this all-consuming, self-destructive focus on my complete failure to carry a child full-term. Possibly *any* child.

Maybe Paul even believes I'm a failure too?

With tears streaming down his face, I fail to see Paul is grieving in his own quiet way as well. Paul has quietly bundled up what is left of our tiny baby and has taken it outside to bury it in the garden. With no such medical knowledge between us, we can't even tell what sex our baby was, since the fetus is so very tiny. Even in our numbed state of disbelief, we instinctively decide not to torture ourselves any further by knowing what he or she could have become one day.

The following morning, I have no choice now but to call Dr O'Connor to tell him what transpired the night before. After listening to my sad tale, with sobs of misery hiccuping my words the whole time, he tells me to come to his surgery *immediately* and to bring the foetus with us.

However, I am totally unprepared for the doctor's next reaction when I tell him Paul has already buried the fetus in the garden.

'HE DID WHAT?' Dr O'Connor shouts over the phone, then quickly pulls himself together. 'Sorry, Isabella, but perhaps I didn't hear you right. Did you just say your husband has actually buried the fetus in your backyard? What was he thinking?'

He sounds really angry now, despite his best intentions to speak calmly to me.

'Yes, he did, doctor. Is there a problem? I mean … aren't we supposed to do that?'

'NO! You AREN'T supposed to do that, Mrs Meier!' (Oh dear! He must be really mad at us not to call me by my first name anymore!)

'But why, Dr O'Connor? Why are we supposed to bring the fetus to you? I don't understand what it is we've done that's so wrong?' I'm on the defensive now and fully prepared to defend Paul's actions if I have to.

I hear him take a deep breath over the phone. Obviously to cool his temper down.

'Well, Mrs Meier. Let me explain it to you then, shall I?' I hear him take one more deep breath for good measure before continuing. 'Whenever a woman miscarries, a thorough examination of the fetus is most important to determine why your baby spontaneously aborted before its full-term. For reasons we don't always understand, your baby may not have been fully formed. Sometimes Mother Nature rejects a fetus for reasons of her own. Either way, we might have been able to find out *why* it happened and to stop it from happening to you again in the future.'

'I do apologise, Dr O'Connor, for our rash decision, but how are we supposed to know all this? After all, this *is* our first baby, and besides,' I throw a little more reasoning into our defence, 'I remember reading somewhere that some island cultures bury their unborn children all the time. Isn't that true, doctor?'

'Yes, this is very true, Bell.' (*Ah! back to first names again, thank goodness!*) 'I do apologise for yelling at you like that. It's just I've never had any dealings with this sort of thing in this day and age. If I was a country doctor maybe, but definitely not in the city. Anyway, Bell, I would still like you to come in and see me sometime *today* please. I'll need to give you a D&C as soon as possible.'

'D&C? Sounds serious. Please enlighten me, doctor. If you would be so kind?'

'Dilation and curettage. I need to clean out everything that may still be inside you. It's very important to do this so that you can successfully conceive again.'

'Oh I see … I never knew that. Okay, Dr O'Connor, I promise I'll be in today, then.'

'I know you are most likely berating yourself as a woman over this miscarriage, Bell. There is no need for you feel bad about all of this happening to you so early in your marriage either. Miscarriages happen to all kinds of women all the time. Like I said before, it's Mother Nature's way of wanting to get it right each time. As you are beginning to realise now, Bell, not all pregnancies work out exactly as you plan. Besides, you have already proved you can conceive easily, so I am confident enough to predict that your second time around should be a much more rewarding experience for you and your husband.'

Not only is Dr O'Connor a wonderful doctor, but he can read minds too!

***

Thanks to Dr O'Connor, I start to treasure my womanhood again. Mother Nature is obviously pleased with me too, because less than three months later my morning sickness has returned and I know for sure I'm pregnant again. By this time, Toby-Lee is also pregnant. Luckily for her, she can still sit down at the table and eat anything she likes, whereas I still can't hold anything down for too long at all, regardless of the time of day.

Living close to my in-laws always requires a certain amount of patience. Hans is okay *most* of the time—when he's not pacing backwards and forwards in his bedroom, mumbling to himself. On the whole, Hans and I get along quite well.

Erika, on the other hand, requires an entirely different approach. No matter what I do, Erika finds any excuse to shoot me down with sarcastic comments every chance she gets. I was beginning to wonder for a while there if the Erika who was being so nice to me when I first arrived here (by hosting that luncheon for me), was really a stand-in actor for the *real* Erika she'd hired to make herself look good to the neighbours. Maybe the *real* Erika is still playing sneaky games with me, sending me crazy mad in the process?

One of the inconveniences of living in a trailer in my in-law's backyard is that it doesn't have an inside toilet, so we have no choice but to make use of the one in the house. The problem with this idea is that Erika insists on locking up the house every night, which of course also includes the back door, giving us no access to their toilet overnight.

With Erika being a late riser, the back door remains securely locked until around ten o'clock each morning. Only then will she unlock the door again. For Paul it's never much of an inconvenience. Being a man, he can discreetly go out and pee on a bush in the garden, which thankfully is secluded enough from the neighbours. As for me, Paul has thoughtfully bought me a bucket to use in the trailer. Particularly for me to use during the night, so he's naturally very upset with his mother for not having more consideration for me, especially when I fall pregnant again. His protests always fall on deaf ears where Erika is concerned. Her usual excuse of, 'What? Leave the back door unlocked, son? That's *never* going to happen! I'll not have some robber break into our home and steal everything from under our noses! There is no way I'm going to leave this house unlocked at night and that's that!'

We finally have to accept that for as long as we live here, a bucket will have to do.

I always have to make sure my designated laundry day doesn't interfere with Erika's schedule either. Since she doesn't have an electric clothes dryer, I usually hang my wet laundry outside on the clothesline. During a long winter, though, I prefer to hang my washing down in the basement near the furnace, otherwise every item of our washing would soon become frozen solid within minutes.

One morning when it's my turn to use the laundry, I find our neighbour from across the street working on the washing machine. Mr Halliwell is such a kind and friendly older man, and even though he's retired, he enjoys having something to do every day. Thankfully for us, he's very handy at fixing broken things.

I sit down beside him to wait for him to finish whatever he is doing and place my laundry basket full of dirty clothes right beside me and out of his way. This is Mr Halliwell's cue for him to lean over in a covert way, to whisper to me, 'I feel obliged to tell you, Bell, that your mother-in-law blames you for breaking her washing machine.'

'Really? I don't understand.' I am quite baffled to hear this today of all days, especially when Erika recently remarked to me about how gentle I am with most things. Particularly in the way I peg my washing on the line. She constantly tells me how rough her daughters can be with her wooden pegs each time they use them, as they always seem to end up broken afterwards.

'Ah! Don't you pay her no mind now,' Mr Halliwell reassures me. 'Anyway, this wouldn't be the first time I've had to try and breathe life back into this blasted machine. Maytag may have made these washers to last forever, but believe you me, this old girl is on its last legs for sure.'

One morning as I'm looking out my trailer window, I see Erika coming towards the trailer with a very sour look on her face. *Oh dear! What will she blame me for this time?*

After she's banged on the trailer door a few times, I calmly open it to greet her.

'Good morning, Erika. How are you?'

'Don't you good morning me, girlie! What've you done with the basement door key?'

'I don't know. It should be on the peg where it always is. You can't find it, then?'

'Do you think I'd be asking you if I already knew where to find it?'

Anger spews from her mouth.

I can't for the life of me understand what she's going on about. Erika always hangs the only key on the peg beside the basement door each night, which amuses me. Every time I see the key on its home peg, it always reminds me of the Walt Disney movie about Snow White, where the seven dwarfs work all day in the diamond mine and each night they lock the front door to the cottage and hang the heavy key on the nail outside.

I swear to Erika I haven't touched the key, but it's then I remember, Paul had to go into to the basement last night for some reason. Even still, I'm still very surprised he hasn't returned the key to its rightful place like he always does. Regardless of what really happened, I'm determined to ignore Erika's cattiness for now. I even offer to help her look for it and follow her back to the house.

As soon as I look down near the door to the basement, I can see the key lying there on the cement. Being such a chilly night, in his haste to get back to warmth of our heated trailer, Paul obviously forgot to make sure the key was securely replaced back on the peg again.

Erika doesn't even apologise to me. She just grabs the key and hangs it back on the peg before storming upstairs without another word. She is obviously too embarrassed to admit to her mistake to me, but from then on, nothing more is said about the basement key ever again. My mother-in-law can be very mean at times, but I try not to let her bother me too much. There are in fact times when I do get along with Erika and one of those times is when she wants to go grocery shopping. I usually go with her when she invites me, even though I never really feel completely at ease in her presence.

One particular winter morning, when the streets and footpaths are all slippery, we set off towards the store with both of us being careful not to fall over as we gingerly watch our steps along the slippery sidewalks covered by sneaky, layers of treacherous black ice, ready to catch any reckless pedestrians completely unawares.

Funnily enough, when we do these trips to the supermarket, she seems so much more relaxed away from home. So, on this particular day, as she's busy chatting away to me, all of a sudden I realise she's no longer by my side. I turn around to see where she is, only to find her lying flat on her back on the pavement, unable to get herself up. Being a roly-poly sort of a woman, the sight of her lying there helpless with her favourite thick woollen skirt way up around her hips and her beanie now covering her face, really tickles my funny bone. Not maliciously, mind you, but it really is such a funny sight to behold.

Trying very hard not to laugh, I make my way back carefully, on the icy sidewalk to lend Erika a helping hand. After all, even though I am concerned about slipping on the sidewalk myself—especially mindful of my own *delicate* state—I don't want her to think I'm heartless about seeing her in an embarrassing situation such as this.

All I can think of now is what the women in the nearby houses must think when they look out from behind their curtains at us. Here we are, with me trying desperately to get this lump of a woman back on her feet again without also slipping and sliding in a heap beside her.

Thankfully, Erika can also see the funny side of it too. At this point, we take one look at each other and start laughing. We laugh so hard we can't stop, until our weakened bladders mercilessly start to trickle out onto the icy sidewalk.

They say humour can cure all ills, and in this instance, I definitely agree. Spontaneous humour certainly has helped to relieve the animosity between my mother-in-law and me.

Well, for a while at least …

***

Whenever I have to go to the toilet during the daylight hours—for more than a piddle—it always means the inevitable trip inside the house. On one particular morning, as I step out of the trailer, I am completely taken aback by what I'm seeing. A whole area of the ground in front of me is covered with snakes! Paul offhandedly mentioned to me at one time the little snakes are called garter snakes. He assured me at the time they are completely harmless, but after seeing them slithering all over the lawn in front of me, I'm not so convinced. According to Paul, in early springtime, the snakes often migrate over this way from the large, overgrown field alongside the property, to enjoy the warm balmy sunshine after their long winter hibernation. Well, whatever the reason for them being here outside my trailer, is irrelevant right now. To my horror, there seems to be hundreds of them *everywhere* and my skin crawls at the very sight of them. I just want to stay inside our trailer until they slither away someplace else to sun themselves. However, since I desperately need to use the toilet, staying in the trailer is not an option. *You'll just have to go for it. You know the bucket will be useless for you this time.* So I am left with no choice but to brave a treacherous path to the house.

As I move slowly along the garden path, one fearful step at a time, I make a point of looking off into the distance rather than down. But as I suddenly hear a sound at my feet, I have no choice but to make sure I'm still on the pathway. I spot one snake in particular with its beady eyes staring me down. It's hissing at me too. I take a few deep breaths as I start to run as fast as my little feet can move me forward. I can't get inside the house fast enough. After using the toilet, I dread going back outside, but what else can I do? Once again, I have no choice. I certainly don't want Erika to think I'm a wimp. I did end up confessing my fear to Erika later that day about had what happened about the snakes, but she only laughed and said, 'Oh, they won't hurt you!'

I guess Erika is used to them. Every summer, she grows a lot of vegetables in her home garden and this summer has told me to help myself. One afternoon, I leave the safety of the trailer to pick some carrots, but as I start to grab the tops, a snake suddenly wriggles out from under my fingers. Instinctively, I want to scream and run away, but I continue anyway. The whole time I'm picking the carrots, my skin is crawling at the very thought of any more slithering creatures lurking nearby, just waiting to crawl up my arms then all over me! The whole backyard scene reminds me of some creepy movie made from nightmares. Even if there is daylight all around me.

***

Like I said before, many men who returned home after the war have no real civilian work skills to fall back on. Besides, many of them signed up to fight for Uncle Sam right out of high school. Before long, this problem is brought to the attention of the US government. Before the men even began returning home, the governemnt introduced what became known as the G.I. Bill, which basically means that *all* ex-military men are now to be given the opportunity to learn various trades at the cost of the US government.

Understandably, Paul is really excited about this news. Even though he already holds a private pilot's licence, this incentive will give him a better chance to work up enough flying hours to obtain his commercial pilot's licence for future employment.

It doesn't take him very long to sign up at one of the local flying clubs, and before we know it, he has an arrangement in place with the men who run the club to take up one of their planes for an hour or so, whenever he's able to.

It's perfectly obvious to me Paul is in his element. Apart from his model planes, flying is the one thing in life he has been totally enraptured with since he was just a young boy. Before too long, he has already connected with a casual group of pilots, and every Sunday morning, they pick a different destination to fly to where they can all meet up and have breakfast together. The wives are allowed to fly with their husbands as well, so Paul asks me if I'd like to go with him, and as some of the other wives are going along with their husbands, I too agree to go with much enthusiasm, *And why not?*

The flight itself is supposed to take an hour, but with it being a cloudy morning, I can't help but feel apprehensive at the thought of flying *anywhere* in such a small plane. I've never even been in an aeroplane. Although as a teenager at Essendon Airport in Melbourne, my adventurous soul always dreamt of doing so, as I watched the planes from the ground land on a field nearby and take off again, wishing it was *me* flying up into the wide blue yonder.

The take-off goes smoothly, so I'm immediately reassured of Paul's flying ability as I watch him at the controls. He certainly seems to be confident and efficient enough to fly such a small plane, but whenever we pass through a thick bank of clouds, I find myself gripping my seat with so much fear my knuckles turn white.

To make matters worse, as we near our destination and are just starting to descend through a thick mass of clouds, I happen to glance off to my right and am immediately alarmed to see another plane flying far too close to us. Much too close for comfort for my already jangled nerves. After this incident, I declare to Paul that I never want to accompany him on any of his early morning breakfast flights ever again.

36
Paul

1947
Wrong navigation equals dire circumstances

I can understand why Isabella isn't too comfortable with flying in a small plane. On our first flight together to a social gathering, I could see just how fearful she really was, with her hands gripping her seat the whole time we were in the air. Of course, almost running into that other plane, didn't help to elevate her fears one little bit. *Damn*, it scared me half to death at the time too! It was a close one, that's for sure—especially with the other pilot being just as 'rusty' as me with his flying techniques.

Flying in small planes is not for the faint-hearted, that's for sure. Even pilots who have flown for years experience moments of pure fear at odd times. Good weather is no guarantee of a smooth flight from start to finish either. Particularly when the plane they're in control of at the time belongs to somebody else.

***

To log in some additional hours of solo flying time towards gaining my pilot qualifications, I've decided it might be a good idea to go visit my aunt and uncle who live on a farm just beyond a small town in the state of Illinois. Thankfully, their farm is just one hour from my usual flight boundaries—depending on the winds. I haven't seen my Uncle Gerhart or Aunt Anna since well before the beginning of World War II. So, apart from adding some hours to my solo flight times, I figure now will be as good a time as any to pay them a visit.

Uncle Gerhart is an inventor of all sorts of creative, mechanical implements and has set himself up nicely for his passionate endeavours inside a large, specially built workshop at the back of his property, which in itself consists of several acres of workable land. This way I'm able to easily land the plane, then park it close to his back door. Perfect!

On the morning of my intended solo flight, I awake with a buoyant sense of anticipation for the day ahead. Today is not all about clocking up my solo hours towards gaining my pilot qualifications, but a chance to spend some 'guy' time with my brilliant and inventive uncle. I'm also itching to tap into his vast knowledge and practical experience of creating all things mechanical again too.

After kissing Isabella goodbye and assuring her I'll be back before dark, I leave our trailer home around midmorning and head straight for the aero club headquarters.

The first leg of my solo flight goes better than I could ever hope for. At last, I'm able to let go of those nagging jitters in the pit of my stomach and regain the thrill of sitting in the pilot seat for my first solo flight since returning home after the war.

As I approach my relative's property, I decide I'll fly over their house first to let them know I've arrived. To make sure they were definitely going to be home, I'd already let them know beforehand I would be coming for a visit today.

Within a few seconds, I can see my aunt and uncle rushing out from the back of their house to wave to me, so I acknowledge their warm greetings by dipping one of my wings. I'll be with them real soon.

My Uncle Gerhart is also a pilot and has his own small crop duster stored in a shed nearby, so he already knows what landmarks to look for ahead of time when lining up to his own runway from a distance. He has made it easy for himself, and now me, by planting a long row of small bushes close together to run parallel to his fence line. Thankfully, the bushes are far enough away from the fence line width-wise to allow for a small plane to land on his makeshift, runway with relative ease.

After much hugging, we sit around talking a mile a minute over a satisfying lunch of cold meats, salad and homemade lemonade my aunt prepared for when I arrived. This gives us more time to get to know each other all over again.

I secretly think the real reason for the ready-made lunch is my Aunt Anna's intuitive way of knowing the two 'whiz kids' of the family (her words, not mine), will want to get on out to the shed ASAP to talk about—but mostly to play with—Uncle Gerhart's latest inventions.

My aunt is absolutely right too. We most certainly do get to have loads of fun together. With me also being an inventor of sorts, I am naturally very interested in all of the various projects my uncle has been working on since I saw him last. One of his latest inventions is a faster, more efficient, mechanical way of distributing hay bales out onto their paddocks for a number of livestock. Gerhart anticipates this new machine will cut their harvesting time by one third. I am always so impressed with whatever my uncle comes up with, and I tell him so. His sharp mind never stops mentally processing better ways to make life easier.

***

We're having such a grand time together. I can already tell my uncle is enjoying himself just as much by the way he's talking enthusiastically about his many new projects on the horizon.

In fact, we have been enjoying each other's company so much, I fail to keep an eye on the time. This is when I realise too late just how quickly the day has slipped away from me.

I've failed to remember, that with me still being a probationary pilot, I must always abide by the club's strict safety rules. One of the main conditions of me borrowing one of the planes is that I must be back at the airport well before dark.

To make matters even worse, I'm suddenly mindful there are no directional equipment or radio on this plane to refer back to after the sun goes down. So, if I *do* get into trouble on the way home, I will be, in effect, flying blind.

Flying in the dark tonight could be even more treacherous for me than I previously imagined, but despite my present predicament I'm still reluctant to tell my uncle of my fears. This is only because I don't want him or my aunt to worry about me unduly.

Besides, why spoil a good day? I reason. I have to learn sometime ... right?

Inwardly, without letting onto my uncle—by word or by any rash actions—I'm actually shaking in my boots! To allay any real or imagined fears, I soon start nutting out for myself a workable survival plan to fall back on. I figure the only way I'm going to be able to navigate safely home tonight will be to quickly jot down on a scrap of paper the various towns, railroads, rivers, etc. I will be flying over. Maybe this way, each landmark will seem more familiar to me, so mentally I can cross each one off my list as I pass over them.

Ten minutes into the flight, night is already descending much too fast for my peace of mind. Thank goodness I was able to take off a bit before sunset at least. After all, any light I have left in the sky to guide me back home is better than no light at all.

Son of a bitch! I know only too well by now I'm bound to be in trouble with the owner of this plane, for sure. I also know deep in my gut I don't have a hope in hell of beating the ominous cloak of darkness. Before too long, my worst fears come true in another way too; not only have I managed to stray off course, but within my current rapidly developing nervous state, I seem to have completely forgotten my navigational bearings.

Heaven help me! My only course of action will be to fly around for a bit to see if I can make out any familiar sights on the ground.

Unfortunately, I can't even spot one thing remotely familiar to use as a reference point to navigate my way back home.

Each of the worse-case scenarios I mentally tried to prepare myself for—even before this trip—are all starting to become disastrously inevitable, one by one.

Hell! I really am in big trouble now!

My most desperate fear of all right now, though, is if I run out of fuel and start to drop like a stone to the ground below.

Tears of frustration and regret pour out of my eyes uninvited, as Isabella's beautiful face flashes before my eyes. In another image, I see her looking down at our tiny baby in her arms, crying her heart out for what could have been.

I won't ever get to say goodbye to her. Not only that, but I won't even get a chance to hold our baby in my arms. She's too young to become a widow and a lone parent. What am I doing? I'm so sorry, Isabella! Please forgive me?

I continue to blubber away for a few more minutes whilst preparing myself for the worst. That is until I spot a silver streak below me and over to the left a bit. My heart misses a few beats when I quickly realise it is actually the moon shining down on the Fox River meandering its way through the hills and into the distance.

I'm back! So, God, you aren't ready to reclaim my mortal soul after all, huh?

I finally have the navigational reference point I need to find my way back home.

***

When I finally do reach the airport, it's in total darkness, so I fly around it several times to let the owner know I am back at last. The poor guy must be beside himself by now, wondering where in the hell that crazy young pilot could have disappeared to in his precious plane.

Upon hearing the familiar drone of his plane overhead at last, he must have immediately guessed what had happened and why I am so late returning.

The owner has obviously overcome his initial surprise because the next thing I see on the ground is the beautiful sight of a whole lot of headlights lighting up the runway for me. The headlights beaming out are no doubt from the cars of other club members also anxiously waiting for my safe return.

Thank God! The row of headlights lighting up all along the runway are more than enough to guide me back to ground level at last.

Once we're all back in the clubhouse, the owner predictably yells at me and threatens that I won't ever be able to fly his plane again, but thankfully that's all it is: an empty threat.

37

Isabella

1947
And baby makes three

Summer gradually turns into fall—or autumn, as I still think of it. With all of this splendour before me and with fallen leaves cloaking the surrounding landscape with a glorious kaleidoscope of colour, it must surely be God himself who has applied an all-inspiring stroke of genius to the landscape from his own heavenly paintbrush. Yes, the autumn leaves of the trees—starting in the month of April—certainly do impress Melbourne's appreciative citizens each year with the vibrant bursts of colour cloaking the hills and country areas with such splendorous vistas. Although, I must admit here, in the United States, fall somehow seems to have the ultimate power to make us mere mortals feel truly alive. Warm tones of deep red, tangerine and gold seem to visibly pulsate with a vibrancy all of their own.

Another new experience for me since coming to America, is on the weekends when Paul and I love to take long scenic drives together. This is when the spectacular colours of autumn can literally take one's breath away. Even as a little boy, and now as a full-grown man, Paul tells me how fall is always his favourite season of the year. I can understand why now. It's fast becoming my favourite season too.

By the end of October, all of the leaves have fallen from the trees as an inevitable reminder that the ghostly persona of winter is about to cloak the land in pure white. The onset of winter also reminds Paul and me that our first child is about to make their entrance into our world any day now.

***

In the early hours on the morning of November 2nd, it's obvious our little bun in the oven is at last ready to make a dramatic appearance into our previously well-ordered life.

My waters break first. Just as I am heading over to the bucket to pee, but as soon as my feet hit the floor, a sudden gush of fluid starts pouring out between my legs. Dr O'Connor warned me that such a thing might happen when I least expect it, but it's still embarrassing to think I might have wet my pants instead.

Since our baby is already two weeks overdue, we've tried everything to hurry the final trimester of my pregnancy along. Doses of castor oil and driving over bumpy roads haven't made bit of difference. We soon come to the conclusion our unborn child is simply determined to make an appearance at a time of their own choosing. This reminds me of my parents telling me about my own birth, just past Christmas in 1921. It's obvious our little one is also refusing to be rushed into the world, just to please others.

Around 10am, we decide it's time to leave for the hospital. Paul has already been in touch with Dr O'Connor to let him know we are on our way, especially with it being a Sunday morning. Evie, my former work friend back in Australia, had previously advised me via our occasional phone calls not to go the hospital too soon.

'Keep walking around as much as you can,' she said. 'Believe me, Bell, this will be far better for you in the long run, rather than spending endless hours in the labour ward, or lying flat out and strapped onto some unfamiliar hospital bed.'

After we pull into the parking lot at the hospital, I ask Paul if he'd mind if we could just stay in the car for a while.

'But, honey, we don't want you to have the baby out here in the parking lot, do we?'

'No, of course not, Paul, but Evie told me labour can take forever once I'm inside the ward, so it would be far better for me to walk around for a while. Well, at least until the labour pains become too strong to manage.

'Well, I guess she would know,' Paul agrees. 'The women on the South Pacific Islands all seem to work right up until the baby is about to be born, then after the birth, they go straight back to work.' Paul stops talking for a minute when he sees the bemused look on my face. 'Not that I'm suggesting for even one minute you should do such a thing.'

'I know you're not suggesting such a thing, darling ... Well, at least I hope not, anyway,' I laugh. 'I promise to let you know when I'm ready to make my move inside, or if the pains become too intense for me.'

So that's what we do. In fact, we've been casually reading the Sunday comics for half an hour or so when Dr O'Connor pulls up in the parking lot and spots us still sitting outside the hospital in our van. We act like we have all the time in the world before the baby comes.

When he pokes his head into the van, he shakes his head, probably as a way of responding to the strange couple who insist on doing things *their* way. 'What on Earth are you two doing *outside* the hospital *AND still* in the parking lot, I might add?'

'Oh, nothing really, doctor. We're just killing a bit of time reading the Sunday comics, before the labour pains kick in,' I answer casually.

He doesn't mince his words with us now. 'Well, I don't mean to spoil your casual Sunday morning or anything, but *please* get yourselves inside this hospital *right now,* if you expect me to deliver this baby of yours sometime today!'

With that said, he storms off into the hospital, expecting us to follow him *pronto!*

Paul stares after the doctor. 'I think that's our cue to head in now, don't you think?'

'I guess so. If we don't, I fear we may have to deliver this baby ourselves. Let's go!'

***

Patsy Leigh finally makes her timely appearance much later that same day. From this day forward, I know my life will never be the same again.

Even knowing our lives will be completely disrupted, her mother and father are completely besotted with their little daughter. With a fierce mother's heart, I know I will always try to protect her from any harm, wherever and whenever I can. I am so in awe of the adorable little bundle in my arms, but I am also only too aware that I have hereby been assigned to be completely responsible for her physical and emotional wellbeing forever onwards. *Am I up for the task?* Yes, I most certainly am!

I try to put her to my breast, but she turns her head away or screams in protest. She is no doubt picking up on my nervousness, but I'm still determined to keep trying. Once I leave the hospital, she cries even more and every time she does, I start to question my abilities as a new mother.

Admit it, Bell, you are fast becoming a nervous wreck.

This is when my Australian friend, Evie, steps in with her motherly advice. 'Forget breastfeeding, Bell. You should be bottle-feeding this little one from now on. That's what I did with my boys and they survived okay. To me, bottle-feeding isn't such a guessing game anymore either. Like what you are going through now, I was never quite sure if my babies were even getting enough breastmilk each time I tried to feed them.'

So I followed Evie's advice, but in hindsight, I'm not so sure it was the right thing for my baby after all. As a first-time mother and since I didn't really know any different, I managed to convince myself I was doing the right thing by switching to bottle-feeding, but deep down, I knew I wasn't really giving breastfeeding a fair go.

For the first few months, I had a very unhappy baby, and no matter what I tried, I couldn't seem to do anything right. According to my doctor, Patsy is probably sucking in too much air through the teat instead

333

of milk, which tends to cause colicky pains inside her immature little tummy.

One morning in my doctor's surgery, I suddenly burst into tears, then couldn't stop crying for most of my appointment. Dr O'Connor tried to console me by merely saying, 'You are being much too hard on yourself, Bell.'

Ha! What does he know, anyway? I thought to myself. Easy for him to say! He isn't the one at home with a crying baby day in and day out.

Listening to my inner thoughts, I soon realised what I was thinking and chuckled to myself. *Maybe my rebellion against doc proves I still have some fight in me, after all.*

To add to my feelings of inadequacy, during our first few months back at home, I can sense Erika's disapproval. Especially when Patsy refuses to settle down to sleep or when she cries constantly. Why can't Erika realise whenever she keeps on frowning or 'tut-tuts' out loud like she does it only makes me even more nervous. Unfortunately, whenever I get nervous around Erika, Patsy picks up on it and cries even more. It would be really nice sometimes if I could turn to Erika for some useful advice, but I never feel like I can ask her for any kind of help at all.

At around three months, I must be doing something right at last, because Patsy finally starts to settle down and sleeps like I imagine *all* babies should. She certainly is much more contented these days. She even looks like a healthy baby should, despite her still-inexperienced and overly anxious mother in charge of her ongoing care.

Because Toby-Lee's son, Charlie, came long just two months before Patsy arrived, during the day when our husbands are away at work, we get together whenever we can to compare notes about each of our baby's progress—as new mothers love to do.

When it comes to how we raise our babies, there's certainly times when I don't agree with Toby-Lee's ways. Now her baby has started to crawl, she puts him in a playpen, and there he stays. Even when he cries and puts his arms up to get out, she refuses to pick him up or cuddle him. When Patsy starts to crawl and I go over to visit Toby-Lee, she insists I put her in the playpen with Roy. I always hate to keep her restricted in this way for very long, so after only a few minutes, when Patsy starts to fuss, I pick her up immediately. This is when Toby-Lee always becomes very upset with me. If I don't put her back in the playpen straight away, she says to me, 'No, leave her in there, Bell. She'll soon get used to it.'

I soon learn Toby-Lee isn't about to let her children make demands from her. Ever!

***

It isn't very long before I realise I am pregnant again, and for some reason, I find myself reluctant to tell my family back in Australia for probably a few months more than necessary.

Time and time again, I try to rationalise why I didn't tell them that I was pregnant from the start. The only reason I can come up with is because I was somewhat embarrassed. After all, Patsy was only five months old when I fell pregnant with my second child, so in reality, there was only a three-month gap from when Patsy was born to when I fell pregnant again. Barely even time for a period of grace. I must be some kind of human rabbit breeding babies all over the place. Who would've thought such a thing, anyway? Least of all me.

Spring has arrived, so I've decided to make Patsy her first Easter outfit. Since I don't own a sewing machine, I set about hand stitching the whole thing, which includes a little dress with a matching coat and bonnet. It has taken me weeks, but I consider this outfit for my first child to be a labour of love. Besides, I have lots of time to accomplish it, which I usually manage to do when Patsy is asleep during the day or when she's lying on the seat right beside me, gurgling happily and kicking her chubby little legs the whole time as she watches me sew. I don't think it really matters what we do during our quiet moments together, really, since she is always happy for me to be close by. I love it too when she stares up at me so intently—as most babies do.

When I make my very last stitch on Patsy's Easter outfit, I'm feeling very proud of myself. Even Erika remarks on how cute she looks, all dressed up in her new outfit for church on Easter Sunday morning.

***

When my second pregnancy is confirmed, we immediately start our search for an apartment. We will, of course, need more room now with two babies to care for. It's hard enough with one child in a small trailer, especially when it comes down to our existing laundry set-up at my in-laws' place. Besides, I'll be doing a whole lot of extra washing now, what with another child added to our existing load.

We are lucky enough to find an apartment quite by chance. A woman on Paul's mail route told him about a family living in her same building who will soon be vacating, prompting Paul to ask her for the name and address of the owner of the building.

As soon as Paul steps into the trailer later this same afternoon, I can tell he's excited about something. He beams his usual Paul grin, which I know I can always count on. Without a doubt, to me Paul has the most beautiful smile in the world, and when he's really happy—like he is right now—his smile has the power to light up a whole room. It isn't until he suddenly pulls me towards him and dances me around on the one spot a few times that I know for sure something really good is definitely about to happen.

'Paul! What's going on? What on Earth has got into you?' I even start to giggle as he spins me around. Paul's happy mood is so infectious, even Patsy is smiling at her crazy daddy as he twirls her mommy around and around in some silly dizzy dance.

'Honey, I think I may have found us an apartment!'

'Really?' My eyes must be like saucers now, daring to believe good luck has come so easily to us. 'Oh, how wonderful, Paul! How did you find out about it?'

'A lady on my mail route told me about it this morning. A family in her building is due to move out soon. She gave me the phone number of the owner of her building, so we can go to see him right now if you're up for it. I just happen to have enough for a deposit at least, so we can secure it today. That is, of course, if you are still happy with it after seeing it for yourself. The money we get from the sale of this trailer should be enough to help with the rent for a while.'

'Oh, Paul, I can hardly believe it! Patsy and I are ready whenever you are! Let's go!'

While I gather a few diapers and some other items together into a carry bag, Paul reaches down to the woollen rug on the trailer floor to take Patsy into his arms for one of his extra-special Daddy cuddles with his baby girl. Once I'm ready to go, we head for the van outside. Thankfully, the drive over to the apartment owner's home isn't too far at all.

As we pull up to the apartment building, he is already waiting for us beside his car. After a quick greeting, he asks us to follow him up to the apartment currently on offer. We are more than happy to oblige of course.

I love it from the first moment I walk through the door. The whole place is infused with so much light and soft muted colours on all the walls AND SPACE! Lots of space! It even has central heating, a blessing come winter for sure. I can tell Paul loves it too. His happy grin says it all. We smile at each other from opposite sides of the open-plan living room, content in knowing this cosy apartment will soon be home for our little family.

We tell the owner we will definitely take it, and Paul arranges with him on the spot to lease the apartment before anybody else can. Without hesitation, Paul puts down the deposit required, which he has secretly been stashing away for a moment such as this.

We bid goodbye to our new landlord in a calm, orderly way, but once we have left our new apartment and even before getting back into the car, we immediately do a fair imitation of an Irish jig, up and down on the spot so excitedly. We hug and kiss each other over and over again, including Patsy in my arms and in-between us. We can't help but feel totally jubilant over our success in finding this place so easily. The waiting list for apartments anywhere within the whole of Chicago is notoriously long. Now thanks to this tip-off from Paul's customer, we have successfully managed to beat everyone else before word could even get out there about it.

Instead of returning to our trailer straight away, we decide, on the spur of the moment, to go somewhere to celebrate our victory. This is indeed a good enough reason to hang the expense for one night at least. We drive up and down the main street for a while, finally settling on a local Italian restaurant. As well as a full-sized pizza, we order some wine for us and a child's size chocolate gelato for Patsy. She adores the gelato, but when it's completely devoured, she soon tucks into our pizza as well, dipping into the thick sauce with her chubby little fingers at every opportunity. I can't help but notice our daughter has definitely inherited her father's wonderful smile.

'I think our daughter may be more Italian than German. What do you think, Isabella?'

'I think you might be right! She's even happy to take some of this Italian food home with us too—all over her!'

***

In no time at all we are able to sell our trailer and move into the apartment. I am so very happy to have a place of our own at last. For the first few days I walk around as if in a dream, constantly running my hand over the shiny stove, the walls, I even open and close every closet in every room. Probably more times than is necessary, but I don't care. I take to turning the lights on and off, just to make sure they are still working. My greatest thrill of all, though, is to be able to flush the toilet every time I use it. Especially during the night. This alone makes this place feels so much more like home already. There will be no more using a bucket at night to pee in, and thank Heavens, no more waiting for Erika to open the door to her house in the mornings when I am at last allowed to use her bathroom even for just a few desperate minutes. I even catch myself running my hand over our new preloved washing machine. Even if it has belonged to somebody else before, it's ours now. No longer will I have to stand in line to use the washing machine. Nor will I have to wait to use Erika's outside clothesline, as I now have an electronic clothes dryer in our apartment, and even though it is also preloved, I don't mind at all since it works really well. Come summer, we also have the use of an outside clothesline at the back of the apartments, available for the tenants of our apartment block only.

Paul wastes no time in organising some of his friends to help him move the piano from his parents' house into our living room. He so enjoys being able to play it every day now. He confessed to me one night, that even before I'd arrived here in America, he spent very little time in his parents' house. I never realised until now just how much Paul has been affected by the underlying tension between Erika and me. Since he has never once complained about it, I just assumed he didn't really care what goes on between his mother and his new wife while he's away at work. I guess I was so caught up in my daily dramas with Erika I never once stopped to think about how much it was impacting Paul—or even Hans, for that matter. I can't believe how blind I've been all this time about so many things.

***

It's such a joy for me to hear Paul play the piano each night. Many an evening after dinner, Paul sits at his piano and plays all the modern songs, starting with Glenn Miller, Artie Shaw and a whole lot of soul, jazz and some lively boogie too. I never knew, until now, he has such an ear for music and a natural ability of listening to a new melody only a few times, before playing it from start to finish, without sheet music. Once learnt, never forgotten with Paul.

38

Isabella

Late 1948
Another flight best forgotten

During this same summer, after we've moved into the apartment, Paul and I decide it would be nice to fly down to Texas to visit Evie. With Evie being a war bride like me, it's so good to be able to talk to her about certain challenges in my new life here in America that I can't talk about to just anyone. Not even Paul sometimes. Evie talks to me too about certain things and we just put it down to women's business. Even living a fair distance from each other these days, we still manage to keep in touch on a regular basis.

Despite still being hesitant about getting back into a small plane again, I know only too well a road trip is out of the question. Yes, time is one factor, but money is the main issue.

Since Erika has agreed to watch Patsy for the time we are away, we set about making plans for our upcoming trip. Before any flight, every pilot has to mark out their course on various maps, noting down towns, railway lines, highways, etc.

'How are you coming along with our flight route, darling?' I wander over to ask him once Patsy is asleep in her cot for the night. 'You sure do have a lot of maps here.'

Paul, with a pencil in his mouth, removes it now to scratch his head.

340

'Well, honey, I'm going to need every one of these maps.'

Once he is aware I am standing right beside him, Paul stretches his free arm outwards to wrap around my waist to effectively pull me in closer. 'The thing is, I need to figure out the layouts of each area we will be passing over in the plane, and anything on the ground to guide us to where we need to go. Since your friend Evie and her husband Peter live in a small town further down south, each of the states we will be passing through all have different maps that I need to refer to along the way. When you plan a trip in an automobile, you simply jump in and follow the road with usually just one map to your destination. It's not so simple in an aeroplane. To map out our route, I have to factor in not just the highways below me, but also major landmarks, such as rivers, forests and nearby cities or farms as well. It's all part of the navigation process I need to learn each time I fly.'

'Oh dear! I'm sorry, Paul. I never really understood until now just how difficult this trip is turning out to be for you. Would you prefer not to go?'

'Of course I want to go, honey. Even with the extra planning involved, it's all good. Besides, it's always a good thing to broaden our horizons … Wouldn't you agree?'

'Yes, of course I agree. We'll still go but only if you're absolutely sure.'

***

Two days later, on a mild-weathered Saturday morning, time for take-off has arrived at last. After first dropping off Patsy to Erika, our next stop is the flying club, where Paul is to take charge of a Piper J-3 Club loaned out to him until midday Sunday morning.

'This is a great little plane, honey. It might look small, but it's mighty. You'll love it!'

I must be seeing this *mighty* little plane with much different eyes. To me, it looks more like a pocket-sized model plane. It might be wonderful to pilot it, but to its passenger onboard, it seems much too fragile to withstand any turbulence.

I still give Paul my best smile, but my nerves are starting to quiver with fear. To make the most of our daylight hours of flight, we take off before seven in the morning. According to Paul, this kind of weather, with fluffy white clouds scattered all around, is perfect for flying. Even though we are on our way at last and even if I am looking forward to catching up with Evie again, I'm *still* not exactly thrilled about the flying part. Nor am I happy about leaving our little Patsy behind without us. I will just have to keep reminding myself that this is the only way we can possibly cover the distance to Evie's place in the shortest possible time.

So far, I've only flown with Paul once and even if we did *nearly* crash into another plane coming out of some clouds, I'm still determined not to let that stop me this time. As I settle myself into my seat behind Paul, the noise of the Piper's engines makes it almost impossible for us to have a normal conversation. Even if it is a small plane, does it have to have such a thunderous beating heart?

I haven't expressed to Paul openly yet, but I'm already having my doubts about this whole crazy adventurous idea. It's still a long trip no matter how we look at it. I fear, with me being newly pregnant and with my squeamish stomach, my *condition* could make matters awkward for us, with our highly anticipated time away.

Unfortunately, my hidden fears are becoming a reality. It seems my normally strong intuitive powers are busy working overtime for good reason. As the day wears on, I just *know* we've made a big mistake. Even while flying, Paul has to diligently study his maps all along our planned route, but in the process, he also has to constantly change from one map to the other. In doing so, he soon becomes so distracted he doesn't spend enough time actually flying the plane. Paul ends up having to circle around numerous times over the same spot to get his bearings again. He finally admits to me—and himself—he is now completely lost! Ultimately, he decides he has no choice now but to land somewhere nearby to find out *exactly* where we are.

We eventually land in some farmer's field, and once we land, he asks me to please stay put inside the plane while he runs towards the house for some more reliable directions.

After what seems like an awfully long time, I grow tired of waiting inside the plane and decide to get out to stretch my cramped legs for a little while. I can tell this field I'm standing on is usually planted with corn, but for now, there are only scattered clumps of stubble left after the crop has been harvested. As I start to walk around, I quickly notice some huge spiders crawling in amongst the remains of the corn husks, so I don't waste any time in jumping back into the plane.

While waiting for Paul to return, I immediately make up my mind that I simply can't go any further on this grand adventure of ours after all. Before we even landed in this expansive corn field, I'd caught sight of the Mississippi River, so I knew we still had a long way to go before even reaching Evie's place.

When Paul returns, he is his usual unflappable self. He doesn't even appear to be at all upset or worried about veering off course. This is when I start to reason with myself that perhaps I *am* making a big deal out of nothing, so I decide once again not to say anything negative to Paul at this stage.

Paul taxis to the corner of the field, since he needs as much ground space as possible to be able to reach a certain speed before the plane can take off.

As we race ahead at full speed across the bumpy ground, I can see a clump of trees dead ahead of us. I urgently yell out to Paul, 'Paul, *please!* Just take us up! We're going to crash! TAKE US UP NOW!'

He has no choice but to yell back at me above the noise of the engines, 'I'M TRYING TO, HONEY! BELIEVE ME, I'M TRYING!'

Much to my relief, Paul somehow manages to pull us up. We are *finally* airborne and not a moment too soon. Another second and we would've clipped a few feet off the top of the trees at the end of the corn field. As we fly back over them—*not into them, thank goodness*—I glance back over my shoulder to see those very same trees swaying a bit too much for my peace of mind.

Without me even having to say anything, Paul has already decided to head back home. Our plans for this trip obviously aren't meant to work out for us this time around. Another deciding factor for Paul is the rapidly darkening skies closing in all around us. Once he's made his decision to turn back, he sets a new navigational course in motion. Once he has turned us around full circle, he confidently points the little plane back towards home and I couldn't be happier. I can't wait to see our little girl again. I'm missing her far too much already.

Besides, these light planes can be very dangerous if not handled right. I can still remember back in Australia, my brother Robbie, when he had planned on going away for a weekend with his friend Cal who loved to fly his two-seater plane at every opportunity. At the last moment, Robbie couldn't go for some reason, so Cal asked another friend if he would like to go instead. On the way home from wherever they went that day, perhaps after a few beers too many, Cal misjudged the field and wasn't able to clear some electrical wires overhead. The plane went down in flames and both Cal and his friend were incinerated. Cal was a seasoned pilot too. These kinds of accidents can occur at any time without warning. No thanks!

***

With another summer over, the chill of winter is already starting to breathe its icy breath all over us. It's not hard to miss the unmistakeable hints of its imminent arrival any day now. At least for winter this year, we'll no longer be in the trailer. I'm not likely to forget—or miss—the unforgiving chill from outside of the trailer finding its way inside to us through any new cracks opening up through its rusted seams. Despite us constantly plugging up any possible sources of entry, those relentless frigid winds somehow always managed to rob us of any stored warmth we struggled to maintain each day.

With this new pregnancy, at least I am faring much better with the morning sickness, thank goodness! Apart from the occasional bout of nausea, my health is excellent this time and Paul often says being pregnant gives me a certain glow.

I have to admit, I do feel more content within myself the second time around.

***

A week before Christmas, Paul and I go in search of our first Christmas tree for our apartment. Patsy is a growing little girl, and to her proud parents, she *definitely* seems more advanced in her development at thirteen months old than most babies her age. She certainly is an active child and so delightfully inquisitive about everything around her. Of course, because of this very same inquisitive nature, she is getting in to everything, keeping me ever attentive and vigilant during her waking hours.

With Paul setting up the tree last night, Patsy and I spend the morning decorating it with little trinkets and colourful tinsel ropes. Along with the hanging of baubles, Patsy never ceases to delight me with a whole lot of giggles and smiles thrown in for good measure. To her besotted mother, she is always such a delightful little girl to be with. One day I will tell her just how much she has helped me in other ways too. Without really understanding why, my sweet little girl has helped to take away the now familiar pain of missing another Christmas season with my Australian family I left behind. I do so wish my parents could have been here to meet their new granddaughter this Christmas. But for now, I'll have to be content with picturing each of them in my mind's eye and hold them ever close to my heart.

Despite me still longing for my Australian family, this year has turned out to be a special time with Paul's family here in America. Erika has outdone herself with a Christmas feast to remember. Just like every other year, as far back as Paul can remember, Erika has gone all-out to cook their traditional Christmas dinner of a beautifully roasted turkey and all the trimmings, including a huge jug of delicious warming eggnog.

She has even baked several pumpkin pies as well, which is no doubt destined to become an American tradition for me to embrace over time. Growing up in Australia, I ate lots of pumpkin with Mum's baked dinners, or as a side vegetable during the week. As far back as I can remember, my mother only ever served cooked pumpkin as a savoury vegetable. Back home, pumpkin is always something we love to eat with our Sunday lamb or chicken roast, along with lots of crunchy golden roast potatoes, white sweet potatoes, carrots and usually with green beans or peas. I don't ever remember Mum cooking it as a sweet pie like Erika does, with the enticing fragrant scent of cinnamon escaping from the centre.

Even before I came to live in America, I already knew pumpkin pies played an important role on the American table every Christmas. I eventually learn how to cook them myself. Secretly though, I don't really care much for the taste of them and probably never will. Although I would never dare tell Erika this of course.

Paul's sister Lillian, her husband Bill and their two children, Jessica and Mason, have come to stay with us for the festive season. Because they live in a small country town outside of Chicago, they will be staying over for a few extra days since it's too far for them to visit here just for Christmas Day alone.

Paul's other sister, Vanessa, lives in Montana with her family so they aren't able to come this year. Even though I won't get to catch up with Vanessa for Christmas, I already met her during my first summer here in America. She had three children at the time—two girls and one boy—but one more boy and girl have come along since then. I must admit, I really do like Vanessa, who is so very different to her younger sister, Lillian, who is more like Erika in both looks and personality. Unfortunately, just like Erika, Lillian has over time built a defensive shell around herself. Perhaps it could be because of her dysfunctional childhood, but whatever the reason, she can be just as stand-offish as her mother at times. Thank goodness both Paul and Vanessa don't fit the same pattern.

39

Isabella

Early 1949
To the hospital, and be quick about it!

January of 1949 rolls quickly around and I'm getting very close to the expected arrival of our second child. In the early hours of the 18th, I know it's time, but I don't bother waking Paul up just yet. When he does wake just on seven, I announce a bit offhandedly that *today* is the day for me to go to hospital.

For the past week, Paul has been preparing himself with the thought. He has even organised with his employer to have a day off around the birth—just in case he or she decides to come during one of his workdays. So here I am, telling him ever so casually now it's time for me to go to the hospital just as if I was about to head off to the supermarket.

Paul calmly makes breakfast for us. We sit and eat it just as calmly too. I can't help but notice, though, Paul's handsome face wearing a worried look just the same.

Even so, he never says one word to me or even tries to hurry me along. Nor does he try to warn me he has this very strong feeling we really should be going to the hospital sooner rather than later! In the same deceptively calm state, Paul notifies his boss that he won't be in today. The whole time he is on the phone, I continue to sit quietly and finish off my tea and toast.

After breakfast, Paul can't stand it any longer. He grabs my hospital bag in one hand, hoists Patsy up onto his other arm, then makes sure I am directly in front of him as we head out the door. He makes certain he has locked our apartment door securely before we take the elevator down to our vehicle in the undercover car park. Before we head for the hospital, we have to make a quick detour to drop Patsy off at her grandmother's, since Erika has already promised to mind her for us when the time comes for me stay at the hospital. While I calmly hand over Patsy to Erika, along with her diaper bag, clothes and favourite toys, Paul rings Dr O'Connor to let him know we'll be on our way soon. All the while, I am blissfully in denial and still insist I don't need to go to the hospital just yet.

I am remembering now, my first delivery with Patsy and how she took pretty much all day to come, so I must have reasoned to myself it would be silly of us now to show up at the hospital at this early stage, naturally assuming it would be the same this time around too.

Boy, was I wrong!

Paul and Erika finally persuade me it might be better to leave now to beat the traffic, or some such reasonable excuse. Much to their relief, I am *finally* ready to get back into the van. Even when we are outside the hospital, I'm not in distress and I don't even have any labour pains. We certainly don't linger in the car park like we did the last time when Patsy was due to be born. Just as well too.

Once we are inside the hospital, one of the orderlies guides me into a wheelchair, which is always parked by the front reception in anticipation. As I'm still in a calm state of mind; as far as I am concerned the wheelchair is merely there for convenience's sake, not for delivering me with haste to the maternity ward. At a quickened pace, the orderly wheels me along several corridors, with Paul following closely behind with my pre-packed hospital bag. Once the nursing staff take over, Paul is politely and firmly ordered back to the waiting room.

As soon as the nurse examines me, she calls for a trolley to move me to the delivery room. Much to my surprise, my baby is already born. Just like that! I can hardly believe how easy it has been for me the second time around. *Piece of cake, really!* I smile smugly to myself.

***

Shortly after, Dr O'Connor goes looking for Paul to tell him he has another daughter, but he can't find him anywhere. He's not even in the expectant fathers' room. Dr O'Connor finally locates him in the cafeteria, where Paul is wishfully hoping to devour an early lunch while he still can.

When Paul does come into my room, all he can do is stare at me with a really puzzled look on his face. 'Are you sure you've had the baby? Your hair isn't even messed up.'

I think Paul saying this is hilarious, so I can't help but laugh out loud with glee.

Paul sits on the side of my hospital bed and leans over to kiss me tenderly. We cling together with happiness and so much relief to know the birthing process has all gone so well and so easy this time around.

'Have you seen our newest little girl yet?'

'Yes, I sure have. The nurse let me see her for a few minutes just now. She's so beautiful, Isabella. Just like her mother. Like her big sister too, although I think she'll have your dark hair this time.'

'Yes, you're right. Patsy does have your reddish-blond hair, alright. There's no mistaking who her father is, that's for sure. This little one will probably take after the Carlisle side of the family.'

'Man, oh man!' Paul exclaims with a huge grin. 'I can't believe how quickly she came into the world! I'm still trying to get my head around it. One minute we're arriving at the hospital and the next minute, you've given birth. Since it took a mite longer for Patsy to come, I thought I'd go grab some lunch, as it'd probably be a long wait. The next thing I know, Doc is tapping me on my shoulder, telling me our baby has already been born.'

'Speaking of lunch, you should go and finish it while you can, darling. Then come back and see me when you're done. I've just been told I'm about to have some lunch myself soon.'

'Good idea! I didn't get a chance to take even one mouthful before … Don't go anywhere!'

Is if I could.

***

We haven't decided on a name for our newest little girl yet. What I like, Paul doesn't and vice versa. The girl from the registry office downstairs comes by each morning to find out our baby's name, but each day she leaves with her official forms still uncompleted. On my last day at the hospital, we know our deadline to submit her name has finally come. Why is naming this baby so difficult this time around? Then I remember the very pretty girl who was with me in the labour ward when Patsy was born. Yes, that's the one! When Paul turns up later, I tell him our daughter is already named, and thankfully, he is happy with my choice. Our new little bundle of joy is to be named Bethany Lynn.

So, here we are with two babies. Because Patsy is already a very independent little girl, she doesn't even seem like a baby to me anymore, and Beth is the most placid baby any mother could wish for. She has such a sweet disposition and rarely cries. In fact, once we are back home, I often go in to check on her in her crib, to make sure she is still breathing. She was only six pounds, three ounces at the time of her birth, but she grows into a healthy, chubby little baby in no time at all.

***

Six months after Beth is born, another apartment in our building suddenly becomes available and as soon as Paul's sister Lillian and her husband Bill hear about it, they ring the owner to rent it, just like we did before them.

They admit to us they are tired of living out in the country and have been hoping to find a place in the suburbs for a while now. Erika sure is happy about this, of course. Especially since our apartment—and now Lillian and Bill's apartment—are in the same building *AND* within an easy walking distance from her house. Now she can see more of her daughter and grandchildren on a more regular basis.

This new set-up of sharing the same building with Lillian and her husband is not without its challenges, since Paul and Lillian have a tendency to rub each other the wrong way a lot of the time. With Lillian being so much like Erika, there is bound to be friction. When Lillian asks me if she can use our washing machine Paul has already installed in the laundry room at the back of the building, I still lean towards caution with saying yes. So I tell her I'll have to check with Paul first. Predictably, Paul knows how careless Lillian can be with her own things, so he doesn't like this idea one little bit. He tells her so too. I can't blame him in a way. Lillian and Bill have been married for years and I have to wonder myself why they still don't have a washing machine of their own by now. After a few days of Lillian promising Paul she'll be extra careful with our washing machine, he finally gives into her persistent pleas.

However, when I go to use the washing machine one morning shortly after this, I find the rollers on the machine that squeeze out the excess water from the clothes are already broken. Paul is naturally livid when he finds out. The fact that Lillian doesn't even have the nerve to tell us and leaves us to find out for ourselves just makes him even madder.

According to her, the clothes got stuck in the moving rollers some-how, with the result that her washing ended up wound around the rollers so tight she could barely retrieve her clothes at all. After fiddling with the washing machine straight after dinner later that same night, he eventually manages to untangle the rollers and greases the ends of them too. With two babies under three now, he is determined to repair the machine for me as soon as possible. Being as meticulous as Paul always is, by the time he finishes repairing it, it now works even better than before.

Needless to say, Lillian never again asks us if she can use the washing machine.

PART 4

Mid to late 1949
Returning to Australia
for better opportunities

40

Isabella

Mid 1949
Making plans for a new start

As the months pass, Paul and I discuss the idea of returning to Australia.

I think I might have been the one who first came up with the idea, but it doesn't matter who did, really. I firmly believe, once a thought of one's destiny takes hold of our soul, there's really is no choice but to carry through with it. Well, at least until a satisfactory solution is reached. In this case, our decision to go back to Australia will ultimately affect our whole future together as a married couple and for each of our children's individual lives.

I've already been asking myself these past few weeks, *Why would I even want to leave America after less than five years to return to Australia? I must be crazy! Are you really that homesick, Bell?*

Well, I don't feel homesick anymore, and I'm happy to admit this to myself at last. I have come to love America very much. Especially now that we have a family of our own. As a married couple with children, I've made many friends by meeting up with other young mothers at parks, or even bumping into them at our local supermarket.

Toby Lee, of course, being the first American friend I made here, has over time become a special friend. I consider myself lucky to be able to spend time with her pretty much on a daily basis. Paul has also renewed some old friendships from his school days, as well as meeting up now and again with some of his ex-army buddies who live close by.

Life is good! So, why am I even thinking of moving away from this new life of ours?

This idea, taking form in the back of my mind lately, refuses to let go, until I accept it fully.

In doing so, I have to accept this (so far secret) revelation of mine, is not just about my own happiness anymore. This time around, the change must be for Paul. He needs to value his own worth as a man again. Not just to slot himself into one temporary job after another. Under his present circumstances, he is expected to wait for perhaps years and years without any promises whatsoever for something more permanent to magically appear.

Right now, he needs to know his role as his family's sole provider really does count after all. Paul's future employment opportunities are at stake here. I can sense Paul is never going to be content to remain a postman for the rest of his life. This job was only ever meant to be a means to an end when he first took it on. In my eyes, retiring as merely a postal worker at the end of his working life could never be the definitive factor of who my Paul really is.

His talents may be many, but his future employment choices overall these days are both dismal and soul-destroying, to say the least. Not only was Paul trained as a radio operator during the war, but he was also trained to be a fully qualified mechanic. Not just on a limited military range of aircraft models either, but on various types of road vehicles as well. Did I happen to mention, he is almost a qualified pilot?

The training the US government provided for Paul during the war years may no longer pay for his civilian life back home, but at least he has gained a good many skills along the way because of it. So there is no reason why he can't apply *some* of those additional wartime skills to the jobs of postwar employment in the future anywhere in the world.

Paul has never been a man to complain about his lot in life, but it still breaks my heart now to watch him leave home in the mornings to drive a mail van out in all kinds of weather, with no immediate prospects in the way of long-term employment. Certainly not with the US Postal Service anyway.

I can no longer bear to see his abilities and confidence slip away from him more each day. Here he is, already a father of two small children and with a wife to support, trying every day to keep his head above water financially. Something has to change! Which makes me more determined than ever to initiate some kind of change for both of us. If I can.

The time has come for me to broach the subject with Paul. Once the girls are asleep tonight, I'll plant the seed and see what grows. If he isn't happy with the idea, then I'll know I tried at least. I do love my life here and the American people have been so wonderful to me ever since I first arrived, but deep down, I love Paul too much to see him continue to struggle like this.

***

The dishes are done. The girls are both asleep and Paul is busy studying a diagram he drew up himself, to build another model plane. He is so passionate about them, but I don't mind at all. The intricate, miniature planes he designs are so perfect in every detail. By keeping his hobby in this way, it helps his brilliant engineering mind stay healthy and active.

'Paul? I need to talk to you about something.'

'Sure, hon, what's up?' He stops what he's doing to look over my way, letting me know, as he always does, that I have his full attention.

'I've been thinking about this for a few weeks now, Paul, and well, I'm just going to come right out with it … How would you feel about going back to Australia?'

'I love Australia. You already know that, but do you mean permanently?'

'Well yes … It's something I've been thinking about a lot lately.'

'What's brought this on?' Paul asks with a puzzled frown.

I don't answer him straight away. I just wait a bit, for my all-important question to sink in first. After a long pause, he finally responds, much too slowly at first, 'Are you saying you're not happy here anymore, Isabella? Are you homesick?'

'No, darling. I promise you I'm not homesick. Nor am I depressed or unhappy in any way at all. I miss my family in Australia, of course, but I'm also very happy with my life here with you and our little girls.' I pause for a moment to catch my breath. To gather together the words I need to follow through with this potential minefield of miscommunication. 'What I'm not happy about, Paul, is seeing you struggling every day just to make ends meet. I'm not happy either with you still driving a mail van out in snow blizzards or in heavy rain, just to put a roof over our heads. With all of your qualifications, I would have thought the US government would want to make better use of your talents by now. It's been four years since the war and the government still expect their fighting men to return home and pick up where they left off? It's just not right!'

'I have to agree with you. It's taking far too long for ex-military men to be recognised or re-employed for their non-military skills. But what could I do in Australia for work?'

'No matter which way you look at it, Paul, Australia is basically an island, isolated from the rest of the world with not much of a population overall, really. So for its workforce, Australia always has to look beyond its borders for skilled migrants and hard workers. I'm pretty sure my father and brothers will be able to give you a few great contacts for work, to tide you over for a while until you can find something more permanent.'

'You're probably right, honey. Yes, we should at least think of going back for that reason alone, and even though you say you're not homesick, I know you must be sometimes.' Paul wanders away from his model planes to come over to the sofa and sit beside me. 'Even so, with such a major decision to make, we mustn't rush into this. Just let me think about it for a few days and we'll talk about it again on the weekend … If that's okay with you? In the meantime, I have a far more interesting idea on my mind.'

He pulls me towards him and kisses me with a sudden passion that lately we've *almost* allowed to slip away. Due, no doubt, to Paul's lack of enthusiasm for anything other than sleep throughout the working week, plus my own exhaustion in taking care of two active little girls all day. All too quickly, we have become slaves to our unavoidable daily routines, allowing no time for each other anymore. Sex seems to be the furthest thing from our minds as we both crawl gratefully into our bed each night.

What starts as a tentative exploration of lips soon ends up with us ripping each other's clothes off like a pair of sex-starved teenagers. *Good Heavens!*

All for the thrill of a spontaneous quickie on the sofa.

What is this madness that has possessed us to behave this way? I think with a smile.

***

I'd already planned to approach Paul again about Australia this coming weekend, just as he himself had suggested we do. Well, the weekend is here now, but we do need our discussion time to be at *exactly* the right moment for *both* of us. After all, our whole future rests on Paul's decision today.

'So, Paul, have you thought anymore about the idea of us moving back to Australia? It's been a few days now and you haven't broached the subject with me since … I take it you're not so keen on the idea at all?'

With our backs leaning up against a tree close to a picnic table in our local park, just a ten-minute drive away from our apartment, we're slowly sip our piping-hot coffee out of enamel mugs from our trusty stainless-steel flask, watching the girls play happily together on a picnic rug beside us with their favourite toys.

'It's funny you should say this now, Isabella, because I was just about to bring up the subject myself.' Paul shakes his head in wonder. We both agree it's always so uncanny to us just how many times we tend to think the same thoughts at the same time.

'I certainly have thought about it, sweetheart. At first, I thought of all the reasons why we shouldn't go, and as you can well imagine, the logical side of my ordered mind kept coming up with all the obvious disadvantages. All of my objections covered the usual things of course, with the main one being the cost of packing up everything we've scrimped and saved to buy for our home so far. Then there's the cost of air travel for all four of us to fly thousands of miles and set up home all over again. Not to mention, me finding some sort of job to support our family budget as soon as possible. We simply *must* financially separate ourselves from your parents too, you realise? I have to warn you, Isabella, this is one thing I won't ever compromise on. I never *ever* wanted to live off my own parents when I returned home after the war, so I will always refuse to live off your parents too. Apart from these obvious drawbacks, though, you already know I love Australia very much.' Paul stops talking for a moment with his brows knotted together in deep thought. *Paul stalling with his final answer must be his way of putting me off altogether. It's perfectly obvious to me, he doesn't wish to discuss it anymore. Ah well! My idea was fun to think about for a while at least.*

When Paul does speak again, assumptions over his answer prove me totally wrong. 'To be completely honest, darling, the prospect of living in Australia full-time excites the hell out of me! So, I guess the answer to your burning question has to be a resounding YES! Let's do it!'

'Oh, darling, do you really mean it?' I wrap my arms around him now and kiss him, not really caring who is watching us from the other picnic tables. 'You won't regret it!'

In our excitement, we pick up one daughter each to hug and kiss them, then swap over to do it all over again. Picking up on their silly mommy and daddy's excitement, our little girls start bouncing up and down and are soon giggling with excitement as well.

Paul and I are suddenly talking a mile a minute. There is just so much to organise! All at once, all of these new exciting ideas are freefalling right into our laps. In the midst of organising our scattered minds, a few important issues manage to gain momentum, pushing away all the other trivial thoughts jostling for attention.

'I know you might not want to do this, Paul, but we'll probably have to stay with my parents to start with, but hopefully, it'll only be for a few months. I most definitely do agree with you on one thing too. We *do* need to stay financially independent from both sets of parents—for the sake of our own self-respect at least. One other thing will be in our favour too. When we do arrive back in Australia, with the girls still being babies, we won't have to worry about sending them off to school for a while.'

'That's right!' Paul agrees. 'By the time they do start school, we should be well and truly on our feet and settled by then.'

'You know what, Paul, I think we should head back to our apartment right now! We need to sit down today and write these important points down as we think of them.'

We're like two excited wound-up kids by now, laughing and teasing each other as we gather up our girls. Not only do we need to pack up our babies, but all of their toys, the picnic basket and rug, along with everything else in double-quick time, into the back of the van. Thank goodness by the time Beth was born, Paul had already converted our van into a four-seated people-mover with still plenty of space at the back for his mail-run job.

On the drive back home, we don't talk much at all. This is because our busy minds are making up for the spoken word. Our combined thoughts are fairly buzzing with activity, with both of us determined to have a serious plan nutted out by the end of today.

Another thing we are in total agreement on is that our future as a married couple with young children is now in the balance, so we have no time to waste.

Time is of the essence!

41

Isabella

1949
No major move is without its problems

Once we make our decision to move back to Australia, we move fast! One major thing at a time, though. The one main thing overall that we must stick to is to be on our way to Australia by early August if possible. This way we can enjoy the last of the warm summer days here in the Northern Hemisphere, but arrive in Sydney at the start of spring in Australia, thereby skipping the chilly onset of winter in Chicago come September.

Our passports are still in order, thank goodness, so that's one less thing to worry about. Our plane fares are officially booked too. Because the girls are both still under three, we only have air fares for Paul and me to worry about. Next, we set about either selling or giving away our furniture, fridge and various other household items to either friends, family or donating them to our local Goodwill store. We pass the washing machine onto Lillian, so any future repairs of broken rollers will be up to her. Paul figures that if Lillian is financially responsible for it, then *maybe* she might be a bit more careful with it from now on. The one thing we can't bear to part with permanently, though, is Paul's piano. With his parents' help, we transport it back to their house for safekeeping, so *if* we should ever decide to return to America one day, it will always be there waiting for him again.

In the end, in regard to the packing up of everything, we stick to our resolve to keep aside only what we need for the trip. Mainly clothes, one favourite toy for each of the girls and a few small keepsakes I treasure and have carried with me all of my life.

My favourite of these special keepsakes is a tennis trophy I won in my own childhood backyard. Being the smart man my father is, when he decided to build a tennis court on our property at Pascoe Vale, he built *two* tennis courts instead. Dad always loved the game himself, so naturally he wanted his children to develop a love for it too. To add some extra money to the family finances he came up with the brainwave of renting out the tennis courts on weekends to various sporting groups and even a few nearby church groups, so when one of the players in the church group took sick, I was asked to fill in. At the time, no-one was more surprised than me when I won the game in the tournament. Hence a trophy to prove it. Winning against that snooty church girl, who swore she could never be beaten, was so much more satisfying to me than winning the game. The trophy itself is not all that big, but I still carry it around with me to remind me of my surprising triumph over unbalanced odds.

As well as the tennis trophy I always keep close to me, I also have another small trophy presented to me at the school assembly for the most promising student. The third collection in my little keepsake box is just a few family photos too precious to ever part with. Everything else has to go. As far as we are both concerned, this move is to be permanent.

We have already decided, at the onset of our plans, there is to be no change of heart for either of us. No last-minute regrets either. Not now or in the future.

***

With all of our trans-country relocation plans finally in place, it is now time to say goodbye to Paul's family, his childhood friends, and of course, his newer army buddies. Last, but not least, we bid farewell to good friends we've made together as a couple. Because we have already accepted we might never see them again, suddenly, our goodbyes become so much more poignant. Toby Lee and I are the first to promise to always keep in touch, despite the time and distance between us. I just hope this will still be the case after a year or two. Even though my friendships with Evie and Mavis are kept alive by the letters we send to each other, when all of our goodbyes are said and done, we'll just have to accept we will probably never see each other again.

After all of the intense preparations we have put in place, the saddest thing for us is to be leaving our first home as a married couple and as a family, here in Chicago. In spite of these second thoughts niggling at us sometimes, I do believe we are now finally all packed and ready to go. Unnecessarily, we remind each other one more time; there is no turning back now. This, as they say in the movies, is it!

Patsy, at nineteen months old, is thankfully no longer in diapers. Beth, now seven months old, is as placid as any baby can ever be. Though very young they may still be, I can't wait for them to meet their other family in Australia. I give pause now to wonder—as any mother of young children would too, I'm sure—how they will travel? How am I going to be able to keep them amused the whole time? Even though these persistent concerns are starting to nag me a lot more by now, I am still very mindful about keeping any such worries to myself. I hardly think Paul needs to see his wife stressing openly about every little thing. Regardless of his positive attitude about this move, inwardly Paul must indeed be worried about certain things, such as finding a job wherever we eventually settle. This moment of reflection reminds me once again of my worrisome thoughts when I left Melbourne to sail across to America, only this time, my worries of reaching my final destination are in reverse. Who would have thought I would be going back to Australia so soon?

Even if both of us are over the moon about returning to Australia, at the same time, we are also being very mindful about not pushing Paul's family's feelings aside. Especially with any excited jabber thrown in their faces all the time. In private, though, we feel a sense of pride within ourselves of how we've managed to organise everything in just a few weeks with two babies under the age of three. Not bad at all, really, but it's much too early to become smug about this whole new adventure just yet. We know we still have to drive to San Francisco to catch our flight to Australia. As far as we are concerned at this point, any unforeseeable obstacles or challenges from now on will just have to be dealt with as they happen.

If they should happen at all. Let's just hope they don't.

***

To save us even more money getting from Chicago to San Francisco, Paul has come up with the idea of approaching an auto firm who are in the business of hiring drivers to deliver new cars to various destinations across the United States. This way, the only cost to Paul as the driver will be the gasoline we'll need throughout the trip. Brilliant! I love this idea and tell him so. This ultimately means that once we reach San Francisco, we won't need to try and sell our vehicle before catching our flight to Sydney.

The day before we're due to leave the car, Paul organises for a buddy of his to drive him into the city to pick up the car, which turns out to be a brand-new, candy apple red 1949 Ford. It even has that distinctive smell of new leather wafting our way from the beautifully crafted, buttercream colour contrasts.

When Paul drives into the entrance of our underground parking area, the girls and I are already downstairs waiting for him to take a quick spin around the block. Paul is obviously getting a real kick out of showing me its many wonderful features along the way, which, he declares, will soon become permanent state-of-the-art features in this model.

'Mark my words, Isabella, this little baby will one day be one of the more popular new automobiles Ford has started to manufacture since the war.'

Just sitting in this car gives me such a thrill. Especially the shiny dash-board with its contrasting red and cream panels. Even the steering wheel looks impressive enough to me, let alone all the other features Paul rattles off, as any true car enthusiast would. I don't feel in the least bit guilty about enjoying this beautiful car. I set out to prove it too, by allowing myself the luxury of sinking back into the beautiful creamy leather seats. Neither of us can resist the temptation to cruise around the neighbour-hood, waving to everyone happily as we go. Why not? For just a little while, we are getting a small taste of what it must feel like to be one of those instant millionaires we've started to hear about these days.

While still planning our initial trip to San Francisco, Paul suggests we should take this one and only opportunity to make an extended detour to visit his sister, Vanessa, her husband Charlie and their family, who live up in the wild, breathtaking state of Montana. Yes, it will mean going out of our way for miles, but this is what we really want to do.

Besides, we figure we should have just enough time to visit Vanessa and Charlie and still be back in San Francisco to catch our flight to Australia. No problem. So that's what we agree upon. Montana here we come!

***

It's a hot late-summer morning already when we set off on the road to Montana. Unfortunately, there is one major thing we completely failed to notice when we first checked the car out the day before; despite all of its impressive new state-of-the-art features, it doesn't have any kind of air conditioning to speak of, *at all!* With our two little ones riding in the back, along with some of our luggage packed all around them, we soon begin to feel the outside heat unmercifully seeping into the interior of this beautiful car. Once the sun starts beating down on us around mid-day, we quickly realise the warming effect from the cherry red exterior of this car probably doesn't help much either. Luckily, we've brought four cotton scarves along with us. At each gas stop we pass along the way, we make sure we soak the scarves in cold water. Once soaked, we wrap the scarves around the children's necks and our own as well. It helps for a short time, anyway.

***

After two long days, we finally reach the border sign welcoming us so beautifully to the state of Montana. Vanessa and Charlie's place is still about an hour's drive over the border, but when we finally pull up outside their front door, we can't wait to escape the stifling confines of the car and stretch our legs at long last.

It is so wonderful for me to catch up with Vanessa again, but the happiness of seeing them is quickly quashed during our first dinner with the whole family. One of the vegetables Vanessa cooks is steamed carrots. I never did like carrots all that much—cooked or raw—but I found if I squashed them with my fork just a little bit and ate them with each mouthful of mashed potato, I could somehow manage to force them down. However, Toby, their five-year-old son, has a problem with carrots as well. I can tell he doesn't like them much either, by the way he screws up his face at the very sight of them, but his mother insists on him eating them. He isn't even allowed to leave the table until his plate is empty. I could never be that strict with my own children and feel sorry for the poor little kid. Toby keeps gagging on them, but he is expected to eat them anyway. After everyone else has left the table, poor little Toby is still there, trying to make those dreaded carrots disappear somehow.

Paul tells me later his mother did the same thing when he was growing up. He and his siblings weren't allowed to leave the table until every last bit of food was gone. I must admit, though, Paul has never been a finicky eater, thank goodness. Whatever I serve him, he's happy to eat. *Just as well,* I think to myself. Especially at the beginning of my marriage, I was such a terrible cook and could never hope to compete with my mother's cooking—or even Erika's—that's for sure.

***

After bidding Vanessa, Charlie and their hoard of five children goodbye,

370

we set off very early the next morning for San Francisco. Because we chose to make a detour so far out of our way to Montana, we now will have to try and make up for some valuable lost time along the way. As a consequence of not fixing this disastrous miscalculation of ours *before* leaving Chicago, Paul now has to drive pretty much most of the day and well into tonight. By the time we do reach San Francisco, his eyes are severely bloodshot.

Paul has to drop us off at the airport first, before delivering the car to its final destination as promised. With this part of his agreement fulfilled, he then has to catch a taxi back to the airport again.

Our overnight stay at the San Francisco airport is a long one. After finding two seats together to lay our girls down, Paul and I manage to catch a bit of sleep here and there by stretching our feet out on the seats opposite us. For the most part, our girls continue to sleep soundly throughout the remaining darkened hours and into the early morning light. Luckily, our waiting area isn't too crowded at this time.

During my quiet waking moments on these unforgiving, inflexible airport chairs, I can't help but think to myself, how when I first arrived in San Francisco by sea, I was only able to view the city from a distance. I was left to take in only a hint of the beating pulse of this famous city from the deck of the SS *Monterey*, because I was unable to enter the bay due to some custom entry requirements.

***

The next morning, we are finally allowed to board our international flight back to Australia and back to the first home I ever knew. Even though I have only lived in America for close on five years, it seems like a lifetime ago since I married Paul in Melbourne, leaving my childhood and teenage years behind to come and live in America. Cupid is a mysterious imp, indeed, to successfully entice a whole lot of young women to fall in love, then tempt them again to throw caution to the wind by marrying some handsome stranger from another land so easily. I know, because I was one of those women.

After taking our seats inside the aircraft, we are intent on settling our little girls in with us for take-off, with the seatbelts snapped into place, Patsy on Paul's lap and Beth on mine. Once all the passengers are checked in and seated, three of the flight crew, numbering six in all, spread themselves out evenly along the centre aisle to wait for one of the other stewardesses to give us a safety talk over the loudspeaker in case of an emergency. Despite a bigger plane this time with a full flight crew to attend to our every need, I still feel apprehensive about this flight. Never mind all this safety talk about oxygen masks, life jackets and whistles to call for help, if this aircraft can just make it over the ocean that's between America and Australia without crashing, I'll be ecstatic!

As we take off, the pilot banks out over the picturesque Bay Area, so passengers can get a good look at the Golden Gate Bridge. Even though we have booked window seats because of my fear of flying, and even if this aircraft is a *lot* bigger than the small plane I was initiated into flying with Paul as the pilot, I am still much too scared at first to even take a peek.

Paul finally coaxes me to move over closer to the window.

'Come on, Isabella! Please? Otherwise you will always regret not seeing this.'

I finally relent and lean over carefully towards the view beneath the rounded aircraft window. Like Paul just said, I would have indeed regretted missing out on such a spectacular sight. As I look out for the first time, a low cloud cover immediately tries to block my view by settling down real low over the Golden Gate Bridge. The distinctive vermillion cables still triumph, rising above them anyway.

My last memory of San Francisco and its vibrant gateway across the bay has managed to, without even trying, completely capture my heart forever. Even if it is only from a passing distance. What a view! I don't think I will ever forget it for as long as I live.

***

The captain of our flight informs us in his welcome speech that this flight is likely to take twenty-nine hours, with a few scheduled stops along the way. Just as well! How on Earth can any airline company expect their passengers, apart from necessary bathroom breaks, to stay seated for more than twenty hours anyway? Not to mention keeping two young children occupied for this amount of time? Impossible!

During the night we land at Honolulu for a stopover. Just like the city of San Francisco, I seem to be destined to view the beautiful island of Hawaii from some distant port or airport. Memories of my journey by sea on the SS *Monterey* return. A lot of water certainly has passed under the bridge and over the ocean waves since then.

Even if we are to refuel at Honolulu for one hour only, at least this time, passengers are permitted to leave the aircraft to stretch our legs for a short while. Despite being allowed to leave the aircraft, we still have to remain restricted within airport boundaries. When we do board again, we find our seats have been converted into beds, with a curtain between us, running all along both sides of the centre aisle for privacy.

During the long night following Honolulu, I am woken again by the realisation that our aircraft is lowering its landing gear. After our few scheduled stops on the way back home these sort of sounds are becoming more familiar to me by now. With other passengers in the seats nearby sleeping, one of the stewardesses whispers to me that we are about to land at a small atoll, out in the middle of the Pacific for another necessary fuel stop.

The next morning, we land in Suva, Fiji. Thankfully, this time, we are allowed to disembark and walk around the city of Suva for a few hours to stretch our legs. I am totally fascinated with the local policemen here. They are all tall, black men with tight fuzzy hair that stands straight up for about a foot above their heads. How intriguing! Their uniforms are like no other police uniforms I have ever seen before. All of the police officers are immaculately dressed in navy blue braided jackets, over spotless white skirts—not pants. Their skirts are strangely cut in a zigzag fashion to knee length. Most likely, the hemline is meant to simulate their native grass skirts. They are also barefoot. One of the officers gives Patsy a big toothy grin when she looks up at him and for some reason she calls him 'Dada!' Paul thinks this is hilarious, especially since he and this Fijian policeman look nothing alike.

***

Throughout this international flight of twenty-something hours, Beth being the contented baby she is, never once gives us any trouble. I don't remember her crying even once throughout the entire flight from San Francisco to Sydney. Patsy being Patsy, is content to amuse herself during her waking moments by running up and down the aisles talking to people. More likely, though, the other passengers have spoken to her first. With Patsy being the charming captivating child she is to her own parents, we can well understand why there will always be smiles all round her, no matter who she interacts with.

The woman sitting across the aisle smiles at me in that familiar united-mother-bond kind of way. She says her name is Angela and she has two little girls as well, although these two seem to be somewhat older than ours. As soon as the plane starts descending into Sydney, both of these little girls' faces suddenly start to turn green. I just know they are about to vomit and their mother is obviously too busy looking out the window to even notice. I finally manage to catch her eye. Just in time too, Angela is able to grab the bags provided in the front of her seat before the first spew of vomit escapes out of each of her daughters' mouths.

Each time we are about to land at any of our designated stops along the way, both of our girls drifted off to sleep, meaning Paul and I awkwardly had to try and carry one sleepy baby each along the cramped aisle while at the same time trying not to bump their little heads against other passengers or the seats. It's the same when we are about to land in

Sydney. Only this time, it dawns on us that we'll have to take all of our hand luggage with us as well.

***

As our plane pulls into the terminal of the Sydney International Airport, I notice a crowd of journalists crowding around, waiting for our plane to come to a complete stop. I suddenly have this crazy idea. 'Paul, let's try and get our photo taken with the girls as we exit the plane. Who knows? Maybe we'll be able to get our photo in the paper, as a memorable record of our return to Australia.'

'We could try,' Paul replies. 'But I don't like our chances of hurrying through this lot.'

With our two little ones asleep again, we bundle them up and exit the plane as quickly as we can, hoping the press will snap a photo of us as a keepsake of the occasion.

But as Paul said, we haven't got a hope of making such a photo moment happening. We should have realised there might well be some famous celebrity onboard our flight. Maybe, if we knew beforehand, we could have managed our timing better, but it obviously wasn't meant to be. We found out later, from reading a Sydney newspaper, that Robert Morley, the famous English character actor, had come to Australia for a stage play and was also on our flight.

Ah well! It *was* nice to brush with fame for a short time at least.

EPILOGUE
Isabella

So, Bell, you're back in Australia! Who'd have thought I'd be back here so soon? I certainly didn't.

Yes, indeed, a lot of living has happened since I first boarded the SS *Monterey* three years ago. Right here in Sydney too. I never could have imagined in a million years how my life would end up making so many amazing detours from all those intensely serious and half-baked ideas I'd made as a young girl.

How would my life have turned out had I not met Paul on my way to Luna Park that evening? Perhaps I *might* have stayed in Melbourne, married and had children with a totally different man. Or maybe, I might even have taken off overseas anyway, because of some other life's quest I wanted to experience, maybe to explore not only America, but what the whole world had to offer me.

Who knows? Regardless of any possible scenarios, I have absolutely no regrets at all.

What I do know is that I can't honestly imagine not knowing a man like Paul Meier! Nor could I ever imagine not waking up to him each morning. To catch him watching me as I sleep, and each time he realises he's been caught out, he just smiles his beautiful smile, reminding me for the millionth time that my day cannot possibly go wrong with a smile like Paul's to greet me each and every morning.

I could never imagine life without our two precious little girls either. They have brought such richness of fun and laughter into our lives. Most of all, they have brought us a whole lot of love wrapped up in two adorable bundles of giggles with some pretty bows on top.

After a short flight from Sydney to Melbourne, I am about to be re-united with my family, who I thought I might never see again. I still can't wait to introduce Mum and Dad to their two gorgeous little granddaughters. And to my dear friend, Coral too, of course, who is also married with two children as well.

We have a lot to catch up on, my best friend and me.

I have been carrying a special secret back home with me too. A secret that not even Paul knows about yet.

I think for this particular secret, I'm going to have to time the unveiling of my news very carefully. Especially where Paul is concerned, who will have to get used to me being pregnant again! Yes, it's true! Our Beth will be just one year old when this new little addition to our family is born. Patsy will be two. A close gap for sure!

No doubt, this latest pregnancy, due around the beginning of March, 1950, will immediately start tongues wagging back in my old neighbourhood.

Appropriate, I would have to say, when I stop to consider that the house I will be returning to, in this very same neighbourhood, is the exact same house where I was born on a steamy summer's night in 1921.

THE END

ACKNOWLEDGEMENTS

I do believe my first choice of acknowledgement should go to the lady herself – the real Izobel.

When I was first invited to read a true memoir of an Australian World War II war bride, I had absolutely no inkling at the time, how it would inevitably impact on my own journey as a writer.

From the very first page of Izobel's true-life story, I was instantly hooked!

Right from the beginning, Izobel seemed to be pulling me into her world more and more with each new page I turned, so that in the end, I had choice but to go with the feeling that everything would work exactly as it was meant to. I somehow knew without a doubt, that Izobel would be with me in spirit to guide me along the way right to the very last page.

Much as I would have liked to have included Izobel's early idyllic childhood years of growing up in Melbourne with her gentle, loving parents and four siblings, I soon realised that I had to either decide to include her whole childhood story which were unfortunately much too long, or to just mainly concentrate on Izobel's developing love story with her handsome American GI instead. So of course, I went for the latter. After all, it was really Izobel's love story that fully captured my heart anyway.

It wasn't until I almost finished this book, that I finally decided it would be better for the whole story overall, for me to split each of the chapters into both Isabella and Paul's points-of-view. Lucky for me, Izobel had included several sections of her memoirs, with what was also going on with Paul's army unit's train trip up though the centre of Australia to Cairns, to go fight the Japanese in the South Pacific. She also included his role as a radio operator during his time on Mindanao Island—with the Philippine army joining forces with the US army – to bravely hold back the ever-tenacious Japanese Imperil Forces, ruthlessly intent on taking over the Philippine islands no matter what.

So with this unchartered task in mind, it was therefore essential for me to do LOTS of research first, about the role of the United States military forces based in Australia and the Pacific region of World War II. So having said that, my next acknowledgement must of course go to the World Wide Web.

What would I have done without it? To fill in Paul's own side of his story, it ultimately meant me going online whenever I needed to, to find out about ALL aspects of the experiences of the American military forces stationed in Australia in the 1940's. Overall, a rewarding and fascinating study indeed!

My next round of acknowledgements also count as major ones for me. If it hadn't been for Izobel's four children – two daughters and two sons – this story might never have been written in the first place. For it was Izobel's children, who originally gave me their mother's story to read and to then give me permission to write this book about their parents. THANK YOU SO MUCH to each one of you.

For my last round of acknowledgements – which undoubtably are equally important – I wish to thank the publishing team at MMH Press, based in Perth, Western Australia. I thank you Karen most humbly, for your superb guidance at the helm of your own publishing house. You always set an excellent example for us authors to follow. Of course, I must also thank Dylan Ingram for enthusiastically filling in the role of my go-to-guy for all things technically creative (as with helping me to design my own book cover this time around). Let's not forget the awesome Eleanor too, for all of your expertise and guidance during the editing process. Your ongoing patience is immeasurable!

A big THANK YOU must go out to all my special friends for your ongoing support, encouragement and feedback (You know who you are), but most of all, to Gary for being the best soul mate ever!

www.ingramcontent.com/pod-product-compliance
Lightning Source LLC
Chambersburg PA
CBHW020251120726
47904CB00001B/165